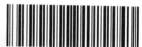

M000073943

THE CURSEBOUND THIEF

FRACTURE PACT BOOK ONE

MEGAN O'RUSSELL

Ink Worlds Press

Visit our website at www.MeganORussell.com

This book is a work of fiction. Names, characters, places, and incidents either are products of the author's imagination or are used fictitiously. Any resemblance to actual persons, living or dead, events, or locales is entirely coincidental.

The Cursebound Thief

Copyright © 2022, Megan O'Russell

Cover Art by MiblArt (https://miblart.com/)

Editing by Christopher Russell

Interior Design by Christopher Russell

All rights reserved.

No part of this publication may be used or reproduced in any manner whatsoever without written permission, except in the case of brief quotations embodied in critical articles and reviews. Requests for permission should be addressed to Ink Worlds Press.

Printed in the United States of America

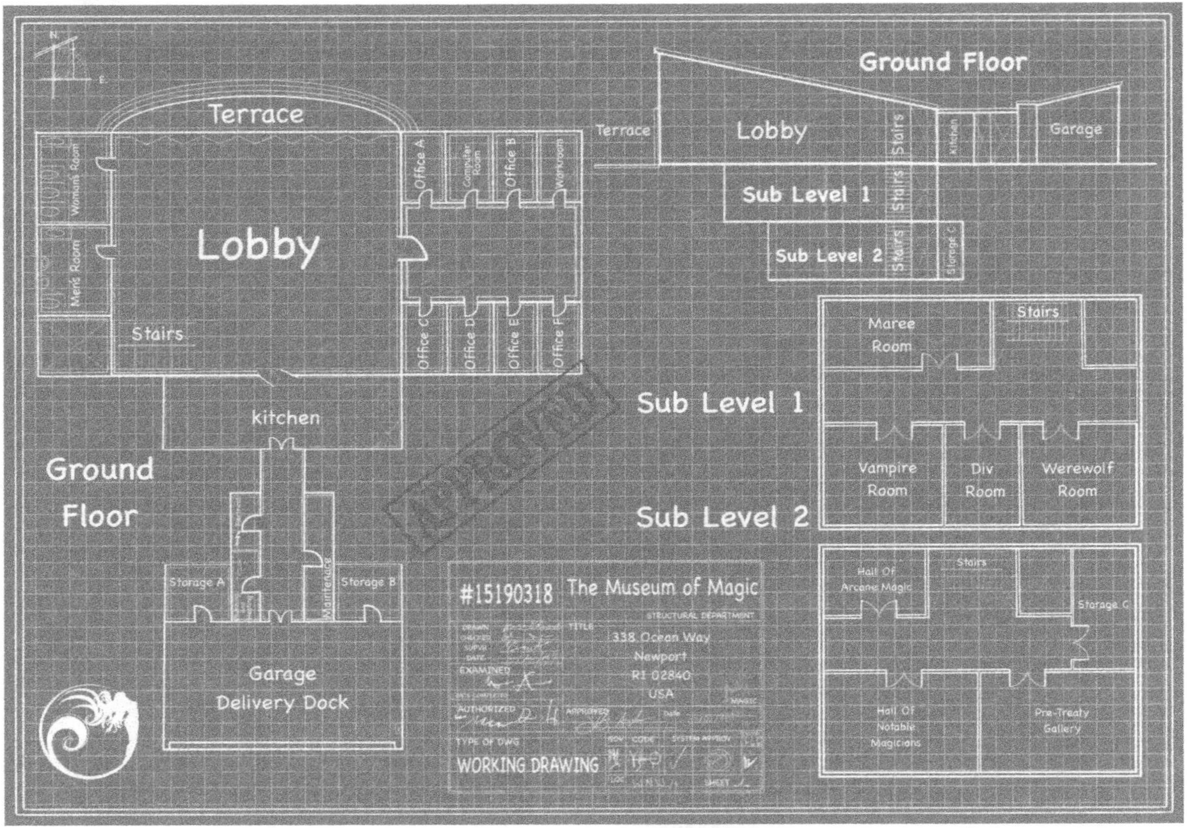
Terrace
Lobby
Woman's Room
Men's Room
Stairs
Office A
Computer Room
Office B
Workroom
Office C
Office D
Office E
Office F
kitchen
Ground Floor
Storage A
Maintenance
Storage B
Garage
Delivery Dock
Ground Floor
Terrace
Lobby
Stairs
Kitchen
Garage
Sub Level 1
Stairs
Sub Level 2
Stairs
Storage C
Sub Level 1
Sub Level 2
Maree Room
Stairs
Vampire Room
Div Room
Werewolf Room
Hall Of Arcane Magic
Stairs
Storage C
Hall Of Notable Magicians
Pre-Treaty Gallery
#15190318
The Museum of Magic
STRUCTURAL DEPARTMENT
TITLE
338 Ocean Way
Newport
RI 02840
USA
EXAMINED
AUTHORIZED
APPROVED
TYPE OF DWG
WORKING DRAWING
SHEET

THE CURSEBOUND THIEF

1

Before

Ari,

You are hereby invited to a heist of the highest order. Danger, deception, and the salvation of the feu are promised to those who commit to attendance.

Please RSVP at your earliest convenience,

Jerek

Jerek,

Sounds thrilling. Who could say no to a party that delivers salvation?

Are you sending a car?

Ari

Ari,

I'm coming to you. Need your help collecting a partygoer before you fly east.

In the meantime, bring our boy home.

Jerek

2

Jerek

Jerek squeezed the bridge of his nose between his knuckles, closing his eyes as he waited for his computer to ding with Ari's response.

The first rumble of a spring storm shook the windowpanes. He didn't spare the glass a glance. The house would hold against any storm. The roof would stay sturdy even as everything else crumbled.

Minutes ticked past. An ache crept up the back of Jerek's neck. He stared at the red-stoned ring on his left hand, trying to distract himself from the gnawing pain in his head. His bag was packed, the plane tickets bought—the time for turning back had long since passed.

A faint mew carried up from the floor as a furry head pounded against his ankle.

"You can't come, Cas," Jerek said. "Cats and burglary don't go well together. You'll have to stay behind."

Casanova dug his claws into Jerek's calf.

"I promise I'm sending you someplace nice." Jerek shut his eyes and kneaded his temples. "The height of cat luxury. You'll never even think of missing your life here."

Jerek opened his eyes to find the white cat sprawled across his keyboard.

Purring rumbled in Casanova's chest.

"I understand." Jerek scratched between the cat's ears. "But we both know there's no other choice."

The computer dinged.

Jerek,

He's on his way. To your house by morning. The Maree aren't happy. Don't think they're just going to send him to you and forget about it. There will be hell to pay for this.

Ari

"Hear that, Cas?" Jerek lifted the cat off the keyboard. "Our brave knight Lincoln is finally coming home."

Jerek kissed the cat on the top of the head before setting him down on the armchair beside the library's fireplace.

No fire crackled in the grate.

He pushed aside the imagined chill that lapped at his neck and allowed himself one long moment to look around the room.

The shelves were packed with texts that held information many would kill to possess. The records and files that didn't need to be hidden had been sorted into an order that would be easy for others to interpret. The pictures of his family had been dusted and perfectly aligned on the mantle.

"Don't mind the sound, Cas. It'll be over soon."

Taking the box of matches from the mantle, Jerek walked through the front door and out into the rain. He didn't need to bother with placing any charges—he'd already run the fuse right up to the stone steps of the entryway.

He touched a match to the fuse and went back inside, not bothering to stay and watch the black car explode. There was too much to be done. Windows to destroy. Glass to scatter.

This was only the beginning of the necessary chaos. Saving everything he loved would require much greater sacrifices than wreaking havoc on his own home.

Jerek Holden didn't even flinch as the boom of the car's explosion shook the floor beneath his feet.

3

Grace

Cheers filled the packed stands. The umpire rolled his eyes as a flock of girls shoved their way onto the front row of bleachers.

Each of the girls carried a handmade sign.

Go all the way Steven!♥!

Homerun for the Homecoming King.

Swing your bat Steven.

Grace tucked her feet under her seat as the girls pushed past, unwilling to tear her focus from the batter long enough to tell the now giggling girls to sit down and pay attention to the game.

Steven strode up to the plate, rolling his shoulders and testing the weight of the bat in his hands.

"Come on, Steven," Grace murmured.

As if he had heard her, Steven glanced up, tossing Grace a wink.

She smiled back, her thrill of joy barely breaking through the surface of her panic as the pitcher drew back his arm.

Her heart throttled into her throat as the ball soared toward Steven's perfect face.

A crack rang around the baseball diamond as Steven hit the ball.

Her lungs forgot how to draw in air. A tingle shot through Grace's chest as the white leather seemed to glow for a moment before becoming nothing more than a pale dot as the ball soared past the outfield, over the roof of Sun Palms High School, and out of sight.

4

Lincoln

"We're booked on a commercial flight?" Lincoln asked as the cab stopped in the long line of cars waiting at the departure gate.

"Did the hills of Italy turn you into such a snob that peasant travel is now beneath you?" Jerek passed the driver twice the money the trip had cost and stepped out of the car, leaving Lincoln in the back seat.

Lincoln climbed out on his side, letting his gaze sweep over their fellow travelers as he looped behind the car to stand beside Jerek. "I'm a Maree, Jerek. I'll sleep in the mud, wade through swamps of blood—"

"And only fly in private jets?" Jerek grinned.

"It's not funny." Lincoln placed a hand on Jerek's backpack, guiding him toward the sliding doors in a less than gentle manner. "You may be my best friend, but I swear you can be such an idiot sometimes."

"Glad to see my top position wasn't stolen while you were away." Jerek walked past the ticket counters and toward security.

"There is someone trying to kill you," Lincoln murmured. "Have you considered that traveling on a plane packed with people could put hundreds of lives at risk?"

"They'll be fine." Jerek pulled out his phone, accessing their digital tickets as they joined the security line. "Just take a breath and act like a normal person who doesn't want to be at the airport."

"I will never understand you." Lincoln clenched his jaw, biting back the lecture he longed to spew as he presented his ID to the dozy-eyed guard.

The guard glared at Lincoln before letting him pass, allowing him to join Jerek in the next segment of the line.

"I just flew across an ocean to protect you," Lincoln said. "We should be in your home keeping you out of sight while we figure out who's trying to murder you."

"No one's trying to murder me." Jerek gave a maddening wink as he placed his backpack on the belt to go through the x-ray machine.

"So the bomb in your car and shots through your dining room window were just some assassin's way of saying hello?" Lincoln dropped his bag onto the belt, worsening his feeling of terrible nakedness.

I should have a sword. And a bow. A damn dagger at the very least.

He held his breath as he walked through the scanner, not exhaling until he'd retrieved his bag on the other side.

"There is no assassin trying to kill me." Jerek slipped his

pack back on. "I blew up my own car, so just relax and try to have a nice flight."

Jerek strolled down the terminal, leaving Lincoln behind.

Lincoln blinked at his best friend's backpack disappearing into the crowd.

"Dammit, Jerek." Lincoln ran after him.

A blond girl with a pixie cut grinned at Lincoln, trying to step into his path as he reached Jerek's side.

"You blew up your own car?" Lincoln ducked his chin, avoiding meeting the blond's gaze as he stepped around her.

"And shot out my dining room windows." Jerek stopped in front of the departure board, scanning the gate assignments. "An assassin wouldn't have been able to harm Holden House. I thought you'd have known that."

"Have you lost your mind?" Lincoln's words came out louder than he'd intended.

"Of course not." Jerek gripped Lincoln's elbow, leading him toward the gate. "I blew up my car and shot at my house while of sound mind and body and without breaking any laws."

"Why?" Lincoln yanked his arm free. "What the hell would possess you—"

"I needed a reason for the Knights Maree to assign you to protect me. What better reason for requiring a personal bodyguard could someone present than multiple attempts on their life?"

"You staged two assassination attempts so I would get sent to visit you?" Lincoln dragged his hands over his face. The ridges of his palms caught the faint traces of stubble on his chin.

Jerek sighed. "No."

A hint of relief eased the tension in Lincoln's shoulders.

"You were already on your way before I blew up the car and shot out the windows," Jerek said. "I had to make sure if the

Maree sent anyone to check on us, they would find adequate damage."

"You've actually lost your mind."

"And, as wonderful as it is to see you, I didn't blow up my car so you could come for a visit. I *do* need your help, and by being here you *will* be saving lives. But the Maree would never have let me borrow you without explaining why, and there are some things the Knight's Council just can't know."

"Talk. Now."

"What do you want me to talk about?" Jerek weaved through the rows of seats at their gate, skirting around the rubble of luggage left haphazardly at the feet of weary travelers. "I've decided I don't like melon anymore and have matured into a greater appreciation of fish."

"You are such an impossible asshole." Lincoln sank into a seat in a row of empty chairs.

Jerek stared at him for a long moment before sitting beside him.

Lincoln scanned the crowd as he waited for Jerek to talk, his training telling him to search for any person that could be a threat, his instincts telling him to shake his friend back into sanity—or to punch Jerek if the shaking didn't work.

"I found a way to fix it," Jerek said.

A stone settled in the pit of Lincoln's stomach.

"You may think I've lost my mind, and that's fine," Jerek said. "But I've hauled you here, and you're going to listen to me. I can mend the Fracture."

"Ladies and Gentlemen, Flight 407 to Las Vegas will begin boarding momentarily." An overly bright female voice filled the gate. "We will begin our boarding with Elite Diamond members, families with small children, anyone needing extra time on the jet bridge, and, as always, members of our armed forces on active duty."

"Too bad normal people don't recognize the Knights Maree," Jerek said. "It would be nice if the sombs let us settle into our seats."

"The point of being a secret society isn't to get priority seating," Lincoln said.

A woman with three small children made her way to the gate, her face almost as red as the cheeks of the sobbing toddler who gripped the back of her pants leg.

A man with an oddly shaped backpack stayed close behind the woman until an elderly couple stepped between them.

The four-year-old began to wail when his mother stopped to present their tickets.

"Jerek," Lincoln said under the cover of the toddler's hiccupping cries, "I know you want to fix the Fracture. We all want things to go back to the way they were before, but it can't be done."

"It can."

"No, it can't. There is no more magic left in the world. It's gone. Destroyed. You should know that better than anyone. Some things can't be fixed. Pretending they can is just a more efficient way of getting yourself killed than blowing up your own car. Which is really, incredibly stupid, by the way."

"Anyone fiercely dedicated to a cause will be considered insane by those who don't believe in their mission," Jerek said. "I can do this, Lincoln. It won't be easy, and I need help. But I can put things right. I can give the feu back the world we were meant to live in."

"I know you want to believe that, but it's not possible. People tried for years."

"I know people tried. But the failure of others does not prohibit my success."

Lincoln shoved aside the bubble of pain in his chest. "I won't let you risk your life for a doomed cause. If that means I have to haul you to Italy and lock you in a cell to keep you safe, so be it."

"You won't even give it a chance? You won't give *me* a chance? The Maree are pledged to protect the feu. Mending the Fracture, restoring magic—what could be more important to the oath of a Knight Maree than that?"

"Nothing. I would gladly give my life if fixing magic were possible, but it can't be done."

"It can." A glint shone in Jerek's eye. "I know how, I know what tools are required, and I know who I need to help me get them."

"Jerek, I..." Lincoln searched the crowd again, wishing for the first time one of his brethren would be amongst the throng, watching him. Judging him.

Ready to tell me how I'm failing and snatch Jerek away from my incapable hands.

"Even if you don't believe me, you're going to come with me. You've been ordered to protect me, and I'm walking into much more danger than I faced while setting the charges in my car." Jerek stood, joining the line waiting to board the flight to Las Vegas.

He looked so rational and normal standing in the queue of travelers. Nothing in Jerek's slim shoulders or unruly brown hair hinted at madness bordering on a death wish.

Gritting his teeth, Lincoln stepped into line right on Jerek's heels. "You do realize that protecting you includes protecting you from yourself?"

"Absolutely." Jerek grinned. "I would expect nothing less of you. But I want you to make me a promise."

"A promise to a madman? And here I thought this trip to the states might be boring."

"When I convince you I can mend the Fracture, you'll do

whatever it takes to help me, and you won't tell the Maree what we're doing until it's already done."

"That's a lot to ask."

"Not if you truly think I'm wrong." Jerek passed his phone to the gate agent, smiling silently until they made their way onto the jet bridge. "And if there's any chance I'm right, wouldn't it be worth risking everything to succeed?"

Lincoln stared at the worn carpet under their feet, trying to imagine a time that had disappeared when he was very young. When flying across the country meant searching out some glorious new adventure filled with the danger and wonder of magic, not playing babysitter to a potentially deranged feu.

"Fine," Lincoln said. "I promise, on my honor as a Maree, I will help you if you've found a way to fix the Fracture. I will stand with you until the work is done. But if you're wrong, if you've lost your mind and developed a penchant for property damage, you have to promise not to fight me when I haul you in front of the Council of the Feu and swear to take whatever help they give you to fix your messed up head with gratitude and a smile."

"Done."

Jerek's confident smirk sent a tingle of fear across the back of Lincoln's neck.

5

Ari

The mist from the massive fountain lent moisture to the desert air. Music pounded through the speakers as jets of water soared high above the pond. Sirens wailed their way down the strip, but none of the tourists cared as they watched the fountains fly.

Ari sat perched on top of a pillar, trying to ignore the chatter of those around her as she watched the water work its own sort of magic. A ballet no human could hope to perform.

The music peaked as the columns of water shot 460 feet into the air. The crowd cheered, and the fountain regained its placid state as nothing more than a pretty pool of water in a sea of neon lights.

"Mommy, make the fountain go again," a child whined from the cluster behind Ari. "I want to watch the water fly."

"We don't have time to wait for the fountain again, sweetie," the mother said. "Mommy and Daddy have a show to see. We've got to get you to the sitter."

"I hate babysitters!"

Ari closed her eyes as the child howled, willing her ears to hear only the soft rustle of the water and not the child's shouts or the endless voices of the Las Vegas crowds.

A breeze picked up, lifting Ari's long, blond hair away from her neck.

A smile curved her lips before Jerek spoke, breaking her moment of peace.

"I should have warned you to dress the part."

"What part would that be, Jerek Holden?" Ari didn't open her eyes. Forgetting the hordes surrounding her was so much easier when she couldn't see all the people hurrying by.

"The role of someone who's more than seventeen," Jerek said.

With a sigh, Ari opened her eyes and looked down at her dress. "Pink isn't just for little girls, Jer Bear. Besides, trying to look older never works for me. I'm doomed to look forever sweet and perfect."

"Why does she need to look older?" A towering boy spoke from behind Jerek's shoulder.

He had the closely cropped hair and muscular shoulders of someone who firmly believed death lurked around every corner, waiting for an untidy moment of weakness to strike.

Ari swallowed her giggle. "Well, I'll be. Lincoln Martel in the flesh. I swear, if I hadn't forced through the orders to get you sent home, I wouldn't have believed my own eyes."

"Forced through the orders?" Lincoln glared at Jerek.

"I had to be sure they would send you and not some other Maree." Jerek shrugged. "The Knights Maree may be filled with honor and sworn to protect the feu, but that doesn't mean I trust them."

"How did you make sure they would send me?" Lincoln shifted his glare from Jerek to Ari and back again. "What did you do, Jerek?"

"He really is as sweetly unaware as you said he'd be." Ari jumped down from her perch. "I thought you were exaggerating."

"No exaggeration necessary," Jerek said.

Pink crept up Lincoln's beefy neck. "I should call the knights right now—"

"You can't," Jerek cut across Lincoln. "You made a promise, old friend. Now it's time for me to prove to you how right I am."

"This might be fun." Ari threaded her arm through Jerek's elbow and leaned her head against his shoulder. "Now, where are we going that I need to look older?"

"To find a seasoned thief for our little escapade," Jerek said.

"Thief?" Lincoln blocked their path forward. "Why do we need a thief?"

"Because even with all our brains and talent, we're going to need help breaking into the most exclusive party the feu have ever seen to steal something worth more than all of our lives combined." Ari winked.

Red crept up Lincoln's neck, swallowing his ears.

"Oh, he's going to be fun." Ari led Jerek around Lincoln, letting the knight trail in their wake as they weaved through the throng.

6

Jack

Jack slouched at the end of the hall, his gaze fixed on the last ray of sunlight peering through the open door.

"You'll learn not to be antsy," Lydia said. "Give it a decade, and you'll want to sleep for a few weeks just to prove you can."

"I never hated spring until I couldn't be in the sun." Jack chewed on his thumbnail. "Days getting longer always seemed like a great thing. Now the sun is just stretching out the time I'm grounded."

"Grounded," Lucas said. "What a stunningly accurate description."

"Hardy-har," Lydia said.

They fell silent, each of them watching for the moment the deadly solar rays truly disappeared, leaving Las Vegas in the grips of a gaudy, man-made glow.

"I need to bring back more," Lucas said. "I've been short the past few nights."

"Don't focus on the bottom line," Lydia said. "If you walk up to a mark with dollar signs in your eyes, the smart ones will always see through you. And the smart ones have the money."

"I try to think of pick-pocketing as a quality-versus-quantity game." Jack rubbed the tip of his gnawed-on thumb. "It doesn't matter how many dollars I come home with as long as I've met some really great people along the way."

"I'm sure they'll love that method when you come up short below," Lucas said.

"I've never come up short." Jack stayed close to the wall as he moved toward the end of the hall, squinting out over the rooftops beyond.

"You could just check the time," Lydia said. "There's science behind when the sun goes down."

"Watches are lame," Jack said.

The sky beyond the neon radiance lost its last hint of orange, leaving nothing but the glow of light pollution in its wake.

"And the sun is down." Lucas stepped past Jack and out into the open air. "May the best man win, and don't forget to go to ground before dawn."

Lucas strode down the street and around the corner toward the main drag where tourists bustled from casino to casino, too drunk on booze and luck to keep close tabs on their wallets.

"I really don't like him." Jack reached his hand out into the open, testing the street for any final rays of sunlight.

"No one likes him." Lydia patted Jack on the shoulder. "But it's a good thing. Having one asshole none of us likes is a bonding experience for the rest of the clan."

"I'll just try to be glad it's not me."

"That's the spirit," Lydia said. "Team up tonight?"

"Sure." Jack stepped out onto the street, savoring the dry desert air despite the scent of gas and sweat tainting the breeze.

It's the freshest air I'll get for a long time.

Lydia led the way past the casinos on the farthest end of the strip, moving toward the pricier part of town.

"You know"—Lydia paused on a street corner, surveying the movements of the crowd—"my take doubles on nights when we team up. They might not say it very often below, but it was a great day for the clan when we found you."

"Great day for me, too." Jack smiled, wincing as his teeth sliced the inside of his lips. Before the taste of blood touched his tongue, the wounds had already healed.

"Them."

Lydia didn't need to point for Jack to know who she had chosen as their first mark of the evening.

A middle-aged woman in four-inch, glittering gold stilettos clung to the arm of a balding man in perfectly tailored pants. The pain of her ill-chosen footwear creased her forehead.

"The shoes are definitely designer," Jack said.

"Perfect." Lydia dodged around a group of tourists and onto the crosswalk.

Jack stayed ten feet behind, careful not to watch as Lydia approached their high-heeled mark.

Lydia stopped in front of the woman. "I'm so sorry, but I just have to know. Who designed your shoes? They are just to die for!"

"Oh, these old boats?" All hints of foot pain melted from the woman's face. "I can barely even remember. I think they're Blahnik."

Jack edged up behind the man, slipping his hand in and out of the man's silk-lined pocket before Lydia could coo her shoe envy.

"They are simply breathtaking. Where can you even buy shoes so beautiful?" Lydia asked.

Jack was out of earshot by the time the woman answered, the man's wallet firmly in his own pocket.

He leaned against the still-warm wall of a casino, staring up at the miniature Eiffel Tower planted on the roof across the way.

He had never been to Paris to see the real Eiffel Tower, but he was certain if he ever made it to the city of love, he would make a killing.

"Any luck?" Lydia leaned against the building beside him, already scanning the crowd for their next target.

"Obviously." Jack didn't pull out the wallet to check their newfound funds. That sort of thing could get you picked up by the police. And being locked in a cell when the sun rose was the very stuff of Jack's worst daymares.

"How about them?" Lydia tipped her head toward a pack of women wearing sashes.

The woman draped in the bride sash already seemed ready to pass out on the sidewalk.

"Not worth it," Jack said. "Those earrings are department store at best."

"Hmm."

They stood in silence for another long moment.

A flock of police officers prowled down the street, searching for something to make their night's work worth doing.

"And inside we go." Lydia laced her fingers through Jack's, leading him toward the doors of the Bellagio Hotel.

7

Jerek

"What are we doing here?" Lincoln asked for the fifth time.

"Finding our resource." Jerek glanced toward the security guards posted around the sides of the lobby. "There are some people whose front door you don't want to go knocking on. I thought it best to meet them in public."

"So you arranged a meeting in a place none of us are legally old enough to be in?" Lincoln asked.

"You never told me he was such a worrier." Ari frowned. "I feel like you should have mentioned that."

"And risk you not helping me get him home?" Jerek said. "IDs please."

"Only if you promise not to change it back." Ari pulled her license from her wallet.

Jerek studied Ari's photo. Her teal eyes shone even in miniature. But it was her blond hair that gave her a radiance beyond the reach of mere humans.

"I'll need yours as well, Lincoln," Jerek said.

"Fine," Lincoln said. "But mine gets put back."

While Lincoln fished in his pocket, Jerek swirled his fingers along the ink of Ari's ID. A tingle buzzed through his fingertips as the ink pulled free, drifting and curving, rearranging to fit Jerek's will.

With a quick puff of breath, he froze the ink in place. "Welcome to twenty-one, Ari."

"Aging four years in a few seconds. I hope it doesn't show." Ari slipped the ID from Jerek's palm.

"You're as gorgeous as ever," Jerek said. "Your turn, old man."

"Old man?" Lincoln said. "I'm not letting you mess with my face."

"Now isn't the time for such extreme precautions." Jerek opened Lincoln's passport, changing the deeply printed ink in a few seconds. "But not all of us can be celebrating our first taste of fully adult freedom. So you get the honor of being twenty-three."

"Why can't you be the oldest one?" Lincoln asked.

"Then I'd have to change my license." Jerek waved them out of the little alcove where they'd been sheltering and toward the casino floor.

"You're seventeen," Lincoln whispered. "You already had to change it."

"Didn't you know? Our boy is twenty-one." Ari stepped between them, looping her arms through theirs.

"That's not true," Lincoln said. "We're both seventeen. Or have you fallen so far into this delusion you don't know what year it is?"

"You didn't read Jerek's file?" Ari said. "I would have

thought a Maree would be more thorough."

"I read the part about the assassination attempts." Lincoln spoke under the rumble of the crowd and vague melody of the background music. "It didn't occur to me that someone I've known since birth would have lies in their Council records."

"I turned eighteen three years ago," Jerek said. "It was really quite magical, fourteen to eighteen in the blink of an eye. It all happened a week after my father died. I decided being an orphaned minor wasn't a life I cared to lead."

"Jerek, I'm sorry," Lincoln began. "If I'd—"

"I'll need to see all three of your IDs." The busty bouncer silenced the ache of old grief in Jerek's chest.

They all handed over their documents, waiting patiently as the woman glanced from photo to face several times for each of them.

The bouncer checked Ari's ID last. "Those eyes of yours real?"

"Only set of eyes I've ever had," Ari said.

"Pity." The bouncer handed back their IDs. "I'd like to buy some contacts that color."

"Sometimes birth defects turn out cute." Ari slipped her license back into her pocket.

"Ha," the woman said in a non-committal way. "Enjoy your evening."

"We will." Jerek bowed Lincoln and Ari onto the gambling floor.

"Now what?" Lincoln asked. "We gamble away the Holden estate?"

"Don't be dramatic." Jerek headed to the craps table at the center of the floor. "Now we wait for someone to rob us."

"You're right, no drama at all." Ari squeezed in between two older men at the table, beginning to giggle before she'd had time to catch on to the thread of their chatter. "I just love craps, don't you?"

"What is she doing?" Lincoln shook his head.

"Making herself an easy mark." Jerek leaned against the edge of the table, flipping the side of his coat casually open to expose the pants pocket that held his wallet.

"Who is she?" Lincoln whispered. "Where did you even meet her?"

"While some people ran off to Italy to train for their great destiny as a knight defending feu and somb alike, some of us had to stay home and survive the brutal reality of the post-Fracture world." Jerek cheered along with the rest of the table as the dealers doled out chips.

The crowd around the table rotated as new players joined the game.

"Ari is a dear friend who happens to believe whole-heartedly in what I'm doing," Jerek said. "Add to that the fact that she's a brilliant hacker and she's the perfect second in command for this mission. Don't worry, that doesn't make your role any less important."

"When I haul you in front of the Council for a psychological evaluation, should I bring her, too?" Lincoln asked.

"Sure." Jerek leapt forward, grabbing for something his eyes had yet to properly see.

His fingers closed around the cold skin of a narrow wrist.

A boy with deep brown eyes, curling black hair, and dark skin that seemed a little too perfect to be human jerked away from Jerek's grasp.

"What's your problem, man?" the boy asked.

A flash of brown leather flicked through the edge of Jerek's vision.

"No problem at all," Jerek said. "I was actually afraid I was going to be stuck waiting here all night. I'd like to speak with Lydia."

8

Jack

Jack frowned at the two boys that faced him, wincing as his teeth sliced his lips again.

He could run. Even the big guy wouldn't be able to catch him. But running would mean calling attention to himself, and that came with the risk of being banned from one of his biggest cash cows.

Jack forced a careful smile onto his face and gave a little bow. "Lydia's too busy for dealing with fans. But I'd be happy to relay your admiration."

"I'm not a fan," the shorter of the two boys said. "I'm an ally here to call in a long-overdue favor. I'd rather not have to follow the clan all the way underground for a meeting. I think we can both agree that would make it a painfully long morning for everyone involved. So please save us all a lot of unnecessary trouble and find Lydia. Tell her Jerek Holden is here to see her."

Jack took a deep breath, trying to catch Jerek's scent over the cacophony of perfume and booze. There wasn't a whiff of fear to him. A seed of worry sank into Jack's stomach.

"I'll go find Lydia and see if she's willing to meet you," Jack said. "I make no promises."

"Of course," Jerek said. "We'll be waiting by the fountains. This kind of chat requires a bit of very public privacy."

"Sure thing." Jack turned to leave.

"Give my friend his wallet back before you go," Jerek said. "I would hate for someone of your talents to be caught stealing from a Maree."

Tension shocked the back of Jack's neck as two teeth at the front of his mouth doubled their length.

Keeping his lips closed, he reached into his pocket, pulling out the brown wallet and tossing it over his shoulder. He didn't wait for the dull thump of the wallet being caught before walking away.

The vibrant colors of the casino blurred around him as he searched for Lydia's scent. Every breath swirled the excitement and fear of the gamblers through him, worsening the worry in his gut.

Calm down. Just calm down.

His body wouldn't listen to his mind.

"You lost, sweetie?" a woman twice his age who stank of old rubber asked.

Jack shook his head, too afraid to open his mouth and risk her catching a glimpse of his fangs.

A familiar aroma caught in his nose. He followed the scent along a row of slot machines, darting around the high-heeled waitresses and to Lydia's side.

She sat perched on a man's knee, a glass of wine she couldn't drink in hand.

The sight of her alive and un-butchered calmed Jack enough for his teeth to return to their normal size.

"Lydia." Jack licked the blood from the corners of his mouth. "I was hoping I might catch you here tonight."

"Get lost kid," the man grunted. "We're having a great time."

"Looks like it," Jack said. "But Jerek Holden stopped by and wants a quick word, something about you owing him a favor."

If Jack hadn't spent most of the last three years trailing around on Lydia's apron strings, he might have missed the flash of fear in her eyes.

"Asshole makes you find me to call in a cigarette I owe him?" She stood, her back to the machine, and kissed the man's forehead. "I'll be back soon, sweetie."

The man didn't even blink as she slipped his wallet from his pocket.

Jack led Lydia past the rows of marks, all lined up and waiting to be stolen from. Balancing their wealth on the edges of their pockets, as though begging him to give them a Las Vegas horror story to bring home so they could share their tale of adventure at their next book club meeting.

I'm going to be short on my take tonight.

The thought wasn't nearly as frightening as the abstract concept of the wrath of the Maree.

Jack slowed to walk by Lydia's side as they stepped out onto the sidewalk.

"What kind of favor do you owe the Maree?" Jack glanced around the crowd, searching for a fleet of highly trained soldiers, wondering how badly being beheaded would hurt.

It would have to be better than sun burning.

"I don't owe the Maree anything," Lydia said. "It's the Holdens I have to repay. Though I didn't think Jerek would be ballsy enough to call in the debt. At least not this decade."

Jack weaved through the crowds toward the fountain. The

music began, and with a flourish, the jets of water burst back to life.

"Lydia, you'd tell me if you were in trouble, right?"

"We're vampires, Jack"—Lydia patted his shoulder a bit too hard—"we're always in trouble."

A girl in a rose-pink dress with long blond hair cascading down her back sat perched on a pillar, her gaze fixed on the dancing water. Jerek leaned against the railing beside her, grinning as Lydia and Jack approached. The Maree stood next to him, his hands behind his back as though hiding the blade that would sever Jack's head from his neck.

"Lydia." Jerek gave a bow as they approached. "It's good to see time hasn't changed your routine."

Lydia didn't bow back. "What do you want, Holden?"

"Your—apprentice, is it—didn't introduce himself while he was picking Lincoln's pocket, I'm afraid." Jerek kept smiling.

Something in his calm replaced the worry in Jack's gut with anger.

Lydia nodded to Jack.

"Jack Slayed." His stomach flipped at his own daring as he bowed deeply to Jerek.

"Huh," the Maree grunted.

"Be nice, Lincoln," the girl in the pink dress warned.

Lincoln's jaw tensed, forming a perfectly chiseled line around the edge of his chin.

"I need your help," Jerek said. "It's a big job, but you'll be paid well when it's over."

"What kind of job?" Lydia said.

"We're going to steal something from a fancy party." The girl in pink didn't look away from the fountains. "Should be a really great time."

"Not a bad way to call in a debt." Jerek shrugged. "You get to do what you love, and the world comes out a better place."

"A better place?" Jack asked.

"Where's the party?" Lydia asked.

"On the east coast at the end of the week," Jerek said. "I'd need you to come now, though. We've got work to get done."

"Sorry, not gonna happen." Lydia crossed her arms. "I'm not leaving Vegas."

A flicker of anger passed behind Jerek's eyes though his smile never faltered.

"You owe my family a debt," Jerek said. "The Fracture might have shattered most magic, but there are bonds that still stand."

Lydia licked her front teeth, letting a drop of blood linger on her lips as she spoke. "You force me to help, you risk the wrath of the clan."

"A debt is a debt," Lincoln said. "Even the clans burrowed deep in the darkness know that."

Lydia glanced around the crowd, searching for Jack didn't know what.

"Look," Lydia whispered, her voice barely carrying over the music of the fountain show, "your mom was an amazing woman. She saved a lot of lives, and I will never forget what she did for me, for all of us. I want to repay the debt, but I can't leave Vegas, not right now. The politics below are far from stable. If I disappear for a week, the balance might shift entirely. Then bye-bye pickpockets, hello tourist drainers. Your mother wouldn't want that."

"Dead people rarely want anything," Jerek said.

Lydia closed her eyes, taking a deep breath before looking at Jack. "Take Jack as my proxy."

"What?" Jack said at the same moment Lincoln said, "Absolutely not."

"I'd say I trained him myself, but the kid's got talent like I've never seen," Lydia said. "Sleight of hand, pickpocketing, lock-picking. The kid was a legend in the shadows before we ever took him below."

"I need someone who's calm under pressure," Jerek said. "This isn't a prank we're planning. There will be danger, and failure is not an option."

"Jack won't let you down," Lydia said. "Will you Jack?"

"Lydia, I..."

She silenced him with a tiny shake of her head.

"Of course I won't." Jack nodded, tucking his hands into his pockets to avoid any temptation to bite his thumbnail. "It's been a while since I left the city. It'll be good to get some fresh air."

"Perfect." Jerek stepped in front of Lydia, looking straight into her eyes. "Lydia Muldrew, if your proxy acts to the best of his ability to ensure the success of my chosen mission, I release you from your debt."

The ten inches of open space between them gave a faint shimmer, as though a blast of steaming air had flown from Jerek's body and into Lydia's.

"If he fails to serve our cause, or causes us to fail, the debt remains an anchor pulling through the next generation."

The air shimmered again at Jerek's words.

Lydia flinched as the second wave met her flesh.

"If Jack gets hurt because of you, I will hunt you down and drain you," Lydia said.

"It would be because of you," Jerek said. "I'm not the one who volunteered him."

"We should go." The girl in pink still didn't look away from the fountains.

"All too true," Jerek said. "We've booked a flight back east, and we don't have the time to risk missing it."

"I can't ride in a plane," Jack said, "even if the flight's supposed to land before dawn. Planes get delayed, or stuck on the runway when they land. I could die."

"Don't worry. We've made arrangements," Jerek said.

With a deep sigh, the girl in pink jumped down from her perch. "You've been booked for first class travel via coffin in the cargo hold. We have to get sweet Aunt Lydia home for her funeral somehow."

"Should we change the name on the papers to Jack?" Jerek asked.

"If they open the casket, they're in for a bigger surprise than Aunt Lydia being a teenage boy," Lincoln said.

"Fair," Jerek said. "Jack, say your goodbyes. We've got to get you packed up for shipping."

The three walked to the edge of the sidewalk, not bothering to watch and see if Jack bolted.

I can't. I can't betray Lydia, even if she bargained me away.

"Just do what they say, and you'll be home next week." Lydia brushed Jack's perfectly styled curls away from his face.

"And if they want me to kill people?" Jack fought to keep his voice from shaking. "We're vampires. They can't just want me to pick a lock. They could find a magician who could do that just as well. They're going to ask me to cross a line I don't want to touch."

"You kill who they tell you to and get home. You won't be the first vampire with body count regret."

"Lydia, please don't make me go. We can send Lucas. He'd like the adventure of it."

"If Holden came out here, it's because he needs the best. I can't leave, you know I can't, so it has to be you. Now quit this whiney toddler shit, climb in a coffin, and try and get some rest on the flight."

"Sure." Jack blinked away the warmth of the tears forming in his eyes. "Keep everybody away from my stuff until I get back."

"I'll sun toss the fool who tries to touch any of it." Lydia kissed his cheek and disappeared into the crowd.

A warm hand slipped into his, the light touch leading him to a cab waiting at the curb.

"Don't worry," the girl in pink said. "We're the good guys, I promise. I've even ordered some really nice bedding for your coffin ride."

9

Grace

Describe King Lear's feelings toward each of his daughters. Include the root of those relationships and how they affect Lear's deteriorating mental state.

Grace's eyes glossed over as she read through the question for the fourth time.

...affect Lear's deteriorating mental state.

She took a deep breath, trying to steer her mind back to the play she'd read only a few days before. Or mostly read.

Steven, beautiful Steven, had been sitting on the couch next to her. His leg pressed close to hers as he fought his way through Shakespeare. His lips formed the words as he read, moving in the most mesmerizing way.

"Pencils down in ten minutes," Mr. Merek called from the front of the class. His eyes were glossed over as well, watching videos on the cell phone he had hidden in his book.

Ten minutes. I can write this out in ten minutes.

Cordelia was the treasure child cast aside, and Regina, no not Regina. That wasn't her name.

Sweat slicked Grace's palms. The time on the clock seemed to speed up as she fought to remember the other daughters' names.

If I don't pass this test...

She couldn't let herself finish the thought. She would pass the English test. She'd never failed a test. Everything was going to be fine.

If I can just remember that damn name.

"Five minutes," Mr. Merek said.

Grace's pencil slipped from her grip. Heat crept into her cheeks as she reached down to grab it.

Steven caught her eye from two seats down the row, giving her a thumbs up before turning back to his paper.

Panic crashed into Grace's lungs, pushing away every reasonable thought.

"Mr. Merek."

Katie's voice barely cut through the thundering of the blood pounding in Grace's ears.

"Mr. Merek!" Katie shot up from her seat, pointing at the trashcan next to Mr. Merek's desk.

Flames licked the sides of the metal can.

Grace forgot her fear as the flames leapt three feet into the air, setting fire to the pile of books resting on the corner of Mr. Merek's desk.

Mr. Merek stared in horror as the flames drifted toward him.

"Get a fire extinguisher," Steven said.

Mr. Merek stood, dropping his phone and knocking his chair over as the fire alarm rang.

With a sputtering hiss, the sprinkler trickled to life.

The students grabbed their things and ran for the door.

Grace snatched up her books, barely giving her test a glance as the sprinkler washed all the words away.

10

Jerek

Aunt Lydia's coffin had been accepted by the airline in Vegas without a hitch, the flight had arrived in Florida ten minutes early, and the van had been parked in the short-term parking lot, waiting right where Jerek had asked it to be.

"Good to see you." Jerek patted the teal and white paint of the VW van, savoring one tiny moment of triumph.

"Somehow, I really thought you were kidding," Ari said. "I mean, I know I should know better, but still."

"You kept your dad's old car?" Lincoln leaned against the driver's door, blocking Jerek's path. "You really think this old clunker is going to get us up the coast?"

"Dad rebuilt this thing with his own two hands," Jerek said. "If any car can get us where we're going, it's this old beast."

"Remind me you said that when we're broken down on the side of the highway," Lincoln said.

"I'm sitting in the back to work." Ari cranked down the driver's window, peeking around Lincoln's head.

"We need to get moving." Jerek shooed Lincoln away from the door. "We can't be late picking up sweet Aunt Lydia's remains."

"Where are you going to put the coffin anyway?" Lincoln opened Jerek's door for him before heading around to the other side.

"We'll shove it in the back with Ari until the sun goes down," Jerek said.

"Lovely," Ari said.

Jerek climbed up into the driver's seat. The worn material felt as familiar to him as his own bed. Finger-shaped grooves had been worn into the steering wheel by years of use. Jerek lined his hands up with the indents.

Dad's hands were the same size as mine.

"We can't leave Jack in the coffin forever." Lincoln closed the passenger-side door. "What are you going to do when the sun comes up tomorrow?"

"Arrangements have been made." Jerek turned the key in the ignition, allowing himself a moment of joy as the engine rumbled to life with a familiar purr.

"You could explain yourself once in a while," Lincoln said. "It might go a long way toward making people trust you."

"Plenty of people trust me," Jerek said. "Even you trust me. If you didn't, you wouldn't be here."

"I made a promise to let you try and convince me. That's not the same as trust." Lincoln clicked his seatbelt closed and looked over his shoulder, glaring at Ari who had curled up with her laptop on one of the couch-like seats that ran along the van's walls. "This tank is going to get us killed."

"Trust the car, knight boy." Ari popped in earbuds.

Jerek pulled out of the parking spot, beginning his winding path out of the garage.

"You do trust me," Jerek said. "Two cross-country flights, some moderate airline fraud, and you're still here."

"Because I'm really hoping my best friend hasn't completely lost touch with reality," Lincoln said.

"I'll do my best not to disappoint you," Jerek said.

11

Grace

"I just don't know what it is with that school." Pop thumped the platter of roast beef down onto the center of the table. "How many incidents do there have to be before they figure out your school was built over a Hellmouth?"

"There's no such thing as a Hellmouth." Dad reached across the table to take Grace's hands in his. The burn scars that marred the back of his left hand caught the light as his knuckles stretched. "If you want an explanation, call it Florida swamp gas. Some kid probably threw a leaky battery away and some confetti caught on fire."

"That's not how fire works," Grace said. "I should know. I've been forced to sit through high school science."

"Our little button is so smart." Pop placed the broccoli on the table with a gentler hand than the beef had received. "She knows the only logical explanation is a Hellmouth."

"You're both ridiculous." Grace shook her head. Her black

hair, frizzed from the fire sprinklers and Florida humidity, bounced around her face.

"Well, whatever it was, we're both glad you're safe." Pop kissed her forehead and took his place at the table.

They sat in silence as Pop dished food onto their plates.

Grace laughed as Dad snatched the serving fork, taking an extra portion of beef.

Pop rolled his eyes and said nothing.

Grace had managed to down two bites before Dad spoke.

"Are you sure you're okay?"

"If you want to talk to us about it," Pop said, "or maybe talk to someone else."

"I'm not going back to therapy." Grace set her silverware down, tucking her hands in her lap. "It would just be a waste of money, because I'm fine. A trashcan caught on fire, and my hair got wet. Honestly, I'm pretty lucky. I get to retake the test next week."

"We never should have let you study with that boy." Pop waggled his fork. "Group dates, that's the ticket."

"We aren't dating," Grace said.

"Our daughter's been through a trauma, and you're worried about dating?" Dad asked.

"There was no trauma," Grace said.

"Even a small fire could bring up old memories," Dad said. "In this family, we don't let emotional wounds fester, no matter how long ago they began. PTSD is a very real—"

"I don't have PTSD." Grace gripped the napkin on her lap. "I just have a lot of luck."

"Your classroom catching on fire is luck?" Pop's eyebrows crept up toward his widow's peak.

"Yeah," Grace said. "Like having you two is luck. Bad luck, good luck, I've got it all in spades. No point in analyzing it. Life just happens."

"Our baby girl is all grown up and philosophical." Pop raised his glass to Grace.

"Still," Dad said, "we're making you an appointment with the guidance counselor."

"Dad—"

"Being well-adjusted isn't something to be taken for granted." Pop added extra broccoli to Dad's plate. "Make us feel better and talk to the counselor. I'll make scallops if you go without arguing."

"Fine, I'll go," Grace said. "But it won't change how my life works."

12

Jack

The uneven road tossing him against the sides of the coffin wasn't the worst part of the trip. At least, Jack assumed he was being driven down a bumpy road—he hadn't been able to see anything but pitch black since he'd been locked inside the casket in Vegas.

The plane had been freezing.

The soft sheets and fleece blankets Ari had lined his coffin with helped, but the hum of the engines pounded into his brain, making sleep impossible.

"This is a terrible mistake. This is a terrible mistake." He repeated the phrase over and over, not stopping until the plane landed with a squeal of its wheels.

Rough voices spoke from just beyond the metal-lined walls around him as he was lifted from the plane. The ground buzzed beneath him for a few minutes. Then the rough voices spoke to other, gentler-toned people.

With a few big bumps, he was moved again. Ending up with his head tipping slightly down.

He'd been like that for a few hours now.

He was back with Holden. He had to be since Ari had shouted through the metal, "We'll let you out after sundown," as the vehicle that now carried him started its engine and drove away.

No, it wasn't the discomfort of the trip, but the absolute lack of control Jack couldn't stand. He didn't even know where exactly the plane had taken him.

"This is a terrible mistake."

Jack didn't have many regrets in life, which was remarkable for an eighteen-year-old, newly minted vampire.

Running away from home four years ago had been the best choice he'd ever made. Following Lydia back to the underground when she'd found him slipping necklaces off women in a theatre lobby on the strip had given him a new home. He'd never regret joining the clan.

And becoming a vampire—the only thing he regretted about that was being made to wait until his eighteenth birthday to be bitten. But that was a clan rule. No one would have dared break it to bite him early, not even Lydia.

And now she's sent me away.

Bitter tears stung the corners of Jack's eyes, but he refused to let them fall even while hidden within the private confines of the coffin.

He wished the vampire myths were true. That he could be locked in a coffin and instantly fall asleep for all the daylight hours. But his blood had rushed to his head from the awkward angle of his prison, and sleep wouldn't come.

What if they want to steal something they can use to hurt people? What if they want me to drain everyone at the party so no one will know what they've stolen?

He would do whatever Holden asked to protect Lydia. To make sure whatever debt she owed would be paid in full.

At least she'll be grateful when I go home.

The hum of the road evened out, slowly luring him to sleep.

At least I don't need too much air.

He had no idea if he'd been out for a minute or hours when the coffin opened with a creak.

"Is he alive?" Lincoln asked.

"Of course he is," Jerek said. "Coffin travel is a time-honored vampire tradition."

Ari's face appeared in the crack first. "He's fine."

"No thanks to all of you." Jack pushed the lid up. The wood met the roof of the van where they'd shoved him, leaving him to scramble out through a crack. "You could have pulled over in a nice dark cave and let me out hours ago."

"We needed to reach our destination for the night," Jerek said. "Now it's dark, and you'll be able to feed."

"I ate two nights ago," Jack said. "I'm good for now."

"Self-restraint," Lincoln said. "I'm impressed."

"Not all vampires are blood-sucking murderers." Jack brushed out the wrinkles in his clothes.

"But enough are that I'm impressed you're not," Lincoln said.

"Just take the compliment." Jerek opened the double door in the side of the van. "Lincoln doesn't offer them very often."

Humid air flooded the car.

"Where are we?" Jack breathed in the scent of damp earth and blooming flowers.

"Middle of Nowhere, Florida." Ari hopped out of the van, a pink backpack slung over her shoulder.

"And why are we here?" Jack climbed out of the teal interior of the VW and onto the cracked asphalt of a hotel parking lot.

"We're running a little collection errand," Ari said. "Have to pick our baby girl up from school."

Jerek glared at Ari.

"Our team still isn't complete." Jerek pulled his and Lincoln's packs from the van, leaving Jack as the only one with nothing to carry.

"Team?" Jack said. "What do you need a team for? If you want something stolen, just point me in the right direction and I'll grab it for you."

"Ha!" A loud laugh burst from Ari before she doubled over, giggling. "Can you imagine?" She gripped Jerek's sleeve. "Just send him and he'll grab it."

"I've stolen diamonds off a lady surrounded by bodyguards, and no one flinched." Jack's fangs sliced his lip. "I'm very good at what I do."

"I never thought I'd be a part of a conversation where being a thief would be a good thing." Lincoln dragged his hands over his cropped hair.

"If it were a matter of walking in and taking something, I would send you in tomorrow evening and we could all go back to our blissfully separate lives, but it's not," Jerek said. "What we need isn't some silly diamond. What we need is infinitely more valuable."

A rusted-out car swerved into the lot, pulling in to park crookedly between two spots farther down the row.

"We should get inside." Ari's gaze kept flicking toward the car as she led the way to the lobby door.

The sign above the entrance feebly shone its promise of free Wi-Fi and a complimentary breakfast.

A woman with skin wrinkled from too many years of avid tanning sat behind the desk, sipping her iced tea.

"Allow me." Jerek stepped up to the desk, pulling out his

credit card and license before the woman seemed to realize anyone had entered the lobby.

"Do you have a reservation?" The woman's gaze fixed on each of the boys before landing on Ari.

"No." Jerek pushed his credit card forward. "But we'd like two adjoining rooms, with a door between if possible."

"We don't rent to anyone under eighteen." She sipped her tea.

"We're all well over age," Jerek said.

"Don't look like it." The woman smacked her lips. "She looks underage as hell, and I don't want that kind of thing happening here."

Ari fished around in her pocket before pulling out her ID. "I just have a young face."

The woman squinted at Ari's ID for a moment before taking Jerek's credit card.

"I'll charge on that deposit if you mess with the room."

Jack tried to ignore the sugary scent of the woman's tea as she made the room keys at the pace of a fatigued sloth.

The outside door dinged open.

The man who had pulled into the parking lot entered, his lips glued to the neck of a giggling woman.

The thick stench of cheap whiskey wafted after them as they headed toward the elevator.

"You going to charge on their deposit, too?" Jack asked.

"Only if they mess with my room," the woman said.

"I'm glad to know you're fair." Jerek took the keys from the counter.

"Breakfast ends at 9 a.m. and I don't feed latecomers," the woman called after them.

"She's a peach," Ari whispered as they stepped into the elevator.

"We're in Florida," Jack said. "I think that makes her an orange."

"You're not awful." Ari nudged Jack's side with her elbow.

As they reached the third floor, the stench of mildew and cheap cleaner filled the air.

Jack lifted his shirt to cover his nose, his stomach rolling though he'd given up his ability to vomit.

Ari rolled her eyes at him and snatched a key from Jerek's hand. "I'll bunk with sucky face."

"That's a little rude," Jack said.

"Bat boy?" Ari slipped the key into the lock.

"A bit better."

"I'll order food." Jerek led Lincoln into the room next door.

Jack closed the door to his and Ari's room and leaned against the fake wood.

"You going to make it?" Ari threw herself onto a bed.

"I'll be fine." Jack pressed his knuckles to his temples.

"Like I said, we really are the good guys, if that helps." Ari kicked off her pink shoes.

"I guess."

"A real talker, you are."

Jack walked over to the other bed and sank down onto its creaking springs. "What kind of good guys force people to help them?"

"I'd say something about the greater good, but that would just sound creepy." Ari rolled onto her side. "I'm not sure you'd understand anyway."

"I'm a vampire, not stupid." Jack picked at the paisley comforter.

"It's not about being stupid. It's about not being around when it happened."

"What happened?"

"The Fracture."

A tingle ran from the back of Jack's neck to the tips of his fingers.

"Let us in," Jerek said from the other side of their shared door.

"What a gentleman," Ari sighed and obediently got up to unlock the door.

"How far have you gotten?" Jerek walked into the room and sat on the foot of Ari's bed.

Lincoln closed the door behind him, leaning against the wall like a bouncer expecting a horde of people to flood in from his own room.

"The Fracture." Ari flopped down onto the bed beside Jack.

"That's a big place to start," Lincoln said.

"Do we really need to do this right now?" Jerek asked. "I'll only have to repeat myself, and no one enjoys that."

"It's time to make good, Jerek," Lincoln said. "I've kept my end of the bargain."

"You really are difficult," Jerek turned to Jack, appraising him for a moment before speaking again. "How much do you know about the Fracture?"

"Everything?" Jack straightened up and met Jerek's gaze. "I mean, it's not like the Fracture is a secret in the vampire clans."

Jerek waved a hand for him to continue.

Jack took a deep breath, willing his fangs not to grow and slice through his lips.

"Twelve years ago, magic broke," Jack said. "One day, everything's fine, the next, crack. The Fracture happens, and magic is shattered. Magicians everywhere end up with flaccid powers."

Ari clapped a hand over her mouth to mute her laughter.

Jerek's eyes narrowed, but he didn't make a move to silence Jack.

"Vampires' powers weren't affected, but things still got really bad for the clans," Jack pressed on. "For all of the feu, I guess. Magicians had been in charge of keeping the peace. The Council of the Feu fell. The treaties and magically created boundaries fell. The Knights Maree tried to figure out what had happened. Went all Grail Quest about it, but they all ended up dead."

Jack looked to Lincoln, waiting for some sign of shame or grief. The knight's face betrayed nothing.

"The Maree had to give up," Jack said. "Eventually, everyone had to give up and move on in the broken, post-Fracture world, which is probably why a powerless magician had to stoop so low as to ask for a vampire pickpocket's help."

"I kind of like him better than Lydia," Ari said.

Jerek clapped, as though Jack had just performed a monologue. "You've learned your lessons in vampire school quite well. But you got a few, key points wrong."

"Such as?" Jack laced his fingers together on his lap, his knuckles cracking as he fought the urge to lunge across the three-foot gap between beds and wring Jerek's neck.

"Magicians didn't lose all their powers." Jerek pressed his hand to the comforter on Ari's bed. The paisley pattern turned from a dull yellow to a beautiful pale pink.

"Pretty," Ari cooed.

"Nice party trick," Jack said.

"Changing the graphic appearance of things can come in handy," Jerek said. "But you're right, it's nothing like the magic we used to have. We've been left with the sad remains of a once glorious world."

Jack tried to imagine being shoved back into the body he'd had only a few months before when he'd been entirely human. "I'm sorry for your loss."

"We all lost a lot in the Fracture," Lincoln said. "But that still doesn't explain what we're doing here."

"The second point you missed," Jerek said, without sparing

Lincoln a glance, "not everyone gave up on mending the damage. The search never ended."

The floor groaned as Lincoln pushed away from the wall.

"Many have been lost in the search, and many have given up and succumbed to grief," Jerek said. "But I never did. And I found it, the way to mend magic for all of us. To put things back to the way they were meant to be, and you, Jack, are going to play a very important role in saving the feu."

13

Lincoln

They waited around the corner for the last of the morning school buses to pull away, taking advantage of the shade beneath a palm tree.

"We shouldn't even be trying to go onto school property," Lincoln said.

"We're high school age," Ari said. "No one will even notice us."

"I've never been inside a high school." Lincoln squinted at the front of the low brick building, searching for signs of security.

"Me neither," Jerek said.

"I spent three years in the cold, cruel halls of high school," Ari said. "It was a real low point for me."

"And you just decided not to go back?" Lincoln asked.

"Graduated early," Ari said. "It seemed like a better plan than dropping out."

"Huh." Lincoln shoved his hands into his pockets. The foreign softness of the shorts grated against his fingers.

"You *huh* a lot, don't you?" Ari said. "That's like your thing?"

"Can we please analyze Lincoln later?" Jerek stepped out of the shade and onto the sidewalk. "We have an errand to run."

"And just how do you think we're going to collect this girl?" Lincoln asked. "We aren't kidnapping her. I absolutely draw the line at kidnapping."

"We just have to convince her in a friendly manner that coming with us is in her best interest," Jerek said.

"This is a terrible idea." Lincoln grabbed Jerek's arm, pulling him back toward the tree. "That school is full of sombs, normal people who have nothing to do with magic, who can't find out about any of us. We can't just drag a girl out here and say *Hey, I'm looking to mend the magical world, want to go on a road trip?*"

"That sounds like a great idea." Ari brushed her hair behind her shoulders. "I'll go in and fetch our girl. You boys stay out here and make sure we aren't attacked by werewolves." She strode toward the school, the hem of her pink shirt fluttering in the wind. She reached the corner and turned back. "You could also take this time to work out your emotional issues, but who am I to judge?"

Lincoln shoved his hands back into his overly soft pockets as Ari slipped through the school's doors.

A beat-up truck peeled into the parking lot. The driver hopped out and ran for the entrance before the stench of singed rubber disappeared.

"We shouldn't have let her go in there on her own," Lincoln said.

"It's a high school, not a war zone," Jerek said. "Ari will be fine."

"We could do the job without the somb." Lincoln leaned against the tree.

"The student we're looking for isn't a somb. If I'm right, she's one of us. She belongs with the feu."

"Then it's even more important that we leave her alone." Lincoln willed his reason to outweigh his worry. "Let her stay a normal person living her normal human life. She could be happy being a somb. Hauling her out of her life, telling her she belongs to a magical world but that world's been broken since before she was taught unicorns weren't real...that's cruel, Jerek."

"Not if we can fix it." Jerek paced the sidewalk. "If we can mend the cracks, then how lucky will she be to join the feu?"

"It's not your responsibility to fix the Fracture." Lincoln kept his feet planted as he watched his friend weave back and forth. "You aren't a failure if you don't try."

"So you believe me?" Jerek stopped. "You think I've finally found where the cracks began?"

"I believe you believe. You think you've found a way to save us all, but if there were a way to do it, wouldn't it have already been done?"

"My father tried. He died trying."

"Jerek." Lincoln pushed away from the palm, his heart thumping too hard in his chest. "The reports said your father died in a household accident."

"He did die in the house." Jerek kicked pebble. "In the library, in fact."

"Why didn't you tell me? Why didn't you tell the Maree?"

"Same answer really." Jerek shrugged. "The Maree think they can fix everything. If I told you, you'd tell them, and they'd come take Dad's research. The Maree might be highly skilled protectors, but they aren't magicians. It's going to take a magician to fix the Fracture. I couldn't risk anyone knowing how close my father had come to finding the answer until I knew where he'd gone wrong and how to do the thing properly myself."

Lincoln looked toward the school. There was no sign of Ari. No hint that any feu had ever even entered the bland somb building. "And you're sure you've got it right?"

"I bet my life on it," Jerek said. "And even if I'm wrong, you gave me your word. You're honor-bound to accompany me as I try to save the feu."

"You could have explained everything two days ago. You would have saved me two days of thinking you had completely lost your mind."

"I had to make sure they hadn't changed you. What if you'd become a Maree drone who wanted to hand all my dad's research in?"

"I should, but I won't." Lincoln ran his palms over the fuzz of his cropped hair. "They could banish me for this."

"Only if we fail." Jerek smiled. "If we get this right, you're going to be a legend among knights."

"There's no way to do this without the girl?" Lincoln turned his gaze back to the school, unable to stare at Jerek a moment longer.

"We need a real magician. She's the only one I've found."

The tinny blare of a fire alarm sliced through the air.

14

Ari

Ari leaned against the beige wall, waiting for the screams and panic to begin. Red lights and wailing sirens filled the hall. Students emerged from their classrooms, not running in fear, but strolling in a bored, put out kind of way.

"Casual. I like it." Ari kicked away from the wall, joining the stream of students behind a girl with shoulder-length, black hair.

The crowd led her around the corner and toward an emergency exit.

With a sigh, Ari toppled forward, knocking down the girl with the black hair.

"Ow!" Ari rolled onto her side, clutching her ankle.

The other girl sat up, pushing her hair out of her face. "Are you okay?"

"I think I twisted my ankle." Ari's lip trembled. "I'm sorry I bumped into you."

"It's fine." The girl stood.

"Everybody out." A male voice boomed down the hall. "I don't want attitude, I want an empty building."

"Dammit." Ari pushed herself halfway up then crumpled to the floor again.

"Let me help you." A boy who looked like he spent more time with free weights than textbooks took Ari's arm.

"She can help me." Ari reached for the black-haired girl. "Please?"

"Sure." The girl stooped low, wrapping her arm around Ari's waist and helping her to her feet.

"Thank you." Ari limped toward the door. "I just want to get in my car and go home. Public school is such a nightmare."

15

Grace

Her shoulders ached from helping the hurt girl limp across the parking lot to the fire rally point. None of the students moved too quickly. They had barely made it past the fire lane when the police and fire trucks zoomed into the parking lot.

"They should just put a fire house here," Katie grumbled. "And maybe provide shade for us to rally under. If I get a sunburn again, my mom is going to be pissed."

"She'll deal." Grace helped the hurt girl to the edge of the pack. "You should sit here. The nurse will make her rounds in a minute."

"You've got this down to a science." The girl grimaced as she poked at her ankle. "Do you have a lot of fire drills here?"

"Probably not a drill." Steven tapped Grace on the shoulder. "Going to introduce me to the new girl?"

Heat crept up Grace's cheeks.

"We haven't really met. We just bumped into each other." The girl gave a little giggle.

"Then I'll do the honors." Steven knelt, holding out his hand. "I'm Steven."

"Ari." Ari grinned as she shook Steven's hand. "How did you know I'm new? Do I stick out that badly?"

"This has got to be your first day. There's no way I wouldn't have noticed you." Steven reached for Ari's ankle. "May I?"

"Sure." Ari's voice fluttered as she spoke.

The perfect damsel in distress just popped into the middle of school and tackled me.

"Ouch." Ari flinched.

"The nurse will be here soon," Grace said. "You should probably just leave it alone."

"I've sprained plenty of things, Gracie. I know a bit about first aid."

Steven didn't even look back at her as he spoke.

"I just fell right over." Ari's perfectly painted pink lips slipped into a pout. "I hate that I embarrassed myself so badly on my first day."

"I wouldn't worry about it," Steven said. "You still make a great first impression."

The police stood lazily beside their cars, waiting for the firemen to find the flames, barely paying any attention to the students, who had already lost interest in the possible inferno in their school.

"I'd really love to have someone show me around," Ari said. "I don't know anything about the town, or even Florida. "

"I'd be happy to help," Steven said. "There's this beautiful spot on the beach, right down the road from here. I think you'd love it."

Grace's heart shattered.

"I love the ocean." Ari beamed.

All at once, the sirens on the fire trucks, cop cars, and inside the school fell silent.

The quiet pressed against Grace's ears. She forced air into her lungs as the students glanced around, more startled by the sudden silence than they'd ever been by the alarms.

"Creepy," Ari whispered.

The cops ducked inside their cars, fiddling with out-of-sight buttons and switches.

"Should I be scared right now?" Ari clung to Steven's arm.

"Nah," Steven said. "Things like this just happen around here. Nobody gets hurt, so no one cares too much. But if you ask me, there's some kind of freak in this school who likes messing with the rest of us. It'll be a bad day for them if we ever find the bastard, that's for sure."

Grace's heart raced, surging at a rate her brain couldn't understand.

The sirens began again, louder and faster than they'd screeched before.

"Some kind of freak is right!" Ari clamped her hands over her ears as she locked eyes with Grace.

"It's too crowded here." Grace didn't care if no one could hear her over the blaring sirens. She took a shuddering breath, trying to slow her still-racing heart, and pushed through the back of the crowd to the sidewalk beyond. She sat on the concrete, taking refuge in the shade of a palm tree.

"Too much excitement for you?" A boy with sea-blue eyes sank down onto the ground beside her.

Grace nodded, wishing she'd noticed the sea-eyed boy before she'd sat. Her legs were shaking too hard to let her stand back up.

"I'm Jerek." He held out his hand.

"Grace." She didn't bother taking his hand. Her own still trembled too badly.

Jerek shrugged and leaned forward to look around her, watching the firemen file back out of the school.

"Waste of taxpayer money," Jerek said. "It would be better for everyone if they figured out how to make the sirens stop going off."

"They've tried. It's the biggest mystery in Sun Palms High School history."

"Pity they're too blind to see the answer's sitting right in front of them," Jerek laughed.

"If you know, why don't you tell them? They'd probably make a plaque for you."

"It would be cruel to turn you in like that."

Grace replayed Jerek's words in her mind, trying to find what she'd missed.

It would be cruel to turn you *in like that.*

"You think I set off the alarms?" Grace pushed herself to her knees. "I was in class, so say what you want, but I've got a room full of alibis."

"Doesn't matter if you were sitting at your desk, at the kitchen table, in the stands at a record-setting baseball game. All the weird things that have ever happened around you—you caused them, Grace Esther Lee-Weiss."

16

Jerek

"Who are you?" Grace pushed away from Jerek, scrambling to stand. "How do you know my name?"

"Which question would you like answered first?" Jerek asked.

"What?" Grace glanced to the crowd standing fifteen feet away.

Jerek took a deep breath, willing his nerves not to betray him and leave him shaking like Grace. "You asked two questions. Which would you like answered first?"

"I don't know." Grace dug her fingers into her hair. "How do you know my name?"

"I've been researching you for months. There, that was easy. What was the other question?"

"Researching me?" Grace stepped back. "What do you mean *researching me*?"

"Internet mostly. If you know what to look for, you can find almost anything with the right tools and a good hacker."

"Hacker?"

"Like, on a computer." Jerek mimed typing.

"I know what a hacker is. You spend time stalking me and you think I'm stupid? That's just great."

"Nothing in my research implied you weren't of a reasonable intellect." Jerek leaned back against the palm tree, staring up between its fronds. "If I thought you weren't intelligent, I wouldn't have bothered coming."

"Coming for what? To accuse me of pulling the fire alarm at my school?" Grace threw her hands wide. She'd finally stopped trembling. "Actually, I don't care. Stay the hell away from me, or I'll call the cops."

"If that's what you want."

Jerek counted to three before Grace turned away.

"Just try not to set your house on fire again," he said before she could take a step. "You seem like a decent person. I can only imagine the guilt you would feel if you caused your fathers harm."

Grace whipped back around. All the color had drained from her face. "Are you threatening my parents?"

"Of course not." Jerek stayed silent as he stood.

Grace watched him, as though judging the danger of his every movement.

"I've never met your fathers," Jerek said. "Have no intention of ever meeting them. I only meant that someone as dangerous as you might cause an accident worse than the one that burned your father's hand."

Grace charged toward him, finger pointed at his chest. "I had nothing to do with that. You sick, creepy idiot. We had a kitchen fire, and Dad could have died. Maybe next time you stalk someone, get your facts straight. I'm not an arsonist."

"I can easily believe you've never meant any harm. But you wouldn't be so defensive if deep down you didn't know you'd started the kitchen fire. And the garage fire. Plus the seven small fires you've had in this school over the last four years. Is anger your trigger? Maybe it's fear."

"I'm getting the principal." Grace spun toward the school.

"Is that really what you want?" Jerek dodged in front of her. "To pretend you've never had an inkling that you are nothing like your classmates?"

"What I want is for you to leave me the hell alone."

Jerek furrowed his brow. "Then you have my sincerest apologies. I'm not often wrong. If there's anything I can do to make amends—"

"Just go away."

"Absolutely. I'm sorry to have bothered you. Best of luck." Jerek reached out to shake her hand.

"Creeper." Grace batted his hand away.

Her skin barely grazed his, but it was enough.

A hint of purple blossomed across her palm, twisting and darkening as it changed the hue of her skin.

Grace gasped as the color swirled, shimmering as it wound up to her forearm, finally settling as a bright violet band.

"What did you do?" Grace backed away from Jerek.

"Explained something without using words."

"What did you do to me?" Grace rubbed her violet forearm with her normal-colored hand.

"Altered the pigment of your skin," Jerek said. "Don't worry, I can put it back whenever I want."

"Then put it back." Grace held her arm out to Jerek.

"I said whenever *I* want." Jerek leaned against the tree, watching Grace's expression shift from fear to utter loathing.

"Fix my skin, or I'll get the cops." Grace spoke through gritted teeth.

"And tell them what?" A laugh bubbled in Jerek's throat. "A weird boy turned your arm purple with a touch? And what logical explanation could you offer for how I had done it? Dye? Toxic chemicals? Magic?"

Grace mouthed wordlessly for a moment.

"You can't tell the police, or the principal, or even your parents," Jerek said. "Because the one word you could use to tell them what I'd done is the very word you refuse to acknowledge."

"Leave me alone." Grace crossed her normal arm over the purple one and headed back toward the crowd.

"I've already promised I would, but a quick word of advice?"

She froze.

"When you're sitting in your room tonight, terrified of the stranger who knew so much about you, and mad as hell that you're going to have to spend the rest of your life with a purple arm"—Jerek crept slowly closer to her, stopping right behind her shoulder—"don't let your emotions channel themselves into destruction that will put your fathers at risk. Think about what I've said, think about the truth buried deep in your soul that you've spent your entire life trying not to know, and then come find me."

Grace shouldered her way into the crowd and out of sight.

Jerek let out a long breath, his shoulders sagging from exhaustion.

"How did it go?" Lincoln stepped out of his hiding place at the back of the pack of students.

"As well as could be expected." Jerek started down the sidewalk, waiting for Lincoln to catch up before speaking again.

"She's furious and confused. I'm honestly surprised she didn't set me on fire, but she'll be with us soon enough."

"Really?" Lincoln said. "Because furious and confused aren't usually on the agenda when you're asking people to help you break the law."

"She didn't fight me when I said she was the fire starter," Jerek said. "Didn't tell me how physically impossible it was. And she didn't laugh when I said the word *magic*."

17

Grace

Grace sat on the edge of her bed, sweat tickling the nape of her neck. Her legs wouldn't stop bouncing. She didn't dare take off the bulky sweatshirt she'd grabbed from her locker and yanked on the moment she got the chance.

It wasn't real. None of it was real.

She reached her trembling hand toward the wrist of her sleeve.

If it wasn't real, then I've lost my mind.

"Which is worse, purple or in need of monumental amounts of therapy?"

She dropped her hand and kept staring at the gray sleeve of her Sun Palms High School sweatshirt.

The sun had already begun to set. She'd begged her way out of family dinner, claiming too much homework. The easiest thing to do would be to curl up in bed and try to sleep.

Wake up in the morning and hope it had all been a bad dream.

"If I don't boil to death in this sweatshirt."

Blood raced back to her feet as she stood and ripped all the covers from her bed. She flopped down on the bare fitted sheet, willing the air conditioning to grant some relief.

Tink, tink-a, tink.

Her phone gave the little chime reserved for messages from Steven.

She rolled over, grabbing her phone from the nightstand.

A message popped up on the screen.

This is Ari. Borrowed Steven's phone to say thank you so much for introducing us! I think Florida life is going to be super great!!

Before Grace could throw the phone, a picture appeared on her screen. Steven kissing Ari on the cheek as the fading sun shone over the ocean.

Grace dropped her phone as though the picture held enough hateful heat to burn her.

But the heat didn't leave with her phone. The burning stayed in her hand, radiating up her purple arm.

"Breathe, just breathe."

She shut her eyes, but the image of Steven and the stupid new blond who had stolen all her dreams in less than a day had been seared into her mind.

"Shit."

The heat on her arm swelled, tingling like ants gnawing on her flesh.

She wrenched her sweatshirt over her head, ready to claw away whatever was biting her.

But there were no bugs on her skin. Only a perfect band of purple.

"Son of a bitch."

She bolted into her bathroom, holding her arm as far from the rest of her body as she could manage, and thrust the offending skin under the faucet.

Biting her lips together, she turned on the tap. But the water didn't wash away the purple. Dripping all over the bathroom floor, she grabbed her loofah and bodywash. She squirted a mound of the vanilla-scented gel onto her forearm and scrubbed.

The soap didn't turn violet. The color didn't budge.

"Shit. Shit. Shit."

She scrubbed harder, turning up the water as hot as she could stand.

"Creepy asshole turns my arm purple, stupid new girl snatches Steven. Did the world just plan a *shit on Grace* day?"

It was too much to happen all at once. Too many coincidences for life to allow.

"That evil son of a bitch."

A perfect girl falling on her. A weird guy screwing with her.

"He set me up." A bubble of rage flared in Grace's chest. "He set me up, and that girl is making out with Steven on the beach. The sick f—"

Flames leapt out of the basin of the sink, burning through the running water.

With a scream, Grace dropped to the floor, shielding her face.

"Stop, stop, stop!"

The light flickering between her fingers faded away.

"Grace, honey, are you okay?" Pop called from the hall.

"I'm fine, Pop." Grace pushed herself to her feet. "Just slipped."

The flames had disappeared from the sink, leaving no sign of damage in their wake.

"Are you hurt?" Pop called.

"I'm okay."

Grace inched toward the sink, her hand shaking as she reached out to turn off the water. Heat radiated up from the ceramic basin.

"Not good. Shit, this is not good."

She looked from the purple on her arm to the sink, then back to the skin on her arm.

"I'm a mutant. I'm a mutant, and I'm being recruited to be on a special team of mutants trying to save the world."

Legs wobbling, she made her way back to her bed.

It seems like your fathers are really nice people. I would hate for them to get hurt.

Flames flickered through her memory. Jumping from the stove to the kitchen table where she'd sat with Dad. He'd been trying to explain to her that the agency hadn't been able to figure out who her birth mother was. Whoever had abandoned her on the steps of the church hadn't left any clues behind.

Fury and sadness had taken over her chest. And then, fire.

"It was me."

Her own words crashed around her ears, shattering her heart on impact.

Her fingers didn't shake as she pulled on her sneakers and a thick, long-sleeved shirt. She locked her bedroom door and turned out the light. She left her phone and wallet on the nightstand. She wouldn't need them to join the mutants. It would be better to leave everything behind.

It would be better to leave her dads behind. She had to keep her family safe.

Safe from me.

The tears didn't begin until she pushed open her bedroom window and the humid night air caught in her throat.

Her knees buckled as she dropped the five feet to the

ground outside. But she didn't feel any pain as she pushed herself to her feet.

Find him. She needed to find him.

Not bothering to wipe the tears from her face, she ran down the sidewalk, heading back toward her school.

18

Jerek

"Do you have a plan b?" Lincoln kicked his feet up onto the dashboard, not taking them down even as Jerek glared at him.

"I don't need a plan b." Jerek turned back toward the window, staring down the sidewalk as he had been for the last hour.

They sat in silence as birds soared between the trees, flying home to roost for the night.

A siren sounded far in the distance.

Before Jerek could spot the flashing lights, the sound had faded away.

"We should move the van," Lincoln said. "Staying in one place will get us spotted."

"Relax."

"We're waiting in a car on a dark street for a girl we don't know who we're not sure is coming." Lincoln lifted his feet off the dash. "Add to that the vampire waiting at the hotel, and Ari being out with a jock who might get handsy, and I really don't think relaxing is the thing to do."

"Of course not. But being tense won't help anything. So put your feet back up and pretend."

Lincoln kicked his feet back onto the dash, letting them land with a thud.

"And don't worry about Ari." Jerek lined his hands up with the worn marks on the steering wheel. "If you have to worry about something, pick anything but Ari."

"Why?"

"Because she's the one thing I don't worry about."

Jerek kept his gaze out the window, even as he felt Lincoln studying him.

Better silence than a hundred questions.

A figure ran around the corner.

"Earlier than I thought."

Jerek climbed out of the van before Lincoln's feet were off the dash.

Grace sprinted toward the school, her dark hair shining in the streetlights.

"Any luck with your arm?" Jerek called across the road.

Grace stumbled a few steps before finally managing to stop.

"Careful, Jerek," Lincoln warned from behind Jerek's shoulder as Grace turned toward him.

"What am I?" Grace's voice cracked as she spoke.

"Got there so quickly?" Jerek said.

"Am I dangerous?" She stopped in the middle of the road, tears streaming down her cheeks.

"The best things in the world are," Jerek said.

A sob shook Grace's shoulders.

"But dangerous doesn't make you evil." Jerek dared to take a small step forward.

Lincoln grabbed Jerek's arm, holding him ten feet away from Grace.

"I could have killed them." She wrapped her arms around her chest, like somehow that could keep her from exploding. "My parents, my classmates. What if I had caught the whole school on fire?"

"It's not your fault," Jerek said. "What you can do is as much a part of you as the color of your hair."

"Black hair has never killed anyone."

"Neither have you." Jerek slid his arm from Lincoln's grip. "And if you learn to use your gifts properly, you never will."

"Gifts?" Grace coughed a laugh.

A bird shot from a tree, terrified by the sound.

Grace dropped to the ground, covering her head as the bird screeched and soared a foot above her.

"We need to go," Lincoln said.

The bird chittered as it soared up into the darkness.

"Magic is the most precious gift this world can offer," Jerek said. "And you were lucky enough to be born with that power coursing through your veins."

"Magic." Grace stared down at her hands.

"We can't stay out in the open," Lincoln said.

"Magicians have roamed the world since the beginning of time," Jerek said. "You are a part of a long line of those given the magical gift. Magic is dangerous. Magic can kill. Magic can also save and be the most beautiful thing in the world if you know how to use it. You can come with us and learn how to use the power you were born with, or stay here and hope for the best."

"Hope I don't kill anyone?"

Jerek knelt in front of her, letting the asphalt dig into his knees. "I can train you. I can teach you how to use your powers and become more than you've ever dreamt of. But it has to be your choice."

A car pulled around the corner, stopping with its headlights shining on Jerek and Grace.

"We're out of time," Lincoln said.

The driver laid on the horn.

"You can stay, or you can come with us," Jerek said. "It's your choice. And I wish you well either way."

"What's wrong with you kids?" The driver leaned out his window. "Get out of the damn road."

"Jerek, now." Lincoln headed back to the van.

"Best of luck." Jerek stood and followed Lincoln, giving the driver a wave as he passed.

Footsteps ran up behind him.

Jerek tensed, ready for a blow.

"I have to come with you." Grace stepped in front of him. "I can't risk hurting anyone."

"Good choice," Jerek said.

"Welcome to the feu." Lincoln pulled open the double door in the side of the van.

19

Ari

Ari leaned on the counter at the front of the diner, waiting for the woman running the register to finally come back from making the slowest pot of coffee the world had ever endured.

Her phone buzzed in her pocket.

Food for four.

Ari shook her head, enjoying the tang of ocean still clinging to her hair.

Already bought our new friend a burger. She hit send and went back to leaning on the counter.

The bell on the door jingled as a trucker strolled in, his greasy skin shining in the florescent light.

His gaze swept the tables before landing on Ari. Grinning wide enough to show his yellowed teeth, he started her way.

"Nice night out there." He leaned against the counter beside her, his elbow only a few inches from hers.

"It's great." Ari pulled her phone back out of her pocket.

Someone else is on diner duty next time. She sent the message.

"Food's on its way, honey." The waitress ambled past, a pot of coffee finally clutched in her hand.

"Thanks," Ari said.

"She'll serve you faster at a table," the trucker said. "I come through here about once a week. She always serves faster at the tables."

"I'm getting my food to go," Ari said.

"I'll give you a ride." He leaned closer to whisper in Ari's ear. "It's not safe for someone like you to be walking around by yourself at night."

"Sex worker or underage idiot?" Ari asked.

"Huh?"

"Do you think I'm a sex worker or an underage idiot who'd climb into a truck with a stranger? If it's the first one, then you must have a ton of cash just waiting in your truck. If it's the second, I should call the cops on your ass."

"I wasn't meaning anything funny, sweetheart." The trucker leaned away from Ari. "Just tryin' to be friendly to a young lady on her own."

She tossed her hair behind her shoulders and gave the trucker a bright smile. "I'm not Goldilocks lost in the woods. I'm the monster under your bed. So watch out, *sweetheart.* You touch me, and I'll destroy you from the inside out."

He stared wide-eyed at her.

"Why don't you go sit at a table? I hear you get much faster service," Ari said.

"Bitch." The trucker headed for a booth in the corner of the room. He sat facing Ari, glaring at her.

"Here's your food." The waitress heaved a bag up onto the counter. "Hope you have enough to pay for all this."

"I've got it covered." Ari pulled a clip of neatly folded bills from her pocket.

"You going to be able to carry that?"

Ari's neck tensed as a young man stepped up beside her.

"I'll be fine." Ari slid the bag off the counter.

"You should call a car." A line of worry creased the man's face, drawing Ari's attention to his chocolate brown eyes.

"I'm not worried." She started toward the door.

"You have people with you?" He stepped in front of her.

"Yes, I have big scary people who will rip your throat out if you try to hurt me."

"Good." He nodded. "Because the creeper in the corner hasn't stopped staring at you."

Ari glanced at the trucker.

Sure enough, his eyes were locked on her.

"I'll make sure he doesn't follow you out." The brown-eyed man smiled.

"Thanks."

"Just get to your big bad friends in one piece." He headed back to the counter where the waitress glared at him as though horribly put out by having to wait to take his order.

Ari ducked out into the night and down a side street, letting the diner's wide glass windows slip out of sight.

20

Jack

The new girl, Grace, hadn't even seemed to notice Jack when Lincoln and Jerek brought her into the hotel room he'd shared with Ari the night before.

She'd let herself be led to the tiny table in the corner without argument. The scent drifting off the girl held a distinct note of fake vanilla, and her clothes were freshly washed. But her eyes were hollow and wide with the horrible mixture of grief and self-loathing Jack had seen from too many people living on the streets before he'd found his home belowground.

"I'll get her some water." Lincoln slipped out of the room, leaving Jerek and Grace alone in the corner.

"Do you want me to fix your arm?" Jerek asked, his tone far softer than when he'd been enforcing Lydia's debt.

"It doesn't matter," Grace said. "I'm a freak. I might as well have a freak arm."

"Being a magician doesn't make you a freak." Jerek took her

hand, waiting for a moment, as though wanting to see if she'd smack him away, before pushing up the sleeve of her shirt.

A band of violet skin wrapped around her forearm.

Jack's insides squirmed at the sight.

Jerek laid his fingers on the purple, draining the unnatural color away in a heartbeat.

Grace stared down at her arm for a long moment. "You're a magician, too?"

"I am," Jerek said.

"And Lincoln?" Grace asked.

"He's human, but he's not a somb." Jerek let go of Grace's hand, allowing both his palms to rest on the table.

"What's a somb?" Grace asked.

"Normal people who have nothing to do with magic," Jerek said. "Lincoln is a member of the Knights Maree. They're the protectors of all magical people. We're called the feu. Magicians, vampires, werewolves, mermaids. There are also divs, who are born to one magical parent and one somb. The Knights Maree watch over all of us."

"This is impossible," Grace said. "It's all a mistake, or a prank, or..."

Her voice trailed away as the table shifted from beige, to green, to bright blue under Jerek's hands.

"It's not a prank," Jerek said. "You and I are magicians."

Grace nodded. Tears dripped from her chin. "Why is this happening to me?"

Jack closed his eyes, fighting the urge to creep out of the room and hide far away from the vanilla-scented magician's heartache.

"You were born magical," Jerek said. "It's who you are."

"But how can magic even exist?" Grace said. "Vampires running around the world? People would know. Everyone would know."

"It's the Knights Maree's job to keep magic hidden," Jerek said. "They've been doing it very well for a very long time."

Heavy footfalls approached the door. A key beeped in the lock.

"Water for everyone." Lincoln held four bottles of water in his broad hands. He gave one each to Grace and Jerek, then set one to the side for Ari before opening his own.

A pang gritted the sides of Jack's throat. His fingers itched to reach for Ari's bottle. But while the thought of drinking cool water might seem wonderful, it would do nothing to slake his thirst.

"Why did you come for me?" Grace said. "Am I in trouble for all the fires?"

"No," Jerek said. "It wasn't even the fires that made me suspect a magician was hiding in your school. It was the sports records."

"What?" Grace held her bottle in both hands, making no move to open it.

"From the time you started at Sun Palms, records have been set in every sport," Jerek said. "But the teams aren't that good. Miraculous catches. Runners leaping twice the height of the hurdles. Those stories caught my attention. From there, it was fairly easy to find you."

"I changed things for our sports teams?" Grace said.

"You aren't just a fire starter," Lincoln said. "Flames just happen to be your stress response. Think of it as your body's fight or flight instinct."

Grace's water bottle crackled as she tightened her grip around it. "Why didn't a knight come for me sooner? Ridiculous field goals, and fires, and all kinds of weird shit has been happening to me since I was little. Shouldn't someone have come to stop me before I hurt anyone?"

"Breathe, Grace," Jerek said.

"The Maree don't search for magicians born outside the feu community," Lincoln said.

"Then why did you come to find me?" Grace looked to Jerek.

Jerek sighed.

Jack sat up a little straighter on the bed, his body preparing to run, though his promise to Lydia forced him to stay.

"Because I'm barely a functional magician," Jerek said. "Something happened twelve years ago that hobbled the powers of every magician...but you."

"What?" Grace leaned as far back as her chair would allow.

"You are unique, Grace. You were spared from the terror that stole so much from the rest of us," Jerek said. "If I had the magic that you do, I would have left you alone. If there had been anyone else who could have helped me, I would have dragged them to this hotel instead. But you are stronger than I am. You may very well be the strongest magician the world has left. We have the opportunity to help the feu, to put right a horrible wrong that stole so many lives, and I need you to help me."

"No." Grace stood, backing away from the table. "You do not get to tear me out of my life and ask me for help."

"I have no other options. You have to help me," Jerek said. "There's a reason I searched for so long for someone like you. The feu need you. It's time to put our world back together."

"I just want to not be dangerous." Grace pressed herself into the corner of the room. "You said you would teach me to control the fire. Tell me how to do it so I can go home."

"It's not that simple," Jerek began.

Pounding kicks on the door stopped him from speaking again.

"Who's hungry?" Ari called from the hall.

Jerek stayed frozen, standing across the table from Grace.

Lincoln didn't seem willing to turn his back on them.

"I'll get it." Jack slid off the bed.

Grace didn't spare him a glance.

Jack opened the door, stepping aside as Ari carried in a bag that smelled like grease and charcoal.

"I brought everyone burgers," Ari said. "It seemed like a safe bet. Sorry, Jack, I searched the menu for a pint of blood to go, but no luck."

"It's hard to find take out for vampires," Jack said.

Ari set the bag down on the once-again beige table.

"You?" Grace glared at Ari.

"Hi again." Ari unpacked the Styrofoam boxes of food. "I really hope you're not a vegetarian."

"Shouldn't you still be at the beach with Steven?" Grace said. "Already tired of being a little sand slut?"

Ari set the last box on the table and stood up straight before turning to Grace.

"Steven is a groping dickhead who's been playing you for months while hooking up with every girl who giggles when he winks. I'd offer to show you his messaging history, but then you might set my laptop on fire and I'd have to strangle you. So instead of calling me a slut, how about going for some gratitude? Maybe a nice *Wow, Ari. Thank you so much for saving me!* Feel free to paraphrase."

"You set all this up." Grace rounded on Jerek. "Had her send me pictures so I would freak out and start a fire? I was at home. My parents could have gotten hurt!"

"You had to see the magic for yourself or you never would have believed us," Jerek said. "We had no other choice."

"Steven would have screwed you over to your face eventually, and what would have happened if we weren't here to be your guides and fire extinguishers?" Ari slid a Styrofoam box toward Grace. "Eat your burger."

The top of the box began to blacken and crackle.

"Burn your food if you want. I'm not going back out for more." Ari grabbed an uncharred box and sat down on the bed.

"If you set the room on fire, we'll have to deal with police." Jerek spoke in a low, even voice. "Take a breath, and let the fire go out."

Grace took a long, shuddering breath.

The curls of smoke stopped drifting from the top of the box, leaving only a patch of black and a terrible stench behind.

"I'll get the window." Jack stepped up and over the bed, easily sliding the window open, despite the layers of paint sealing the frame shut.

"If you want to walk out, I won't stop you," Jerek said. "I'll mourn the good you could have done for the feu and search every shadow in this world for another way to continue this venture. But you? You'll spend the rest of your life not knowing what you're capable of. You'll spend every moment wondering if you could hurt someone, or if you could fly."

Grace touched her forearm where the violet had been. "What do I tell my parents?"

21

Lincoln

The springs in the cot the desk woman had given them poked up through the mattress, each prong seeming to know exactly the worst place to dig into Lincoln's spine.

He'd given Grace his bed. It was the only thing to do. He couldn't let her stay in a room with Ari and risk the entire hotel burning down before morning.

Grace had spent the first two hours crying softly into her pillow. Jerek had gone still after a few minutes, though how he could sleep through the sniffling, Lincoln didn't know.

Once Grace had finally drifted to sleep, Lincoln hoped to do the same. But the cot had other ideas.

Judging the creakiness of each spring, Lincoln rolled out of bed, pulling his pillow and blanket to the floor with him.

A muddy forest floor would have felt cleaner than the carpet, but at least the floor was flat.

He lay on his back, staring up at the shadows on the ceiling. The brightness of the streetlight outside their window made it seem like morning had come.

We'll have to be loaded into the van before dawn.

To go where?

He understood Jerek's goal, but the path to the party was anything but clear. If Grace could hold it together long enough, and if Jerek really had found the actual artifact—whatever that might be—he needed to fix the curse...

If.

He'd raced across an ocean to protect his friend and had ended up in a VW van on a mission that could get him banished from the Maree and disowned by his family.

He slipped his phone from his pocket, carefully hiding the light from the screen under the cot.

He pressed his thumb to the scanner then opened the app marked by the flaming shield of the Maree with a series of four passwords.

A message waited for him.

Check in, Lincoln. Is the Holden situation under control? Do you require assistance?

Lincoln closed his eyes, feeling himself balancing between two worlds. The power to change everything rested within a few taps of his fingers.

The problem runs deeper than expected. May take some time to stabilize. Will update if additional action becomes necessary.

He pressed send without giving himself time to reconsider.

Tucking his phone into his pocket, he rolled onto his back, hoping he might get at least an hour's sleep before dawn.

22

Grace

They were loaded into the teal van before her alarm would have gone off for school. Grace couldn't be sure what made the horrible feeling of dread in her stomach worse—having watched them pack the boy Jack into a compartment hidden behind black drapes under one of the sofa-like seats, or driving away from her home.

"Where to?" Lincoln asked.

The fact that the knight wasn't sure where they were going added an extra level of squirming to Grace's stomach. She sipped her hotel coffee. The watery brew didn't help.

Jerek turned the van onto the highway, not answering until they were firmly headed north. "We've got one more crew member to pick up before the fun can begin."

"Who?" Lincoln asked at the same moment Jack called, "Where?" from below Ari's seat.

"Not too far," Jerek said. "North Carolina."

"Who's in North Carolina?" The edge in Lincoln's voice cut through the remnants of the early morning haze in Grace's brain.

"Gibbs," Jerek said.

"You're kidding," Lincoln said.

"You really are a peach," Jack said, his words muffled by the thick layer of vinyl draped around him.

"We have one shot at this." Ari pulled a pink computer out of her pink bag. "We need all the muscle we can get, and Gibbs fits the bill."

"Why do we need muscle?" Grace asked. "Are you worried I'm going to hurt people?"

"Muscle couldn't keep you from burning us all alive," Ari said.

"You didn't tell her about the job?" Jack asked.

"What job?" Grace downed the rest of her coffee.

"Remember how magic was broken? Well, we're going to fix it," Jerek said.

"Fix it how?" Grace asked.

"You two go ahead," Ari said. "Some of us have work to do."

"For a long time, we didn't know how the Fracture started," Lincoln said. "The Knights Maree searched for years."

"What did they find?" Grace scooted closer to the front of the van.

"A steaming pile of nothing," Jack said.

"That it wasn't a natural phenomenon," Lincoln said. "The only viable explanation they couldn't rule out was a curse."

"Someone cursed magic?" Grace asked.

"I prefer *some evil asshole cursed magicians and doomed the feu to years of chaos*," Ari said, "but yours works, too."

"Is that even possible?" Grace asked.

"When all other possibilities are gone, whatever remains, no matter how improbable, must be the truth," Jerek said.

"And you're going to undo the curse?" Grace's heart thumped heavily, making every beat rattle against her ribs.

"*We're* going to undo the curse," Jerek said. "I can't do it without you, Grace."

"But you're going to train me first," Grace said. "We're going to go somewhere where I can learn about magic and how to be safe and then when I'm ready, we'll do this."

"Saturday," Ari said. "You've got to save the feu on Saturday."

"What? Why?" Grace squeaked.

"Mending the Fracture requires an incantation," Jerek said. "Magicians lost the ability to do incantations when magic broke."

"Which is why you're here." Ari kept her gaze locked on her laptop as she typed away at a furious pace.

"Incantation." Grace's voice wobbled on the word.

"It also requires a very special magical artifact, one I have spent a long time tracking down," Jerek said.

"And we're going to steal it from a fancy party," Jack said. "Snatch the thing, do the spell, save the crumbling world of the feu, and restore magic to its former glory."

"We're going to steal from a party?" Grace set down her cup and gripped the edge of her seat.

"We're stealing from the bad guys," Ari said. "It helps if you keep that in mind."

"Uh-huh." Grace nodded as fear clenched her stomach.

"Once we have the whole crew together, we'll work on the plan," Jerek said. "We only have one shot, but I know we can get this right."

"Pull over." Grace crawled toward the door.

"You can't go home, Grace," Jerek said. "You aren't safe around sombs, you know that."

"Pull over!"

Jerek stopped the van just in time for her to jump out and be sick in the grass.

23

Jerek

The sun was still lingering in the sky when they reached the inn at the bottom of the mountain.

Grace hadn't spoken in hours or eaten any of the food shoved her way by Ari. Lincoln looked ready to jump out of his skin. Jack had gone silent after lunch.

"We need fresh clothes. I'm all for traveling light, but there are limits," Ari said as they parked in front of the inn.

Intricately carved trim surrounded the roof, giving the whole thing the look of a fairy tale pastry.

"Nice place," Lincoln said.

"I have good taste." Jerek opened the box he'd tucked under the driver's seat and pulled out one of the stacks of bills. "Get clothes for everyone, and be nice to Grace."

Ari rolled her eyes as she took the money without counting it. "I'll be good."

"Wait until after dark, and I'll come with you," Jack shouted from his hiding place.

"Don't worry, Jack, I'll take care of you. I'm an excellent boutique shopper," Ari said. "I promise, no sad lumberjack clothes."

"Then I guess I'll just lie here until sunset," Jack said.

"Make arrangements to eat," Jerek said. "You've been looking peckish."

"What's he going to eat?" Grace asked, then added in a whisper, "Is he going to kill somebody?"

"*Jack's* never killed anyone," Jack said.

"Sorry." Grace knelt next to Jack's hiding spot. "I'm sorry, Jack."

"Don't worry about it," Jack said. "I get snappy when I'm hungry."

"Awesome. I'll see you all later." Ari swung open the van doors and strode down the street like she'd lived in town her whole life.

"I'll get us a couple of rooms," Jerek said. "Maybe they have a suite available."

"Are we going up the mountain?" Lincoln asked.

Jerek gazed up the side of the mountain. Deep green trees covered the slope, leaving no hint of the terrain below. The tourists who frequented the town and lake stayed safely nestled at the base of the mountain, never venturing into the depths of the forest.

"We'll go first thing tomorrow," Jerek said. "The moon is still full tonight. Better to stay down here."

Don't push too hard, or we'll lose her for good.

Lincoln's gaze slipped to Grace for a split second before he nodded.

The steps of the white porch surrounding the inn creaked under Jerek's feet. He shuddered at the flowered wallpaper coating the hall. Portraits of hunting dogs in various majestic poses hung at regular intervals along the corridor.

I can't compare everywhere to Holden House.

"Can I help you?" An old woman—in every way the opposite of their hostess at their previous accommodations—stepped into the hall. Flour coated her hands and apron and had crept into the wrinkles on her face.

"Do you have room for five tonight?" Jerek asked. "We'd be happy with a suite if you have one."

"Sure thing." The innkeeper offered a warm smile. "You look tired. I'll get y'all set up someplace nice and comfy."

"Thank you very much, ma'am." Jerek pressed a grateful smile onto his face. "We've had a long day of driving."

"Where are you folks coming from?" She dusted her hands off before rummaging in a drawer and pulling out an oversized notebook.

"Florida," Jerek said. "Road trip north to look at some colleges."

"Nice to see young people with ambition."

She tapped a pen on the line where Jerek needed to sign in.

"There's not too much to do in town at night," she yammered on. "Most everything shuts down at dark around here. Though I suppose with how much you've been driving, you'll just want to sleep."

"Absolutely."

The innkeeper—Mrs. Smith, but he could call her Dora—didn't stop chatting as Jerek paid for the rooms and collected Lincoln and Grace from outside, or as she very carefully deposited Grace into one room and Lincoln and Jerek into the other.

By the time Jerek closed the door to his room, he wasn't sure the buzzing in his ears would ever stop.

"Cozy." Lincoln sat on the flower-patterned armchair by the lace-curtained window.

"It suits you," Jerek said. "It's how I like to picture your time in Italy. Morning sword fighting and hand-to-hand combat. Afternoon lessons on the history of the feu and techniques in fighting the powered. Evenings spent sitting by a lace-covered window looking out over rolling hills of vineyards."

"Not really how it is at the compound, but if you like to think of it that way." Lincoln shrugged.

Jerek tossed his backpack onto the bed closest to the door. He hadn't packed very much. One fresh set of clothes, the bare essentials for toiletries, three of his father's notebooks, one faded and tattered text, and a box made of shining black wood.

"You're going to start working with her here?" Lincoln said.

"If she can manage it without vomiting." Jerek opened the box, carefully laying its contents out on the bed.

"How long do you think we'll stay with Gibbs?" Lincoln asked. "It would be easier to work with Grace there."

"Better not to count on the folks up the mountain for too much hospitality. Gibbs will want us, the rest might not." The last thing he pulled from the box was a thin polishing cloth.

He wiped the gem in the ring on his left hand, polishing the red stone until its dark heart shone through.

"We don't need Gibbs," Lincoln said. "If it comes to a fight, I can handle it myself."

Jerek bit the corners of his mouth and moved on to polishing the small crystal sphere he'd pulled from the box, not speaking until he was sure he wouldn't laugh.

"You're an expert fighter, Lincoln. Trained by the best in the world. Pit twelve of me against one of you, and I doubt I could give you a scratch. But there are times when brute force is necessary. Gibbs is our muscle. If we get trapped, I want Gibbs fighting our way out."

"Six seems like a lot. Getting that many in and out of the party without anyone noticing? Smaller might be better."

"So we send Jack in alone and hope for the best?" Jerek peered into the sphere, allowing himself a moment to admire the light caught within the crystal. "We get Gibbs on board tomorrow, then smooth out the plan."

"If you say so." Lincoln looked back out the window.

A light tap sounded on the other side of the door.

"She really does have impeccable timing." Jerek strode over and opened the door.

Grace waited in the hall, the front of her hair wet from splashing water on her face.

"How are you?" Lincoln stepped up behind Jerek's shoulder.

"Completely freaking out." Grace tucked her hair behind her ears. "I've never been this far from home without my parents. Also, I'm a magician. Also, I have to help save the feu, which apparently includes me. So, yeah. Not my best day."

"You're going to be okay," Lincoln said. "I can't imagine being thrown unprepared into magic—"

"Which is why we're going to prepare you," Jerek cut across. "We don't have long to get you ready, so the sooner we begin our work, the better."

"Right." Nodding as though convincing herself it was a good idea, Grace crossed the threshold and stepped into the room. "Quaint."

"Thanks," Lincoln said.

"Over here." Jerek ushered Grace to sit at the head of his bed.

She perched on his pillow.

Jerek lifted the narrow text with the cracked leather cover. He ran his finger along the familiar texture of the binding before holding the book out to her.

"What did Ari tell my parents?" Grace folded her hands on her lap. "Do they think I'm dead?"

"You received a last-minute invitation to an internship in New York," Jerek said. "You sent an apology and have been posting updates of your adventures on social media."

"Are Dad and Pop responding?" Grace swiped the tears from her cheeks.

"I haven't looked," Jerek said. "Ari manages all the computer work. I'm sure they're furious. But with some training, you'll gain the control necessary to move safely among the somb. If you want to go home then, I'm sure your fathers will take you back with open arms. And if you choose to live among the feu, you'll be welcomed as one of the heroes who freed magic."

"I'd settle for going home and not risking hurting anyone." Grace lifted the book from Jerek's hand. "Is this a spell book?"

"More like a theory text," Jerek said. "You have to learn to channel your magic in a non-destructive way before we can chance an incantation."

"And if I can't do it before the party?"

"You have to," Jerek said. "There is no option for failure."

Grace opened the book, carefully turning through the first few pages.

"I don't understand how this is possible. *The energy of the spirit draws from something larger than the soul*?" Grace read from the text. "What's that supposed to mean?"

"Magic is..." Jerek searched for the best words.

Truthful, but not frightening.

"Magic," Jerek began again, "is a river. It races all around the world and runs much deeper in some places than in others. The water is hidden, and only people born with magic in their blood can feel and use the strength of the river.

"Sometimes, a somb accidentally stumbles into the hidden places where magic runs deep. If they are that unlucky, strange and terrible things can happen to them because they aren't meant to swim in those waters. You and I were born to spend our lives touching the current. The waters of magic are as much a part of us as the blood in our veins.

"When the Fracture happened, everyone thought the river had disappeared. Like an earthquake had split the ground and magic had tumbled far into the earth, out of our reach. But you, Grace, you can still touch the magic. Which means it didn't go anywhere. Magic didn't change, something changed magicians."

"But not me?" Grace asked.

"No." A bubble of hope surged in Jerek's chest. He splayed his hands out on the comforter, pressing the bubble away.

"Why not?" Grace asked.

"That's a very good question," Lincoln said.

"And we're going to find the answer," Jerek said. "But I need to know more about your magic first. How you touch the water, if you will."

"See how I make the magic work, figure out why I'm different, help you, go home." Grace nodded. "Okay. That's only four things. I can do four things."

"Good." Jerek lifted the crystal from the bed.

The sphere fit in the palm of his hand and, even in the ever-dimming light of the room, seemed to find a bit of sun to hold within its center.

"It's beautiful," Grace said.

"It is." Jerek lifted Grace's hand, placing the sphere on her palm. "Keep looking at it. Let your eyes find the very center. Find the tiny glimmer of light that waits where all the pieces converge."

Grace stared at the crystal. The lines of worry between her eyes faded as the moments ticked by.

"Now, keep your gaze at the center, and let your mind

wander to everything that's happened in the last few days. All the fear, and anger, and confusion," Jerek said.

"I can't do that. I'll set the inn on fire."

"You won't," Jerek whispered. "Trust me. It's okay to be angry, as long as you know how to channel the feeling."

A gasp caught in Grace's throat, tears formed at the corners of her eyes, but she didn't blink.

A glow shimmered into being at the center of the sphere, feeding the light that had already existed. The glow swirled and twisted, forming shapes whose meanings rested beyond Jerek's understanding. The shapes melded together, becoming a dazzling sheet of flames whose light danced in Grace's unblinking eyes.

24

Jack

The dingy bar was the only place in town open after sunset, hidden down a back alley with barely a sign to tell passersby why there was music coming from beyond the shuttered windows.

Jack sat at the bar, fiddling with his beer, wishing he could drink it.

I should have tried cheap beer before I was bitten.

He gave the bottle a sniff and winced at the odor.

Prickles rose on his neck as instinct warned him he was being watched. He didn't bother looking around. Being young, black, or dressed like he had more money than anyone else in the bar could all draw attention. As long no one shouted *vampire,* they could stare all they liked.

"Jack?" a soft voice asked.

Jack nodded and swiveled on his stool.

The man was as handsome as his picture had been—tousled

hair that rested just above his brow, tiny lines by his eyes, implying the usual presence of his easy smile.

"Hello, James." Jack held out his hand.

James's smile flickered away. "Hi."

"You okay?" Jack patted the stool next to his.

"You look a little younger than your picture." James kept his chin down as he spoke.

"Excellent skin care. I think it's worth the investment."

"I don't want any trouble," James said. "Maybe I should head out."

"Hold on." Jack fished in his pocket and pulled out his wallet, sliding the ID aging him at twenty-two down the bar. "Feel better?"

"Yeah." James's shoulders relaxed, and his easy smile returned.

"Great." Jack let his fingers trail over James's for a moment before taking back his ID. "Then what do you want to drink?"

25

Ari

"We really should switch to sleeping during the day and being awake at night." Ari pulled her covers up to her chin, savoring just a few more moments of comfort and warmth. "It must really suck to be Jack, hidden in the van while we drive around, and I honestly loathe mornings."

"You can't just hack the sun?" Grace kicked off her covers and climbed out of bed.

"Your new things are in the bag on the chair." Ari stared up at the ceiling.

The sound of a paper bag opening came from the corner.

"Traditionally, people say *thank you* when someone buys them nice things," Ari said.

"You seem to think I should thank you for a lot of things."

"You should." Ari rolled over to face Grace. "You can start with the shoes and work your way up from there."

Grace said nothing as she dug through the bag of clothes, pulling out the pants, shirts, and boots Ari had chosen for her.

"You're going to need something better than sneakers up the mountain," Ari said. "It's a whole different world up there."

"You make it sound like we're going to Narnia."

"Depends on your view of Cair Paravel." Ari rubbed her eyes and kicked both feet out of bed, instantly regretting her choice as the morning chill of the floor shocked her toes.

She reached into her own bag of clothes, pulling out a thick pair of hiking socks, slim-fit jeans, and a loose, pink button-up to complete the outfit.

Grace had already finished dressing by the time Ari reached for her pink boots.

"How did you know my size?" Grace stood in front of the mirror, staring at her jeans, turquoise tank, and matching boots.

"I looked into your online shopping history. It's really not that hard."

"You hacked my whole life. You violated my privacy."

"And you almost got your whole school killed." Ari yanked on her boots. "So how about you don't cast stones." Grabbing her bags, she headed for the door.

"What have my parents been saying?"

"Your pop says *no questions asked, just come home.*" Ari tightened her grip on her backpack. "Your dad started furious and has quickly degenerated to hysteria. He mentioned something about having the J.C.C. help him put up missing posters."

"This could kill them." Grace buried her face in her hands. "As sure as a fire, this could kill them."

Ari took two steps toward the door before her conscience caught up to her feet. "I'll send them an email from your new boss in New York, telling them how you're moving into intern housing, and an email from you saying you're sorry for running but Steven broke your heart and you had to get out of town."

"They won't just let it go. They'll research the company. Pop will fly to New York."

"And you'll be on a retreat to L.A. when he does. The website will twist them around so many ways they'll start bragging about their baby's new job. Trust me, I've been *interning* in New York for ages."

"Interning as what?"

"Teen liaison for a P.R. company."

Grace's laugh followed her out into the hall.

Once the door closed behind her, Ari allowed herself a real smile.

Not the worst magician to have dragged out of the darkness.

The floorboards creaked as she made her way downstairs, but the chatty innkeeper didn't appear. The boys had already gathered by the van. Jack sitting on the roof, Lincoln and Jerek both leaning against the hood. All of them had dressed in their new clothes.

"Have a nice dinner, Jack?" Ari opened the back doors of the van to stack her bags with the growing mound of the boys' possessions.

"I've had worse. Tasted a bit like bourbon, but that's my own fault for buying him so many drinks. Nice work on the clothes, by the way." He swept a hand over his black V-neck shirt, black pants, and black leather boots. "Not what I would have chosen, but I appreciate the lack of white."

"Seemed right with your dining plans." Ari winked.

"And for me?" Lincoln stepped in front of her, blocking her path to the van's side doors.

Ari traced her finger along the lines of his plaid flannel shirt, which held tight against the ridges of his pecs. "It just felt right."

"Mmmhmm." Jack jumped off the roof and opened the side doors, bowing Ari in.

Ari wiggled her eyebrows at him as she climbed into the van and to her usual seat. She pulled out her laptop as Jack slid into the safety of his den.

"Why the pink?" Jack asked.

"Do you want the actual reason or a movie quote?" Ari opened an internet browser, scanning through the news reports coming out of Florida.

"The real reason."

"Step Daddy number two said smart people never wear pink. He was my least favorite of the step squad. Proving his sexist ass wrong sparks joy every damn day."

Ari lifted her hands from her keyboard, waiting for laughter to drift up from under the seat.

"I'm glad you're trouncing the asshole step's dickish opinion," Jack said. "But you also look really good in pink."

"I know." Ari's shoulders relaxed as she pulled up her search alerts.

Grace climbed into the van, shutting the door behind her. Red lined the bottoms of her eyes, and pink kissed her cheeks. She sat in the far back of the van, her face turned toward the window.

"And up we go." Jerek started the van and pulled away from the inn.

"I hope Dora doesn't make us breakfast," Ari said.

"I warned her," Jerek said.

"People like her don't often listen." Ari shut her laptop as they wound their way to the narrow road that switch-backed up the side of the mountain.

The sun peaked over the horizon as they began their ascent.

"Stay down, Jack," Lincoln warned.

"Don't worry," Jack said. "I'll stay here and hide for the next...really long ass time."

"Good," Jerek said.

Within a few twists of the road, trees covered their view, offering only brief glances of how far up they'd driven.

"Do you think Gibbs will feed us?" Ari asked.

"Barbara will," Jerek said. "Good food, too."

"Nice."

"Maybe don't mention you're a Maree until after you've eaten," Jerek said.

"I don't think Lincoln has to mention he's a Maree," Jack said. "He reeks of honor and duty."

"Thanks," Lincoln said. "That's great."

They drifted back into silence as the pavement disappeared and dirt took over the road. Driveways, so hidden they couldn't be seen until after the van had passed, peeked out of the woods. With no houses visible or signs in sight, Ari's fingers itched to pull out her phone and call up a GPS.

It wouldn't work anyway. There are some times technology fails you.

I'm starting to sound like my mother.

Ari shivered.

Jerek veered off the road.

Ari held her breath, waiting to crash into the trees. But a narrow path waited for them, and a white clapboard house peered out at the end of the trail.

26

Jerek

"One, two, three, four," Jerek counted.

The door to the balcony above the wide front porch opened before he hit five.

A girl with a mane of red, curly hair sweeping around her shoulders stepped outside wearing nothing but underwear and a t-shirt.

Jerek leaned close to the windshield and waved as he stopped the van.

With a grin, the girl jumped over the edge of the balcony, landing on the ground eleven feet below like she'd stepped down from a stair.

"Damn." Ari whistled.

"Wait in here." Jerek stepped out of the van and into the cool morning air, gently closing his door behind him. "Hello, Gibbs."

"No one's called me Gibbs since puberty, *Holden*." She blew a curl out of her eyes.

"Is it Evelyn these days?" Jerek asked. "It does have a nice ring to it."

"Eve, mostly." Eve wrinkled her nose. "Gran's the only one who calls me Evelyn."

"Is Barbara here?" Jerek nodded toward the house.

"Not back yet. She's been running longer these days."

"Good."

Eve raised one red eyebrow.

"We have some things to discuss before she gets back."

"Does it have to do with the Maree and the vampire you've brought up our mountain?"

"Both, peripherally." Jerek closed the gap between them, stopping close enough that her six-foot height became impossible to ignore. "I found him. The man who destroyed both our lives. I know where he is, and I know how to mend the Fracture. I need your help, Eve."

"Whoever is responsible"—Eve's gaze flicked toward the van—"I get to tear his throat out. Deal?"

"As soon as I've gotten what I need to fix the Fracture, I won't care what you do." Jerek held out his hand.

Eve shook it as her grin turned to a satisfied smile. "About time, Jerek. I was beginning to think you'd never come through."

"All things in their time." Jerek waved the others out of the van.

"Why the Maree and vampire?" Eve asked. "Really gives a low taste to the revenge affair."

"We need them," Jerek said.

"For what?" Eve said.

"Hey there." Ari climbed out of the van first, with Grace and Lincoln following behind.

"This is Ari, our hacker. Grace, my protégé," Jerek introduced, "and Lincoln—"

"A Martel Maree." Eve cocked her head to the side.

"Can you smell it on him?" Ari asked.

"Even if I couldn't," Eve said, "that chin, that glower, couldn't be anything but a Martel."

"I'll try and take that as a compliment." Lincoln dipped his chin in a bow.

"Don't bother." Eve headed toward the house, waving them to follow her. "Tell the vampire not to feed on our land."

"He ate last night," Jerek said. "Everyone on the crew will follow the rules of the pack while they're here."

"What rules?" Grace asked.

"Really?" Eve opened the door to the house. "You bring people up our mountain and don't prepare them for the pack?"

"We've had more important matters to discuss," Jerek said.

"Basic rules of werewolf territory. Respect the pack, obey the alpha of the pack, respect the territory of the pack. Don't mess with shit, and you'll be fine." Ari turned to Eve. "Good enough?"

"You forgot *stay inside at night.*" Eve looked to Lincoln. "And don't betray the pack."

"No time for old troubles. We have work to do and can't waste our precious time before Barbara gets home." Jerek stepped past Eve and into the house.

Early morning light shone through the polished windows, bathing the tidy space in a warm glow. Perfectly folded blankets lay across the back of the couch as though the Gibbs family had been expecting visitors. Pictures hung over the mantel, creating a perfectly aligned, immaculately dusted shrine.

Jerek forced his gaze away from the Gibbs family photos and sat in a carved wooden chair, his back to the pictures.

"Give me the name," Eve said.

Lincoln froze halfway down to his seat on the couch.

"If I give you the name," Jerek said, "you have to swear you won't tell anyone in the pack where we're going or why. I can't risk him getting wind we've figured him out before we pull off our plan."

"Fine," Eve said, "you have my word as a Gibbs. I tell no one the name of the murderer or any hint of what we're planning to do to him until his roof is painted with his entrails."

"What?" Grace whispered.

Ari patted her shoulder. "Try not to puke again."

"Louis Chanler." Jerek watched the words swirl around the room.

Ari glared at Jerek as though he'd just sold a brick of gold for a copper coin. Grace glanced between the others, as though trying to decide what she was expected to feel. Lincoln sank down into his seat, the color draining from his face. Eve paced the center of the room, looking every bit the wolf that resided within her.

"That son of a bitch," Eve growled. "That hypocritical, evil son of a bitch."

"I know." Jerek leaned back in his chair, keeping his face calm.

"He came to their funerals. He let Gran sell him my mother's moonstone when we were broke." Eve snatched up a glass from the coffee table and hurled it against the wall.

"He bought a lot of things from a lot of families," Ari said. "He ruined our world and then took advantage of the people left desperate by the Fracture."

"I don't understand," Grace said.

"Louis Chanler," Eve rounded on her. "That asshole—"

"Maybe you'd better let me. Life is easier if we keep Grace calm." Ari pulled her laptop out of her bag.

"You don't have to be rude about it," Grace said.

"Sometimes the truth stings." Ari sat on the floor and

opened her laptop on the coffee table. "Louis Chanler—the richest magician in the United States. Gather round, children. It's time for a story."

"What about Jack?" Lincoln sat on the couch behind Ari. "Shouldn't he be here for this? We've been waiting for days to get this information. He should be given the courtesy of knowing what we know."

"I'll give him a private tutoring session tonight." Ari winked. "Maybe we'll even canoodle."

"You're not his type," Jerek said.

"Well, damn." Ari rolled her eyes. "May I continue, Mr. Holden?"

Jerek stood and went to the back of the couch with Eve, watching over Lincoln's and Grace's shoulders.

"Louis Chanler." Ari clicked open a file, pulling up a picture of Louis.

Chanler stood on the beach in the photo, the wind sweeping through his gray hair. The only wrinkles on his face were the smile lines at the corners of his eyes. His perfect white teeth stood out against the tan of his skin. Louis Chanler looked more like a model than a murderer.

Hatred surged in Jerek's stomach. He dug his fingers into the back of the couch.

Hating him won't help you end this.

"His bank accounts hold more money than all of us could spend in an extravagant lifetime or twenty," Ari said. "He's made even more money and a very philanthropic name for himself in the twelve years since the Fracture. Where most magician family businesses went under without the magical boost they'd depended on, the Chanler assets all boomed. Louis had put lots of money into little things like land and the stock market."

"Because he knew he was going to destroy everything magical," Eve said. "I say we burn him alive."

"As fun as playing witch trial might be," Ari said, "it's Louis's other enterprises that led us to him. When the feu were barely scraping by as they adjusted to the post-Fracture world, Chanler decided to do what any good rich guy would do—start planning for his legacy. Louis began buying up magical artifacts from his cash-strapped brethren."

"Gran couldn't pay the electric bill." Eve rammed her fingers into her curls. "She was so happy she cried when Chanler drove up the mountain and offered to overpay her for Mom's moonstone. Wonder if he felt guilty for murdering her as he laid his blood money in Gran's hand."

"I don't think people like him are capable of normal human emotion," Lincoln said.

"Some guy went around buying up everyone's family heirlooms, and no one thought it was weird?" Grace asked. "Is that a normal thing among the feu?"

"Absolutely not," Jerek said. "My family had been using the same incantation books for generations."

"And your parents sold them to Chanler?" Grace asked.

"No," Jerek said. "My father kept every book, artifact, and talisman for the day magic would come back into the world. He wouldn't let Chanler touch anything from the Holden estate. He wasn't ready to give up on magic."

"Smart man," Ari said. "But Chanler appealed to desperate people with a wonderful plan. If the Fracture had broken magic, then what little the feu had left needed to be preserved for future generations. He wasn't collecting magical heirlooms to resell. Chanler was creating the first ever Museum of Magic."

"The Maree gave him their backing." Lincoln dragged his hands over his face. "Offered to help protect the collection. It's one of the few projects they actually dedicated knights to while the search for the fix to the Fracture was still underway."

"The search never should have stopped," Eve said.

"For some of us, it didn't," Jerek said.

"Which is how we weaved our way through the records of magic and right to Chanler's marble doorstep," Ari said.

"For the artifact?" Lincoln said.

"What artifact?" Eve said.

Everyone turned to Jerek.

"It's your party, Jer Bear." Ari shrugged.

"The heliostone." Jerek let the word settle for a moment. "Chanler's got it, and we're going to steal it."

A string of muttered, multi-lingual curses unlike any Jerek had ever heard rolled from Lincoln's mouth.

"You want to steal the heliostone?" Lincoln asked once he'd run out of profanities.

"What's a heliostone?" Grace asked.

"When can we take it?" Eve asked.

"Ahem." Ari clicked open a new image on her computer.

A scan of an ancient document appeared on her screen.

"The heliostone is an artifact that has been lost and rediscovered about a dozen times since the feu began keeping records," Ari said. "The stone is fabled to be the most powerful conduit of light magic ever known. Ride into battle against evil carrying the heliostone, and your enemies will fall before you. Ferry the stone into a place of deepest darkness, and all will turn to light. Those kinds of things."

"And the heliostone can mend the Fracture?" Grace asked.

"It's a piece of the puzzle," Jerek said. "Just like you."

"You can't tell me Chanler has the heliostone and hasn't told anyone," Lincoln said. "He's not secretive about his collection, and something like that would give him bragging rights around the world."

"I'm sure he'd send a newsletter to every living feu," Ari said. "Trouble is, Chanler doesn't know he has it."

27

Eve

The scent of the frying bacon and eggs didn't calm Eve's nerves. She wanted to run. Tear out of her human skin and bolt through the forest until her limbs could carry her no farther.

In time. Patience, Evelyn.

"Need help?" Jerek stepped into the doorway that led to the dining room.

"I can make breakfast on my own."

Eve scooped the bacon onto a paper towel-covered plate and scraped the eggs into an oversized dish.

"It's nearly nine," Jerek said. "Shouldn't Barbara be back?"

"Gran will come when she comes." Eve handed Jerek the plate of bacon. "Are you afraid of my cooking?"

"No." Jerek's smile lasted only a moment. "I'd just like to see her."

"I'm sure she'll be thrilled you came for a visit. A Holden up our humble mountain."

"There's nothing humble about the pack's mountain."

"Just a bunch of wolves hiding in the woods. Surprised you even remembered to come find me."

"Eve." Jerek set the bacon down and took both Eve's hands in his. "I'm not here out of obligation. I'm here because you and I are in this together. I have spent the last three years tracking down the heliostone—"

"I could have helped you search."

"I couldn't get your hopes up. Not until I was sure where the stone was and who had cast the curse in the first place. Eve, I made you a promise twelve years ago. We fight the end of this war together."

"Then why bring a Martel?" Eve lifted her hands away from Jerek's.

"Because we need a Maree, and he's the only one I trust."

"The Maree are worthless."

"Not Lincoln. Though I'd appreciate your testing him. Who knows what mush they made of him at the compound?"

"Do I have to go easy on him?" Eve grabbed the platter of eggs.

"Of course not."

A thrill of adrenaline shot through Eve's chest. "Could be fun."

Jerek didn't say anything else as he picked up the plate of bacon and followed her to the dining room.

The others were already seated around the table. Even if the vampire had been able to come inside, there would have been plenty of room for more to join.

This house was built to have more people in it.

Eve set the platter on the table with a thunk.

Grace jumped. Ari tsked from behind her laptop screen. Lincoln didn't move at all.

"Breakfast is ready." Eve sat next to the head of the table, holding Gran's seat open.

"Thank you." Grace took a plate from the stack.

"Thanks." Ari emerged from behind her computer just long enough to serve herself.

Lincoln sat still until everyone else's plates were filled.

"Going to starve?" Eve stabbed the eggs on her plate. "Not that I mind, but it does seem a bit dramatic."

Lincoln took a plate, serving himself only a spoonful of eggs.

"Fine," Eve said. "But eat quick, because Gran will be here in a minute, and this could very well be your last meal, Maree."

"What?" Grace shot a terrified look to Jerek.

"Don't worry about it," Ari said.

Lincoln picked up a piece of bacon and slowly crunched through it.

The front door banged open.

"Evelyn, why does the yard smell like bat and the house smell like trash?" Gran called.

"We've got guests, Gran." Eve crossed her arms as a smile lifted her lips. "Holden drove up the mountain with some friends."

"Holden?" Gran stepped into the doorway. She narrowed her eyes at Jerek, scrunching together her freckles so it became impossible to see where one ended and another began. "Jerek Holden, I wasn't sure I'd live to see you come back to pack land."

Jerek stood, giving Gran a little bow. "I had some things to attend to."

"Things to attend to?" Gran said. "Your daddy dies, and you stop coming south? Do you think that's what he would have wanted? A Holden has responsibilities."

"Gran." Eve's smile slipped away.

"It took me a little while to sort myself out, ma'am," Jerek said. "But I'm here now if you'll have me."

"Drag a bunch of ragamuffins into my house *then* ask if I'll have you?" Gran gave a rough laugh. "Our allegiance is to you, Holden, not to a pack of scraps clinging to your coat tails."

"I understand, ma'am," Jerek said. "And I wouldn't have brought anyone here if I didn't have business I needed them for."

Gran examined each person seated at her table before looking back to Jerek. "And what sort of business could possibly involve me and a herd of teenagers?"

"Not you, Gran," Eve said. "Jerek came to see me."

"That, I like even less." Gran sat at the head of the table. "Anything I should know about?"

Jerek looked to Eve.

You could tell her. Tell her about Chanler and go after him right now.

"No." Eve picked up her fork. "We've got it covered."

"Good." Gran dished eggs onto her plate. "Make sure you get the Maree off my land as soon as you can. Not all pack folk are as civilized as we are."

"A few days at most, ma'am," Jerek said. "And we are very grateful for your hospitality."

Gran gave another laugh and chomped down on a crisp slice of bacon.

28

Lincoln

"This is silly." Lincoln paced the wide swath of grass between the back of the Gibbs' house and their old barn, which hadn't seemed to hold animals for a very long time.

"Don't be such a baby." Ari sat beside Grace on the steps of the back porch, unmistakable glee dancing in her eyes. "Don't the Maree teach their minions that practice makes perfect or something like that?"

The hinges creaked as Eve swung open the back door of the house. She'd traded in her t-shirt and underwear for a lavender tank top and black leggings that perfectly displayed her well-muscled body.

"Nice," Ari said. "But I would have gone with a darker color to hide the blood."

"Blood?" Grace asked.

"It's kind of cute that you're so naïve." Ari patted Grace's hand. "I mean, it's going to get old fast, but this morning, still cute."

"Ari," Jerek warned.

"What?" Ari dusted off her pink boots.

"There won't be any blood." Lincoln studied Eve. The way she walked with her weight close to her toes, as though preparing to run. The way she rolled her right shoulder, as though checking on the status of an old injury.

"You really think I'm going to take you down that fast?" Eve walked out to the center of the grass, her head traveling side to side as she tracked Lincoln's pacing. "It's true. I just didn't think you'd be so humble."

"There's no point in fighting amongst ourselves," Lincoln said.

"It's not like a fist fight," Ari said. "It's practice."

"Tonight, we'll begin working on our plan for the party," Jerek said. "We all need to know what we're working with."

"When I beat him, can we send him home?" Eve asked.

"No," Jerek said.

"Damn." Eve stepped into Lincoln's path. "Ready, Martel?"

Her eyes narrowed as she stared at him. Whether in concentration or hatred, Lincoln wasn't sure.

"No stone," Jerek warned. "You won't be able to use it at the party."

"I won't need it."

Eve lunged forward, catching Lincoln hard in the ribs.

Pain pounded through his center. He reached forward, trying to carry her with him as he fell to the ground, but she had hit him too hard. Rather than tumble to the grass, he flew back ten feet, landing just shy of the trunk of a tree. The force of his fall knocked the air from his lungs.

Grace screamed.

"Don't kill him," Jerek sighed. "None of us are dispensable."

"You're really no fun," Ari said.

Lincoln gasped and leapt to his feet. "Cheap shot."

"Worked on you." Eve shrugged. "How much actual fighting have you done?"

"Enough." Lincoln charged forward, leaning low as though preparing to return Eve's blow to the ribs.

At the last moment, Eve leapt four feet into the air.

Lincoln reached up, crashing his forearm into her ankles. She toppled to the ground, landing on her hands and knees.

"See, Grace?" Ari said. "This is about to get interesting."

"They really don't just have you sitting around Italy pruning grape vines," Jerek said.

He'd joined the girls on the porch, standing behind them with his arms crossed over his chest like some sort of gladiatorial judge.

Eve pushed off of all fours, landing on her feet in front of Lincoln.

"What special tricks did they teach you for fighting wolves?" She kicked out, catching him behind the ankles.

Lincoln shifted his weight, stumbling forward instead of falling back. He swung his right fist, catching Eve in the cheek.

Grace squeaked.

Eve blew the hair out of her eyes while punching Lincoln in the middle of his chest.

Again, all the air shot out of his lungs. He brought both fists up, swinging one at Eve's face while pummeling the other down on her right shoulder.

She'd only seen the hand aiming for her eye. She leaned the other way, giving Lincoln more force as he hit her shoulder.

Pain flitted through her eyes.

Lincoln shifted his weight to step away, but Eve swung her hand up, catching him under the armpit and sending him flying sideways like a cast-aside ragdoll.

He hit the ground hard and rolled, gritting his teeth against the moan of pain that tried to escape him as a rock cut into his side.

"That shirt was new," Ari said.

"Sorry." Eve glared down at him. "We done here?"

"No." Lincoln pushed himself to his feet, testing the motion of his arms.

"Are we really going to waste our time letting the Maree play punching bag?" Eve asked. "I'll tell you how this ends. You keep hitting me, I keep getting up. I keep hitting you, you stop getting up. Because that's what Maree do. They quit. They pack it in like a bunch of useless children who shouldn't have anything to do with the feu."

Anger flared in Lincoln's chest. "The Maree are the protectors of the feu." He charged forward.

Eve swung with her fist, but Lincoln kicked her hand aside.

"We have spent generations protecting the feu from the sombs." He twisted around, catching Eve by the back of the neck and tossing her into the dirt.

"And then they gave up." Eve leapt back to her feet. She took two giant strides and jumped, kicking Lincoln in the side of the head.

The world spun as pain pounded through his ear.

"The Maree didn't give up." The ground shifted beneath his feet as Lincoln blinked, forcing his eyes to focus on Eve. "We lost hundreds of knights in the search for an end to the Fracture."

"You ran like cowards." Eve charged.

Lincoln spun, kicking behind and catching her in the stomach.

She fell to the ground with a grunt.

"There was nothing else to do." Lincoln's lungs ached with each breath. "The person who caused the terror didn't leave any clues for us to follow. We didn't even find the bodies of half the knights who went on the search. If we had kept going, the Knights Maree would have gone extinct."

"Then they should have." Eve stood and wiped the blood from the corner of her mouth. "If the Maree can't fulfill their duty, then the world would be better off without them. The Maree are traitors and cowards."

"That's not true. You have no idea how hard the Maree have been working to rebuild."

"I don't need to. I know about all the innocent people whose murderer you stopped trying to find." Tears glistened in the corners of her eyes.

There's been too much pain.

Lincoln watched as she ran forward, kicking high and knocking him to the ground. He didn't fight as she wrapped an arm around his neck, blocking his supply of precious air.

"Enough," Jerek said.

Eve didn't let go.

Spots danced in front of Lincoln's eyes.

"I said *enough.*"

She released Lincoln's neck.

The door to the house banged shut behind her before Lincoln could roll onto his back. The leaves on the trees regained their shapes as he blinked at the sky.

"That went well." Ari stepped into Lincoln's view, hovering over him like a divine and judgmental angel. "I guess I should go grab you another set of clothes from the van."

"Thanks." Lincoln's voice came out rough.

Ari reached down, taking his hand and yanking him to his feet. "If it makes you feel any better, some of us don't think all Maree are traitors. A little ineffectual, but not the maliciously betray type."

"Thanks."

Ari squeezed his hand before walking around the side of the house.

Lincoln could picture her telling Jack all about the fight.

He'll make me spar with the vampire next.

"Good work." Jerek leaned against the clapboard side of the house.

"You wanted me to end up in the dirt?" Lincoln touched the side of his head. Blood stained his fingers.

"It didn't matter who ended up in the dirt," Jerek said. "You two were going to end up hitting each other eventually. Now we've gotten it over with."

Jerek went into the house, leaving a silent Grace and a fuming Lincoln behind.

29

Grace

Grace clutched the cracked leather book in her hands as though its pages held the answer to the terrible riddle her life had become.

To help her family, she had to leave them. To learn, she had to run away from school. To save people, she had to meet with wannabe criminals in a dusty old barn.

A shiver shook Grace's shoulders despite the warm musty air.

Jerek swung open the barn doors, letting in the last traces of the sunset.

"How is the reading going?" he asked.

"I finished the text," Grace said. "Didn't understand half of it, so I started again from the beginning."

"Good." Jerek dragged two sawhorses over from the side of the barn. "I'll give you a different book tonight."

"How many did you pack?" Grace set the book down and helped Jerek lift a sheet of wood on top of the sawhorses.

"Just one. But Barbara has a few, and she said she didn't mind me borrowing them for some light reading."

"She doesn't know the books are for me?"

"There are some things it's best for Barbara not to know."

"But we're meeting in her barn, and her granddaughter is supposed to be coming with us." Grace looked around the cobweb-speckled space. "Doesn't she want to know what Eve's up to?"

"Maybe you should leave Eve's business to Eve." Eve strode into the barn, carrying a tray of snacks.

"I would never dream of doing anything different." Jerek placed his palms on the makeshift table. The dust and grime coating the sheet of wood puffed away as though blown by a giant's breath.

A snap of shock jolted Grace's heart. "Will I able be able to do that?"

"By the time we're done with you, you'll be able to clean the whole barn with a simple incantation." Ari appeared in the barn entrance, pink pack over her shoulder.

"Jack on his way?" Jerek asked.

"As soon as the sun is down." Ari ran a finger over the table, checking the wood's cleanliness before pulling out her computer.

"And Lincoln?" Jerek asked.

"He's your puppy, not mine," Ari said.

Eve shot her a glare.

"Shit." Ari cringed. "Sorry."

Eve said nothing. She ventured farther into the depths of the barn than Grace would have dared, coming back with a crate in either hand.

Jerek set his own bag on the table and pulled out a worn notebook.

Ari eyed the frayed edges of the front cover. "Ever considered digital copies?"

"With hackers like you in the world? Never." Jerek sat on one of the crates.

Ari took the seat next to him then began typing away on her computer.

Eve made another trip to the far side of the barn, coming back with two more crates.

"No chance of some light?" Ari asked.

Eve moved to the door, opened a metal box, and clicked on the lights.

"It's like a real meeting now," Ari said.

"Glad to help." Eve found two more crates then sat at the table facing the door, just in time for Lincoln to appear from the darkness.

Bruises marked his face, and he held his arm awkwardly away from his body.

"Not too sore I hope." Eve grinned. "I would hate for a Gibbs guest to get a bad night's sleep."

"I've slept through worse." Lincoln sat at the table, the corners of his eyes crinkling in pain.

"Here comes bat boy," Eve said.

"So, in Eve land bat boy is okay but puppy is offensive?" Ari asked. "I just want to make sure I know how to piss people off properly."

Grace hurried to the table, sinking into the seat next to Lincoln before Jack walked in from the darkness.

"If this is an intervention, I'm really not in the mood." Jack waited in the doorway.

"It's the first meeting of our full heist team. Really, we should come up with a cute name, like the Fracture Fighters or..." Ari's voice trailed away as Jerek looked at her with one eyebrow raised. "Or we could just be boring."

"I'm Eve." Eve leaned across the table, holding out her hand to Jack.

"Jack." He shook her hand. "Never met a werewolf before. It's a little intimidating."

"Good," Eve said. "You'll do fine on pack land."

With a smile that showed the tips of his fangs, Jack sat with his back to the night.

"If we may begin," Jerek said. "We've all agreed to the job. We're going to steal the heliostone and mend the Fracture. Yes?"

Murmured consent circled the table.

"The trick now is getting the stone. And that won't be an easy task." Jerek looked to Ari.

"Right." Ari spun her computer to face the group.

A picture of a mansion overlooking a cliff appeared on the screen. "I present the Chanler estate in Newport, Rhode Island. Chanler's Museum of Magic is all set to be a one-of-a-kind marvel. Artifacts dating back to the first casters, relics from the magic wars, heirlooms from all over the world. He's spent years building a fortress to protect the collection from feu and somb alike. And where else would you build a bunker of your most treasured possessions but under your super fancy rich guy house?"

She clicked over to a new image—the excavation plans for a set of tunnels and rooms reaching far below the Chanler estate.

"It's taken years to construct the museum," Ari continued. "I mean, digging into the seabed and not flooding your tunnels has got to take a ton of money and time, but our evil Chanler has kept plugging away, building his museum to protect the legacy of the feu and it's finally ready for the big opening night."

"The grand opening of the Museum of Magic." Jerek stood. "Our one chance for getting the heliostone."

"The stone is going to be on display?" Jack asked. "An artifact of that caliber will be surrounded by security. I'm willing to try, but I can't guarantee I'll be able to get within ten feet of the heliostone."

"But"—Jerek held up one finger—"Chanler doesn't know he has the heliostone."

Ari clicked again, bringing up a new image.

A beautiful night sky alight with dazzling stars filled the screen.

"The Caster's Fate," Lincoln whispered.

"What?" Grace glanced to Lincoln. Absolute awe filled his face.

"A work of glass art created more than a few hundred years ago," Lincoln said. "The window sat above the monument to the fallen casters in France. After the treaty established the Knights Maree, the sanctuary that housed the monument was built as a place for the feu and knights to meet in peace.

"The stars in the glass were meant to symbolize the magicians who had fallen during the long conflict. The treaty almost fell apart when rogue magicians burned the sanctuary. I didn't know they'd rescued the window. I thought it was lost."

"Lost, pilfered, almost the same." Ari waved a hand through the air.

"But what's a blue glass window got to do with the stone?" Jack asked.

Ari tapped the screen, zooming in on the glass panel. "Polaris, the north star."

Grace leaned in toward the computer. The stars weren't bits of clear glass as she'd first thought, but stones set into the deep blue. Each stone was unique in shape and size and held its own slightly different hue just as the stars in the heavens did.

Larger than those around it, the stone representing the

north star was completely devoid of color, not even taking on the hue of the blue glass surrounding it.

"What are those marks on the stone?" Jack asked.

Grace squinted at the screen, trying to see what Jack's vampire eyes had detected.

"Nicely done." Ari opened a close-up image of Polaris. Divots cut into the bottom of the stone at regular intervals. "Looks like it might be damage from the window's creation, or if you want to deep dive your magical history, marks left from whatever the stone was meant for before it was taken for the window."

"The Carrier's Staff," Lincoln said. "The marks are from being a part of the staff."

"Ding, ding, ding," Ari said as a picture of a metal staff popped up.

The dark and light metal twisted around in a pattern of ridges like tree branches spiraling up toward the sun. At the top, the different veins of metal separated, creating talons that dug into an egg-sized, diamond-like stone.

"The heliostone in its last known iteration," Ari said.

"How can Chanler not know he has it?" Jack asked.

"Chanler is an idiot?" Eve suggested.

"Hard to see the forest for the trees?" Ari said.

"Because there's no reason the heliostone should have been anywhere near the Caster's Fate," Jerek said. "By all known accounts, the stone was last seen in South America."

"Then how did you find it?" Grace gripped the edge of her crate seat.

"An unhealthy obsession," Ari said.

Jerek shot her a glare.

"Fine," Ari said. "Years of searching and some really great help from me."

"And you're sure this is the stone?" Lincoln asked.

"I'm betting my life on it," Jerek said.

"You're betting all our lives on it," Eve said.

The room fell silent. Only the rustle of the breeze through the trees and the buzzing of the electric lights lent any sound to the night.

"I know," Jerek said. "And I wouldn't ask any of you to come with me to the museum if there were another way. But it's the fate of the feu at stake, and I can't do this alone."

"I'd never let you try," Ari said. "Mostly because you'd fail."

"And why do you think all of us won't fail?" Jack asked.

"Because we can't," Eve said.

"That's great, but it doesn't mean we can succeed, either," Jack said. "How exactly do you plan to get in, steal a glass window, and get back out?"

"Loosely?" Jerek said. "We go to the party, get to the window, shatter the glass, steal the stone, and restore magic before we ever try to get back aboveground."

"Risky." Eve pursed her lips.

"Why don't we steal the stone before the party?" Grace asked. "Wouldn't that be better than trying to get to the window when there are a bunch of people around?"

"You'd think so." Ari turned her computer, typing for a few moments before spinning the screen back to the group.

A new set of blueprints had appeared, showing the museum from the side.

"There are officially two entrances to the Museum of Magic that don't involve trying to dig or blow our way in and risk flooding the entire complex," Jerek said. "The first is the main entrance on the ocean side of Chanler's property. The second is the service entrance. Both are guarded around the clock. No one gets in without permission."

"There's also a great little staircase to nowhere, but..." Ari wrinkled her nose. "Not really helpful either."

"If we can't sneak in, we'll have to walk through the guarded doors. Hundreds of people are going to the opening party. That's the best cover we're going to get." Eve studied the blueprints. "We can sneak in with all of them."

"Exactly." Jerek's eyes twinkled. "Chanler won't even know we're there until it's done."

Excitement bubbled in Grace's chest.

I'll be helping. Not hurting anyone. Doing some good...

"Not to be a downer, but as the only career criminal here, how are we getting in?" Jack counted on his fingers. "What kind of security are we dealing with at the door? Is the window in a case? What's the case made of? Will there be guards in the room? How many of them? How long do you need to do the incantation? Can she even—"

Jerek held up a hand, silencing Jack.

"That's why we're all here," Jerek said. "I've laid out the path to the treasure. Now we're going to work together to figure out how to steal it."

"Oh, Team Treasure," Ari said. "That has a nice ring to it."

"No, Ari," Jerek said.

"I'll keep working on it." Ari spun her computer back around. "Now, who has a brilliant idea about sneaking past a pack of guards without getting the stabby end of a sword?"

30

Lincoln

The gray of dawn had begun to peek up over the horizon, giving depth to the forest surrounding the Gibbs' house. The smell of trees and damp earth filled Lincoln's lungs.

A very small part of him knew he should recognize the scent. He'd spent summers in the woods as a small child, running through the trees, playing and laughing. The dry scent of hot summers and cold stone halls were more familiar to him now.

Sounds carried from inside the house. Whether someone was waking up or finally going to sleep, he didn't know. They'd made Jack a safe room upstairs. He'd still have to stay inside, but it would be better than being trapped under a van seat. They'd all left the barn a little more than an hour ago, and even then, they'd only gone so Jack wouldn't get stranded.

They still had too many *ifs* to work out.

If we can get into the party.

If Grace can manage the spell.

If we can get to Rhode Island without killing each other.

The front door creaked open behind him. The quiet padding of bare feet crossed to the stairs next to him.

Lincoln only had to glance down at the pink pedicure to know who stood by his side.

"You okay?" Ari asked.

"As well as someone can be when they haven't slept in a day," Lincoln said.

"And have had the crap beaten out of them." Ari sat on the step beside him. "To be honest, you did better than I thought you would."

"Thanks."

"I mean it." Ari bumped him with her shoulder. "Eve's a fifth-generation werewolf. As trained as you might be, your blood is completely human. You didn't die. That's pretty impressive."

"Thanks." The word came out with a laugh this time.

"Just imagine what would happen if she went full wolf. At the party. On the guards."

Even as Lincoln forced his hands to stay relaxed on his knees, the tendons in the sides of his neck tensed.

"Granted, we won't be dealing with your standard security stooge lineup. There are Maree guarding the museum and the collection," Ari said. "The knights swore they would protect the artifacts."

"If the Maree knew what Chanler had done, he would have been tried and executed years ago."

"I know. The knights believe in justice, and the Martel family has a long history of noble deeds and good intentions. It's gotten a bunch of you killed, but I admire the consistency."

"We have a sworn duty to protect the feu."

"Which is what your brother must think he's doing. For Martin Martel to be working as a guard at the Museum of Magic at only twenty-years-old...your parents must be so proud."

"Don't." Lincoln gripped his knees.

"Don't what? Point out the truth or talk about your family?"

Lincoln ran a hand over his face. His stubble had started to go soft.

I'd be sent to run for needing a shave this badly.

"Do the others know?" Lincoln asked.

"Jerek does. I was going to mention it at the meeting of the Fracture Fixers, but since you hadn't mentioned your brother working for Chanler, I thought it best to keep quiet."

"If Martin knew what Chanler was, he'd bring him before the Council of the Feu himself."

"There is no more Council of the Feu. At least not that can do anything about Chanler."

"The knights then."

"Are broken and infiltrated." She laid her hand on top of his. "Can you honestly promise there isn't one knight among the Maree who wouldn't side with Chanler and his power and money?"

"Martin wouldn't." Lincoln looked at Ari, searching her eyes for belief or condemnation.

Or help.

"I believe you." Ari turned her face back to the sunrise. "But we can't risk both of you being at the party. He could recognize you."

"Jerek can change my face."

"Family is family. I'm putting through the documents to have your brother transferred west. The knights in Japan are suddenly in desperate need of his help."

"He'll hate it there. He fought for years to get sent home to the States."

"How badly would Martin's honor be damaged if he was working for Chanler when we out him as a traitor to the feu? I'm saving your brother's career."

Lincoln turned his wrist, taking her hand in his.

"Now all I have to do is make sure none of the other Martels get sent over." Ari gave a tired sigh. "That'll be fun."

"They won't take Fred out of Paris, and the rest are too young," Lincoln said. "Won't matter that much, though. I've spent the last twelve years at the compound. I'll know one of Chanler's guards."

"We'll make sure they don't know you. It's going to be okay."

"Thanks."

The delicate size of her hand in his seemed impossible, like a bear being comforted by a butterfly. Still, he couldn't bring himself to let go as the sun climbed over the edge of the mountains.

"How did we get wrapped up in this?" Lincoln asked.

"Accident of birth and an unfortunate friendship with Jerek Holden."

A laugh rumbled in Lincoln's chest, shaking loose the tension he'd been holding on to for days.

"Don't let yourself feel too cheerful." Ari leaned close, whispering in his ear. "It's going to get so much worse before it gets better."

Lincoln laughed even harder.

"I just can't wait for—"

"Shh." Lincoln pressed his free hand over Ari's lips.

A rustling of the trees shocked the tension back into Lincoln's shoulders. "Get in the house."

"Fat chance." Ari stood, dragging Lincoln up with her, her

gaze sweeping the trees. "Who the hell is out there?" Her voice carried across the lawn.

"Go get Jerek. Stay inside." Lincoln let go of her hand and stepped out onto the grass, reaching for the knife hidden in the waist of his pants.

"Jerek!" Ari shouted. "The trees are shaking, and I think it's for you."

"Not what I meant," Lincoln said.

"I told you I'm not going inside." Ari stepped in front of him, planting her feet, her hands on her hips as she gazed down the road. "Jerek will be out in a minute."

Shapes appeared between the trees. A dozen people peered out from the leaves, their gazes shifting between Lincoln and the house.

"If you won't go inside, at least get behind me," Lincoln said.

"Hi." Ari waved to the people in the trees. "Can we help you with something?"

For a moment, no one moved. Then a man stepped out onto the lawn.

Scars marred the man's face, and gray tinged his dark brown hair.

"We're here to see what's been brought onto pack land," the man said.

"You're here to talk to Barbara? It's pretty early in the morning for a visit, but I guess I can check and see if she's up. Barbara!" Ari shouted. "You've got friends, and they seem a little cranky."

The front door of the house squeaked open.

"Harry," Eve said.

Lincoln didn't dare turn away from the pack to look at her.

"What the hell are you doing on Gran's lawn at this hour of the morning?"

"What the hell are a vampire and a Maree doing on your Gran's land at all?" Harry stepped farther onto the lawn.

The other wolves moved with him, matching his stride.

Lincoln reached forward, grabbing Ari's arm and dragging her back to stand behind him.

"Rude," Ari whispered.

"Who we have in our house is our business." Eve stepped in front of Lincoln.

She had put on shoes and pants.

Don't make us fight you.

Lincoln wanted to speak, but the glares from the pack kept him silent.

Let Eve deal with her own.

"The whole mountain is pack land, Eve," Harry said.

"How right you are." Jerek slammed the door to the house open. "A whole mountain's worth of territory. Not many werewolf packs are so lucky."

"Holden." Harry bent his torso in a bow but kept his gaze fixed on Jerek.

The wolves behind Harry bowed as well.

"It's been a long time, Harry." Jerek stopped beside Eve. "Seemed like it was finally time to check on the Holden family land. It's such a strange feeling to own a whole mountain you hardly ever see."

"We are, as ever, grateful for the generosity of the Holden family."

The level of hatred in Harry's voice grated Lincoln's nerves.

A fight not started is a battle already won.

"It's not generosity," Jerek said. "It's a wonderful investment and the Holden family's duty as stewards of the feu. I'm sure you haven't forgotten it was the Holden family who sponsored this pack's petition to the Council for the right to settle on feu-protected land. First pack to receive such an honor and the

Holden family's responsibility to maintain. There are some duties we can't turn our back on. Isn't that right, Lincoln?"

All the wolves turned their glares back to Lincoln.

"It's the duty of the Maree to protect feu and sombs alike." Lincoln dipped his chin. "People might not always like how things turn out, but it's always the intention of the knights to help the feu."

"Help the feu?" Harry asked. "How much help did we get when our kind was slaughtered?"

"Harry, don't," Eve said.

"Don't fight me, little girl," Harry growled.

"You won't win here, Harry. These people are guests on Gran's land."

"Your Gran's land should have been your daddy's land." Harry moved closer, stopping three feet in front of Eve. "But the butcher murdered him. Murdered your mother, your brother, half of your pack, and what did the Maree do?"

"Nothing," Eve said. "They ran back to the safety of their compound and left us with dead to bury and orphans to feed."

"Then what the hell is a Maree doing on our mountain?" Harry growled.

"Lincoln is here for my personal protection," Jerek said. "He's acting as my guard while I check on the mountain of which I am the sole legal owner. So, as much as I would love to chat with all of you about how we might convince the Maree of the terrible wrong they committed by essentially ignoring the slaughter of the werewolves, I'm afraid I've had very little sleep and now is not the time."

"We're not letting the Maree leave this mountain," Harry said. "They ignore our blood, we'll take theirs."

Lincoln gipped the hilt of his dagger, keeping the shining blade hidden behind his back as he slipped it from its sheath.

"You forget, Harry," Jerek said, "my mother was slaughtered

in the same blast that killed your people. I have just as much a right to hate the Maree as you do. But this is not the place for vengeance, and Lincoln was no more than a child when the butcher struck. All of you leave, and we'll be on our way. There are people who deserve to be brought to justice for what happened here. I give you my word, the butcher will finally have to stand and face the atrocities committed. The tides of change are lapping at our feet."

"I don't trust magicians," Harry said. "And I won't suffer a Maree to live."

He reached for the neck of his shirt, pulling out a heavy silver pendant.

"Harry, don't," Eve warned.

Harry flipped the top of the pendant aside, allowing his moonstone to soak in the sunlight of the new day.

"Damn." Ari dodged in front of Lincoln, snatching the van keys from Jerek's pocket before running away.

Please get somewhere safe, Lincoln wanted to shout after her but couldn't spare even that stray bit of thought as Harry's form shook.

His brown hair trembled, growing like a plant on a sped-up video. Fur sprouted from the sides of his face, his shoulders, and arms. His lips twisted and stretched, making room for his lengthening teeth. His fingers distorted, losing the soft look of humanity as nails hardened into claws.

Behind Harry, the others transformed, pulling energy from the moonstones they wore.

"You're making a horrible mistake. One I will not forgive." Jerek stepped in front of Eve, placing himself between her and the pack as she began her own shuddering transformation.

"Give us the Maree." Harry's roar shook the insides of Lincoln's lungs.

"If your choice is made," Jerek said, "then on your own heads rest the consequences."

In a single, blurring bound, Eve leapt over Jerek, pouncing on Harry's chest.

A gray-haired woman in the pack howled, running straight for Eve.

"Lincoln, get the others!" A light flashed in Jerek's palm, lengthening and shimmering into a solid form in his hand.

"You get them." Lincoln charged forward with a shout, crashing his shoulder into the wolf who'd aimed her teeth for Eve's neck.

Jerek slashed out with the bright beam of light, catching a male wolf in the shoulder. Blood spurted from a wound as deep as if Jerek had been wielding a sword.

Eve hoisted Harry from the ground, tossing him over the heads of the wolves who charged forward.

Teeth pierced Lincoln's arm. Sparks of pain danced through his vision. He swung his blade up, cutting into the neck of the wolf who had bit him. Warm blood coated his arm as the teeth relinquished their hold.

Eve grabbed the shoulders of the bleeding wolf, tossing her aside.

Lincoln turned, standing back-to-back with Jerek and Eve.

The pack closed in around them.

"I'm so sorry," Jerek said.

"Don't be," Eve said. "If they've fallen this far, you can't hold yourself responsible for who ends up in the dirt."

With a snarl, a blond wolf large enough to match Lincoln's size threw himself at Jerek's throat.

31

Jack

I wish I couldn't hear.

It had never occurred to Jack when accepting the bite that amplified hearing would be the part of the gift he would loathe first.

"What the hell are a vampire and a Maree doing on your Gran's land at all?" A man's voice carried easily to Jack through the walls of the house.

The seven layers of blankets Grace and Eve had strung up to protect him from the sun did nothing to block out the noise.

The front door squeaked open and slammed shut.

This isn't going to end well.

He could scent the loathing of the wolves on the wind. It stung his nose and wound an instinctual knot of fear in his stomach. That many angry pheromones did not allow for a peaceful ending.

"Who we have in our house is our business," Eve said.

"I knew I liked you," Jack whispered.

"Jack, get in the closet." Grace knocked lightly on the bedroom door.

Jack slipped into the closet, shutting himself in.

A thin line of light spilled in from the hallway as Grace opened the door.

"Jack, we have to get out of here," Grace said. "Something bad is happening outside."

"Yeah." Jack leaned against the wall, letting the old clothes curl around him, forcing himself to take a casual stance though he knew Grace couldn't see him. "An angry werewolf pack on the front lawn is rarely considered a good thing."

"We have to get to the van and go," Grace said.

"I can't." Jack's fangs grew, piercing his bottom lip. "You all go. I'll wait here until dark and figure out how to find you."

"We can't leave you. We all have to go together."

"I can't go outside, Grace. Sun's up. You go. I'll be fine."

"Is he in the closet?" Barbara's steady footfalls thumped into the room.

"You have no idea how many times I heard that phrase in my childhood," Jack said.

"Squeeze into the corner," Barbara said. "I'm passing in a bag."

"Bag?" Jack wedged himself into the corner, ducking behind the row of old clothes.

The closet door opened just long enough for an old rucksack to be tossed onto the floor.

"Climb in," Barbara said.

"What?" Jack said. "I'm not getting in a bag."

"You are climbing in that bag right now, young man. Then I am carrying you to that van so the lot of you can get out of pack territory before we have a second Blood Mountain on our hands."

Jack lifted the heavy canvas from the closet floor. "I'll burn."

"The whole house will burn if you stay here," Barbara said. "Pack yourself in with clothes and let's go."

"Lincoln, get the others!" Jerek's shout pounded into Jack's ears.

"If I die doing this, you have to promise me something." Jack ripped clothes down from their hangers, wrapping them around his body to cover every inch of bare skin.

"You're going to be okay," Grace said.

"What's the promise?" Barbara asked.

"Have Ari help you find my family." Jack stepped into the rucksack, shimmying the thick fabric up over his hips. "Tell them I forgive them and I'll see them all in Hell."

"You have my word," Barbara said.

He curled into a ball, barely squeezing into the sack. He snaked the cords of the bag in over his head, pulling the top shut. "I'm in."

The closet door opened, and strong arms heaved him into the air.

"You're going to be okay, Jack," Grace said. "I promise you'll be okay."

"I've heard that before." Jack closed his eyes, trying to give in to the helplessness of his situation.

He bounced in Barbara's arms as she ran down the stairs.

"You know," Jack said, "I really wish my grandmother had been as badass as you, Barbara."

"You're too kind," Barbara said.

The door creaked open, and sunlight touched the outside of the bag.

Jack gasped as traces of the rays burrowed their way through the fabric to his skin.

"You're okay!" Grace shouted.

Barbara's pace quickened. They were behind the house. The sounds of the fight curved around the solid structure.

Grunts, screams, the impact of bodies clashing together—Jack gritted his teeth against the burning pain, wishing he could move enough to cover his ears.

A slam and the revving of the van's engine came from the right.

"Over here!" Grace shouted.

Too loud, Grace.

Over the screaming as a blade sliced flesh, one thundering set of footsteps carried around the house.

"Someone's coming," Jack said.

Barbara cursed.

The van stopped next to them.

"Get him inside!" Ari shouted as the van's side doors opened.

Barbara stretched out her arms, lifting Jack toward the van.

Something hard slammed into her back with a shuddering thump.

Jack flew out of her arms, landing half-in/half-out of the doors. The canvas tore as he tipped toward the ground.

Pain. Searing, all-encompassing agony ripped through his flesh. He didn't know which parts of him burned, only that fire had stolen him.

"Jack!"

He couldn't recognize the voices that screamed for him.

"Jack!"

His head hit something, and blood trickled into his mouth as hands pushed and shoved him into the darkness.

32

Grace

"Jack!" Grace screamed his name as she shoved him into the safety of his compartment under the seat. "Jack!"

His only answer came as an unending scream of agony.

"We have to get the others," Ari said.

Barbara slammed the van doors shut, leaving herself on the outside. Her newly formed claws tore into the face of her attacker.

"Barbara." Grace reached for the doors but toppled sideways as Ari began driving around to the front of the house. "We can't just leave her."

"She'll be fine," Ari said. "Hang on, and be ready to open the doors."

"But—"

The van swerved, its wheels spinning in the grass as they tore onto the front lawn.

Eve, Lincoln, and Jerek stood back-to-back, fighting off the attacks of the pack.

Jerek swung his sword made of glistening light at the throat of a rearing wolf. Blood spurted from the monster's neck.

Bile soared into Grace's mouth. She gripped the door handle, letting the pain of the edges digging into her skin anchor her to something above sheer panic.

Ari aimed the van straight for the center of the fight.

A horrible thump came from the front of the van as she plowed into a wolf with long, mousy hair.

Grace swung open the side doors, the impact radiating into her arm as the metal smashed into the back of a male wolf with gray dotting his dark brown hair.

He spun to face Grace. His gaze met hers. He snarled, baring his bloody teeth.

A spike of light burst through his chest as Jerek stabbed him from behind.

A scream tore from Grace's throat as she scrambled away from the blood.

"Come on!" Ari shouted.

Jerek leapt in through the side doors, dragging Lincoln in behind him.

Eve threw herself in after, slamming the doors closed.

Ari stomped on the gas, hitting another wolf as she raced down the narrow drive.

"Barbara." Grace's voice wobbled as she fought to draw air into her lungs. "We have to go back for Barbara."

Eve turned to her. Blood had mixed in with her red hair, matting her curls to her forehead. Claws had grown from her hands, and blood stained her sharpened teeth.

"Gran will be fine. Keep driving." Eve crouched next to the door, watching the woods for wolves chasing them.

A howl carried from the house as they turned onto the dirt road that led down the mountain.

"We can go back," Lincoln said. "We can help her."

Eve closed her eyes. "Gran doesn't need our help to kill them all."

Jack's groan from under the seat kept Grace from begging to go back and find a way to stop anyone else from getting hurt.

"What happened?" Jerek crawled over to the covering, favoring his left leg.

"Sun touched," Ari said.

"We need to help him," Lincoln said.

The color had drained from his face, and blood dripped freely from a wound on his forearm.

"We need to help you, too," Eve said.

"Ari, where's my bag?" Jerek tapped the end of his sword of light, shrinking the blade to the size of a needle and storing it in his pocket.

"Passenger seat." Ari took the turns at top speed.

Grace held her breath, waiting for the van to tip.

"You're wonderful, Ari." Jerek grabbed his pack.

"I know," Ari said. "You can adore me later."

Jerek pulled out the black, shining box. "Grace, I'm going to need your help."

"What?" Grace squeaked.

"You help me now, or Jack dies."

33

Jerek

"What do you need me to do?" Grace grabbed stray clothes that had been strewn across the floor, taking an aging shirt and reaching for Lincoln's wounded arm.

"No." Jerek opened the shining black box, his eyes searching for something even as his mind raced to settle on what exactly he needed.

"We need to apply pressure," Grace said. "We should take him to a hospital."

"And what could a somb doctor do for Jack?" Eve took the old shirt from Grace's hand, pressing it to the wound on Lincoln's arm. "No one is going to a hospital."

A tiny bit of gold twine lay in the corner of the box. Jerek snatched it up, feeling the familiar coarseness of the fibers between his fingers.

"We don't have a choice," Grace said. "We need to find an Emergency Room."

"Grace." Jerek set the box down, sliding as close to the flap of Jack's safety as he could.

"Lincoln could bleed to death," Grace said.

"And how would you explain the werewolf bite?" Eve said.

"Grace!" Jerek shouted.

She finally turned to him. Tears streamed down her cheeks.

How lucky would she be to never have to understand?

Jerek shoved his sympathy aside. "Grace, I promise we are going to take care of Lincoln. But right now, Jack has a lot less time. I need you to help me. I can't heal Jack without you."

Panic filled Grace's eyes as she crawled to Jerek's side.

"There is magic that can help Jack," Jerek said, "but it requires an incantation."

"I don't know how to do an incantation."

"You don't have to. We're going to piggyback the spell." Jerek passed Grace the other end of the twine. "You're going to lend me your magic while I do the incantation. Okay?"

Grace nodded, her whole body trembling with the movement.

"Good." Jerek slipped carefully under the black and into Jack's hiding spot. He hadn't noticed how horribly still Jack had gone until they were both crammed into the same tiny space.

Jack's chest rattled with each breath. A low moan escaped him as Jerek traced his fingers along the bottom of the springs above them, yielding a gentle light.

"It won't hurt you," Jerek said. "This light can't hurt you."

He raised his head to look at Jack, biting the insides of his lips to keep from gasping.

Dark blisters covered Jack's face, oozing blood that trailed lazily down his cheeks. Skin flaked off the backs of his hands, falling away in large chunks.

Calm, Jerek. Calm.

"Grace"—Jerek kept his voice steady—"I need you to focus on the end of the twine in your hand. Use it as you would the center of the crystal."

"I'm not good with the crystal," Grace said. "I don't know how to use magic."

"Do as I say, or Jack will die," Jerek said. "Focus on the end of the twine in your hand. Push your magic toward the tip of the gold. I need you to funnel every bit of energy you can, Grace."

"Okay, okay."

Jerek closed his eyes, focusing on the coarse bit of string in his hand.

Nothing more than a string. A tiny bit of twine to save a life. We're not even halfway there, and people are already dying.

A warm tingle touched the center of his palm as a faint energy danced across his flesh.

"You can do this," Eve said.

The tingle surged, shocking up his arm in a terrible jolt.

Jerek gasped, his chest rising off the ground as magic coursed through his body.

Blissful fire consumed him. Every nerve in his being danced with magic. His head spun as his mind tried to grasp the wonderful terror filling him.

Power.

The power to work the world around him to his will. To bend the laws of nature and create true magic.

Jack wheezed and went still.

"Jack." Jerek clamped his eyes shut, fighting for reason beyond the power that filled him. "Jack!"

Jack lay frozen.

Jerek twisted, reaching his free hand up to drape across Jack's forehead.

"*Illi santu, mandrova. Illi santu, varen.*"

Magic poured from his palm, trickling into Jack's body.

"Varen timosty, en trada saren."

Jack shuddered, coughing blackened blood as the skin beneath Jerek's palm smoothed.

"Venitsi carum, illi santu. Alondra tendum."

Jerek savored the last word of the incantation on his tongue.

The taste of sunshine and salt on the wind.

Grace.

He lifted his hand from Jack's face as the last of Grace's magic faded away.

Blood stained Jack's skin, but the terrible blisters had vanished. The backs of his hands had healed.

"Jerek?" Grace's voice wobbled. "Is he alive?"

Jerek laid a hand on Jack's chest.

His ribs rose and fell steadily.

"Jerek?"

"He's okay," Jerek said. "He's going to be okay."

He let go of the thread. The last of Grace's magic ebbed from his chest, leaving a horrible void in its place.

"Keep the light out," Jerek said, adding in a whisper, "Rest well, friend."

"We're ready," Eve said.

Jerek slid out from under the seat. Blankets and clothes had been draped over him, keeping any hint of light from reaching Jack's skin. When he was finally free of the flap, Grace and Eve pulled the blankets off.

"You okay?" Ari asked from the driver's seat.

"Fine." Jerek's head spun as he sat up.

Grace took his arm, steadying him. Their eyes met. A flicker of understanding beyond any words traveled between them.

I know the touch of your soul. I have felt it mix with mine.

"Lincoln." Grace pulled Jerek with her toward Lincoln.

All the color had drained from his face, and blood seeped through the wrappings on his arm.

"You have to do the spell again." Grace pressed the end of the twine into Jerek's palm.

"I'll be fine." Sweat beaded Lincoln's brow. "Save your energy."

"You're losing too much blood," Eve said.

"We can do it," Grace said.

Jerek wiped Jack's blood off his hand before placing his free palm on Lincoln's arm.

The words flowed out of him without thought, the power brought forth by foreign magic.

You have to know the spells, Jerek. His father's voice echoed in his head. *One day, magic will come back. If we give up on the knowledge of magicians, we condemn ourselves to darkness. Learn the words, son.*

The bright burn of magic buzzed at the edge of his mind, caressing his thoughts.

"*Alondra tendum.*" He finished the incantation and dropped the twine.

The magic vanished from his chest, leaving a darker and more terrible void than before.

"Let me see." Eve lifted Lincoln's arm, unwrapping the filthy shirt.

Blood stained his skin, but the bite had knit neatly back together.

"All better." Lincoln picked up another discarded shirt from the floor, wiping his arm with a shaking hand.

"Is he..." Grace's voice trailed away. "Is he a werewolf now?"

"No," Lincoln said at the same moment Eve said, "In his dreams."

"A wolf has to be fully transformed for a bite to hold magic." Jerek heaved himself up onto the bench above Jack. "The pack had only used moonstones to transform. Blood loss was the greatest risk."

Weight pressed on the void in Jerek's chest.

Sleep. I need sleep.

"Where did all these clothes come from?" Lincoln picked up a pair of worn jeans.

"Dad's." Eve leaned against the back of the driver's seat. "Gran could never bring herself to empty out any of the closets."

Grace looked down at the blood on the clothes and the floor of the van. "I'm so sorry. You said there was a way to magic things clean." She looked to Jerek. "Can we fix it?"

"Not now." Jerek shook his head. The teal interior of the van swam in his vision. "I—"

"Don't worry about it," Eve said. "This stuff should have been thrown out a long time ago."

"We need to find a place to wash up," Ari said. "We can't be a bunch of teenagers driving around covered in blood. We can't afford that kind of attention."

"Won't be safe to stop until we're farther from pack land," Eve said. "I know a place an hour from here."

Lincoln pushed himself up on the seat opposite Jerek. He studied Jerek for a long moment. "You need to rest."

"So do you," Jerek said.

Grace sat on the floor, gathering up all the clothes. She didn't shake from the magic she had forced out of her body, didn't show a hint of fatigue.

Jerek fought to keep his eyes open.

"Sleep, Jerek," Ari said from the front. "Trust me, I've got this."

Jerek drifted to sleep before he could think of an adequate reason to refuse.

34

Grace

Grace sat on the floor in the back of the van, trying to avoid the blood on the carpet while not spreading any of the deep red from her clothes to the clean parts of the upholstery.

Jerek slept on one bench and Lincoln on the other. Ari drove while Eve navigated from the front passenger seat.

Don't panic. Whatever you do, don't panic.

The golden twine lay on the floor in front of her. She had funneled her magic into Jerek. Felt him at the edges of her being. Felt his determination and will joining with hers as her magic reached through him.

Don't panic. Don't you dare panic, Grace Esther Lee-Weiss.

"You okay back there?" Ari asked.

Grace nodded then realized Ari couldn't see her. "I'm fine."

"They'll be okay," Ari said. "You saved them."

"I know." Grace's heart rattled against her ribs. "Sorry. I didn't mean for that to sound snobby."

"It didn't," Eve said. "It's a fact. I ripped out a guy's eyeball with my claws, you saved Jack and Lincoln. Those are facts."

"Yeah." Grace dug her nails into the carpet.

"We're going to have to get the van cleaned," Ari said. "We'll have to find someone who doesn't ask questions."

"You don't know anybody?" Eve asked.

"Not out here," Ari said. "I'm from Vegas."

"Hmm," Eve said.

"I'm sorry, but is this normal for you?" Grace crawled to the clean spot on the floor between the two front seats. "Are bloodstains a normal part of life for the feu?"

"I've been used to blood for a long time," Eve said.

"Ari?" Grace looked to the blond, still dressed in perfectly clean pink.

"I mean, it's not like I love blood, but it happens," Ari said. "Everybody's going to live, so just hold on until we find a place to clean up. I promise, once you've washed, you're going to feel a lot better."

Don't panic.

The screaming in her head pushed past productive thought.

"We shouldn't be here," Grace said. "We should call the knights or the Council."

"Too big a chance of someone being in Chanler's pocket," Ari said.

"Then your grandmother," Grace said. "Barbara can get the stone."

"Gran's place is on the mountain," Eve said. "The pack needs their alpha."

"Grandma Alpha. I like it." Ari gave Eve an appreciative grin.

"Okay," Grace said, "but there has to be someone. An adult, a real adult."

"Like who?" Eve twisted in her seat. "My parents are dead, so that counts them out of saving the day."

"Nobody in my realm," Ari said. "Do your dads want to hop on the grand theft train?"

"But what about Lincoln's parents," Grace said, "or some wise old guys who live in isolation. There has to be someone else who can do this."

"That would be nice, wouldn't it?" Ari said. "I should have looked into wise old guys who fix problems instead of spending so much time looking for you. Stupid lack of time management."

"We can either go to someone who's no better off than we are, or someone we can't trust. I get how this is hard to understand, you're new, but"—Eve leaned against the window, staring up at the sky—"imagine you've spent most of your life, ever since you learned to read and tie your shoes, knowing there was something wrong in your world. A very bad person did a ton of really awful things, and somehow, they got away with all of it. They've spent years getting away with it. Living their life while good people who should still be alive are rotting in the ground.

"Now imagine someone comes along who knows who slaughtered your family, someone you know for an absolute fact couldn't have been in on it from the beginning or sat on their ass while the butcher lived at large. Do you take the info and run to people who are either incompetent or corrupt, or do you go after the bastard and tear out his intestines yourself?"

"You maybe should have stopped before intestines," Ari said.

"I..." Grace tried to reason through it, to make herself choose the wise course. "I wouldn't let the information out of my hands until I could be sure it was done. I wouldn't risk a traitor or dumbass screwing up the world for the next set of kids. I wouldn't risk the murderer being able to hurt my family ever again."

"There you have it," Eve said. "We're taking Chanler down ourselves, no matter what it takes."

"Welcome to Club Vengeance," Ari said.

"Nah." Eve shook her head.

"I'll keep working on it," Ari said.

Grace leaned against the side of Eve's seat. The rumble of the road beneath them dragged her eyes closed.

You have to mend the Fracture. You have to make magic safe for the next little girl. It's the only decent choice you can make.

The decision to take action soothed her nerves. The throb of panic in her chest settled into a dull ache of anxiety.

"Get off here," Eve said.

The hum of the road changed as they left the highway.

"Jack'll need to eat tonight," Eve said.

"I can find him someone," Ari said. "Food for Jack and a clean van. We can rest today and keep heading north tomorrow."

"Is it going to mess with Jerek's plans?" Eve asked.

"Sometimes you have to save Jerek from Jerek," Ari said. "He needs rest as badly as the other boys."

"Was he hurt?" Grace's mind raced back to the moment where her magic connected with him. Of all the sensations she had felt, injury hadn't been one of them.

"Not *wounded* per se," Ari said, "but Jerek's a magician who hasn't had pure magic run through him in a long time. He just did the magical equivalent of downing a bottle of tequila while climbing Mount Washington. He'll survive, but he's going to pay for it."

Grace clutched her hands to her chest, remembering the bliss of magic soaring out of her. "I didn't mean to hurt him."

"You didn't hurt him," Ari said. "Chanler hurt him. And

when we mend the Fracture and everyone else is suffering a magic use hangover, Jerek will be just a little bit better off than the rest because you reintroduced him to the hard stuff."

"You saved two people," Eve said. "Just be happy with that and move on. Left here."

Ari followed Eve's instructions as they weaved onto ever-smaller roads. Trees reached over them, blocking out the morning sun as it rose higher in the sky.

"We'll be there soon," Eve said.

"Did anyone die today?" Grace asked, the question popping out before she could think better than to ask.

"People die every day," Eve said.

"But the wolves," Grace said. "Do you really think your grandmother killed them?"

"Probably," Eve said, "but they attacked an alpha, so that's what they get. Hell, we might have killed some before we left."

"I hit one really hard with the van," Ari said.

"Is being okay with people dying a part of the heist?" Grace gripped Eve's seat as the van bounced over rocks.

"We hope for zero casualties," Ari said, "and accept that some things are bigger than one life."

Grace nodded, trying to let the words sink in in a way that didn't bring back the panic.

Some things are bigger than one life.

"Here," Eve said.

Ari pulled the car over on the side of the two-lane road. No real shoulder reached beyond the white lines, just an edge of dirt and a wide ditch beyond.

"No one will bother us here." Eve swung open her door and hopped over the ditch, striding out into the woods beyond.

"Jerek, Lincoln." Ari twisted in her seat. "We have to clean up so we don't look like serial killers."

Keeping her head low, Grace walked to the boys, tapping each of them on the shoulder.

"Wake up," Grace said.

Jerek's eyes fluttered open. Their sea-blue hue pummeled her breath from her lungs.

"We have to wash the blood off," Grace said.

"We can't afford to let anyone see the blood on our hands."

35

Lincoln

Lincoln lay still for a moment, running through a list of everything that should be in pain the moment he moved. His arm, his ribs, the back of his hand.

All of me.

Gritting his teeth against the oncoming agony, he sat up.

A dull ache pulsed through his body, but the throbbing pain he'd expected didn't come.

"Didn't think the spell would work so well?" Jerek asked, one eyebrow arched high.

"Didn't know it had done anything besides stop the bleeding." Lincoln opened and closed his hands. A lingering stiffness had taken the place of broken bones.

"There are anatomically specific spells for healing," Jerek said. "But I don't know all of them. A blanket healing seemed like the best plan."

"And how much did it cost you?" Lincoln asked.

Jerek shrugged.

"We should go," Ari said. "Eve's already run into the woods. If we don't hurry, we may never find her again."

Lincoln stood, hunching over as he climbed out of the van.

"Watch out for the ditch." Ari hopped out of the driver's seat and slammed the door behind her.

"Careful with the van," Jerek said.

"Sometimes the van likes a little spanking. You're just too soft to understand her wild side." Ari leapt over the ditch and headed toward the trees.

Grace stepped out of the van.

Lincoln offered her a hand, steadying her as she jumped over the ditch.

Jerek climbed out behind her. "Going to lift me over the puddle?"

"Do you need me to?" Lincoln held his hands out, offering to take Jerek's waist.

Jerek shook his head, the small movement throwing off his balance just enough for Lincoln to see the stumble.

"How often have you piggybacked magic?" Lincoln kept his voice low enough that Grace wouldn't be able to hear.

"Come on." Ari waved for them to follow.

She and Grace had reached the edge of the trees.

Lincoln leapt across the ditch. He turned back to steady Jerek, who ignored him and made the jump on his own.

"I'm not frail," Jerek said.

"No, you're drained," Lincoln said. "It wasn't safe."

"You and Jack were in much more danger than the spell ever placed me in," Jerek said, the snap of fatigue crisping his tone. "I've never used the twine to siphon magic from a magician untouched by the Fracture. Obviously I haven't as we've only recently found quite possibly the only living one."

"But you've piggybacked spells before?"

"Only once. Chain enough hobbled magicians together, and you can almost work a proper incantation," Jerek said. "It hurt like hell, but Dad managed to keep the wards around the house working. I don't know if any other feu home can boast the same."

"When did your dad manage that?" Lincoln said.

"The day after the Maree retreated to Italy. Called in every favor he could. He didn't want me to be taken the same way as Mom."

Lincoln walked toward the trees, studying the spring leaves, the intertwined roots, anything to keep from looking at his friend's face.

"I never blamed him for the pain casting the wards cost," Jerek said. "Better a day from Hell than being blown to pieces, but I could never understand why he didn't try it again. Why magicians didn't all just join together and live in packs like wolves so we could still work magic. But then I suppose when you hobble a magician's primary defense, you can't expect them to trust anyone enough to open up what little power they have left."

They walked in silence for a minute.

"I think that was the cruelest thing Chanler did." Jerek studied his palm. "Not stealing magic, or even people's lives, but robbing the feu of the ability to trust. Not the knights, not feu of other kinds, not even fellow magicians. Everyone became a threat. Everyone became the enemy. Fear stole our last chance of living a life of magic. Chanler brought down an entire civilization with a single curse."

The gurgle of running water cut through the trees. The bright peal of Ari's laughter rang over the soothing sound.

"Jerek." Lincoln stopped before the edge of the treeline. "Thank you. For healing me and Jack."

"Of course. I'd do it again no matter how bad the hangover.

How are we going to rebuild feu society if we don't start trusting and sacrificing for each other?"

"Jerek," Ari called. "Come wash the blood off. The water's fine."

They stepped through the trees and onto the banks of a creek.

Ari sat on a stone in the middle of the water, letting her feet drag along with the current. Grace knelt on the bank, scrubbing her hands. Eve had moved farther upstream and stood naked in the waist-deep water, washing blood from her hair.

"I don't know what I find more stunning," Ari said. "The fact that she ripped out eyeballs or the fact that she does so well maintaining her curly hair."

She laughed when Lincoln's head snapped toward her.

"Don't worry." Ari winked. "However beautiful you and Eve might be, you're safe as hell from me. Broody and damaged isn't my type."

Heat rushed to Lincoln's cheeks.

Grace laughed, turning the sound into a cough as she kicked off her shoes.

"Now I know where I went wrong." Jerek stripped down to his boxers and waded out into the river, scrubbing blood from his arms.

"You never stood a chance, Jer Bear. Too close to incest." Ari splashed water on her face. "You and I are destined to be platonic soul mates."

Jerek flicked a bead of water in her direction. "It's comforting to know our bond will never change."

Ari rolled her eyes then tipped her head back, smiling as the sun played across her face.

"I know it would kill him, but it's terrible Jack can't come out here." Grace examined her now clean nailbeds. "I don't know if I could give up the sun."

"You'd be amazed what you can sacrifice when the ends are valuable enough." Jerek ducked below the water, scrubbing his head.

"Come on, Lincoln," Ari said. "We don't have all day. Take off your shoes and wash away the traces of our battle."

Lincoln carefully untied his boots. Blood caked the laces and had soaked through to his socks.

"I'll find you new clothes tonight," Ari said. "Next time Jerek says everyone has to pack light, I'm going to punch him."

"I can rinse them." He stripped off his pants and shirt, staying, as Jerek had, in his underwear. He waded into the river, carrying his clothes with him.

The current pulled the red from the fabric, whisking the blood downstream and diluting it beyond the point of recognition.

"I'll find a drycleaner when I find someone to clean out the van." Ari pointed to Lincoln's shoulder. "Sick tat, bro."

Lincoln glanced down at the flaming shield marked on his shoulder.

"Didn't think the Maree gave out tattoos until eighteen," Ari said. "Your file didn't mention you being taken as a full member."

"I'm not officially." Lincoln scrubbed his shoelaces. "But they swore me in at sixteen. The knights have been doing it with everyone."

He glanced up in time to see a look pass between Ari and Jerek.

"There aren't enough of us, otherwise. Four hundred knights are being asked to do the work of more than a thousand. They try to keep the young ones at the compound, or running errands like protecting Jerek, but if a battle comes, everyone sixteen and up is sworn in and ready to die protecting the feu." Lincoln fixed his gaze on the flowing water. "You think the

Maree abandoned you, but you're wrong. We're doing everything we can to rebuild, so we can help the feu rebuild. I didn't spend my childhood hiding in Italy. I spent it training so one day I would be able to fight for all of you!"

He didn't realize he'd been shouting until he looked up and noticed all the others frozen, staring at him.

Eve stood twenty feet upstream, shirt loosely draped across her front.

"You spent your childhood at the Maree compound with your parents and brothers and sisters as you learned how to fight feu and somb alike." Eve waded closer, not breaking eye contact with Lincoln. "Well, thank you for your service, Sir Knight. I'm sure you found it rough living with so many like-minded and determined people."

"Eve," Jerek said.

"What? You don't want me to hurt the golden son's feelings?" Eve said. "Sorry if his fragile sense of nobility can't handle the fact that some of us watched our families burn at the hands of the butcher. Some of us didn't get to hide and wait to be ready for death. Some of us almost starved and froze because their home was decimated. The knights failed, Martel. Calling it *rebuilding* is pure cowardice."

She sloshed out of the water and stalked into the woods, leaving her shoes behind on the bank.

"Eve," Lincoln called after her.

"Leave it," Jerek said. "Let her cool down."

Lincoln trudged out of the water, dropping his clothes and chasing Eve through the trees. Twigs tore at his feet, and branches scratched his arms.

"Eve."

She ran faster, slipping through the woods like the animal buried in her blood.

"Eve. Cowards run."

She stopped, leaving her back to him. Her shoulders rose and fell with each angry breath. Beads of water coated her back, shimmering in the sunlight, casting a glow on the white ridges that marred her skin.

"I can't change choices that were made when we were young," Lincoln said. "And yes, I'm lucky. I'm the only one I know whose whole family survived the Fracture and the fallout. One third of the feu gone in a month, more than half of the Maree dead within a year, and my whole family stayed safe."

"Makes your lot look like traitors if you ask me." She yanked her shirt on and turned to face him.

"We aren't traitors," Lincoln said. "We just got lucky. Dad's quest to fix the Fracture failed, but he made it home safe. Mom was just far enough from the blast in Belford to not get hurt. My brothers and I were too small to be a part of anything. We were at my Grandparents', safe within the wards until we were sent to the compound."

"Such a lucky family."

"We didn't ask to be spared. You don't have to like the Maree, you don't have to like me, but at least believe I'm not a traitor. My family wants nothing but peace and safety for the feu. Just trust me that far."

"Trust is earned, not given. Help us get the stone and stand guard while I take care of Chanler. You do that, maybe I'll start to buy that not all knights are cowards."

A curl fell across her forehead. A hint of softness breaking through the ferocious anger. A crack in the armor that kept her alive and fighting.

"I've already agreed to the plan," Lincoln said. "If that's what it takes to convince you, I'll be patient."

"Huh."

"In the meantime, at least give me a chance to be a person

separate from the Maree." He held out his hand. "I'm Lincoln. I like burgers and speak crappy Italian."

"Eve. I like fresh air and long walks." She turned away and strode toward the van, leaving Lincoln with his hand outstretched.

36

Jack

The rumble of wheels and mumble of voices carried to him through the pain.

Agony faded away, replaced by a horribly persistent ache that warned him against the perils of movement.

Sense came as the van stopped for the second time. Doors opened and soft voices spoke.

"Jack?" Ari said from just beyond the safety of his cave.

"Yeah?" Jack's voice came out raw, grating against the dryness of his throat.

"I got you a date for tonight," Ari said. "He'll be here twenty minutes after dark. Come inside and get cleaned up when you can. I'll have fresh clothes for you."

"Thanks."

"Once you feel better, want to come meet some nefarious people with me?" Ari asked.

"Sure," Jack said. "Maybe I'll snag myself an after-dinner snack."

"Sounds like a plan," Ari said. Movement rustled then stopped. "Jack?"

"Yeah."

"I'm glad you're not dead."

"Thanks."

The van doors closed behind her.

He stared up at the springs of the seat above him. A glimmer caught his eye. A faint glow of something that didn't hurt his skin.

If he poked back through the memory of the pain, he could remember Jerek making the light. Jerek healing him. The others not abandoning him when they could so easily have left him on the ground to die.

"These are good people, Lydia."

He wished she were there to answer.

The stagnant air pressed down on him. The urge to burst out of the darkness sent shivers to his fingers.

"It's worth it. It's worth it."

He repeated the phrase over and over, waiting for the time until dark to tick away.

Ari had found a date for him. Jerek had healed him.

"There are good people in the world. People beyond the clan, Lydia."

He could picture her shaking her head in judgment as she whispered back, *I told you there were good people. Just because you came out of Hell doesn't mean the whole world is filled with demons.*

37

Ari

"I don't judge what you drink for dinner. You don't get to judge me either. Also, you're welcome for prowling through your man app long enough to find someone hot with hematolagnia on their fetish list." Ari took a long drink of her chocolate milkshake, the stench of chemicals and motor oil only moderately marring her liquid dinner

Jack opened his mouth to speak. The high pitch whir of a blade cutting through metal silenced him. He crossed his arms as he waited for the sound to stop.

Ari took another drink of the chocolate delight, wiggling her eyebrows at Jack.

"Thank you for Mr. Sexy Pants. And I'm not judging the milkshake," Jack said. "I'm worried about your nutritional intake."

"You're far too kind." Ari batted her eyelashes.

"Hey, you two." A man in ripped jeans and a worn button-up waved them over to his desk. A single light bulb covered by a torn lampshade hung overhead. Papers sat in three uneven piles, surrounding his computer, which had definitely seen better days.

"Prince Charming calls." Jack placed Ari's hand on his elbow, walking arm in arm with her to the desk.

"I don't know what you kids did in that van—" the man began.

"You don't want to," Jack said.

"But it's going to cost you to get it clean," he pressed on. "Cash up front."

"Why do people doubt we have money?" Ari reached into her pocket, pulling out a fat wad of bills. "It's rather insulting, don't you think, Jack?"

"Ridiculously so," Jack said. "I mean, the most I've carried is $50,000. But beyond that, there's really no point in lugging around cash. Who's going to take the time to count through it?"

Ari tipped her head back and laughed, letting her blond hair cascade down her back.

The sounds of work halted as the men stopped to stare at the two teens with lots of money.

"Well," the man said. "Is there anything else we can do for you fine folks?"

"Now that you mention it," Ari said. "There are a few hard-to-find items I'd love to get my hands on."

"You've come to the right place." The man smiled, showing his perfect white teeth.

"I know," Ari said. "I'm good with research."

38

Lincoln

Lincoln leaned against the headboard, wishing he were in his room in the compound instead of trapped in a one-star motel. The knights hadn't allowed him to keep very much in his quarters, but at least he'd had a desk and chair. A computer to work on. Access to a one-of-a-kind weapons locker.

He tipped his head back against the uneven grooves of the cheap bedframe, staring at the popcorn ceiling.

Do the right thing.

He grabbed his phone from the nightstand, not letting himself think as he typed in the series of passcodes.

There were no new messages from the Maree. No summons bidding him to come home at once, or orders on how to handle Jerek.

They're counting on me.

They trust me.

Lincoln wished he could silence the voice whispering in his head.

He clicked open a new message and typed.

There is more at work here than I thought, and too many things I still don't know. Ignore the orders coming from above. The blood to be spilt will count for more than disobedience. When the time comes, you'll know.

His fingers hovered over his phone screen. He wanted to say something more, to send love or apologies.

Send the bottom five to the bay. I don't care the cost.

He finished typing and hit *send*. In an instant, the message window closed. He quit the app, leaving his phone as nothing more than a dull weight in his hand.

The lock from the hall beeped open.

Jerek came in, carrying bags in both hands.

"Clothes and food," Jerek said. "I don't know where we're going to put all of this in the van. It's getting crowded."

"It'll fit." Lincoln set his phone back on the bedside table. "We won't be in the van too much longer anyway. It'll be a day to your house, then we can lay low. Perfect the plan until it's time for the party."

"I—" Jerek furrowed his brow, unpacking the food from the paper bag as though he hadn't spoken at all.

"You what?" Lincoln asked once Jerek had handed him a fork.

"I don't think we can go back to the house," Jerek said.

"But you told me this morning Holden House still has wards. It's going to be the safest place for us to wait it out."

"We have somewhere else we need to be."

"Don't tell me we're going to find someone else. It's too—"

"Risky, I know. It's not a person. It's a thing." Jerek sat on the edge of his bed, eating his spaghetti and meatballs.

Lincoln opened his own box of food, finding the same mushy spaghetti.

"It didn't occur to me until today," Jerek said. "In fact, we should all be grateful you and Jack were so badly wounded. If I hadn't tasted Grace's magic, I wouldn't have realized how deep the curse goes."

"You do know you haven't actually told me what you're talking about?" Lincoln devoured his meatballs.

"I thought the curse had just gone out into the world," Jerek said. "Floating down the rivers of magic and casting away all who had touched the sweet waters of her power."

"Poetic, but not really helping me understand."

"Grace had already touched magic before the Fracture. I could feel it. Her familiarity with the current of power going all the way back to birth. Touching magic is as natural to her as breathing, she just never knew what it was she was feeling."

"And if the curse poisoned the river, Grace was already drinking the same water as everyone else." Lincoln set his food aside. "But then how? How was she not affected and everyone else was?"

"The curse never touched magic. It never banished power from the earth as the knights thought, or tainted the flow of magic as my father thought. It targeted magicians directly, blinding each of us to the power around us."

"But then why not her?" Lincoln stood to pace the room. "If bolts of lightning streamed down from heaven, striking every magician, why was she spared?"

"What if the curse wasn't aimed at magicians? What if Chanler had a very specific list of people in mind and only those on that list were affected?"

"Grace was abandoned as a baby. If whoever gave birth to her was determined enough to hide her existence that they left her outside a church, they wouldn't have registered her anywhere."

Fear and understanding sent a surge of energy through Lincoln's body, filling him with the need to run or fight or...steal.

"It's impossible." Lincoln's chest deflated.

"We already have a crew."

"We'd need a miracle."

"Finding Grace is a miracle."

"So we just stroll in and take it?"

"We make a plan," Jerek said. "Think of it as a dress rehearsal for the party."

"Breaking into a museum is one thing—"

"We can't succeed without the list. If it was used in the curse, we'll need it for the cure."

Lincoln closed his eyes, forcing his thoughts to a building with white marble halls. "You're sure you need it?"

"There isn't any other explanation. Can you think of another way the curse could have found everyone but Grace?"

"No." Lincoln pinched the bridge of his nose. "We're going to be hanged for this."

"People don't hang heroes."

"Heroes don't usually steal the Blood List."

39

Jerek

Jerek hated the freshly cleaned stench of the upholstery, like the van was somehow supposed to have become a new car through the thorough scrubbing of the carpet. The traffic around D.C. wasn't helping his temper either.

It seemed horribly unfair he should have to wait in traffic while trying to save the feu.

I should have a siren on the roof.

There's probably an incantation for that.

He imagined the bliss for a moment. A few simple words and traffic would part in front of him. None of the drivers knowing why they had the sudden instinct to move out of his way, but all obeying the silent orders of his spell nonetheless.

Sadness tightened his throat. He pressed on the horn, taking out his anger on the drivers around him.

"I don't know why you decided to drive through the city,"

Ari said from her spot on the seat in the far back. "It would have been a lot faster to cut a wide path around the beltway."

"Around to where?" Eve asked.

"Holden House," Ari said.

"We're making a detour," Jerek said.

"Obviously," Ari said. "And it's taking forever."

"I mean a detour into D.C.," Jerek said. "We have an errand to run."

"What kind of errand?" Grace asked.

"Why do I feel like I'm going to hate this?" Eve said.

"Because you will," Lincoln said.

Ari shut her laptop, laying her hands on top. "What errand are we running on our way to steal the heliostone, Jerek?"

"We're going to the Council of the Feu," Jerek said.

"To turn ourselves in for theft before we bother stealing anything?" Ari asked.

"We're stealing the Blood List," Jerek said.

"Oh, casual," Ari said.

"Why would we want to do that?" Eve asked.

"We need it to mend the Fracture," Lincoln said. "We think the curse was placed using the list. If we want to free all the magicians on the list, Jerek's going to need it with him at the Museum of Magic."

"Interesting." Ari flipped open her laptop.

"And when exactly did you figure this little detail out?" Jack asked from under the seat.

"When I was helping to heal you," Jerek said.

"Great," Jack said. "Glad I've been of use."

"And how do you intend to steal a document sacred to the treaty?" Eve asked.

Jerek merged left, inching his way forward in traffic. "Walk in and take it."

"We're going to die," Eve said.

"I'm missing something," Grace said. "If you need a list, can't Ari just hack into a database and get it for you."

"I'm good," Ari said. "But there isn't a way on the planet to hack the list."

"There is only one Blood List," Lincoln said. "It's kept in the headquarters of the Council of the Feu at all times. The list hasn't left that building in almost a hundred years."

"What kind of list is so important?" Grace said.

"You know," Jack said, "it's nice, as a new vampire, to not be the person who knows the least on this adventure."

"I'm proud of you, Jack." Ari patted the top of his cave.

"What is the list?" Grace asked.

"Lincoln"—Jerek glanced to his oldest friend—"you're the treaty scholar."

"The Blood List was created by the same treaty that formed the Knights Maree," Lincoln said.

"Treaty between who?" Grace asked.

"The feu and those who would become the Knights Maree," Lincoln said. "I'm not sure where to begin explaining."

Ari huffed a sigh. "A very long time ago, sombs were terrified of witches. Evil people went around hunting for witches, vampires, werewolves, anything that wasn't strictly human. Eventually, some less evil but super stupid people who didn't understand the feu at all, decided they wanted to be cool and kill witches, too. But those people weren't good at finding actual witches, so they ended up massacring a bunch of sombs. The evil people were all like *Oh shit, bigotry is bad. Now humans are dying because we hate the feu. We've been evil and wrong this whole time. This has to stop.*

"So, they found some witches and decided to strike a bargain to stop the witch hunts in exchange for the feu hiding their existence from the boring human sombs. Which they were already trying to do anyway, but whatever. So, the feu formed the Council, the witch hunters formed the Knights Maree, and while they were figuring out the details of how to live in peace and form the secrecy pact, the Blood List came to be. There, Lincoln, now you can explain."

"Thanks," Lincoln said. "The Blood List was written into the treaty for two reasons. First, to help the Knights Maree keep track of the magicians they were sworn to protect. Second, to give the knights information that allowed them power over the magicians."

"And the magicians agreed to being stalked by Big Brother?" Grace asked.

"You're forgetting that magicians could do a nice little spell and kill a dozen of Big Brother's minions without having to twitch a finger," Eve said. "It helped level the playing field and keep the peace. Giving the mice the cat's address doesn't really hurt the cat."

"Unless an army of mice with pitchforks and torches shows up," Jack said, his laugh muffled by the thick fabric around him.

"Like I said, levels the playing field," Eve said.

"And all the magicians just said *cool, sign me up*?" Grace asked.

"No," Lincoln said. "Signing the list wasn't mandatory. Magicians didn't have to put their names down."

"And the list has to be signed in person," Ari said. "So it took a long time to get everyone on board."

"But magicians not on the list weren't protected by the Maree," Lincoln said. "Think of it as not being on the fire department's list of houses to protect. It's fine...until a fire starts."

"Then it's suddenly not fine and you end up dead," Ari said. "Enough disasters happened that the feu started counting on the Maree's protection. The general consensus is after about 1892, all magicians were named on the list."

"The list is a record of every magician," Lincoln said. "And if Chanler cast the curse on everyone on the Blood List—"

"We have to snatch the list to lift the curse," Ari said. "And here I was looking forward to relaxing at Holden House."

"I'm not on the list?" Grace asked.

"If I'm right, then no." Jerek gripped the steering wheel. "If you are, then we won't take it."

"Right," Grace said. "Sounds good."

"How are we going to get close enough to the list to take it?" Eve asked.

"The new mistress of Holden House and I are going to register our new baby," Jerek said.

"Who's the new mistress?" Jack asked.

"I was hoping one of the girls would volunteer." Jerek merged onto the downtown exit.

40

Eve

Gran had never taken Eve to D.C. Life on the mountain took too much work to leave time for trips north to the capital.

Eve walked along the avenue between the museums, watching the children filing out of the fancy buildings, their faces filled with wonder.

I would have been happy coming here.

She could imagine it so easily. Her mother and father trying to herd her and Mark through the crowds. She'd be picking on Mark, her duty as the older sister. They'd bicker, then they'd all eat ice cream together and laugh.

Pain dug into the center of Eve's chest. She let out a slow breath, tucking away the memories of her family's faces for a different time.

I'll see you when I'm stronger.

"Eve." Lincoln jogged toward her from the end of the street. "Eve?"

The others had reached the corner. They'd all turned around to stare at her.

"Sorry." Eve weaved through the crowd toward the rest of the group. "Thought I recognized someone. We can't risk any wolves having followed us from the mountain."

"No." Lincoln kept close to her side. "If anyone found out why we're here, we'd be—"

"Dead," Eve said. "The word is *dead*."

"Yeah," Lincoln said.

"The only way out is success." Eve brushed a curl away from her eyes. "So don't screw it up, Maree."

"I'll do my best," Lincoln said.

"We're doomed."

"You okay?" Ari asked as Eve and Lincoln reached the group.

"Just scouring the crowd," Eve said.

"Then let's keep moving." Jerek voice was crisp, harsh even.

"Don't be so antsy." Ari poked him in the arm. "It's a beautiful day and a nice walk. Let's enjoy what could potentially be the last taste of freedom we ever get."

"Please don't say things like that," Grace said. "It makes me nauseous."

"I'm not antsy." Jerek turned away from the row of museums, cutting down a street filled with coffee shops and restaurants catering to tourists. "If you must know, I'm worried about leaving Jack stuck in a public parking garage. I know he'll be safe in the van. It just feels rude."

"I knew you had a heart." Ari ruffled Jerek's hair.

Jerek scowled and patted his hair back into place.

They fell into silence as they walked through the city.

There wasn't anything to talk about.

Ari smiled benignly as they moved on to less crowded streets, enjoying the afternoon like she hadn't a care in the world.

I wish I could be her. So happy, so carefree.

So stupid.

If not smiling while walking into danger is a fault, I don't mind being guilty of it.

"You okay?" Jerek asked.

"Just enjoying thinking about all the ways this could go wrong," Eve said.

"It'll be fine," Ari said. "This is a happy occasion. It's time to sign baby Holden up for a lifetime of treaty protection. It's nice to have such a caring baby daddy."

"You are the love of my life, dear." Jerek kissed the back of her hand. "Young or not, you are the only one who could ever capture my heart."

A group of school children walking the opposite direction surrounded them. A stumpy boy knocked into Eve with his giant red backpack.

"Watch it," Eve growled.

"Then get out of my way." The kid flipped up his middle finger.

"You little punk." Eve turned, starting toward the kid.

"Come on." Lincoln linked his arm through hers and took her hand. "He's not worth it. Just keep moving."

"Kid needs to learn to not be a dick." Even as Eve spoke, she let Lincoln lead her away.

"And life will teach him the hard way," Lincoln said. "But tossing him up into a tree will make a scene, and that would be a very bad idea right now."

"He still deserves it," Eve said.

"I know." Lincoln relaxed his grip on her hand but kept his arm linked with hers.

"I'm not an animal, you know." Eve tucked her anger aside. "I am capable of controlling my temper and the wolf."

"I know that, too. I'm still breathing. That's impeccable self-control."

Jerek stopped at a corner café, choosing a round table and pulling a chair out for Grace. "This looks like a nice place for you to wait."

"I'm not good at waiting," Eve said. "We should all go in."

"Five teens walking into the Council of the Feu to register a baby?" Ari said. "You're right, that wouldn't be suspicious at all."

"We need you and Grace out here," Lincoln said.

"You mean Grace can't come inside and someone has to sit with her," Grace said.

"He means we need you out here," Jerek said.

"I don't like it," Eve said. "There're too many things we don't know."

Ari squeezed Eve's hand. "And that's why you're staying out here. You're vital to our plan."

"Yes. Drinking coffee is so important," Eve said.

"Absolutely," Ari said. "We might need you to save our asses."

"Fine." Eve sank into a chair, the metal of the seat cool despite the warmth of the day.

"See you soon," Jerek said.

"Don't get killed," Eve said.

Ari threaded her fingers through Jerek's, her blond hair cascading down his arm as she leaned against his shoulder. Lincoln stayed two steps behind them as they rounded the corner and disappeared from view.

41

Jerek

He'd been in the Council of the Feu headquarters at least a dozen times in his life. Still, Jerek had to convince himself he was headed toward the right door.

Situated between two grand buildings meant for important sombs to do important things, the front door of the Council of the Feu looked like nothing more than a side entrance to a wide-windowed breezeway between offices. Only the *CFH* carved into the marble above the door confirmed Jerek hadn't lost his mind and had indeed found the right place.

He pressed the small black buzzer and waited.

His pulse quickened as seconds ticked past.

We've done nothing wrong.

Yet.

"Is it a holiday?" Ari asked. "If we came all this way and it's a holiday, Jerek Holden, I'll never get in a car with you again."

"How can I help you today?" A chipper voice came through a hidden speaker.

Jerek spoke to the plain front of the door. "Jerek Holden with Ariel Love here to register a newborn on the Blood List, accompanied by Knight Maree Lincoln Martel."

"Welcome to the CFH, Mr. Holden." The door opened without a sound.

"I'm not sure I can do this." Ari pulled on Jerek's arm, backing away from the entrance.

"We have to, Ariel." Jerek slipped his arm from her grip and placed his hand on the small of her back. "It's what's best for the baby."

Tears sparkling in her eyes, Ari nodded, leaning on Jerek as he guided her into the long hallway.

The windows that lined the entry from the outside were invisible from the interior. Rather than clear glass dotting the space, paintings hung on the solid white marble walls.

"This way." The voice beckoned them left, past the painting of a funeral pyre with a writhing figure trapped within the flames.

"You'd think they'd make the décor a bit more cheerful," Ari said.

"I think *austere* was the style they were going for." Jerek wrapped his arm around her waist, keeping her close to his side.

The echo of their shoes carried down the hallway, warning everyone of their approach. Not that there was anyone in sight to warn.

They traveled down the vacant corridor, passing painting after painting. At the end of the hall, the only choice they were given was to turn right.

The new corridor had been built of the same marble as the

first, but here, alcoves had been carved into the walls with statues filling each niche—busts of great magicians and knights, a life-size marble replica of the sword and shield of a Knight Maree, a statue of a werewolf and vampire standing beside a magician with images of fauns, centaurs, and mermaids swirling beneath their feet.

An open pair of double doors waited at the end of the hall. Three women sat behind desks in the room beyond. None bothered to look up at the sound of approaching footsteps.

The moment they stepped through the door, the familiar scent of coffee and ink reached Jerek's nose. A calm that had nothing to do with their present situation washed over him.

"Hi," Ari said, her tone missing its usual ease. "We're here for the Blood List."

The woman at the rightmost desk looked up. "I'm the registrar. How can I help you?"

"We're here—" Ari took a shuddering breath. "We're here to register a newborn."

The other two women looked up, too.

"Where is the child?" the registrar asked.

"I..." Ari's voice faded away, lost in her tears.

"The child has been sent to a better home than we could provide." Jerek reached into his pocket, pulling out a vial of blood. "It's still our duty to register him."

"I'm glad you came prepared," the registrar said.

Jerek's stomach turned at her sympathetic smile.

"And how can we help you today, Maree?" The registrar looked to Lincoln.

"I've been assigned to protect Mr. Holden," Lincoln said. "In the CFH or not, it's my duty to keep him safe."

"Lilly, will you run a check in the Maree files," the registrar said. "I hope you don't mind, but procedure is procedure."

"I would expect nothing less." Lincoln bowed, looking every bit the trained Maree his time in Italy had chiseled him into.

"And what names are we filing the parentage under?" The registrar clicked away on her computer. "We have to put the child in the right place."

"Jerek Holden, father," Jerek said. "Mother not on the list."

The registrar's head snapped up. "I'm sure you don't mean you've brought a somb into the CFH."

"Ariel Love, div," Ari said. "I'm feu."

The middle secretary typed for a moment. "She's here." She squinted at her computer screen. "Oh dear." Her face paled. "You're doing the right thing, you know. You're a very brave girl, Ariel."

"Thanks," Ari said. "Even a half-breed div has a duty to do what's right."

The secretary on the end gave a pointed cough. "Lincoln Martel, assigned to Jerek Holden after multiple assassination attempts. What on earth is this world coming to?"

"It's been a rough year all around," Jerek said.

"I'm so sorry." The registrar stood, brushing imaginary dust from the front of her blazer. "If you'll follow me, I'll get you in and out in no time."

"Thank you," Jerek said.

Ari clung to his arm, silent tears trickling down her cheeks.

The registrar led them to a bookcase at the side of the room. She ran her finger along the spines of the books on the second shelf down, stopping on a black volume titled *The Cost of Conscience*. She pulled on the top edge of the book. A pop and a hiss sounded from inside the wall.

Ari clung harder to Jerek's arm as the bookcase swung backward, revealing a plain stone hallway.

Iron and glass wall sconces hid the electric lights from view in a failed attempt at making the corridor appear ancient.

Flaming shield symbols marked the walls at regular intervals, each with a panic button hidden in the center.

Jerek's neck tensed with every shield they passed.

How quickly can the registrar reach a button? How fast can the guards respond?

There were no alcoves or passages leading out of the hall, no place for someone to hide or hope for escape.

A solitary wooden door blocked the end of the corridor.

The door swung open, letting a woman in her eighties into the hall. She narrowed her eyes at Jerek and Ari before giving the registrar a nod.

"Afternoon." The registrar nodded back, leading them around the woman and to the waiting door.

The registrar laid her palm on the iron handle. The metal shimmered for a moment before the door swung open.

The registrar stepped aside, bowing the others across the threshold.

Jerek's heart leapt into his throat as they stepped inside the Blood Room. He flinched as the door thumped shut behind them, grateful that Ari's eruption into tears covered the sound of his gasp.

No furniture gentled the somber air of the hexagonal room—no place to sit, nor any implication of comfort. A wrought iron chandelier hung from the ceiling, providing the solitary source of light. The only break in the plain stone was a pedestal carved of cherry wood and the scroll that lay on top.

"Is that it?" Ari let go of Jerek, stepping toward the scroll.

"That is the Blood List," the registrar said.

"Wow."

The scroll was smaller than Jerek had remembered it being. The parchment only seemed to wrap around the twelve-inch rods at the top and bottom a few times.

"Are you sure that's right? It looks too short to be the real

Blood List." Ari swiped the tears from her eyes. "I don't want the baby written down on some fake list."

"The list was created long before the Fracture," the registrar said. "If you were to thoroughly unroll the scroll, it would reach down the block. Thankfully, the creators envisioned the treaty and the Blood List lasting for many generations."

"We are humbled by the foresight of our forefathers." Lincoln gave another little bow.

Jerek clenched his fists against the sudden desire to punch his friend in the stomach.

"Shall we?" The registrar gave another maddeningly compassionate smile.

"Right." Jerek took Ari's hand, guiding her to stand at the side of the pedestal.

"Pardon me." The registrar reached under the scroll, pressing on the wood.

A narrow drawer that hadn't been visible before popped open. A gold-tipped, red-feathered quill and crystal inkwell lay on a bed of black velvet.

"Wow," Ari said again.

"You'll need to use the blood as the ink." The registrar touched the parchment. A faint shimmer of gold gleamed on the scroll for a moment before the rods began to twist, winding up from Ethan Helmer to older entries. The deep red words blurred as the parchment raced through seventeen years' worth of names.

"Here you are," the registrar said as the scroll shuddered to a halt. "Jerek Holden, son of Richard and Risa Holden. Is that correct?"

"Yes ma'am." Jerek blinked at his parent's names hovering together right above his.

He tried to think of it. His parents alive and happy, holding their son as they added his name to the unbroken family lines dating back to the creation of the list.

"If I may have the blood?" The registrar held out her hand.

Jerek reached back into his pocket, pulling out the vial of blood.

"I can't do this." Ari shook her head, stepping away from Jerek, backing against the stone wall.

"Ariel, we have to." Jerek reached for her. "We have to do what's best for the baby. We made a promise."

"We can't just write down his name and walk away." Ari clutched her stomach. "Everyone will know. All the feu. Let his new parents put him down."

"I'm afraid that's not possible," the registrar said. "If a child's name isn't added to the list by a blood relation, they have to wait until they come of age."

Ari collapsed to the floor, her whole body shaking with a fresh round of sobs.

Lincoln stepped discreetly to the registrar's side. "I'm so sorry, could you give us a minute?"

"Maybe it would be best if you came back another time," the registrar whispered.

Jerek knelt beside Ari, holding her close.

"If we leave, I don't think we'll ever get her to come back," Lincoln said. "Like Jerek said, it's been a rough year, and I would hate for their child to pay such a terrible price."

Jerek looked up to the woman, as much begging in his eyes as he could manage. "She can do this. I know she can."

The registrar nodded. "I'll be right outside. When you're ready, it'll take less than a minute." She slipped into the hall without another word. The door closed silently behind her.

"Oh, thank god." Ari brushed her tears away. "My throat was starting to hurt from all that crying."

"Are they watching us?" Jerek held Ari's face in his hands, pressing his lips to her forehead.

"One camera above the door." Lincoln faced away from Jerek and Ari as though giving them space.

"Right." Jerek stood, burying his face in his hands and walking toward the door.

He turned back to the room, studying the details of the pedestal and six corners of the stone walls through his fingers.

He reached back, touching the wall behind him.

A spot of energy danced within the stone, a lens of moving pictures in a sea of stillness.

His magic reached for the lens. He closed his eyes, willing an image of the room to grow across the glass, picturing Ari's hair sticking to the tears on her cheek. The rounding of Lincoln's spine as he hunched over the scroll.

It only took a moment. The magic required barely tingled in his chest.

"They can't see us," Jerek said. "But we have to be quick. They'll only buy we're standing frozen for so long."

42

Lincoln

"Give me the blood." Lincoln reached for the vial.

"You're sure we can't just search Grace by name?" Ari's voice crackled, her tone still muffled from crying.

"Her dads named her." Jerek pressed the vial into Lincoln's hand. "Grace Esther Lee-Weiss won't be written anywhere on this list."

Lincoln pulled the stopper from the vial and dripped the blood into the crystal inkwell.

"You're sure this is going to work?" Ari leaned over Lincoln's shoulder.

"As sure as Jerek is about needing the list." Lincoln dipped his finger into the blood. Ignoring the feel of it on his skin, he wiped off all but a drop before lifting his hand and pressing the blood to the parchment.

The list glowed red for a moment as the blood disappeared.

"Where did it go?" Ari asked.

"The list doesn't allow stray drops to fall," Jerek said. "The parchment has to remain pure."

"Find the blood." Lincoln spoke to the list.

They all froze, waiting for something to happen.

"This isn't going to work." Ari glanced toward the door.

"It will," Lincoln said. "It's how the knights identify dead magicians."

"You always know the comforting thing to say," Ari said.

Jerek dipped his finger into Grace's blood and smeared the red across the parchment. "Find the blood."

Again, the scroll shimmered red before fading to nothing.

"She's not on the list," Jerek said. "I was right. Chanler used the Blood List for the curse."

"Then we're taking it." Lincoln's hands hovered above the scroll. He flexed his fingers, seized by the unshakable feeling that moving his hands forward the few inches to seize the Blood List would somehow alter the rest of his life.

"Wait." Jerek reached into his pocket, pulling out two black rods with blank parchment wrapped around. The ends of the rods shimmered as the perfect black paint chipped and gained texture, as though it were aging hundreds of years. He unrolled the counterfeit scroll a few inches and grazed the white with his clean fingers. Deep red names appeared on the paper.

Richard Holden

Risa Holden

Jerek Holden

The fake list looked perfect.

"Do it," Jerek said.

Lincoln lifted the real Blood List from the pedestal as Jerek slid his newly made forgery into place.

Lincoln held his breath. His pulse thumped in his ears as he waited for sirens to sound, shouting to the world that they'd done something horribly wrong.

"We need to go." Ari headed to the door.

The lights dimmed as she reached for the handle.

"Shit." Ari stepped back.

A hum began in the walls, shaking from deep within the stones.

For one horrible moment Lincoln thought the walls would slide in, shrinking the room around them. He pressed the Blood List into Jerek's hand. "Get this out of sight."

Jerek shoved the priceless scroll into his pocket.

"I'm sorry." Lincoln drew his fist back and punched Jerek hard in the face, knocking him to the ground.

"Jerek!" Ari screamed.

"Open the door," Lincoln ordered.

Ari grabbed the handle, swinging the door open and running head on into the registrar.

"Help! I need help!" Ari screamed.

"Why is the Blood Room upset?" The registrar started toward the pedestal.

"Please get me out of here!" Ari grabbed the registrar's arm, dragging her toward the door.

"Don't you dare move!" Jerek stood, blood dripping down his face. "Ariel, what the hell is happening?"

Terror filled Ari's face before she turned and sprinted down the hall.

"Ariel!" Jerek tore after her, slamming his shoulder into the registrar.

Lincoln leapt forward, steadying the woman as she tipped toward the floor.

"What is going on?"

Lincoln blocked the registrar's path as she started for the pedestal and forged scroll.

"We won't be needing the list today." Lincoln held both hands up. "Apparently, the child isn't half-magician after all."

"Oh dear." The registrar turned around just in time to see Ari slap Jerek hard across the face.

Ari ran to the now solid stone wall at the end of the hall. "Let me out!" She pounded on the stone.

"Ariel, just tell me whose it is." Jerek chased after her.

"Shit." The registrar tore down the hall after them.

Lincoln shut the door to the Blood Room, leaving only a faint hum that couldn't carry above Jerek and Ari's shouts.

"Let me out!" Ari shrieked.

The registrar reached the door and pressed on the side of the stone.

A gap the size of the bookcase on the other side shimmered into being.

"I need help out here!" the registrar shouted.

"I hate you, Jerek Holden." Ari shoved past them and into the office.

The registrar grabbed Jerek's arm. "What the hell happened in there? The room is giving me a warning."

"The walls started buzzing when Ariel punched me." Jerek wrenched his arm from the registrar's grip and tore after Ari.

"Get back here!" The registrar chased him, Lincoln only a step behind.

Six men in dark suits ran out of a door that hadn't existed when they'd been in the front office only minutes before.

"Lock the building down!" the right-most secretary shouted.

Lincoln bolted past her as the dark-suited men reached the first long hallway.

With a dull clunk, the ceiling at the front and back of the statue corridor shifted, sliding down sheets of marble to block the way in and out of the hall.

Ari slipped under the far wall, rolling into the painting

corridor. Jerek leaned forward as if to follow then froze, letting the marble block him in.

"Get the girl." The registrar planted her hands on her hips as she panted.

"She won't get out the front," the security guard at the front of the group said. "Who wants to tell me what's going on?"

"The baby isn't mine." Jerek slid down the wall, burying his face in his hands. "It was never mine."

"We need to check the Blood List." The security guard pressed a finger to his ear. "Safety check the scroll."

"The scroll is fine." Lincoln stepped forward. "We need to get to Ariel."

"She won't be able to get out," the security guard said. "She can wait."

"She's a div," Jerek said. "You can't trust her kind to be rational. How could I be so stupid?"

"Neither the knights nor the Council of the Feu can afford an incident involving a vulnerable young girl," Lincoln said. "I need you to appreciate the delicacy of the situation and the respect owed to the Holden Family name."

The guard glared at Lincoln for a long moment.

Lincoln kept his chin up, his face impassive. A Maree performing his duty. Nothing more, nothing less.

With a wave of the guard's hand, the wall on the far side of the room shuddered and slid back up into the ceiling.

Jerek leapt to his feet and bolted down the portrait gallery.

"Thank you," Lincoln said. "We would be happy to sit with her and wait while you check the Blood Room alarm for what went wrong. I didn't think the warnings were sensitive enough for a punch in the face to set the whole room humming."

"Ariel!" Jerek shouted.

The sheer, very real panic in his voice shot a jolt of fear into Lincoln's chest.

"Mr. Holden!" Lincoln sprinted around the corner and into the portrait corridor.

At the end of the hall, Ari banged against the metal door to the outside with bloody fists.

"Ariel, don't you dare!" Jerek reached Ari, grabbing her shoulders and yanking her away from the door.

A crack shot dread into Lincoln's lungs. Sparks flew from the edges of the doorway, shooting toward Jerek and Ari.

Jerek knocked Ari to the ground, covering her body with his own.

"No!" Lincoln sprinted toward them as flames followed the sparks.

Bright red lights sprouted from the ceiling, swirling their beams across the shining marble.

A calm female voice filled the corridor. "Please find the nearest emergency exit."

"Ariel, I'm sorry." Jerek pulled her to her feet as the flames around the door faded to smoke. "I'm so sorry. I didn't mean to lose control."

"You sick bastard." Ari smacked Jerek across the cheek with her bloody palm and lunged for the door.

"Stay right where you are," one of the security guards shouted, reaching for the pocket of his coat.

"I will not allow you to aim a weapon at Mr. Holden." Lincoln stepped between the guards and Jerek.

Ari flung open the door and sprinted onto the street.

"Ariel!" Jerek tore after her, disappearing through the still-smoking door.

"Get them." Four guards dodged around Lincoln, each pulling a slim silver object from their pocket.

Two guards remained, both pointing a silver dagger at Lincoln.

"I'm a Maree, not a magician." Lincoln displayed both his

palms. "I'm protecting Holden under Maree orders. While I appreciate the independence of the CFH guards, I can assure you, you do not want to interfere with the will of the Knights Maree."

The larger of the guards reached into his other pocket, pulling out a pair of black handcuffs. "Put these on and you can wait for Holden and the girl to be brought back."

"Mr. Holden got a head start," Lincoln said. "You aren't going to catch him."

With a flick of his wrist, the smaller guard sent a shaft of light flying from the tip of his dagger. The light twisted in the air, reaching for Lincoln's arms.

Lincoln leapt forward, dodging the light and thrusting the heel of his palm into the larger guard's sternum. He snatched the dagger from the guard's hand as he thrust his elbow up into the man's chin.

The man crumpled to the floor.

"You son of a bitch." The smaller guard lunged forward, slicing his blade through the air.

A ribbon of red light flashed toward Lincoln's chest.

Lincoln raised his newly obtained blade, slicing the spell in half. A shred of the thin shimmer reached him, striking him in the stomach. White-hot pain blazed through his gut. He kept his eyes open wide, focusing on the face of the man who had hurt him. He stabbed forward, shooting a web of magic at the guard, who yelped and toppled backward as the spell wrapped around his chest.

"Do not stand against the mission of a Knight Maree." Lincoln snatched the dagger from the web-wrapped guard.

"They'll banish you for this." The guard spoke through clenched teeth.

"Report it, and you'll be banished yourself." Lincoln stepped over the guards and strode to the door, shoving the daggers into his pockets and breaking into a sprint as soon as he reached the sidewalk.

The other guards were well out of sight, chasing Ari and Jerek who knew where.

They can't have caught them.

Lincoln ran left, away from the café where they'd left Eve and Grace.

What do I do if the guards did catch them?

He rounded the corner and slowed his pace, ducking into the first restaurant he came to. He weaved his way slowly through the dining room, searching the tables as though looking for a friend.

A woman a few years older than him sat alone at a table for two in the corner.

"Hi." Lincoln gave his most bashful smile. "I'm really sorry to bother you, but my ex-girlfriend just walked in with the guy she cheated on me with, and I'd rather not be spotted. The last thing I need is for her to be posting all over the internet that she saw me eating alone."

The woman looked up from her phone, sliding her gaze up and down Lincoln.

"I swear it's nothing weird," he said. "I just want to blend in with the crowd."

"Five sympathy minutes, and no funny business."

"Thank you." Lincoln sank into the seat opposite her. "You have no idea how badly I don't want to be recognized right now."

43

Ari

The cream stung Ari's fingers as she packed it around the hinges of the CFH door.

I will murder you if this doesn't work, Jerek Holden.

It didn't matter if the failure wouldn't be entirely Jerek's fault. The man at the garage might have only been useful for cleaning blood out of upholstery. He might have sold her the wrong ingredients. Jack's mixture might have been off. Her own reasoning in using magic to ignite the sketchily purchased explosives might have been flawed.

"Oh, I will murder you, Jerek Holden."

The rumble of the marble dividers grinding through the walls echoed down the empty hall.

"Dammit." She pulled the vial from her pocket, dumping the rest of Grace's blood across her palm and smearing the red over the acrid pale cream she'd already spread.

"Let me out!" She pounded her fists on the door. "Please let me out!"

"Ariel!" Jerek's footfalls pounded up behind her.

"Let me out!"

Jerek grabbed her. His fingers grazed the slick of Grace's blood on the doorframe.

Ari screamed over the crack of magic.

Sparks shot from the hinges.

Pain jolted through her hip as Jerek tackled her to the ground.

Flames leapt from the door, bringing with them the stench of iron and sulfur.

"Please find the nearest emergency exit." A woman spoke calmly as red light flooded the hall.

Jerek rolled off Ari and grabbed her arm, dragging her to her feet. "Ariel, I'm sorry. I'm so sorry. I didn't mean to lose control."

"You sick bastard." She smacked him hard across the face, biting the insides of her cheeks to hide her grin.

Ari launched herself at the door, striking the hinged side with her full weight. Pain throbbed in her shoulder, but the door didn't give.

"Stay right where you are."

Ari ignored the guard's shout.

"Don't do this to me," she muttered to the door.

She took a step back and threw herself at the metal again.

The door gave with a crack, crashing forward and onto the street.

The sun dazzled her eyes as she turned right and bolted down the sidewalk, tucking her hands firmly in her pockets.

"Ariel!" Jerek's shout followed her down the street. Instinct begged her to turn around, to run back to Jerek and make sure he was safe.

"Ariel!"

Follow the plan.

She ran down a side street, stopping in the shade of a tree.

"Sorry about this." She placed her bloody palms on the side of the tree.

Water seeped from the bark, surrounding her hands, washing away the blood. In less than five seconds, the red had been absorbed into the tree, leaving Ari with only one spot of red staining her pale pink dress.

"You boys had better have gotten out of there." She whipped her hair up into a tight bun and sauntered down the street, gazing up at the buildings around her as if she hadn't a care in the world.

44

Jerek

The thrill of magic zapped through Jerek's fingers as the faint power within him joined the burning potential of Grace's blood. A surge of heat was all it took to ignite the explosive paste Ari had planted on the hinges.

A spark singed his fingers as the magic took hold. He leapt back, tackling Ari to the ground, covering her head with his chest.

She gasped as her hip struck the marble floor.

I'm so sorry.

He kept her pinned down as flames licked the metal, eating through the hinges.

Red lights filled the corridor. A female voice spoke in a comforting tone. "Please find the nearest emergency exit."

Jerek rolled off Ari, yanking her to her feet.

He raised his voice so the guards could hear. "Ariel, I'm sorry. I'm so sorry. I didn't mean to lose control."

"You sick bastard!" Ari drew back her hand, slapping him hard across the face.

He clamped his mouth shut against the smear of blood.

Ari threw herself against the door, stepped back and rammed the metal again.

"Stay right where you are!"

The hinges gave, and the door burst open, freeing Ari.

One down.

"Ariel!" Jerek screamed after her.

Lincoln stood behind him, facing off with the guards.

Don't mess this up, old friend.

"Ariel!" Jerek shouted her name and ran onto the sidewalk.

A very small part of him expected lightning to streak from the sky and strike him down for daring to steal from the Council of the Feu. Or worse, for the Blood List to burst into flames or shrivel up and disappear away from the protection of the CFH.

He headed down the street he'd walked with Ari and Lincoln only a short time before.

A man trailing a herd of dogs behind him took up the whole sidewalk.

Jerek darted around them and onto the street, leaping back up onto the sidewalk as a blue jeep raced by.

The café came into view before the thundering of boots pounded behind him.

"You! Stop!" a CFH guard bellowed.

Grace and Eve still sat at their table in front of the café.

A woman in a long, floral-print dress pointed at Jerek's face and gasped. "I think he needs help."

Damn, the blood.

Grace stood and stepped into Jerek's path, still deep in conversation with Eve.

He rammed into Grace, knocking her to the side.

"Watch it, asshole," Grace shouted after him.

Jerek didn't pause to see if she'd been hurt or what the bang and shattering of glass behind him might be.

He ran a hand over his face, seeping the color from the blood, leaving the wetness as a thick and sticky translucent smear.

A crowd of tourists packed the sidewalk. Jerek weaved into the horde, dragging a hand through his hair, tinting the strands a vibrant red with barely a thought. He brushed off his shoulder, changing his shirt from black to turquoise.

The guards ran into the crowd, shoving their way through the tourists who murmured excitedly as though being knocked around by men in suits was nothing more than an amusement park ride.

"Back the hell off, man." Jerek jerked away from a guard who had stepped on his foot.

The guard didn't give the boy with the bright red hair a second glance.

45

Eve

"Breathe, Grace," Eve said. "You know what to do."

Grace shook her head so hard her entire body moved, sending coffee sloshing out of her cup.

"If worse comes to worst, just set the street on fire, and everyone will be too busy running for their lives to look at us," Eve said.

"Not funny." Grace glared at Eve.

"Got you to stop panicking." Eve shrugged. "If everything goes really well, we won't see them at all."

Eve leaned back in her seat, watching the people passing by. She sipped her coffee slowly, the tension in her gut tightening as her drink grew cold.

The waiter came by to refill their cups. Eve slipped cash onto the table and smiled at the man.

Don't you dare try and make me leave this table.

He eyed the cash, but didn't take it. "I'll be around in a few minutes in case you ladies need another refill."

"Thanks," Eve said.

"They should have been back by now." Grace chewed on her bottom lip. "Something went wrong."

"Or there was a line," Eve said. "Or the registrar was on a coffee break. Or they had to fill out a stack of forms. They're fine. They'll be here."

Grace stared down the street toward the CFH.

"Relax," Eve said. "Panic kills plans."

"Right." Grace leaned back in her seat, sloshing coffee from her cup again.

A man with six dogs on leashes strolled past, heading toward the CFH. All the dogs turned their noses to sniff Eve, whining in her direction.

"Aw, come on guys." The dog walker yanked on their leashes, dragging his charges past Eve. "Sorry about that."

"No problem." Eve smiled at the man, her hands curling into fists as the temptation to tear the leashes from his hand and set the dogs free surged through her.

"Oh no." Grace whimpered.

Eve followed Grace's gaze down the street.

Jerek ran toward them, blood streaked across his face and two guards gaining on him.

"Is that my blood?" Grace whispered.

"We can hope," Eve said. "Just stay calm."

Grace stood, taking a step away from the table and onto the sidewalk proper, keeping her eyes locked on Eve. "This is a terrible idea. I don't know why we thought this would work."

Jerek darted around the dogs and onto the road.

Eve's heart leapt into her throat as a jeep barreled toward him.

He jumped back up onto the sidewalk as Eve rose to her feet.

Grace bit her lips together, waiting for the blow.

Jerek drove his shoulder into her side, knocking her to the ground. She fell between two tables, clutching a scroll with black rods to her chest.

"Watch it, asshole!" Grace rolled to her hands and knees.

Eve watched Grace slip the scroll under her shirt but couldn't spare the time to help her to her feet.

The guards were too close to Jerek. They'd catch him before he could slip away.

"Are you okay?" Eve leaned down toward Grace and kicked back, hitting the underside of their table.

The table flipped over, smashing into one of the guards who tumbled into the path of his comrade. The table rolled sideways, knocking into the next table over.

"Oh, sorry!" Eve started toward the fallen guard, but he was already on his feet, chasing after Jerek.

Run faster, Holden.

"Sorry!" Eve turned toward the table her own had knocked into. Coffee cups had tipped over, soaking through sandwiches and clothing alike.

"I'm so sorry." Eve clapped her hands over her mouth. "I'm such a klutz." She grabbed napkins from the nearest undamaged setting and dabbed at the spills on the table. "I'll pay for your lunch. I really am sorry."

She barely caught a glimpse of Grace walking down the street and turning out of sight.

46

Ari

The side doors of the van unlocked before she reached for the handle.

"It's okay." Ari patted the teal side panel. "Everyone's going to make it back okay."

The van didn't answer. She knew it wouldn't, but speaking to the mostly inanimate object somehow made her feel better about being the first back from the CFH.

From the mission.

She wasn't entirely sure if calling it a mission made the worry rolling through her stomach feel better or worse.

"Ari?" Jack called from under the seat before she stepped up into the van.

"Yep," Ari said. "I'm surprised Grace's blood on my dress didn't throw you off."

"I can smell that too," Jack said. "But your base scent is totally different."

Ari shut the doors behind her and crawled up to the front, unrolling the windows.

"Where's everybody else?" Jack asked.

"Didn't go quite as quietly as we'd hoped. We had to scatter. Everyone will be here soon."

"Are you okay?"

"Fine." Ari lay on the floor next to Jack's hiding place. "I'll have to wash my dress, and my eyes are swollen from crying about giving up my fake baby that wasn't actually Jerek's. I hate playing dumb slut. It's emotionally exhausting."

"And completely out of character. No one would ever call you dumb or slutty."

"Oh, it's happened. Trust me. I've had both things screamed in my face. Somehow, it still stings." Ari wiped away the fresh tears burning in her eyes before they could fall.

"Point me at them, and I'll tear their throats out. I'm not hungry, but that never stopped me from bingeing ice cream in my human days."

"Thanks." Ari laughed.

"I wish I could give you a hug right now."

"Yeah. That would be nice."

Ari stared at the ceiling of the van, studying the pattern in the quasi-carpet fabric.

"Next time you all abandon me in a parking garage, can we make sure we're parked belowground?" Jack asked.

"You got it."

The crunch of footsteps came from outside the van.

"Who is it?" Ari whispered to Jack.

"Jerek."

Ari sat up, crawling toward the front seat as Jerek opened the driver's side door.

"Are you okay? Do you have the Blood List?" Ari searched Jerek's face for signs of damage.

His left cheek was bright red and a bruise had begun to blossom under his right eye.

"Sorry about your face," Ari said.

"What happened to his face?" Jack asked.

"Lincoln and I hit it a couple of times." Ari couldn't keep her laughter out of her words.

"Next time we steal something, can I come?" Jack asked. "I feel like I missed out on a lot of fun."

"It was charming," Jerek said. "Grace has the Blood List. I had security chasing me, and I couldn't risk getting caught."

"Poor thing is probably hyperventilating by now," Ari said.

"She's stronger than you give her credit for," Jerek said.

"Is that why you push people so hard?" Ari asked. "Because you think they're stronger than they are."

Jerek reached back, taking Ari's hand in his. "I know how strong people are, and I never push when there's another choice."

"Sure."

He pressed his lips to the back of her hand and mouthed *I'm sorry*.

Ari rolled her eyes and leaned forward, nestling her head against his side.

Minutes ticked past. There was nothing to say. No plans to go over. Life froze while they waited for the others to arrive.

Ari's fingers itched to be busy on her computer. Finding out more about Chanler. Checking on Grace's social media messages.

Nothing to do but wait.

"Eve and Lincoln are coming," Jack said. "Grace isn't with them."

"Then where the hell is she?" Jerek said.

47

Grace

Grace walked down the street as slowly as her panic would allow.

I'm not on the list. They wouldn't have taken it if I were.

Tears stung the corners of her eyes. She'd tucked the Blood List under her shirt, gripping the scroll to her stomach like somehow pressing it close to her skin would make her name appear on the parchment. The magic of the ancient list would devour her whole being until she truly belonged.

How much did my mother hate me if she couldn't even write my name down?

What would my name have been?

The sage words of a dozen therapists floated through her mind.

The reasoning of others can't always be understood.

A found family can be stronger than blood.

There are hundreds of reasons a mother might decide she isn't a fit parent. You have to believe she wanted the best for you. And look at the amazing family you ended up with.

"Not good enough."

Grace cut off the street, heading toward a patch of trees.

A harassed-looking mother bounced a sobbing baby on one knee, while a toddler played on the ground by her feet.

Grace gave the woman a nod and searched the streets around her for men in suits. There were plenty of well-dressed men around, but none seemed intent on finding anyone.

She pulled the Blood List out from under her shirt. Her hands shook as she unwound the parchment.

Richard Holden

Risa Holden

Jerek Holden

Their names appeared together. Permanently attached in the records of the feu.

"Tommy, do not put that in your mouth," the mother shouted.

"Yummy," the toddler laughed.

"Where am I?" Grace whispered to the Blood List.

The paper shone faintly in her hands, the rods vibrating so gently she could barely feel the magic pulsing through them.

She held her breath as she waited for the names on the parchment to change.

Maybe they hadn't stolen the Blood List because she wasn't on it. Maybe they had found her and taken the list to prove who Grace's family really was.

The light faded from the scroll, leaving the Blood List as nothing more than old paper.

Tears fell from Grace's cheeks and onto the scroll, streaking through Jerek's name. The long-dried blood didn't smear. The

Blood List absorbed her tears like Grace hadn't existed to cry them.

A sob shook her chest.

"Are you okay?" the mother asked.

"I'm fine." Grace re-rolled the scroll, tucking it back under her shirt. "Thanks, though."

"You hang in there, okay?" The mother gave her a smile.

Grace nodded. "You have beautiful children."

The mother glanced from the still screaming baby to the toddler who now had a stick poking out of his mud-covered mouth.

"Ta-da!" The toddler spit out the stick with a grin.

"You want them, you can have them," the mother snorted.

Grace forced out a laugh as she half-ran out of the trees.

Another sob clutched her lungs. Gasping for air, she stopped running.

I shouldn't be here. I shouldn't be a part of this.

Grace searched the street, looking for someone she could give the Blood List to. Then she could resign from this horrible plan to help a world that wanted nothing to do with her.

I'm not a part of anything.

I never will be.

Pain burst through her chest.

She gasped, trying to drag air in past the stabbing panic that seized her lungs.

"No, no, no!"

With a crack and a pop, smoke drifted up from the front of the car parked next to her.

"Shit." Grace turned to the crowd. "Get back! Everybody get back."

Some of the passersby scrambled to get away from the car, but others stayed frozen, as though interested to see what might happen next.

"Move!" Grace shouted.

Flames leapt from the engine.

"It's going to blow up!"

Those seemed to be the words the crowd needed to hear.

Screams filled the air as everyone scattered.

Bang!

Heat licked the back of Grace's neck.

She kept running, letting her feet carry her down the street as sirens blared to life blocks away.

She ran past museums, restaurants, and offices, not caring if people noticed the crying girl tearing past them, gripping her stomach like she might be sick at any moment.

The parking garage finally came into view. Eve stood next to the concrete partition three stories up, searching the streets beyond. She disappeared as soon as she spotted Grace.

Disappear. Run away. It's fine, just do it.

Her legs begged her to stop as she ran up the incline toward the waiting van.

"Grace." Jerek stepped out, blocking her path before she could reach the third story. "Where have you been?"

"Take it." Grace pulled the Blood List out from under her shirt, thrusting the scroll into Jerek's hands. "I don't want it near me. I don't want any part of this. I'm done."

"Grace—"

"No! You come bursting into my life and steal me from my home. You tell me I'm a part of something, but I'm not. Do you know how long I waited for someone to show up at my parents' door looking for me? Someone who could tell me why my eyes are so dark, or whose black hair I have. Someone who could tell me why the hell my mother would leave me outside in the middle of the night. But you can't tell me any of that, and no one ever will!"

"Grace." Jerek stepped forward, reaching for her hand. "You are a part of something. You're one of us. You're feu."

"The feu don't want me. I'm not on your list. I'm a freak who can't be human and doesn't belong with magic." Her shoulders shook as she sobbed. "I'm nothing. I don't belong anywhere. No one loved me enough to write my damn name down."

Jerek wrapped his arms around her, drawing her close to his chest.

"You belong with us." Jerek's lips brushed her ear as he whispered. "You belong in a broken world with broken people. None of us are whole. That's why we're here."

"You're only trying to convince me to stay because you need me." She didn't pull away from him. She didn't have the strength to deprive herself of the thin comfort of his warmth surrounding her.

"That's not true. We can't succeed without you, but wanting you to stay is more than that. If you want to, you can go back home, tell your dads New York was a bust. Beg their forgiveness, but where would that leave you?"

"With a life." She laid her cheek on Jerek's shoulder.

"It would leave you with nothing but a hollow place where magic should be, trying to survive the lie that you're normal. I've dragged you too far down this road for you to turn back. Hate me if you want, but don't hurt yourself by walking away."

"I used to dream someone would come to school and tell me I was a princess from an exotic country. I'd been given away so I could be safe from rebels who had tried to destroy my family and it was my destiny to rule my homeland and save my people," Grace said. "It never once occurred to me that having people count on you could feel suffocating and awful."

Jerek took Grace's face in his hands. "Life is suffocating and awful. But there are people waiting in the van who want to try and survive the suffocating awfulness with you. And they're all a lot more likely to survive until next week if you come with us."

Grace looked up the ramp to the van. Ari, Eve, and Lincoln stared back at her through the windows.

"It may not be the destiny you dreamt of," Jerek said, "but we're what you've got."

He took her hand, leading her to the van, opening the side doors for her.

"You don't have to come with us," Jerek said. "But we all want you here."

"You saved my life." Jack spoke from under the seat. "It would be rude to abandon me before I can return the favor."

Ari reached back from the front seat. "Get in the van, Grace. You'll spend the rest of your life wondering what you could have been if you don't come with us."

"Ari," Lincoln said.

"She's right," Eve said. "You're part of the Band of Bandits now."

"Still not quite the right name," Ari said.

"Please." Jerek looked straight into her eyes. There was no begging in his gaze. No fear of her disappearing. Only the clear acceptance that, broken as she might be, Grace was meant to be with them.

"Okay." The single word snapped through the hopeless anxiety in Grace's chest.

The faint sound of clapping came from under the seat.

"Just so you know, I blew up a car." Grace climbed into the van. "There's probably roadblocks, so don't head back toward the museums."

"Somehow, it feels right," Jack said.

48

Lincoln

Fire trucks raced past the entrance of the parking garage, all headed toward the museums.

How long will it take the Council to figure out magic caused a car to explode?

They won't.

The horrible realization shook Lincoln in a way he didn't think possible. The Council of the Feu and Knights Maree didn't know about Grace. The CFH would figure out the scroll currently in the Blood Room was a fake—perhaps they already had—then the CFH would notify the Council proper and the Knights Maree. The Maree would contact Lincoln, wanting to know exactly what had happened and where the hell the Blood List had gone.

Lie. Tell them the room glitched and no one had touched the list. Call it a set up.

Lincoln pinched the bridge of his nose. No one would

believe a Holden had been present for chaos and somehow not been a part of it.

"You okay, Lincoln?" Ari asked.

"Just a headache," Lincoln said. "I think we should stop for a bit once we get out of the city. Take a moment to breathe."

"I would think a Maree's instinct would be to get as far away from trouble as possible," Eve said.

"Ari should check for chatter about the list," Lincoln said.

"Already doing it." Ari peeked around from the front passenger seat. "Nothing about the Blood List or Jerek Holden on the usual sites."

"They've got to know it's gone," Jerek said.

"It makes sense for them to keep it quiet," Ari said. "Magicians would panic. It's the legacy of their kind."

"But the CFH knows Jerek was there." Lincoln dragged his hand over the stubble on his chin. "Even if they can't prove it, they've got to know we have the list."

"And we're not giving it back until we're done," Eve said.

"But we're in Jerek's dad's van," Lincoln said. "Heading up the coast to Holden House."

Lincoln paused, waiting for someone to argue.

"We can't go to Holden House," Jerek said.

"Damn." Ari leaned back in her seat. "I wanted to see Casanova."

"I know somewhere safe we can go," Jerek said.

"And the van?" Lincoln asked.

"We're not ditching the van," Jerek said. "I can switch out the color and change the plates."

"We need to stop somewhere out of sight and get it done," Lincoln said. "The Maree and the Council might not be what they were before, but we can't take any chances. If we get caught—"

"Then I don't get to gut Chanler," Eve said.

"There's a nice park not too far from here." Ari zoomed in on her laptop. "Decent tree cover to do magicky things."

"Perfect," Jerek said.

They sat in silence as they made their way out of D.C. and onto the highway. Even then, only Ari spoke, directing Jerek away from the main roads.

Lincoln stared at his hands resting on his knees. He'd spent years learning to use those hands to fight, to help people.

This isn't what your teachers had in mind.

He studied the faint pink on his knuckles from punching Jerek. He hadn't even hesitated to hit his oldest friend in the face.

Jerek drove them into a town, following the signs for the state park.

"We should get food," Eve said.

"After Jerek's changed the van," Lincoln said.

Eve shrugged.

"We should pack snacks," Jack said. "Not for me, obviously. That would be weird. But a cooler wouldn't be a bad idea. Have nice little thief picnics."

"We'll remember that next time we go on a larceny binge," Ari said.

The wheels of the van crunched on the gravel lane leading into the park. Trees draped over the drive, lending a sense of security Lincoln wished could be real.

"It'll take me a bit to rework her," Jerek said. "It's a lot of surface area to cover."

"I'll just be here," Jack said. "Hiding under a seat."

"Ari, take Grace and the crystal." Jerek pulled the sphere from his bag.

"I think I've had enough magic for one day," Grace said.

"We don't have time for that to be true," Jerek said.

"Besides, I'd rather you not catch the van on fire. That would take a lot more work to fix than altering the paint job."

Grace glared at Jerek. Purple streaks marred the skin under her eyes.

"Don't worry." Ari took the sphere from Jerek. "It'll give us some time away from Mr. Charming. And isn't that the greatest gift of all?"

Grace managed a half-hearted laugh.

Lincoln swung open the side doors and climbed out to hold them open for Grace. "I'm going to stretch my legs."

"Antsy from punching Jerek?" Ari hopped down from the passenger seat. "I found slapping him to be a soothing experience."

"You're too charming for your own good, Ari," Jerek said.

Ari slammed the van door behind her.

"More like tense from marble walls sliding down around me," Lincoln said. "I just need some air."

"Don't wander too far." Ari leaned close to his ear. "You haven't given me a look at those lovely daggers in your pockets, so..." She stepped away, one eyebrow raised. "Come on, Grace. Let's go channel some angst."

Ari took Grace's hand, leading her through the trees to the grassy meadow beyond.

Lincoln watched them walk away.

They believe the heliostone can save them. They believe in Jerek.

"Martel." Eve stopped at the back of the van. She tipped her head for Lincoln to follow and walked back up the park road toward the main streets beyond.

Giving one last look toward Ari and Grace, Lincoln followed Eve.

She didn't stop until the van was almost out of sight.

The color of the back panel had already shifted from teal to a deep, cherry red.

"Listen," Eve said, her tone low and quiet. "I wanted to say you did well."

"Thanks." Lincoln glanced back toward the van. The cherry red had changed to fire engine.

"I just mean walking into the CFH and knowing they would ask for your name." Eve dug her fingers into her curls. "I would have bet seven to ten you weren't going to come out with Jerek and Ari. Six to ten none of you were going to come out at all."

"We need the Blood List," Lincoln said. "There wasn't another way to get it."

"Doesn't matter. I know what it's like to be raised to be loyal to a pack. Going against them, even if it's for their own good, can't be easy."

"No." The honesty of the word tore at Lincoln's resolve.

"I just wanted to say"—Eve looked up to the trees above them—"maybe you aren't as useless a traitor as I thought."

"Thanks. I appreciate that."

"Credit where credit is due." Eve shrugged. "But if you screw up me getting my hands on Chanler—"

"You'll eviscerate me. I got it."

"Good." Eve patted him on the shoulder hard enough to leave a bruise. "Nice talk."

She strode back to the van, which had morphed to a deep shade of violet.

Shaking his head, Lincoln ventured farther down the road.

He hadn't lied about needing air. The urge to run a marathon or climb a mountain, even leap into a sparring ring outmatched by opponents, pounded through his veins. He needed to do something hard, something painful.

Something to make me forget.

Up ahead, a small parking lot held three cars. All empty, with no drivers in sight.

One Virginia plate, one Maryland, and one very dusty car from Texas.

Lincoln pulled his phone from his pocket. Such a small thing to be so important. Chips and wires and a screen. A lifeline tying him to the Maree. To his whole family.

He closed his eyes, picturing some poor family from Texas being pulled over by a black van. They'd be questioned and searched and sent on their way, with no hope of explaining to the somb police that a secret order of knights had ransacked their car.

"I'm sorry."

With one last glance around, Lincoln knelt, reaching up and into the curve of the bumper. His phone barely made a sound as he let it slip from his hand.

He stood and headed back to the now bright yellow van, a weight gone from his pocket, while a heavier burden pressed on his chest.

49

Grace

"Don't try so hard," Ari said. "If you push, you won't be able to focus."

Grace resisted the urge to roll her eyes as she stared into the center of the sphere. The green of the meadow and trees surrounding them lent the orb an emerald hue. "I still don't know how making a crystal ball light up is going to help us steal a rock and save the feu."

"You need to be able to use your magic," Ari said. "Think of this as the training wheels version of being a magician. All the fire, none of the insurance claims...or explosions."

"I just don't understand." Grace pressed her palms against her eyes, trying to stop their throbbing.

"We have a plan."

"Jerek has a plan. We have the bits and pieces he's chosen to gift to the rest of us that we just have to hope will work out."

Grace opened her eyes and glanced toward the trees that hid the van.

"Get the heliostone, break the curse." Ari leaned sideways, blocking Grace's view. "That's really all we need to know."

"But how exactly do we break the curse? You at least know those details, right?"

"Nope." Ari lay back on the grass.

"And that doesn't bother you? I mean, you're like his right-hand man. Shouldn't you be in the circle of trust or whatever?"

"First of all, we can go with right-hand girl. Having a man at your right hand does not make you more powerful. Second, Jerek trusts me as much as he trusts anyone."

"And how long have you been helping him work on this plan without knowing where it's leading?" Grace asked. "How long did you help him watch me?"

"Longer than you want to know. Look, I trust Jerek. However he wants to get the heliostone and make you into a magician capable of breaking a curse that's ruined the lives of the feu for a dozen years is fine with me. Because believe it or not, Jerek is the good guy. Whatever he's doing, he's doing it for the good of all of us."

"But why won't he—"

"It doesn't matter. I can read Jerek better than anyone, and the thing he's worried about right now isn't where we're going to stay tonight or if Lincoln and Eve are going to tear each other's throats out before we ever get to Chanler's party, or even what color he wants to turn the van. He's worried he backed the wrong magical horse and when the moment comes you won't be able to pull through and do the incantation we need instead of just catching the party on fire. So, just take a breath, stare into the magic sphere, channel your energy, and leave the planning to Jerek. You've got enough to worry about."

The temptation to throw the crystal at Ari's head gnawed at the edges of Grace's mind.

"Fine." Grace looked back into the center of the sphere, focusing on the tiny point of glowing light, trying to see it as more than a bit of stray sunshine.

The light was a part of magic. Magic that coursed all around the world and called to her being as fresh water called to animals dying of thirst.

"How did you meet him?" Grace asked.

"What happened to focusing?" Ari rolled over to face Grace.

"I focus better when I'm distracted."

Ari gave a dramatic sigh. "Weirdo. I met Jerek when I was too little to remember him. His mom worked for the Council of the Feu, as like an ambassador or liaison, I don't know what her title was. But she worked everywhere. Reaching out to feu, trying to connect them with the community. Building trust and stronger bonds among all magical people."

All magical people.

A whole world of people to which she, Grace, belonged.

As a random stranger who wasn't even on the guest list trying to bash her way through the door.

"Mrs. Holden came to my house a few times," Ari said. "Brought Jerek with her. I didn't think I'd hear from any of the feu again after the Fracture. I thought I'd be left alone. Trying to cope with being different. Doomed to live life in the shadows."

"Sounds awful."

"It was. Until Jerek reached out. Went through his mom's old records looking for people and found me."

"And you just so happened to be the hacker he needed?"

"It had nothing to do with computer stuff. Or maybe the computer stuff has to do with everything. I don't know if you'd understand."

"Try me."

"Being a part of magic when I was really little," Ari began slowly, "it was like I belonged in this web of wonderful that reached all over the world. Even if I was feeling like a freak walking through a crowd of totally normal sombs, I knew somewhere in the world there were other people like me. I knew we had to hide, that I could be passing them in a crowd and not even know it, but they were out there and I would meet more of them and see amazing things because, hidden or not, I was connected to all the feu."

A tug pulled at the center of Grace's chest. A hint of longing for something she'd never even known she'd lost.

"That's why I like computers and the internet so much," Ari said. "I'm connected to everything. Not in the same bright, shiny, magical way. But I'm a part of the world. I can touch places I've never been."

"Hack into the lives of people you've never met."

"Oh, come on. Don't pretend you're still mad about that. If I hadn't done some moderate pilfering of your information to help Jerek, you'd still be the mystery fire starter of Sun Palms High School. You wouldn't know anything about magic or the feu. You'd be living your life in the dark, wondering why there's something deep inside that never feels quite right."

"It was still rude and wrong." Grace tamped down her anger, pushing the fire it formed in her chest out toward the sphere.

The glow inside the crystal crackled like a log spitting flames.

"That's better," Ari said. "You're going to help us rebuild the wonderful web of magic that connects all the feu. There won't be any more little feu girls crying in their rooms because they know there will never be anywhere for them to truly belong. Tell me that isn't worth breaking a few rules."

The fire in the crystal sizzled away, taking the glow with it.

A terrifying void filled the center of the sphere, but before Grace could toss the crystal aside, another shape formed.

A thin line of light spun into being, drawing another line out of the blackness. Then another.

The lines didn't stay trapped at the center of the sphere, but spread out, reaching toward the very edges of the crystal.

"That's more like it," Ari said. "Now shift the current. Bring all the strings together to make one amazing whole."

"I don't know how."

"Sure you do. Stop whining and make it happen."

With a force like a punch to Grace's chest, the thin threads shifted, snapping together into one whole that shone out of the sphere with a light brighter than a bonfire.

The gleam bounced off the trees and grass. Flecks of dancing light, like the most magnificent glitter, sparkled on Ari's face.

"Awesome." Ari beamed.

"Mommy, mommy, what's she got?" A little boy dragged his mother through the grass toward Grace and Ari.

"Playtime is done, honey." The boy's mother didn't look up from her phone. "It's time to head home."

"And that's our cue to go." Ari lifted the crystal from Grace's hand, slipping it into her pocket as the light faded from the sphere.

A pain tugged at the corners of Grace's mind as she pushed herself to her feet.

It wasn't until they were walking across the grass with the sphere tucked out of sight that Grace recognized the feeling.

Grief.

50

Ari

The taste of the sea air reached Ari two miles before they ever saw the beach. The setting sun sparkled its last rays on the water as it dipped behind the trees. A giant white house sat just above the sand, a wide porch and balcony looking out over the Atlantic. Turrets rose from the north and south corners, giving the home the silhouette of a place where magic belonged.

Dim lights of distant islands glimmered across the waves, an impossible-to-ignore reminder of the path that lay ahead.

Ari took a deep breath, letting the salty air fill her lungs.

"What is this place?" Grace leaned close to the van window.

"A rental," Jerek said. "And I had to give them a massive security deposit, so try not to catch anything on fire."

"Ha ha."

Ari hopped out of the van, dragging her backpack with her.

"How long are we here for?" Eve asked.

"Until the party if all goes according to plan," Jerek said. "We've booked the place through Monday."

"Can the reservation be traced to us?" Lincoln unloaded the bags from the back of the van.

"Nope," Ari said. "Not unless someone wants to track a fake identity back a few years."

"Don't worry," Jerek said, turning to Grace who stared at the house with pursed lips. "I pay the fake identity's credit card bill with real money. It just won't look like it's coming from me."

"A very special Ari kind of magic." Ari tossed her hair dramatically and took her bag of clothes from Lincoln. "We have to go shopping for the party," she called into the van. "I'll check around and see where we want to spend Jerek's money."

"You're a doll." Jack jumped from the side doors, stretching his arms and tipping his face up to the dark sky.

"Is anywhere around here going to be open?" Eve asked.

"We're in a rich people's playground," Ari said. "Everything is open if you have the money to pay."

"Right." Eve grabbed her bag and headed to the house.

"Some people don't appreciate the finer things," Jack whispered.

The rest of the pack filed to the porch together, catching up to Eve, who leaned against the doorframe. The door itself had a clear window latticed through with a pattern of silver. Soft white curtains blocked the view of the inside of the house.

A code box hung from the handrail of the porch steps.

"It'll be nice to be in one place for a day," Jack said. "Not that I don't love my vinyl palace."

Jerek popped open the lock box and pulled out a set of house keys. "We'll need food, too."

"Ahh, the practicalities that get in the way of larceny," Ari sighed.

"I can go get food," Lincoln said.

"Good. Grace and I will get straight to work." Jerek unlocked the front door, giving the group their first peek at their new home.

"Damn," Jack said.

"Damn is right." Ari peered into the shadows.

Jerek flicked a switch, lighting the crystal chandelier that hung above the wide, sweeping staircase leading to the second story. The perfectly polished wood floor sparkled in the light. Paintings of lush seascapes hung on the pure white walls above the carved chair rail.

"We have five bedrooms, so no one will have to share," Jerek said.

"Are you sure you can actually pay for this?" Grace whispered.

"Sure he can." Eve headed up the stairs. "He's a Holden."

"Of course she's going to pick her room first." Ari tightened her grip on her bags. "If we weren't doing something so dangerous, this would be a lovely vacation."

"I'll head down for my room." Jack walked to a door under the stairs.

"Game room with only one window," Jerek said. "We'll be able to block it pretty easily."

"Oh, thank the setting sun." Jack threw open the basement door. "I'm going to pace all day just to prove I can."

"I was thinking more about planning," Jerek said.

"I can pace and plan." Jack disappeared down the stairs.

"I'll drop you off to find clothes while I get food," Lincoln said to Ari before rounding on Jerek. "Do not let Eve leave the house while I'm gone. I'll feel better knowing she's with you."

"Oh really?" Jerek leaned against the handrail.

"Fake orders or not, I was assigned to keep you safe." Lincoln headed up the steps, his heavy boots thumping on every stair.

"I don't want to be pushy," Grace said, "but I can ask my dads to help pay for this, when it's all over I mean."

"I really can pay," Jerek laughed.

"While all the other magician families of old were using their powers to create jewelry beyond compare, grow crops at unbelievable rates, miraculously heal the sick and make the best wine this world has ever tasted," Ari said, "the Holden family went a more sustainable route."

"What?" Grace asked.

"Real estate, mostly," Jerek said. "Partial ownership of an array of different small corporations, and a large investment in the education of the feu."

"Don't worry." Ari patted Grace's hand. "Jerek can pay."

"Good." Grace nodded. "Not that I thought you *wouldn't* pay. It's just so much money, and—"

"Quit while you're ahead," Ari whispered.

"Right." Grace grabbed her bags and headed up the stairs.

Ari waited for the sound of a door clicking closed.

"A house by the ocean, Jerek?" Ari kept her voice low.

"We're an easy drive from the party," Jerek said. "We've only got one more full day to prepare. It seemed like a wise choice. Besides, the rental listing said the sunrise from the balcony is magnificent."

Ari kept her glare fixed on his sea-blue eyes.

"And it's my way of saying I'm sorry," Jerek said. "And I am...very sorry."

"Are you?"

"I'm not saying your coming into the CFH wasn't necessary. Taking Grace would have been too dangerous, and there's no way Eve could have pulled off an act like that."

"Too true."

"But I know what it cost you." Jerek laid his hands on her shoulders. "I don't ever want to see you hurt, Ari. I hated tearing open the wounds you hide so well. You are the best of us. You deserve every ounce of respect and adoration the feu can muster. Sometimes, I wish you weren't so terribly brave and clever. Then I wouldn't have to rely on you so much."

"And you'd never have made it this far." Ari bit the inside of her bottom lip. "For what it's worth, I'm not mad. Not for anything you said, or anything you did. You had to."

"But it still hurt."

"Yeah." She put her bags down and wrapped her arms around Jerek's neck, pressing her cheek to his. "I just hope when you save the world, you can find a way to make it a better place than it was before."

"You'll do it without any help from me." Jerek held her tight. "And you'll be breathtakingly brilliant."

Ari laughed, blinking away the tears that threatened to form in the corners of her eyes. "I really do love you, Jerek Holden."

"I know." Jerek stepped back and pressed his lips to Ari's forehead. "And I really do love you, too."

Footsteps came from below.

Ari stepped away from Jerek, running a hand through her hair.

Jack swung open the basement door. "Are we ready to shop?"

"Always," Ari said. "Lincoln, come on or we're leaving without you."

"Do you need measurements?" Jerek pulled out his wallet, passing a credit card to each of them.

"I am sworn to work to the best of my abilities to ensure this mission's success," Jack laughed. "While I may be a damn fine pickpocket, a master of sleight of hand, and the occasional *blow things up* type of guy, I am equally valuable in the world of fashion. Every one of you will be perfectly dressed to fill your role, and I swear the shoes will fit. Because I may be a wayward teenage vampire, but I sure as shit am good at what I do."

Ari applauded. The sound of her clapping bounced off the white walls of the foyer.

"Everything okay?" Lincoln appeared at the top of the stairs.

"You just missed a rousing speech." Ari headed to the front door. "Be good, Jerek. Be a kind and patient teacher, and don't forget to leave the porch light on."

"Be careful in your happy place," Jerek said. "Enjoyment often lends itself to a false sense of security."

Ari blew Jerek a kiss and took Lincoln and Jack by the hands. "Come on, boys. Let's go freak people out by throwing Jerek's money around."

51

Eve

The moonlight was strong enough to tingle her skin, but she missed the raw power of the full moon.

Eve tipped her face up to the sky.

I want to run and jump and claw.

She took a deep breath, catching the scents of the dozen small creatures that roamed through the tall grass by the house.

I want to not be human for a while.

Her hand drifted up, clasping the pendant at her neck. A tiny flick, and the moonstone would glow. Claws, adrenaline, strength, all at the tips of her fingers.

A bright light burst from an upstairs window, followed by a shriek from Grace.

Eve stared at the window, waiting for a bloodcurdling scream or a howl of pain. The light faded away, replaced by the rumble of Jerek's voice.

"Glad we have such a strong magician on our side." Eve

turned away from the house, walking another wide circle through the grounds.

The chill of the night air wasn't enough to cut through the heat of her skin.

Tear it off. Tear off my skin and run.

She let out a deep breath.

"Running won't get you Chanler. It's only two more nights. You can hold on for two more nights."

A squeal of glee carried from the house.

"What am I doing, Gran?"

Gran's voice tugged at the edge of her mind.

You're doing what's best for the pack. The pack comes first, whether they like it or not.

Eve slid her fingers away from her pendant.

For the pack, she could be patient. For them, she could survive in her skin.

She reached back, touching the raised lines on her shoulder. She closed her eyes, remembering the pain as fire lapped at her feet and glass sliced through her flesh. The wails of the long dead pounded in her ears. Her throat tightened, ready to scream as she had twelve years ago.

Silence surrounded her. The pain drifted away.

"I can be strong for all of you." She turned toward the house. "I can make it a little while longer."

Eve didn't look back to the moon as she walked up the porch steps. She flinched as she shut the front door behind her, cutting herself off from the night.

"Eve," Jerek shouted from upstairs.

"Yeah," Eve said.

"I need something glass that won't be missed," Jerek said. "A wine glass perhaps?"

"You got it," Eve called up the stairs. "By the way, the

grounds are clear and we aren't being invaded by Maree who want to execute us for treason against the treaty of the feu."

"Wonderful," Jerek said. "But we really do need that glass."

"I'm being good, Gran," Eve whispered as she headed down the white hall to the kitchen. "Keep on my shoulder, because I'm really trying to be good."

52

Jack

The texture of the silk sent tingles up Jack's spine. The emerald green gown didn't have any beading or flourishes. Only a plunging neckline and high slit marked the garment as anything special.

"Are you sure about this?" Ari bit her bottom lip. "I don't know if it'll go over very well."

"It's a gorgeous gown." Jack stepped in front of the mirror, holding the dress up to admire the lines. "I don't care about going over well."

"It really is divine." Macy beamed over Jack's shoulder, fulfilling her role of upscale saleswoman to such perfection, Jack wanted to applaud her perfect use of a coy and indulgent smile. "I'm sure it will be lovely on..."

"A friend," Ari said. "That's the problem with hanging out with people who procrastinate. You end up playing personal shopper."

"It doesn't seem like you mind," Macy said.

Jack twisted to the side, picturing a silver shoe sticking out from the long slit. "Oh, I don't mind at all."

"Me neither," Ari whispered.

She took Jack's hand, sliding her fingers through his and stepping up to stand at his side. Her scarlet gown cinched in at the waist, giving her the unmistakable figure of a fairy princess.

"We make quite the pair."

Ari leaned her head on his shoulder. "We are beautiful."

"What else do you need for your"—Macy pursed her lips—"wedding reception, did you say?"

"It's more a union celebration," Ari said. "Basically an excuse to throw a huge party."

"Isn't that what all weddings really are?" Jack passed the green dress to Macy. "We're going to need one more."

"What do you have in mind?" Macy eyed Jack. "Perhaps a gown for someone with a slim figure and darker skin tone?"

"That would make my dreams come true," Jack said. "But I'm afraid it's a different dark-haired beauty we're dressing. I won't be wearing a gown to this particular party."

"Pity," Macy said. "I have some things that would be stunning on you."

Macy disappeared into the back room of the boutique.

Jack smiled after her as though she could see him through the back of her head.

"You okay?" Ari slipped out of her luscious scarlet gown.

"Fine." Jack tossed Ari her sundress. "Well-fed, surrounded by beautiful things, what more could a biter ask for?"

"Don't lie, Jack. It's not one of your more developed skills."

Jack inhaled, reveling in the clean scent of fine fabrics. "I'm everything I ever wanted to be. I'm powerful and deadly, I spend my evenings with men, and I'll tear out the throat of anyone who says what I feel is wrong."

"But?" Ari turned away from Jack, looking back over her shoulder as he finished her zipper.

"I have this sharp fear lodged behind my heart that someone is going to barge through the door and tell me I'm going to burn in Hell for being in a dress shop." Jack bit his lips together. His teeth didn't pierce his skin. They stayed terrifyingly rounded and human.

"Sweetie"—Ari took Jack's face in her hands—"if you're going to Hell for anything, it's being a vampire. That's way more worthy of damnation."

"I'm not sure my parents would agree."

"Oh Jack." Ari pulled him into a tight hug, nestling her head on his shoulder.

Her scent flooded his nose and caught in his lungs, the fresh perfume of windblown shores threatening to drag tears from his eyes.

"If I ever have the pleasure of meeting your parents, I'll slap them then tie them down so they can listen without distraction while I tell them how wonderful their son is, and how badly they screwed up by driving him away," Ari said. "Or I can just hack into their bank accounts and ruin their lives tonight. It's up to you."

"Let them keep their money." Jack stepped back, taking Ari's hands in his. "I've got one not-so-asshole sibling they need to put through college."

"*Ech.* Fine. But as soon as non-asshole is free of the family, let me know, and I'll make sure they never get to retire." Ari kissed Jack on the cheek. "We runaways have to stick together."

Macy emerged from the back room with a fresh selection of gowns in hand. "What look are we really going for?"

"Belle of the ball with a hint of deadly," Jack said.

Macy nodded. "Perfect. I have some really exceptional choices for you."

It took another half-hour to complete the four sets of party clothes.

Tears sparkled in Macy's eyes as she rang up the totals.

"Can you tack on an extra $200?" Ari said. "Just as a service fee since you stayed open so late."

"You really are too kind." Macy punched in the extra numbers without hesitation.

Jack looked outside, trying not to see exactly how much of Jerek's money they'd blown through.

The bright yellow van waited on the street, Lincoln leaning against its side.

"Our chariot awaits." Jack lifted their stack of chain-store bags in one hand and the boutique purchases in the other.

"Do you need some help?" Macy asked.

"He's got it." Ari unlocked the shop door, holding it open for Jack.

"Have a great night." Jack turned back just in time to watch Macy jump up and down behind the cash register.

"Need help?" Lincoln pushed away from the van, reaching for Jack's bags.

"So many people wanting to help poor little me," Jack cooed. "What ever will I do?"

"You better have bought some decent food." Ari opened the back doors of the van.

"I bought enough to get us through," Lincoln said.

Jack rearranged the mound of grocery bags, creating a flat place to lay the girls' gowns. "Lincoln, you know we're only at the house for a few more days and one of us doesn't eat anything bought in a grocery store, right?"

"I figured it was better to overestimate," Lincoln said. "I've spent my whole life surrounded by knights who have to eat three-thousand calories a day to keep up with their expended energy, and I'm one of eight kids in my family. My perception of how much food people need might be a little bit off."

Jack climbed into the passenger's seat. "Ah, the pleasures of needing a seatbelt." He gleefully clicked the clip.

"You should have told us you were out here waiting." Ari climbed into the back as Lincoln started the van. "You could have come in and tried on your clothes. You're going to be devastating, darling."

She fainted dramatically onto the back seat.

"I lost my phone. I didn't want to interrupt by knocking," Lincoln said.

"Lost your phone?" Ari crawled up to kneel between the front seats. "Where?"

"Must have fallen out of my pocket in D.C." Lincoln pulled the car out into traffic, barely making it two feet before he had to stop for a line of drunken vacationers stumbling across the road. "I'm not too worried. Once this is all over, either I'll be banished and won't need a Maree-issued phone anymore or honored and the knights won't mind giving me a new one."

"I know your phone's fancy, but I could try and trace it," Ari said. "I'm sure the Maree could trace it for you, too."

A middle-aged woman tipped over in the middle of the street, grabbing the front of the van for support. "Linda. Linda! I'm drunk."

Linda wobbled back into the street to claim her friend. "Sorry." She flapped a hand at the windshield. "Sorry."

"If the Maree could trace your phone," Jack said, "maybe it's good it fell out of your pocket."

"Maybe," Ari said. "Would have been nice to take a peek inside the programing, but whatever."

The road finally cleared, and Lincoln turned the van toward the house.

Women in designer dresses and cheap shoes prowled the sidewalks.

Not her. Not her. Maybe him.

Jack sized them all up as marks. None would yield the sort of money he had grown accustomed to in Vegas.

"Next time we leave the house should be for the party," Ari said. "Kind of puts a weird spin on things."

"I don't know," Jack said. "I've only known about the party for a few days, so it seems right that this freight train is just tearing down the tracks."

"How long have you known about it?" Lincoln glanced back at Ari.

"That would spark a deeper conversation you don't want to have," Ari said.

"Ooh," Jack said. "That sounds juicy."

"How long ago did you and Jerek decide to steal the heliostone from the museum?" Lincoln asked. "I think it's a legitimate question. I'm the first one who got pulled into this, and—"

"I knew Jerek wanted to go for the party about twenty minutes before you received your orders, if you must know," Ari said. "Giving Jerek information doesn't mean he'll do anything with it, at least not in the way you'd expect. If you'd been around to take care of your *best friend*, maybe you'd know that about him."

"It's not like I wanted to move to Italy," Lincoln said, his calm tone somehow worse than screaming. "When the Fracture hit, we were all kids. None of us had a choice in anything that happened."

Jack closed his eyes, picturing himself in his dark sanctuary under his seat.

"But some of us grew up," Ari said. "Some of us didn't have the luxury of holding on to the apron strings of safety disguised as duty and honor. I gave Jerek the information. He decided to move on it. Don't tell me you're having doubts, Martel. You lost your phone. You can't message home for help anymore."

The vinyl of the steering wheel crackled in Lincoln's grip.

"What we're doing is right," Lincoln said. "The Fracture has to be fixed, and there's no one else to turn to."

"But?" Jack said.

"But I keep running the math in my head," Lincoln said, "and it doesn't add up."

"Add up how?" Ari asked. "We came up with this plan together. Do you not like your role at the party? Because I'd be happy to trade."

"No, it's just..." Lincoln stared at the red light in front of them.

Jack watched Lincoln's face. He didn't move or speak until the light changed and it was time to press on the gas.

"I've been trained as a knight since I was a kid," Lincoln said. "I've been raised to risk everything for the feu and the Maree, and I'm not afraid of any of it. I don't think we can come up with a better plan than what we've got. It just feels like I'm missing something."

"Then we should go over the plan again," Jack said.

"It's not the plan," Lincoln said. "It's just a paranoid feeling in my gut, that there's something I'm not seeing."

Jack's teeth pierced his lip. "What kind of thing?" The familiar taste of blood touched his tongue.

"It feels like there's a word left out of a sentence," Lincoln said. "And I don't know which one of us is changing the phrase."

53

Ari

Darkness.

The absolute thrill of pure freedom racing through her veins as oxygen blasted full force into her lungs.

No monsters to fight. No secrets to discover.

Perfect, uninhibited bliss.

She dove deep, racing over the uneven terrain, then surged up to swirl high above in the shimmering moonlight. The speed demanding so little energy she could have kept going for forever.

Endless bliss. No hands to hold. No problems to solve. Just freedom.

She let her movement slow as she basked in the silver gleam rippling over her naked body.

There could be no secrets here. No wondering if someone would be against her when the time for change came.

She longed to close her eyes. To let herself drift away and leave the rest to themselves.

I've given them everything they need. All debts are paid.

The lure of the dark horizon pulled at her chest, begging her to let go of what was past and follow the current to places none of the others could follow.

I can't.

Taking one last breath, she let the world claim her. The wind pummeled her skin, dragging her away from her haven, leaving her with nothing but shadows lurking in the night and the path she had laid out for all of them.

54

Jerek

Jerek knew how to cook well enough—he'd been making his own meals for years—but he'd never tried to make food for more than two people and one cat at a time. Light had already begun to creep into the morning sky, but from the back of the house, the sunrise couldn't be seen. There was no trace of the sun glimmering on the ocean from the kitchen window.

Probably best not to be distracted.

Jerek cracked ten eggs into a pan, stirring the yolks together before the bottom of the pile of goo began to brown. They would want more to eat than eggs, he was quite sure of it, but the house hadn't come with a toaster.

Daring to leave the stove for a moment, he started the coffee pot. By the time he turned back to the pan, the eggs near the bottom of the sludge had browned.

"Damn." He clicked the heat down, frantically stirring the

eggs.

"Need help?" Grace stepped up next to him.

He'd been too distracted to hear her approach.

Don't let yourself slip, Holden.

"I don't know." Jerek squinted at the eggs. "Is brown and runny a style usually served at breakfast?"

Grace lifted the pan from the stove and tossed the eggs into the trash. "How about you get plates and I'll worry about not poisoning us."

"Sounds perfect." Jerek opened the cupboard. Plasticware took up one half and china the other. He pulled down a stack of china plates.

"Do you have servants at Holden House?" Grace cracked eggs into the pan, moving with an enviable economy of motion.

"I had a nanny when I was younger," Jerek said. "My parents traveled all the time before the Fracture, and after, Dad wasn't in a fit state to raise me alone. The nanny moved on to a new family when I turned thirteen."

"But no one else?" Grace pulled out a baking pan, bread, and butter. "No butler, no cook?"

"No." A tiny smile curved the corners of Jerek's mouth. "Mom and Dad liked their privacy."

"Butter the bread?" Grace held out a knife.

The mundane task of smearing butter on bread eased the tension at the edge of his mind.

Grace hummed a tune he didn't recognize.

When was the last time I listened to music?

She dished the eggs out onto each of the plates and placed the pan of bread into the oven.

"How did you learn to cook for so many people?" Jerek asked. "You're an only child."

"Only child with tons of cousins." Grace poured coffee into a flower-painted teacup. "Both my dads come from big families.

Put all the cousins in the same house, and there's not a table big enough to fit everybody."

"Sounds nice."

"It is." Grace's face fell. "*Was*, I guess."

"*Is*. You're going to get to go home when all this is done."

"Right." Grace sipped her coffee. "You're right." Her hand trembled as she set down her cup and picked up an oven mitt. "What about you? Tons of extended family running around the feu?"

"No. I'm the last."

"Please tell me someone made lots of coffee." Ari's rumpled pajamas hung loosely around her frame as she leaned against the doorframe.

Jerek pulled the pinkest cup he could find from the cupboard and poured her coffee.

"You aren't as horrible as I sometimes believe." Ari breathed in the steam from the cup. "We taking breakfast downstairs? Go over things with Jack while we eat?"

"Probably for the best." Lincoln came down the hall completely dressed. His eyes lingered on Ari's pajamas for a moment before he looked to Jerek.

"We can do a fashion show, then decide where to hide everyone's illicit materials," Ari said.

"I need to practice the incantation," Grace said. "I'm not—I need as much time as I can get."

"You just have to try on the dress. Jack and I will do the fancy stitching." Ari took a plate of eggs. "Thanks for not letting Jerek poison us."

"No problem." Grace winked at Jerek.

The others chatted as they sorted out coffee, eggs, and toast.

Eve came downstairs, stone-faced and silent.

Too quickly. It's all moving too quickly.

Grace laughed. The others joined in.

Jerek didn't know what had brought so much joy.

Jack hid in the corner of the basement until the door above closed behind them. He'd surrounded the ping-pong table with an odd assortment of chairs and pulled off the net to give them a wide space to work. Hand-drawn sketches on large pieces of brown paper showing the route in and out of the party lay on the chipped green surface.

The chatter continued.

Lincoln pointed to parts of Jack's map.

Jerek felt his mouth move but couldn't push far enough out of his own head to know what words his lips had formed.

None of them looked at him. None of them seemed confused or afraid.

I'm making sense. I can't think, and I'm making sense.

Eve set a bag on the table, pulling out the items Ari had procured from the man who'd cleaned the blood from the van.

Ari took Jerek's arm, digging her nails into his skin.

The pointed pain jerked his mind back into the present.

"The problem is security," Jack said. "Are they going to figure out we're trying to smuggle stuff in? If they do, what's our move?"

"Find Chanler," Eve said.

"Security won't know what we have," Jerek said.

"Lock picks, a little bang-bang powder, a priceless scroll," Jack said. "You're right, why would anyone notice that?"

"None of it is enough to draw the Maree's attention. They'll be looking for magical weapons though, so I'd be more worried about the daggers." Ari turned to Lincoln. "Or aren't you planning on packing those?" She sipped her coffee.

"What daggers?" Eve asked.

"The ones he took off the security guards at the CFH," Ari said. "Fancy ones. Magician made, probably irreplaceable at this point. At least until we mend the Fracture and save the day."

Lincoln stared at Ari.

"Where are they?" Eve asked.

"What are they capable of?" Jack asked. "Can they cut through glass?"

Lincoln reached down, pulling a blade from each boot. He set them on the table, keeping his hands on the hilts.

"Why didn't you tell us?" Grace asked.

"Because they are weapons infused with stores of magic," Lincoln said. "The Maree are guarding the party. There's no way we could get these past security."

"So says you." Ari reached for a blade.

Lincoln tightened his grip on the hilt.

"They should stay here," Lincoln said. "Once this is done, they can be given to the armory of the Maree."

"Once this is done, the Maree can get magician help to make whatever weapons they want," Jerek said.

No one moved for a long moment.

"We don't need them," Lincoln said. "Smuggling in weapons will only lead to more people getting hurt. We don't need anything this dangerous."

"So I should stay behind?" Eve said. "I'm more dangerous than those daggers could ever be."

"That's not what I meant, and you know it," Lincoln said.

"Give the daggers to Ari," Jerek said. "When this is over, we'll gladly return them."

"What would she need them for?" Lincoln asked.

"If you're so against using them, I don't think you need to know," Ari said.

"Absolutely not," Lincoln said.

"Do it, Knight Maree." Jerek laid both his hands on the table.

"Is that an order, Mr. Holden?" Lincoln said.

"If it has to be," Jerek said.

Lincoln stood, carrying the daggers around the table and laying them in front of Ari. "Any blood they shed is on your hands, not mine."

"I'm okay with that." Ari didn't touch the blades. She left them sitting in front of her as Lincoln walked back to his seat.

It's for the best.

"Well," Jack said. "I can sew the lockpicks into my jacket, no problem."

"Lincoln will have to carry the eater," Eve said. "Too risky to leave it with any of us."

A tiny siren screeched in the basement.

Lincoln and Eve both sprang to their feet.

Ari cursed and dug in her pocket.

"What the hell is that?" Eve said.

"My phone." Ari didn't look up from her phone screen.

"You couldn't choose a less startling ringtone?" Jack asked.

"Not a normal ringtone." Ari tapped and swiped on the screen. "Shit."

"What?" Jerek pressed his palms to the tabletop, forcing his body to remain relaxed.

"Someone found us." Ari dragged her fingers through her hair, pulling it away from her face.

"People are here?" Grace's face paled.

Lincoln reached toward the daggers.

"Not us here," Ari said. "Fake us I planted."

"Explain," Eve said.

"I wanted to know if anyone was following us," Ari said. "So I created a trail for fake us after D.C. Ran some credit card charges under an alias loosely associated with Jerek and booked him into a hotel last night."

"And someone found my hotel?" Jerek dug his fingertips into the table, darkening the green of the paint.

"According to the 9-1-1 I paid the concierge a ton of money

to send," Ari said. "We now have a friend booked into the room next to ours. He's just waiting for us to come back so he can give Jerek a birthday surprise."

"But that's okay then," Grace said. "They found the fake trail, so we're safe here."

"That depends on who found it." Jerek forced his voice to stay steady.

It would be so much easier to think without all of them watching me.

"We should go check it out," Eve said. "Bring your *friend* his very own birthday surprise."

"Or we could just hide here and wait it out," Jack said. "The party's tomorrow. They found the easy trail, so let them spend some time sitting in the wrong place."

"Unless they were sent by Chanler," Jerek said. "He cast the curse, he's got to know we'd need the Blood List to reverse the damage. If he knows I have it and is looking for me, he might guess I'll come after him. Heliostone or no, the party would be the best time to get onto Chanler's estate."

"Then let's go check it out," Eve said. "Maybe we'll get lucky and Chanler decided to run the errand himself."

"I should go," Lincoln said. "It might be a Maree—"

"Then you're the last person who should be anywhere near that hotel," Eve said.

"Well, I'm going to stay here and not die." Jack shrugged.

"I can go," Ari said.

"You have other work to do, Ari," Jerek said. "Eve and Lincoln can go."

"And leave all of you unguarded?" Lincoln said. "No, Eve has to stay."

"Like hell, Maree."

Jerek held up his hands. "We aren't unguarded. We have

the only known, untainted magician here to protect us, and we will, in turn, protect her."

"Fine." Lincoln pushed away from the table. "Can we at least take the daggers in case it's an ambush?"

"Eve can protect you," Jerek said.

Eve coughed a laugh.

Lincoln's face sank into a scowl.

"The daggers are needed elsewhere." Jerek pulled the van keys and his phone from his pocket. "Take the van, and keep in touch."

"And be careful," Ari said. "I don't know who dug deep enough to track the fake Jerek, but whoever found Lionel James is going to be pissed as hell."

"Don't worry." Eve reached across the table, squeezing Ari's hand. "I can use my big girl teeth if I have to. Come on, Maree, let's go kick some stalker ass."

She headed up the stairs.

Lincoln followed, not bothering to say goodbye to anyone.

It's better that way. Let it lie.

"They should have finished their breakfast," Jack said. "I remember eating breakfast. I used to hate eggs."

"Good thing you don't have to eat them," Grace said.

"Fair." Jack leaned back in his chair.

"So now what?" Grace asked.

"You and I go work on your spells," Jerek said.

Fatigue seemed to settle on Grace's shoulders at the mere thought, but she nodded.

"I'll play tailor of mystery," Jack said. "Wanna join the fun, Ari?"

"I have a little work to do. But I trust you. We'll all look fabulous." Ari slid the daggers off the table.

"Where are you going to put them?" Grace asked.

"Far away from our Maree." Ari headed toward the stairs.

Trust her. Above all, you can trust her.

"Ari," Jerek called after her. "Be back soon."

"Pinky promise."

With a flick of her blond hair, she disappeared up the steps.

55

Eve

Eve stared out the window, watching the countryside pass by.

Schools with wide lawns and sports fields with well-kept stands. Houses with cheerfully painted front doors. People walking their dogs and going for runs.

"You could have driven, you know," Lincoln said, breaking the fifteen minutes of silence.

"I've only ever driven Gran's truck," Eve said. "And that wasn't my favorite. I'd rather run where I need to go."

"The hotel is fifteen miles from the beach house," Lincoln said. "How long would it take you to run there?"

"Isn't there some sort of Maree formula for that?"

"Not really. I know changed, the max speed for a werewolf is a two-minute mile. Unchanged, four."

"Well, there you go."

"But that doesn't mean all wolves are that fast."

"Only that you should be prepared for a pack to move at that speed if you're trying to attack." Anger rumbled in Eve's chest. "The study was tactical, not personal. I understand."

"Our job is to protect Weres, not hurt them."

"Unless they go rogue. Or you have to run and hide."

The area around them changed from sweet little homes to shops and offices.

"Do all wolves hate the Maree this much, or is it just your pack?" Lincoln asked.

"Is that not in your Maree files?" Eve twisted in her seat to face him.

"No."

"Well, I don't know either. Cross-pack communication doesn't tend to be friendly."

Lincoln rubbed his thumbs across the top of the steering wheel, his lips locked in a straight line.

"What?" Eve asked.

"Just wondering what the odds are it's one of yours or one of mine."

At least he's smart.

"I'd give us a third each." Eve leaned back against the side window. "One third pack come for revenge after Gran took out so much of Harry's misplaced rebellion. One third Maree come to take you away for going rogue."

"And one third Chanler come to kill us before we can out him and try to undo all his destruction."

"Yep."

The blinker clicked a maddening rhythm as Lincoln waited to turn left.

"What do we do about it?" Lincoln asked.

"If it's one of Harry's, we kill them before they kill us and run like hell before the cops come."

"Same for Chanler."

"And your brothers in arms?"

Lincoln glanced toward her. Wrinkles pinched between his eyebrows. "You want me to say we should kill them."

"I'm looking for an answer, not a lie to keep me cooperating."

"I don't know." He looked back toward the road. "If a Maree has been sent to collect me for breaking my oath, I can't blame them. Not the knight, they'd only be following orders, and not the Knight's Council for sending them. I have broken my oath. They'd be right to take me to stand trial."

"I get it."

Lincoln's worry lines shifted as he glanced toward her again. "You do?"

"Sure. If the Maree sent some innocent kid to come drag you home, it would be wrong to kill them for not knowing enough to stay out of our way. But we can't let them interfere. And it's not like we've got enough people to leave someone behind to sit on a prisoner while we rob Chanler."

"I know."

"That leaves us where?"

Lincoln let out a shuddering breath. "Hoping someone has come to kill us."

Eve's stomach shook, jostling a laugh out of her before she knew anything was funny.

Lincoln laughed with her, the low sound of it lighter than Eve had thought possible.

Tears trickled down her cheeks, and she gasped for air.

They pulled into the parking lot of the hotel. Well-tended grounds and tastefully lit signs greeted guests. The yellow van stuck out amongst the classy cars of the other patrons.

Eve's laughter died as Lincoln turned the key and the engine shuddered to a stop.

"If things get messy, we can't tell Grace." Eve brushed the tears from her cheeks. "The others can take it, but—"

"We can't risk her panicking this close to the party."

A mother dragged three giant suitcases toward the front of the hotel, two bickering children following in her wake.

"Any tips for how to do this in your fancy training?" Eve asked.

Lincoln reached under his seat, pulling out a box. He flipped open the lid and grabbed a handful of cash. "Try asking nicely and go from there."

"Sounds like as good a plan as any." Eve instinctively touched her pendant before opening her door.

Lincoln crossed around to her side of the van and held out his hand. "Might as well practice for tomorrow."

"We aren't going to the party as a couple."

"But we're going to have to be in character." Lincoln kept his hand out. "Think of it this way, if you can pretend to like me, you can do anything."

"More fancy Maree training?" Eve took his hand, placing her palm against his.

"More like my mom trying to get eight kids to be nice to each other."

Eve let out a whistle. "Brave woman."

"Orders from the Knight's Council. Knighthood has to be inherited. We lost too many searching for a way to save the feu, so the repopulation order came down."

Eve's throat tightened. "I'm sorry."

"Don't be. My youngest brother's only two, and if the way he charms people now is any indication, I'm going to be related to the first President of the World."

"Are Maree even allowed to run for office?"

"If anyone can find a way, it'll be little William."

Eve let her laugh ring out as Lincoln opened the lobby door.

The mother of two stood at the lobby desk, her face turning red as she argued with the concierge about early check-in times. In the far corner of the lobby, an old man poured himself a cup of coffee.

The single elevator had been tucked against the opposite wall with the fire stairs right beside.

Eve took a deep breath, scenting the air. Orange cleaner, stale smoke, coffee, liquor, microwave popcorn, and domesticated dogs.

"Not one of mine," Eve said.

"Are you positive?"

"Unless they sent a non-wolf as a proxy." Eve smiled at the concierge as she caught the harassed woman's eye.

"Is it a Maree?" Lincoln raised one eyebrow.

"There's too much somb stink for me to tell."

"I really am sorry, ma'am," the concierge said. "But there is no check-in available before 2pm."

"Well congratulations, my children are going to destroy your lobby." The mother dragged her bags over to the beige couch in the center of the space.

In the moment it took Eve and Lincoln to step up to the counter, the kids had already begun running circles around the polished tile floor.

The concierge closed her eyes for a moment, then pressed a bright smile onto her face. "How can I help you today?"

"Hi." Lincoln reached across the counter, shaking the concierge's hand. "We received your message about a birthday guest for our friend Lionel James. We just wanted to make sure our guest was settling in okay."

The woman's smile widened, making her look like a badly painted, overly-excited doll. "Your guest is in room 304."

"I'm so sorry to ask." Eve leaned closer to the desk. "But do you happen to know our friend's name? I've been so busy arranging guests, I've completely lost track of who might be checking in here."

A hundred-dollar bill appeared in Lincoln's palm. He slid the bill across the desk.

"Mr. Roscoe," the concierge whispered. "Nice gentleman. I don't think I've seen such stunning blue eyes on a handsome boy like that in a long time."

"Could I get a key to his room?" Eve winked. "I haven't seen Roscoe in a very long time."

"That's not usually allowed..." The concierge's protest faded away as Lincoln slid another hundred across the counter.

She picked up a key card and handed it to Eve. "Pleasure doing business."

"I thought you said there was no early check-in." The mother stormed over to the desk.

Eve ducked out of her way, leading Lincoln toward the staircase.

"She had the key pre-made," Lincoln said. "How much did Ari pay her?"

"Does it matter?" Eve let go of Lincoln's hand and pushed open the stairwell door. "Holden's got more money than he'll be able to spend in his lifetime."

"I bet a lot of people think that until they run out."

They fell silent as they climbed to the third floor.

The hairs on the back of Eve's neck prickled as instinct beyond the human part of her blood warned her something was off.

What the hell came looking for us?

Eve paused at the door to the third floor, waiting for someone to sprint up the stairs ready to attack.

Nothing.

Lincoln stepped past her, opening the door.

She didn't have it in her to bristle.

A middle-aged woman in plaid pajamas wandered down the hall, squinting against the artificial light, ice bucket in hand.

Eve gave the woman a sympathetic smile and gripped Lincoln's wrist, holding him in place until the woman closed the door to room 321 behind her.

They walked silently toward room 304.

I wish I could take off my boots.

Can't afford to use the moonstone in here anyway.

Maybe.

They stopped in front of 304.

Eve held up the room key then mimed kicking in the door.

Lincoln pointed to the room key.

Eve shrugged and slipped the key into the slot. The lock beeped. She turned the handle and shoved the door open.

Lincoln leapt in front of her as a voice shouted, "What the hell do you think you're—"

In a blur of blond hair, Lincoln knocked a boy onto the bed, pinning him down with a knee pressed into his back.

"I thought I was supposed to be in charge of knocking people down," Eve said.

"You were on door duty," Lincoln said. "It seemed like a good division of labor."

"Get off me!" the boy growled.

"He doesn't seem very polite." Eve shut the door, fastening all the locks behind her. "Or very smart."

A rolling suitcase lay open on the floor. A laptop and the remains of a pizza waited on the desk.

Eve knelt behind Lincoln, feeling the boy's pockets for weapons. She found nothing but a cellphone with a cracked screen.

"You stalk us and don't bother bringing any weapons?" Eve checked under the pillows and in the nightstand drawers.

"I'm not stalking you, ginger," the boy said.

"Watch it." Lincoln twisted the boy's arm behind his back.

The boy whimpered.

"It's okay," Eve laughed. "I've been called way worse than *ginger*."

"Please, you have the wrong guy."

"Really?" Lincoln looked to Eve. "Should we let him go? He says we've got the wrong guy."

"It's true," the boy said.

"So somebody else has been stalking Jerek Holden?" Eve said.

The boy stopped fidgeting.

"Oh, so you *have* been looking for Jerek?" Lincoln twisted the boy's arm again.

"If that son of a bitch sent you here to beat the shit out of me then fine, just do it. Two against one. Sounds right to me."

"I'm not going to beat the shit out of you. Yet." Eve moved to the side of the bed, kneeling to be eye-level with the boy. "First, we chat. I find out why you're here, then I decide if you're going to limp out of here, be taken out in an ambulance, or if I'm going to have to sneak your corpse out in a laundry cart."

"This is some kind of a sick joke," the boy said.

"You know, I never really thought about the practicalities, but I think you're right," Lincoln said. "He wouldn't fit in his suitcase, so a laundry cart really would be the best option."

"Sometimes movies get it right," Eve said.

"Don't kill me," the boy said. "Ari will be pissed if you do."

Lincoln glanced to Eve.

"Ari?" Eve said. "I know Ari. I think she'd like the laundry cart idea."

"She wouldn't want you to hurt me," the boy said. "Ask her. Ari will tell you not to kill me."

"Maybe," Eve said. "But if I ask what she wants, I lose the fun of deciding for myself."

"How do you know Ari?" Lincoln dug his knee into the boy's back.

"Ask her if you want to know," the boy said.

Lincoln switched his grip on the boy, pressing his thumb toward the back of his hand.

"She's my girlfriend," the boy shouted. "I'm Ford. Ari is my girlfriend. I'm only here to convince her to come home."

56

Lincoln

Lincoln tightened the last knot, securing Ford to the pipes under the bathroom sink.

Ford glowered at them from the floor.

"We'll be right back." Eve took Lincoln's arm, pulling him back to the bedroom and shutting the door behind him.

"We need to call Ari." Lincoln pulled the phone from his pocket. "Figure out what she wants us to do."

"Do you believe him?"

Lincoln closed his eyes, trying to picture Ari and Ford as a pair. The vision sank a stone in his stomach.

"I have no idea." Lincoln dialed Ari's number.

Jerek answered after the first ring. "Is everything all right?"

"Define *all right*," Lincoln said. "I need to talk to Ari."

"She's indisposed," Jerek said. "What do you need?"

Lincoln dragged a hand over his face. "We found the person who found fake you. He says he's her boyfriend."

Jerek let out a muttered string of profanity.

"Have you met him?" Lincoln asked.

"Ford?" Jerek said. "I've met him."

"Blond-haired, blue-eyed?" Lincoln said.

Eve leaned close to speak into the phone. "Looks like he and Ari were weirdly cast out of the same mold?"

"That's Ford," Jerek said. "Did he say why he followed her across the country?"

"To bring his girlfriend home," Eve said. "Could be romantic if it wasn't creepy and chauvinistic."

"What do you want us to do?" The tension in Lincoln's shoulders tightened as he waited for Jerek to speak.

"Make sure he doesn't have anyone else with him. Then bring him here," Jerek said. "We can always lock him in a closet while we go to the party."

"Is there anything we should know about him?" Eve asked. "Does he have claws? Will he shoot sparks into the poor van's engine?"

"None of the above," Jerek said. "The only thing Ford is capable of is hacking. Sorry to disappoint either of you, but I'm afraid you managed to catch a somb."

"You have got to be kidding me."

"We can't bring him back to the house," Lincoln said. "We're working on feu business. We can't have a somb there."

"We'll keep him isolated," Jerek said. "Besides, the fairy is out of the woods on this one. Ford found out about the feu a while ago."

The tension in Lincoln's shoulders crept down to his fists.

"Just get him here as quietly as you can," Jerek said.

"I'll gag him if I have to," Eve said.

"Make it happen." With a beep, the phone went silent.

"We can't do this," Lincoln said. "He's a somb. We can't put him in Jerek's van, let alone bring him to a house with Jack."

"What about me?" Eve crossed her arms. "Am I not as big a risk as Jack?"

"You're a bigger risk, but he's already seen you." Lincoln slipped Jerek's phone back into his pocket.

What the hell were you thinking, Ariel Love?

"Let's tell our new friend we won't kill him if he stays quiet." Eve opened the bathroom door.

"She told you, didn't she?" Ford said. "Ari told you I'm her boyfriend so you can't hurt me."

"No such luck." Eve loosened the strips of towel, untying Ford from the pipes. "Ari wasn't interested in talking to us about you, but we were told to move you without killing you if it could be done discreetly. Would you like to walk nicely out of this hotel, or do you want my friend and me to arm wrestle over who gets to play piñata with your head? Your choice."

"Is Ari going to be where you're taking me?" Ford asked.

"I can't promise you'll get to see her, but yes," Lincoln said.

"Then I'll come quietly." Ford stood up straight and puffed up his chest, though he still barely came up to Lincoln's nose. "But if I find out you hurt Ari—"

"Ari's safe," Eve said. "It's your own neck you need to be worried about."

"Can I pack my things?" Ford asked.

"Like hell," Eve said.

"I'll grab them." Lincoln took the laptop and zipped it into the suitcase. "Ari will want to look at how you found us."

"Finding you wasn't that hard," Ford said. "When Ari went missing, I knew Holden had to be behind it. I tracked her passport to the east coast. Then I was sure. Took me a bit to figure out how Holden was paying for things, but he should have tried harder if he didn't want me to find her."

"You are such a creep." Eve locked her arm through Ford's, holding his bicep with her other hand.

He grimaced as she gripped him.

"Be good while we get through the lobby," Eve said.

Lincoln held open the door and followed them out into the hall.

"You didn't find Jerek, by the way." Lincoln pressed the elevator button. "He never checked in to this hotel. Ari made a payment with the Lionel James alias's credit card in case anyone was trying to find us."

"She's brilliant." Ford closed his eyes, a look of absolute rapture filling his face. "God, I love that girl. She must have known I'd be looking for her."

Eve dragged Ford into the elevator.

Lincoln stepped in behind, pressing the lobby button.

"Yeah, not so much," Eve said. "We thought you were going to be someone way cooler and harder to handle."

57

Ari

Ari stopped at the edge of the waves, enjoying one more moment in the water.

"I'll come back soon," she whispered.

The sea grass caressed her ankles as she walked up the path that led to the house.

Lincoln waited on the front porch, leaning against the door with his arms crossed.

"What is it, Daddy?" Ari skipped the rest of the way to the house. "The sun's only just about to go down, so I don't think I missed curfew."

"We found the person who found fake us," Lincoln said.

Ari rocked back on her heels. "And you want me to find a place to lock them up, or a place to hide the body?"

"Oh, we've already got Ford Roscoe locked in the closet in Eve's room."

Ari blinked at Lincoln, trying to find a way mesh the words said with the person speaking.

"Ford Roscoe?" Ari said.

"Yep, your boyfriend tracked you down, and now Eve's guarding the closet door."

"You have got to be kidding me." Ari shoved Lincoln aside, opened the front door of the house, and sprinted up the stairs.

"Ari," Lincoln called from the bottom of the steps.

"That prying, selfish, low-level, obsessive prick." Ari fought to keep herself from screaming.

"Ari!" Ford shouted the moment Ari stormed into Eve's room.

Eve sat leaning against the closet door, reading a book. "Hey, Ari. Found your creepy boyfriend."

"Ex-boyfriend," Ari said.

"That's not true, and you know it." Ford pounded on the closet door.

"We weren't even really dating," Ari said.

"I've told you a hundred times I'm in love with you," Ford said.

"That doesn't imply dating." Ari dug her fingers through her hair.

"Should I let him out?" Eve's voice shook with an ill-concealed laugh.

"Am I allowed to strangle him if you do?"

Eve shrugged.

"Ford, why are you here?" Ari sank down onto the bed.

"They brought me from the hotel. That was an excellent trail you laid. I really thought I had found you."

"But why were you looking for me in the first place?" Ari said.

"I tried calling, but you didn't answer." Ford's words came out muffled, like he had pressed his face to the door. "I checked all the boards, and you'd gone dark. I even went to see your mom."

"You shouldn't have done that." Ari gripped the seashell-print bedspread.

"I was worried about you, Ari. Your mom said you were interning in New York, so I knew you'd run off. I had to look, you know I did."

"You really didn't."

"Well, it looks like I was right to be worried," Ford said. "Was that a Maree who almost broke my arm at the hotel?"

Eve sat up straight, furrowing her brow as she watched Ari.

"And, from the look of the pendant she's wearing, the girl guarding the door to this surprisingly musty closet is a werewolf," Ford pressed on. "I don't know what Jerek's roped you into, but if there's a wolf and a knight working together, I'm glad I found you."

Shit.

Shit. Shit. Shit.

"You have no idea how much damage you could do here." Ari made herself let go of the bedspread. "People could die because you turned up at the wrong time, Ford."

"As long as it's not you who gets hurt," Ford said.

"Ford, I have to go talk to people downstairs," Ari said. "Stay in the damn closet or I'll feed you to the vampire."

"Ari?" Eve whispered at the same moment Ford said, "You shouldn't be getting involved with vampires."

"Just stay."

Eve growled.

"Not you." Ari jumped off the bed and headed out into the hall, going down the stairs without waiting for Eve to catch up. Lincoln waited at the bottom of the steps, arms still folded.

"Oh, stop with the disappointment routine." She flicked Lincoln on the nose. "Jerek. Jerek!"

"He's in the basement with Grace," Lincoln said, "who we're going to have a really hard time convincing shouldn't tell her dads about the feu now that you told your boyfriend."

"First of all"—Ari stalked to basement door—"not my boyfriend. Second, I didn't tell him about the feu. Your precious Council did."

"What?" Eve chased Ari down the basement stairs.

"Jerek." Ari didn't stop at the bottom of the steps. She ran right up to Jerek and spun him away from Grace mid-sentence. "You let them bring him here?"

"I wasn't sure what else to do." Jerek shrugged. "Death seemed like too stiff a penalty for being obsessed with protecting you, but leaving him to his own devices could ruin our plans and we've come too far for that to be allowed."

"You told your boyfriend about the feu?" Grace stormed around the ping-pong table, fury dancing in her eyes as she glared at Ari. "After all the shit you fed me about having to keep the secret? After lying to my parents and keeping me from contacting them for days?"

"I never told Ford anything!" Ari's voice ricocheted around the basement and slammed back into her own ears.

"Damn, girl." Jack gave a whistle from his seat in the corner.

"Then how does he know about wolves and the Maree?" Eve stood halfway down the stairs, her arms crossed and jaw set.

Lincoln had taken a ludicrously similar pose one step above her.

Ari couldn't even bring herself to laugh at their posturing. "You can stop with the interrogation routine as neither of you actually has a right to question me."

Jerek took her hand, kissed it, and held on tight, anchoring her against the chaos. "Does he know about Chanler and the heliostone?"

"Of course not," Ari said. "You and I are smart enough to keep our business off the internet."

"Then we lock him up until after the party," Jerek said. "We'll leave him in the closet with food, water, and a good book to read. Grace can work an incantation to keep him trapped. When it's all done, we'll let him out and send him home."

"With knowledge of the feu?" Lincoln said. "I'm willing to stretch the rules to mend the Fracture, but letting a somb who knows about all of us run free is pushing too far."

"You're right," Ari said. "Let's just kill him. That'll fix everything. Glad I'm hanging out with the good guys. Gotta love those daring knights who want to slaughter innocent people."

Eve snorted a laugh.

"Don't pretend you're any better," Ari said.

"We're not the ones who told him about the feu," Eve said.

"Neither is Ari," Jerek said. "Everyone sit."

"Why?" Lincoln said.

"Because this feels like a standoff, and quite frankly the lot of you are emotionally exhausting." Jerek sank into a bright-blue painted chair.

Ari sat to his right, not letting go of Jerek's hand as the rest moved into their places.

"Would you like to explain, or shall I?" Jerek said as Lincoln finally sat in the bright pink chair farthest from Ari.

"You wouldn't get it right." Ari shut her eyes for a moment before looking to the rest of the group. "The feu are morons is basically what it boils down to."

Jack raised an eyebrow, but the rest only glared.

"Before the Fracture, there was all kinds of magical communication," Ari said. "But unless you were a magician, there wasn't anything better than the good old internet. Maree started using digital communication, then the wolves jumped on, vampires, divs, everybody had their own encrypted message boards on the internet. After the Fracture, even magicians hopped on. How do you think Chanler stayed in touch to gather his hoard of artifacts and advertise the opening of his museum?

"Sure, the sites are secure and hidden in tiny corners of the web where no one who doesn't know what they're looking for should ever think to poke around, but that doesn't make the sites impenetrable. The feu got so used to their magic being untouchable by sombs, they thought the magic of fancy coding would protect them, too."

"It didn't," Jerek said. "Not as the Maree or any of us had hoped."

"I'd been patrolling on the sites for years," Ari said. "I'd only noticed a few names coming through that didn't belong. I tracked most of them to make sure they didn't go spreading what they'd found. Crashed everything they held most dear if they did. Ford was the first one to start tracking me."

"He was stalking you?" Eve asked.

"More like digital cat and mouse." Ari shrugged. "Hacker-style flirting. I wasn't even positive he was a somb until I met him in person."

"Did you crash his life?" Lincoln asked.

"I burned through his system three times," Ari said. "He may lack my digital finesse, but when it comes to straight up information, he's as good as I am. Depending on the task, he might even be better."

"And now it's all in his brain," Jack said. "You'd have to hack his head off to actually remove the information."

"Bingo," Ari said.

"You should have told the Maree," Lincoln said.

"And let them lock him up or worse for finding information they left unguarded?" Ari said. "Never."

"We can't just let him walk around knowing about the feu," Lincoln said. "It puts all of us in danger."

"It doesn't." Ari buried her face in her hands.

"What puts the feu more in danger is the information the Maree never sought to protect," Jerek said. "I may not enjoy Ford's company, but I personally guarantee he will never try to out the feu."

"People always promise not to out you," Jack said. "Words slip out by accident, people get tired of keeping a secret. What happens when Ari breaks up with him?"

"I've done it," Ari said. "I've broken up with him four times."

"Six," Jerek corrected.

"He may think he's in love with me, but really it's the feu." Ari tipped her head back, wishing the right words could be written on the ceiling as clearly as they would pop up on her computer screen. "He's an outsider who's spent his life searching for something that would mean he could belong somewhere, anywhere. Finding out about the feu—"

"Doesn't make him one of us," Eve said.

"No, but it makes him the keeper of a secret thousands of people are desperate to protect. He's been helping me crash sombs who find the feu for the last two years. He is the protector of the feu none of you knew existed." Ari looked to Eve. "People have found traces of the pack's mountain, and he erased it." She turned to Grace. "All those sports championships coming out of Sun Palms High? Yeah, people seeking mutants had pinged your school as a hot spot. You can thank Ford and me for stopping the three middle-aged men who wanted to find the freak and use them to make bank betting on pro games."

Grace shivered, cupping a hand over her mouth like she might be sick.

"The Maree aren't discreet enough when they move knights en masse," Ari pressed on. "And there's a reason blood dates have been getting easier to find in Vegas. The web chatter screams that Vegas is where the real hematolagnia action thrives. All of you are so damn cocky, and Ford has been spending his time trying to protect us. So yeah, it's super inconvenient that he showed up now, but if any of you turn him in to the Maree, I will add you to the FBI most wanted list and make sure you spend the rest of your days hiding out in a dank corner. Am I clearly understood?"

Jerek squeezed her hand.

She took a shuddering breath.

Air. I need more air. I don't belong up here.

"Okay," Jack said. "I'm all about protecting the unsung hero. If you say he's one of the good guys, I trust you."

"How did sombs find the pack's mountain?" Eve said.

"You'll have to ask Ford," Ari said. "I was working on Grace, so he ran point on that one."

"I can't believe sombs almost found us." Eve dug her fingers into her curls. "If people came after the pack, it would be a massacre."

You don't even know which side would lose more.

Ari bit her lips together.

"I won't tell," Grace said. "And I get why it's different than my dads. Making them keep what I am a secret would be a burden to both of them, and I'd be tossing them into danger they couldn't defend themselves from. I can't believe some random guy's been protecting us."

"The Maree should know," Lincoln said.

Ari glared at him, wishing she had something within reach to throw. "If you even think of turning him in—"

"If our online security is that bad, it needs to be fixed," Lincoln said. "Even if Ford turns in everything he's found anonymously. Once the Fracture is mended, the feu are going to come out of the woodwork. It's going to be a golden age for magic, and that'll mean more online chatter. The knights monitor the internet, but not on this scale. We have to rethink the way the Maree have been protecting the feu."

"Well," Jerek said, "if you make it through tomorrow without being banished, perhaps you can put out some feelers for the Maree hiring a somb to protect their digital information."

Ari laughed and sank back in her chair.

"We'll keep him locked in the closet," Eve said. "I don't think he'll like it, but if I promise not to gut him, he might see reason."

"We should let him come out for a bit," Grace said. "He could at least eat dinner with us. The more he sees us as decent people, the less likely he is to ruin our digital lives forever."

"You learn quick." Ari winked at Grace.

"I'm going to go for the unpopular opinion here." Jack stood.

"You're not biting him," Ari said.

"Ha ha. We've been working on a plan for six," Jack said. "And it's a good plan, but it's tight. Ari's part especially, and none of us can fill in for her. There's too many working pieces, and if one person gets waylaid, we're screwed."

A trickle of realization tightened Ari's stomach. "No."

"When life hands you someone who's willing to aid and abet, it seems wrong to lock the willing set of hands away," Jack said. "Trust me. I'm the only actual criminal here."

"He's not feu," Lincoln said. "Not turning him in is one thing. Using him to help steal the heliostone is pushing way too far."

"Is it?" Jerek leaned back in his seat. "It would free Ari up."

"Free me up for what?" Ari said.

"To keep an eye on things," Jerek said. "Make sure nothing goes wrong. Get us out of whatever trouble we haven't seen lurking inside Chanler's estate."

"I don't like it," Lincoln said.

"For once, I agree with the Maree," Ari said. "We have a plan, we shouldn't change it, not this late in the game."

"Eve?" Jerek said.

"I'm with Jerek," Eve said. "I'm the muscle, not the planner."

"Grace?" Ari said.

"I..." Grace rubbed her knuckles on her bottom lip. "If Ford takes your place, then you could be closer to me and Jerek. It's always felt like we were going to be too exposed. This would fix that."

"The plan doesn't need fixing," Ari said.

"Four to two it does." Jerek pushed away from the table. "I'll go see if Ford is willing."

"Everyone else might as well stay here." Ari pressed her palms to the table. "Ford's going to jump at the chance. Jerek will be back down with the new member of the Slippery Seven in two minutes."

"I was going to bet on three." Jerek disappeared up the stairs.

"You're the one that vouched for him," Jack said.

Ari dug her nails into the table's chipped, green paint. "Vouching for someone and wanting to drag them into danger are two very different things."

58

Jack

Jack half-listened as Jerek explained the former plan to Ford. Then the others chimed in as they redistributed duties, making sure Ford understood exactly where he was meant to be.

Ford made suggestions.

Ari rolled her eyes.

I can't even tell if she loves him. Jack felt a flicker of disappointment at the lack of certain love connection.

But poor Ford was probably better off if Ari didn't love him, even if he couldn't see it yet.

"No one knows your face," Eve said. "Which will be a huge advantage."

"And save me quite a bit of time," Jerek added.

They spread out the map, using board game pieces to mark where each of them belonged. Jack's place was marked by Miss Scarlet. It felt right on more than one level.

He went back to stitching the lockpicks into the lining of his jacket. His fingers enjoyed the tedious motion.

"You really mean to tell me that the dolt never noticed what he had in his own collection?" Ford asked. "What kind of idiot curator did he hire?"

"Callen LeBlanc," Ari said, "curator and asset manager for the entire Chanler estate. Either he's too dumb to know he's working for the devil or too crooked to care."

"It would be nice to know which," Ford said.

"Well, if you run into him, be sure to ask," Eve said.

"Alright." Ford turned back to the map.

He might actually be serious.

Jerek and Ford kept talking as the others rounded up dinner.

Jack stayed sitting beside them, altering Eve's dress.

There was never a stench of fear wafting around Ford, only the scent of fervent belief, which was somehow more terrifying.

You may have backed the wrong horse this time, Vegas.

They ran through the plan again as the others ate, bouncing the pieces around as though tossing a ball, testing everyone's ability to catch the pattern their lives depended on.

"Jack and Jerek arrive first," Ari said. "They blend in and wait for the party to begin in earnest."

"The rest of us arrive in fashion," Eve said. "Stroll right in like we own the place."

"And everyone will believe that you should." Jack moved on to taking in Grace's dress. "I'm going to have to scrounge something for Ford."

"He'll look magnificent, I'm sure," Ari said.

"Obviously," Jack said.

"Then Jack will find me," Ford said. "And we sneak away to work my own brand of magic."

Jack grabbed a slip of paper and began sketching. Something he could build from supplies in the house that would fit in at a fabulous party.

They kept circling through the details over and over. Jack ran upstairs, broke into the locked attic, and raided the dusty trunks for material. When he got down, they were still hammering through the plan ad nauseum.

"The trick is keeping the room clear," Grace said.

"That isn't for you to worry about," Lincoln said. "I'll make sure you have the time."

It went on until after midnight. Ari declared the meeting over and dragged Ford from the room. The rest drifted away to sleep in their own corners of the house.

Jack didn't need sleep. He wouldn't need to rest for a few more days. So he waited in the basement, sewing. Counting the stitches until sunrise.

59

Ari

She yanked the covers up to her chin and dragged herself as close to the edge of the mattress as she could.

Ford rolled over, bouncing the bed. "I really was worried about you."

"I know," Ari said. "And I really am grateful someone in the world cares enough to freak out when they think I'm dead."

"I do." Ford reached out, touching her arm.

"Me agreeing to let you risk your life does not mean we're back together. Not even a little."

"I know." He didn't move his hand. "But I'd rather be here not dating you than at home worrying about you."

"You're impossible." Ari rolled over. "You realize this is dangerous, right? Like, if Chanler catches us, we are all going to die."

Ford shrugged his top shoulder. "I've spent the last ten years reading about the feu online, and now I'm going to walk into the

Museum of Magic. Cut protecting you out of the picture, and I'd still have to say yes to going, Ari."

"That makes me feel a little better about your potential demise."

"Good." Ford tucked her hair behind her ear. "Now get some sleep. We've got to save the future of the people who don't want us around tomorrow."

"They do want me around." Ari rolled back over to face the hall.

Someone walked past the door, their shadow setting shapes to dance on the floor.

"They love the useful bits of you," Ford said. "I love all of you, even the broken pieces. You're braver than any of them, Ari. You're the only one who's going to lose something if Jerek actually fixes the Fracture."

Tears stung the corners of her eyes. She shut them tight, forcing her breathing to become even, relaxing her shoulders like he would believe she'd fallen asleep.

"Just remember I'm here," Ford said. "No matter how things turn out, I'll always be here."

60

Jerek

He hadn't brought a sweater to guard against the chill night air. He didn't want to be comfortable.

He loved the goose bumps on his skin. The shiver of his shoulders. Sure signs that he, Jerek Holden, was alive.

He sat on the balcony facing the sea, waiting to watch the sunrise.

Minutes ticked by, but he didn't mind. He savored each moment of the night, just as he would cherish the dawn.

A creak sounded behind him as the door to the upstairs hall opened, allowing another person into his sanctuary.

He felt the glow of Grace's magic, like heat flowing through his chest, seconds before she spoke.

"Is it bad if I'm glad I'm not the only one who couldn't sleep?"

"No," Jerek said. "It's a big day. It's normal to be nervous."

Then why aren't I?

Grace stepped out to the very edge of the balcony. "Can I sit, or would you rather be alone?"

"Sit," Jerek said before his mind had time to consider the joys of solitude.

"It's nice out here." Grace pulled the comforter from her bed tight around her shoulders.

"It is. I've always liked the ocean, and the sunrise."

As if the sun had heard his compliment, her first orange rays burst up over the horizon, wobbling on the water like a foal fighting through its first steps.

"We can do this, right?" Grace asked. "I mean, I know we have a plan and..."

Jerek reached out and took her hand, lacing his fingers through hers. The warmth of her magic raced up his arm, banishing the goose bumps from his skin.

"We can do this," Jerek said. "Our contingency plans have contingency plans."

"But what if"—Grace whispered—"what if everything goes right, and we get to the Caster's Fate and we get the heliostone out, and I can't do the incantation?"

"You can. All you have to do is say the words and channel the magic. I'll do the rest."

"I still don't know if I can."

"I do. I'm sure enough for both of us. Don't worry about the magic. That's like worrying if you'll know how to breathe fresh, clean air."

The arc of the sun appeared, now confident of her place in the sky.

"It's beautiful." The tension ebbed from Grace's hand.

"The universe's promise that no matter what happens, a new day will dawn. None of us are big enough to stop the sun from rising. Not even the most powerful magicians in history could do it."

"Did they try?"

"A few." A smile touched Jerek's lips, and a weight lifted from his heart. "But none ever managed it. So the sun keeps coming up, and new days dawn. And all of us are too small to stop the world from spinning around and around."

"Tomorrow will be a lot different from today." Grace leaned her head on Jerek's shoulder. "I wonder if magicians will feel the Fracture mending right away, or if word will have to spread that magic works again."

"They'll feel it. Like their first breath of air after twelve years of drowning. Every magician alive will know as soon as it's over."

"Do you think they'll know it was us?"

"Every feu child will know our names. None of us will ever be forgotten."

The sun climbed higher. Jerek watched the color of the waves shift, trying to memorize the beauty of each shade.

61

Grace

The smooth, black silk tingled the tips of Grace's fingers.

"You look devastating." Jack peeked over her shoulder, watching her study herself in the mirror.

Pink crept into Grace's cheeks.

I'm beautiful.

"Thanks," Grace said. "You picked a wonderful dress."

The fabric twisted as it wrapped around her, draping all the way to her feet. Shots of silver broke through the plain black, sparkling even in the dull light of the basement. The neckline dove far lower than she would have been bold enough to choose for herself, and the back dipped all the way to the base of her spine, daring the eye not to stare at the warm hue of her skin.

"It's okay to think you look fabulous," Jack whispered in her ear.

"Thanks."

"Now let Ari doll you up while I deal with Wolfy McGrumpyPants." Jack shooed Grace away from the mirror.

Ari had set up shop on the ping-pong table. Curling irons, straighteners, hairpins, and more makeup than Grace had ever seen outside a store had all been lined up in a way that implied some strange order.

"Sit down, and let me work," Ari said.

"This is ridiculous." Eve stood next to the mirror in a t-shirt and underwear. "We're going to steal things. I shouldn't be wearing a full-length gown."

"It's a party. You need to blend in," Jack said.

"Then give me a sensible pantsuit. I'm the one who's expected to fight if shit hits the fan, remember? Do you really want me defending all of us in these?" Eve held up a pair of three-inch, silver stilettos.

Grace bit back a laugh.

"Don't move your head." Ari ran a brush through Grace's hair.

"This is more prep than I did for prom last year," Grace said.

"Clearly you need more feminine friends," Ari said.

Grace tried to picture it. All of them just being friends from high school. A group of quasi-misfits banding together to slog their way through the trauma of public education.

It wouldn't work. We'd never have made it through one lunch together.

"Ari." Ford ran down the stairs. "While I appreciate the subtlety in your Viva la Feu trojan, I think you could amplify its efficacy if you make a few tweaks to the bug's coding."

"Are you really criticizing the programming skills of someone who has a hot curling iron in her hand?" Ari brandished her weapon.

"I'm not criticizing." Ford cringed. "I'm being a second set of eyes."

"Bring it here." Ari looped the curling iron into Grace's hair and began chatting, in what might as well have been a foreign language, to Ford.

"Please don't burn my hair off," Grace said.

"The lack of trust." Ari flicked the back of Grace's head.

"I cannot fight in a full-length skirt," Eve said. "Give me a tux."

"You are not wearing a tux," Jack said. "You are not wearing a pantsuit. You, my ginger goddess, are going to wear this green gown whether you like it or not. If you have to go all wolf, feel free to run around the party in your underpants with your boobies out. Until that time, put on the damn dress."

"It's almost time for us to go." Jerek jogged down the steps. He wore a uniform of a black jacket and pants over a white shirt and red vest.

"You could be dressed like Jerek and me," Jack said. "Wouldn't you rather be pretty than stuck in a bad production of *Hello, Dolly*?"

"Are you ready?" Jerek asked.

"If I could get Eve into her dress, I'd be ready to get into my monkey suit." Jack glared at Eve in the mirror.

"Fine." Eve pulled off her t-shirt and tossed it aside.

"And there's her boobs," Jack said.

"Give me the dress," Eve said.

"I really want to keep your hair simple," Ari said. "It's your eyes that should pop."

"Lincoln," Jerek called up the stairs, "time for your new face."

"There, I'm in the gown," Eve said.

The emerald green practically glowed against her skin. The

fabric hugged her curves, giving her the look of an Amazon warrior.

"Wow," Grace said.

Jerek studied Eve before giving a nod. "Nicely done, Jack. Everyone will be so busy marveling over how gorgeous she is, no one will think for a moment she's dangerous."

"A wolf in sheep's clothing," Jack said. "Except the sheepskin is silk."

"Promise whatever you change on my face you'll be able to put back." Lincoln thundered down the stairs, already dressed in his tux.

"He gets pants," Eve said.

"You look beautiful." Lincoln gave Eve a little bow.

Eve rolled her eyes and stormed away from the mirror.

"Don't go too far," Ari warned. "You're up after Grace."

Eve plopped down into a chair.

"And careful how you sit in the dress." Jack wrinkled his nose at his catering uniform. "I would have loved to get you all dressed and pretty later, but I'm afraid preparing for cocktail hour calls me away."

"Are you ready?" Jerek looked to Lincoln.

Lincoln let out a long breath. "Sure." He stepped in front of the mirror.

"Chin up." Ari lifted Grace's chin to dab cream under her eyes.

"Hmm." Jerek surveyed Lincoln as a sculptor would stone.

"Hair, chin, nose, eyes." Ari waved a powder brush at Lincoln. "All of them are too Martel."

"Right." Jerek ran a hand over Lincoln's cropped hair, changing the color from dark brown to dirty blond.

"Keep him handsome," Ari said. "He needs to be attractive enough to play his role."

"You don't think he could do it on charm alone?" Jack straightened his red tie.

"Never," Eve laughed.

Lincoln flinched as Jerek flicked his eyelids, changing his irises from brown to vivid green.

"Sexy." Ari grabbed a tube of pink and started on Grace's cheeks.

"This is where it gets a bit more difficult." Jerek pinched the bridge of Lincoln's nose. As he pulled his fingers apart, the skin seemed to widen, leaving a slight bump behind. He ran his hands along Lincoln's cheeks, sinking them just a bit, and poked him in the chin, creating a cleft.

"What do you think?" Jerek spun Lincoln to face the group.

"They could be related, but it's not Lincoln," Eve said.

"I agree," Ford said. "Different enough, but not like botched plastic surgery."

"Pink up his lips a bit," Ari said. "We need him to look excruciatingly kissable."

Jerek squinted at Lincoln. "Fair." He brushed his fingers along Lincoln's lips, leaving them an enviable shade of deep pink.

"Like a berry ripe for the picking." Jack stepped in front of the mirror, brushing off the sleeves of his catering uniform.

"Looking good," Eve said.

"My first day of honest work and we're going to steal something," Jack said. "Somehow, it feels right."

"Eyes closed," Ari said.

Grace shut her eyes, trying not to flinch as Ari used brushes and fingertips on her lids.

"A little darker on the hair," Ford said. "No, too much."

"Maybe add a little plump to your cheeks," Eve said. "More. You don't want anyone to suspect you've spent your days inside plotting a heist."

"That's good," Lincoln said.

"And open." Ari tipped her head, examining her handiwork.

The boy in front of the mirror turned to look at Grace.

Reason told her it was Jerek, but her heart sank as she looked into his now dark brown eyes.

I miss the sea-blue.

His plump, rosy cheeks gave him the look of a worry-free seventeen-year-old. One who hadn't taken the fate of the feu on his own young shoulders. His now dark brown hair swept perfectly to the side in a way Jerek never quite managed.

"What do you think?" Jerek asked.

"It's perfect," Grace said. "I wouldn't even know you."

"Good." Jerek smiled, crinkling the corners of his eyes.

At least that's the same.

"We should go," Jerek said.

"What about Ari?" Eve said. "She went into the CFH. Aren't you going to make her a brunette?"

"Changing my features is beyond the powers of a mere mortal like Jerek Holden," Ari said. "I'll have to rely on a centuries-old weapon to hide myself."

"What?" Fear tumbled in Grace's stomach.

"Makeup, my dear." Ari held up a palate of shimmering eye shadow. "And I took a massive personal hit by choosing a scarlet gown instead of my signature pink, so clearly I'll be completely incognito. Besides, I'm not a Holden or a Maree. No one is going to be looking for me."

"Maybe hit up the contour palate. You're pretty enough for people to remember you even without a fancy family name." Jack lifted hangers of clothes from the edge of the stairs and held them out to Ford.

A black blazer, white shirt, kilt, and pouch hung together.

"Congratulations, Ford," Jack said. "You're Scottish tonight.

Please don't argue. You did crash the Good Guy Gang last minute."

"Still not the right name," Ari said.

"Are you kidding, it's great!" Ford took the hangers. "I've always wanted to wear a kilt."

"See how easy it can be, Eve?" Jack said.

"Hand him three-inch heels and see how he feels," Eve said.

"He'd be thrilled for a chance to show off his calves," Ari laughed.

"I'm ready," Jack said.

"Right." Jerek looked around the basement. "Well, we'll see you all at the party."

The flurry of preparation froze. The air in the basement hung heavy with the weight of doubt and the desperate need for it not be to time for them all to separate.

We'll never act if we wait to be ready.

"Let's go save the feu," Jack said.

"Ari." Jerek took a step closer to her.

"Don't worry." Ari waved him toward the stairs. "Just save me some good hors d'oeuvres."

Jerek smiled, but the wrinkles didn't crease the corners of his eyes this time. "Will do."

Jack climbed into the garment bag he'd lined with layers of space blankets.

"It would be easier for me to carry you if I weren't in a dress." Eve zipped Jack into the bag and hoisted him over her shoulder.

"But see how capable you remain even when glamorous?" Jack's voice faded as Eve carried him up the stairs.

Jerek nodded to the group and headed up the steps, closing the door behind him.

62

Jerek

The view from the bridge to Aquidneck Island should have been breathtaking. Jerek wanted to enjoy the sun sparkling off the water and the breadth of the waves far beneath him. But his capacity for joy had drifted away hours ago.

It's for the best. Nothing to do now but succeed.

"I wonder what people will think," Jack said from under the seat.

"About what?"

"The fact that the feu were saved by teenagers," Jack said. "I wonder if the adults will have the decency to feel guilty about not fixing the Fracture themselves."

"There are some things adults aren't capable of," Jerek said. "At least not the normal ones. They spend so much time worrying about bills and responsibility, they forget the importance of possibility. They slip into the trap of trying to survive and forget there's more to life than merely living to see another sunrise. So it falls on people like us who are still learning about the world to ask the right questions and be determined enough to find answers."

"Jerek, I'm glad Lydia wouldn't come with you."

"Me, too."

They drifted into silence as Jerek pulled into the traffic of downtown Newport.

Normal adults. Jerek's father would have hated being called normal.

He wasn't one of the ones Jerek was talking about anyway.

But Richard Holden hadn't lost his life searching for possibilities in the world, only salvation for his son. Pain pinched Jerek's throat at the memory of the frantic gleam in his father's eyes as he pored over books for hours, hunting for some way to mend the horrible wound that had hobbled magicians.

He wanted to protect me. To give me a world where I could protect myself.

Jerek gulped down air, fighting to breathe through the panic rising in his chest.

"You okay?" Jack asked.

"Road rage."

"Damn tourists. Awful drivers wherever they go."

You started it, Dad. But I'm going to end it.

His nerves calmed as he pulled out of town proper and onto a street lined with old mansions. Sweeping gardens and marble walls graced homes built by people who had no idea magic existed and yet somehow wanted to create fairylands of their very own. Hordes of visitors piled into the estates, buying themselves a few hours of storybook perfection.

Past the mansions tourists were allowed to invade, a road wound along the ocean where modern money had built its home in houses hidden by rocks, hills, and high stone walls.

Jerek slowed as he neared the address for the Chanler estate. Up ahead, the ocean cut sharply inland, forming a canal where the water foamed with each crash of the waves.

Rising high above the frothing channel, a gray stone mansion engulfed a ridge, growing out of the rock as though the house had burst up from the ground fully built. Light glinted from a row of windows cut into the cliff itself.

Chanler even forced the stone to bend to his will.

Across the bridge, over the canal, and around the corner, a high stone arch with a wooden gate blocked Chanler's private entrance to his estate. Farther down the road, a wrought iron gate marked with the letters MOM led to the museum where the guests would be arriving in a few hours' time.

Jerek kept driving around the curve, cutting down a dirt road. He looked east, stealing one final glance of the ocean battering the rocky shore.

Give them hell, he imagined the waves whispering.

The thought, however foolish it might have been, brought comfort.

He allowed his face to brighten into a smile, the newly formed roundness of his cheeks pushing up toward his eyes in a foreign way.

A sign had been stuck into the ground next to the dirt road.

Event crews this way.

The road cut sharply to the right, veering into an underground tunnel that headed back toward Chanler's house. The tunnel twisted, and the sun disappeared from view.

"You can come out," Jerek said.

"Oh, thank God." Jack slid out from under the seat. "Next time we do something like this, can we get an RV with a sunproof backroom?"

"I love my van," Jerek said.

"I love sitting up." Jack climbed into the passenger seat. The tunnel widened into an underground parking lot.

Vans labeled with everything from *catering* to *table rental* had already pulled in. Workers bustled in and out of three sets of wide doors at the end of the garage.

Jack whistled. "This is a swanky affair."

"Let's go crash it."

They hopped out of the van and started toward the catering truck.

A heavyset man with a comb over and a scratched-up clipboard stood at the opened back doors of the truck, giving orders to the catering staff.

"What are you doing?" The man frowned.

"What?" Jack asked.

Jerek searched the garage for a place to lure the clipboard man. Jack would have to knock him out. They'd wait for a new manager to take over and—

"I needed all my catering staff here twenty minutes ago," the man said. "This guy is busting my balls, and we weren't even supposed to start loading in for another ten minutes. Special event, my ass. Rich people and their damned theme parties, am I right?"

"Can't stand them," Jerek said, trying to ignore the boss's strong scent of whiskey and cigarette smoke.

"Don't hurt your back," the boss said. "I'm not paying for workman's comp."

Jerek turned.

Jack had lifted two giant crates of silverware.

"No worries." Jack flashed a smile. "I'm actually a lightweight lifter at school."

"I might actually forgive you for not being a half-hour early," the boss said.

Jerek lifted one crate of silverware, his arms instantly protesting the strain.

"You not a weight lifter?" the boss asked.

"Librarian in training," Jerek grunted.

"Well, you're worthless." The boss shook his head. "At least keep your feet moving."

"Yes, sir." Jerek followed Jack through a door that led out of the garage.

"He's a peach," Jack said.

"At least he didn't ask for our names," Jerek said.

The corridor had been built of plain concrete with exposed wires and industrial light fixtures running along the ceiling.

Has Chanler ever walked this hall?

The metal doors branching out of the corridor were marked with stenciled words.

Plumbing and Heating

Wiring and Cables

Maintenance

The last door in the hall had the white word *Kitchen* painted on the metal.

Jack kicked open the door, holding it aside for Jerek.

But the door didn't open into an industrial kitchen. A short hall led to a carved wooden door, which swung open as Jerek approached.

A bustling kitchen with chefs already at work waited beyond.

"Silverware over here!" shouted a woman whose frizzy red hair fought against the confines of her high bun.

Jack weaved through the kitchen toward Frizz.

"Leave these here and get another load," Frizz said. "When the silver is done, make sure he sends the napkins next. The idiots at the shop didn't fold them. You two lucky boys get to help me make four-hundred napkin swans." She gave a raspy guffaw and shooed them away.

Jerek headed back toward the door to the garage, pausing for a moment to catch a glimpse through the swinging door that led out of the kitchen in the opposite direction.

A giant crystal chandelier hung from the lobby ceiling, its light dancing on the parquet floor far below.

"Who is in charge of the bar?" A man burst through the kitchen door. The wrinkles on his brow accentuated the widow's peak of his dark hair, and though the man was no taller than Jerek and had an even slimmer build, the whole room froze at the sound of his voice.

"I'm the head bartender tonight, Mr. LeBlanc." A blond stepped forward, a bottle of vodka in her grip.

"Chanler wants to try the champagne." Mr. LeBlanc tapped his clipboard. "Now."

"Yes, sir." The blond raced back across the kitchen to the walk-in fridge.

"Come on." Jack tugged on Jerek's sleeve.

Neither said anything until they were back in the concrete corridor.

"We didn't know about the second set of doors between the loading bay and the kitchen," Jack said.

"I know."

"What else don't we know about?"

63

Grace

"Next time," Ari said, "can we please just rent a limo?"

"Hiring a driver was an unnecessary risk." Lincoln glanced in the rearview mirror.

"That's easy for you to say. You're not crammed in back here." Ari wiggled in her seat, knocking Ford, who had been made to sit in the middle, into Grace.

Grace slid as close to her window as she could, staring at the line of fancy cars stretching out in front of them.

"It's only fair that people six-foot and over get the front seat," Eve said.

"I didn't think there would be this many people at a museum opening." Ford leaned forward, giving Grace extra room to breathe.

"It's more than a museum," Lincoln said. "It's the first opportunity the feu have had to feel truly magical in a very long time."

"And we should have sprung for a limo for the occasion," Ari said.

"In my defense," Lincoln said, "I didn't know there would be five of us riding together when I booked the car."

"Sorry about that," Ford said.

"Don't be sorry." Ari patted his knee. "You didn't request to be brought to the ball, Cinderella. Fate just dropped you in the wrong basement at the wrong time."

"I don't think it was wrong at all." Ford laid his hand on top of Ari's.

She didn't pull away.

They chatted mindlessly as the line leading up to the wrought iron gate cleared. The letters MOM loomed over them. The script had a swirl to it, making the initials look light and fragile, but Grace's heart still raced at the sight of the three letters.

Chanler had named the museum. Chanler had chosen the script for the gate. Chanler had collected the artifacts, and planned the party, and destroyed the world of the feu for his own gain.

And we're going into the monster's lair.

Lincoln pulled forward, stopping beneath the archway. Men in dark suits waited at the gate. One held a clipboard, the other a flat disc he ran along the length of the car.

Lincoln rolled his window down.

Don't do it. Don't give them a name, just drive away.

"Name, sir?" The man was the right age to be in college, not much older than any of them.

Do you know what Chanler has done?

"Derek Miffler," Lincoln said. "Here with Ellen New and our guests."

The man scanned his list. "You're lucky. First I've seen with more than just a plus one."

"We know the right people." Eve smiled. A twinkle burned in her eyes.

The man didn't recognize the danger of that glint.

Run. Run before she tears you apart.

"Well, I hope you enjoy the party," the man said. "Pull right up to the lawn and the valet will take your car from there."

"Perfect." Lincoln rolled his window back up.

"I'm riding home in the van," Ari muttered.

The drive didn't cut straight up to the museum entrance. The lane had been carved into the side of the hill, winding back and forth more than was truly necessary to get from one place to another.

It was as though Chanler had walked through his estate and pointed to all the things he wanted his guests to see before they could be allowed to reach his museum.

Visitors had to admire the view of the great Chanler mansion with the sun just beginning to sink behind. The evening sky lent color to the gray stone, giving the house a majestic beauty it could never have hoped to achieve on its own.

The guests had to drive between massive boulders, large enough to crush the car—whether to appreciate the natural sheen of the stone or be terrified by their size, Grace didn't know—past trees dripping with exotic blooms that didn't seem to belong in the spring season this far north along the shores of the Atlantic, then to the edge of a carefully roped-off rose garden, teasing at luxury not meant for any but Chanler himself.

Finally, the entrance to the Museum of Magic came into view.

The doors themselves were nothing more than simple glass cut into the side of the hill. But a wide, white marble veranda reached onto the lawn, looking out over the ocean. Beneath the steps, the grass had been set with dozens of high-top tables.

The road stopped fifty feet below the first table. A long, midnight-blue carpet cut through the grass and all the way up the marble steps.

"Here we go." Lincoln stopped at the carpet.

Men dressed in black with red vests opened all the car doors, extending hands to the girls, stepping aside for the men.

"Thanks." Grace felt herself blush as she took the gloved hand offered her. She didn't let her ankles wobble in her heels, didn't let her gaze search the face of every boy wearing a red vest.

She took a deep breath, letting the fresh Atlantic air steady her.

Lincoln dropped the keys into the valet's hand.

The stranger drove away, leaving the five of them at the end of the blue carpet.

"Shall we?" Ari stepped to the head of the group. "If I don't find some kind of delicious seafood dripping with butter, I'm going to call the whole night a bust."

Ford chuckled and offered Ari his arm. "I will make it my personal mission to find you a delightful snack."

Ari tipped her head back and laughed. Her silky hair tumbled down her back like a cape. She looped her arm through Ford's and sauntered up the carpet.

So easy. So relaxed. How are they so good at this?

"Shall we?" Lincoln said, the stiffness in his tone proving it wasn't only Grace who felt wholly out of her depth.

"Let's go."

Eve didn't reach for Lincoln's arm, and he didn't offer. The three of them trailed behind Ari and Ford as distinct entities. Grace wished she had someone to cling to. Someone to anchor her as instinct screamed for her to run.

I'm not alone.

Eve had a slight smile on her face, and the dangerous gleam still shone in her eyes.

She's hunting.

If Grace hadn't known what Eve was after, it might have looked like she was searching for a date for the evening.

Lincoln scanned the crowd in a bored way, like he was waiting for something to pique his interest without holding much hope of success.

Grace studied her friends. She had nothing to be looking for. Her part in their mission wouldn't come until the very end. All she had to do for now was exist. Be a girl at a fancy party enjoying an evening with an ocean view.

She forced her shoulders to relax and studied the easy sway of Ari's hips. Dropping her hands to her sides, Grace tipped her chin up and let herself saunter.

Heat shot to her cheeks as a young man in a tux stared at her from his high-top table, his eyes alight, not with suspicion, but anticipation.

More eyes found their group as they walked up the long carpet. Most of the men's gazes halted on Ari and Eve, but some found Grace.

Well done, Jack.

They climbed the marble steps to the veranda where couches and poufs had been laid out for guests who preferred to sit.

Without seeming to search, Ari headed left to a square of midnight blue and silver couches where a group of teens lounged.

"Mind if we join?" Ari didn't wait before sitting on the arm of a couch next to a girl with tan skin and auburn hair. "If another forty-year-old man offers to show me his yacht, I just might scream."

"I will never understand why they want you to see their yachts." The girl with the auburn hair looked up at Ari. "The ones with the boats worth seeing are never the ones who want to bring you along."

"It's a pity beautiful girls can't enjoy a party in peace," Lincoln said. "And hard not to step out of place to defend them."

The girl with the auburn hair waved for all of them to join. The rest of the teens shifted their positions to make room for the four of them.

And there were only four of their group left. Ford in his kilt had disappeared.

Grace didn't dare search the crowd for him. She hadn't even felt him drift away.

A girl in a deep red dress waved Grace over to share her pouf.

"I'm Derek, by the way." Lincoln offered the auburn-haired girl his hand. "Derek Miffler. Thank you for offering us sanctuary."

"Mariah Chanler." The girl smiled but didn't take Lincoln's hand. "If anyone really bothers you, I'll just toss them out of Daddy's party."

The group laughed, and Grace joined in.

Do you know what your father did? Do you know what your life will be after tonight?

Of course Mariah didn't know. How could she? She'd only been a kid when her father had destroyed magic.

Mariah waved a hand, and servers appeared with trays of champagne and no intention of checking IDs.

Lincoln leaned toward Mariah from his place on another couch, asking questions about the estate and listening to her answers with rapt attention. Ari still perched above Mariah, laughing on cue and studying the bubbles in her glass.

Eve sat on a couch that had been empty but was now filled with young men vying for her attention.

Grace pressed her champagne flute to her lips, letting only the tiniest trickle of bitter sweetness pass over her tongue. The chill evening breeze swept in from the ocean, lifting her hair from her neck.

"Mariah." A man with silver hair, a chiseled jaw, and a tan to match Mariah's stepped up to their group.

"Yes, Daddy?" Mariah leaned around Ari to look up at her father.

64

Eve

Louis Chanler didn't look like a monster as he took his daughter's hand, leading her away from the group and toward the glass doors of the museum. Louis Chanler looked like nothing more than a man as he smiled with his perfect white teeth.

The muscles in Eve's legs tensed, begging her to pounce. She reached toward the pendant at her neck.

It doesn't matter if he's a monster. I am, too.

"Ellen." Ari leaned across the gap between couches and dug her nails into Eve's knee. "If you're not in the mood for bubbles, I'll gladly take yours."

Eve looked into Ari's unnaturally teal eyes. There wasn't warning waiting for her or even fear. Just a simple, readable question.

Would you really sacrifice everything we've been planning?

Eve gripped her pendant.

Chanler didn't deserve to take another breath of fresh night air. He didn't deserve to eat fancy food, or laugh, or walk with his daughter by his side. He should be ripped open on the steps of the palace he had built on lies and murder, his guts laid bare for all to see.

The wealthy hero Louis Chanler was nothing more than a murderous man. He would bleed like a man and die like and man. And when everyone ran in fear and turned their backs on his greatness, the birds would feast on the remains of the butcher who had destroyed the feu.

"I'll let you keep it." Ari leaned back.

Chanler stopped in front of the glass doors. Lights Eve hadn't even noticed before dimmed as a single beam brightened on Chanler.

The guests' conversations drifted away as everyone looked up to the museum doors.

Now. Kill him now while everyone is looking. Let them all watch the end of their tormentor.

"Ladies and Gentlemen." Chanler's voice drifted out over the veranda. "I am deeply honored that you have traveled from all corners of the world to join me for the opening of the Museum of Magic."

Less than five seconds to get to Chanler. Less than two to kill him. Where are the Maree? There have to be some roaming through the crowd.

"For more than a decade, I have been working to preserve the legacy of the feu. Collecting artifacts that too easily could have been lost to time."

Jerek and Grace can do the incantation after Chanler is dead. It would be easier. No time constraints to panic Grace. No Maree to keep away while the magic happens.

"But I could not sit idly by and watch the greatness of our people slip away. The history of the feu needs to be preserved for future generations. For my daughter, Mariah."

Mariah stepped up to her father's side, giving a coy wave before taking his arm.

It would be impossible to keep her father's blood from touching her. She would taste it, feel the sticky warmth on her skin. She would never forget that moment. Her father's last scream would haunt her dreams for the rest of her life. The taste of his blood would taint every meal she ate.

Mariah tossed a wink to their group. At her friends.

She's just a girl. Just a teenage girl dragged to her father's party.

If I drench her in his blood, I'll be the monster she hates, not him.

Eve let her hand fall to her lap.

"I know how excited you all are to see the collection. Some of you"—Chanler pointed to the back of the crowd—"have been hounding me for years."

A wave of laughter rolled over the lawn.

"And I promise you, soon, very soon, you will all be allowed into the museum to witness the wonder of centuries of feu history. In the meantime, eat, drink, and enjoy this beautiful evening. Because tonight, on the edge of the ocean, nestled deep below the ground, you will witness wonders your grandchildren and great-grandchildren will be begging to hear about for years to come. Ladies and Gentlemen—" Chanler raised his glass.

The crowd did the same.

Eve let her arm rise, holding her glass in the air, saluting the man who had destroyed her family with blood and fire.

"Tonight, we step into the past to embrace the future," Chanler said. "To the Museum of Magic."

"The Museum of Magic," the crowd chorused.

65

Lincoln

The lights brightened, returning to their low, discreet level, and music that had been a gentle hum in the background grew to be a noticeable force over the buzz of the crowd.

"I think that's our cue to dance." A tall boy with dark skin and a well-groomed beard stood and offered his hand to Eve. "I would be honored if you would dance with me, Ellen."

Eve smiled and took the boy's hand.

One step closer to the door.

Mariah left her father's side, weaving her way back toward the group. Lincoln stood and strode straight to her.

"Excuse me, Mariah." Lincoln gave a little bow. "Would you care to dance?"

The words felt obscure in his mouth. Left over from lessons the grandmothers taught at the compound. The matriarchs' way of rounding out the violent edges post-Fracture life had carved into the children of the Maree.

"Wanted to beat the others to the punch?" Mariah tipped her head to the side, appraising Lincoln from his well-polished shoes to his newly altered hair.

"I didn't fancy waiting at the end of the line." Lincoln shrugged.

Mariah laughed and took Lincoln's hand.

A server appeared from nowhere, taking their glasses as Mariah led Lincoln to the open space on the white marble veranda right in front of the doors.

"It's a relief, actually." Mariah placed Lincoln's free hand on her waist. "Honestly, it's the same flock who have been crowding me since we all hit puberty. It's sort of sad. You'd think they'd have figured out by now I'm not the princess to fill their bank accounts."

"Is that what you think?" Lincoln swayed to the music, keeping his hand firmly on Mariah's waist.

Strength to support, not to control. His Grandmother's voice echoed in his head. *Smile, but only as you listen.*

"I know it." Mariah laughed. "Are you the same? Come pecking around for scraps like a seagull?"

"Not at all," Lincoln said. "Hors d'oeuvres, champagne, the great mysteries of the museum, but that's all."

"Hmm." Mariah ducked away from Lincoln, spinning under his arm before easing back into his grasp. "And where are you from, Derek?"

"All over. Took my family some time to settle into life after the..." He let the word *Fracture* hang in the air. "We lost most of our people, but dad made a life for us out in Arizona."

"Arizona?" Mariah tipped her head to the side again. The simple slant of her chin exposed the supple side of her neck. "I didn't think many of our kind ended up that way."

"That was how Dad wanted it," Lincoln said. "We lost Mom and both his parents. He gathered what was left and made a life sans magic."

"You've been hiding with the sombs?"

"Haven't we all?" Lincoln said. "There are somb staff at this party. That never would have been allowed before."

"Daddy paid them very well to come work his *theme party*. Honestly, having a fake museum for a mythical magical population is far from the most absurd thing the staff have seen in Newport." Mariah leaned close to whisper in Lincoln's ear. "If you're very lucky, I just might tell you about the pirate ship hired to raid the neighbor's sweet sixteen party."

Lincoln spun her, guiding her closer to his chest as the song ended, daring someone to try and slide between them.

A new song began without anyone interrupting their pairing. Though two of the boys from the couches lurked in the shadows, watching Lincoln and waiting for their chance to cut in.

Ari danced with a man in his twenties. Her laugh bounced around the dance floor. Grace swayed in the grip of a boy who seemed more eager to talk than dance. Eve had retired back to the couches where three boys surrounded her, and four girls sat opposite, glaring daggers.

Mariah didn't speak again until they'd found the rhythm of the new song. "I don't think you've been as isolated as you pretend. You showed up here with friends. You must have kept in contact with some feu."

"I don't think I could survive in complete isolation."

Mariah leaned close to his ear again. "It's awful." Her breath whispered on his skin. "Daddy tried to keep me away from people for ages after the world ended. LeBlanc finally told him I would end up an antisocial narcissist if I wasn't allowed friends."

Her gaze drifted over Lincoln's shoulder. He resisted the urge to turn and see what had captured her attention.

"LeBlanc?" Lincoln asked.

Mariah looked back to him. "Our estate manager."

"And LeBlanc"—Lincoln said the name slowly as though it hadn't been in the information he'd been studying for days—"has he arranged it so you can leave the grounds? Perhaps run away for a picnic on the beach?"

"And abandon the party?"

"I meant tomorrow," Lincoln said. "I'll still be in town."

Mariah bit her lips together. "Sorry, Derek, but I don't think that would work."

A shock of panic shot through Lincoln's heart. "I'll have to content myself with dancing, I suppose."

"Not necessarily." Mariah stepped away and wiggled a finger at him to follow her back to the couches.

Lincoln trailed behind her, forcing his pulse to stay steady.

Confess some deep secret. Pretend to panic or be ill. Actually be ill.

"Rachel," Mariah said.

A girl with black hair shot through with purple looked up.

"Lincoln here is still looking to dance, and my feet just won't take it." Mariah sank down onto a couch. "Be a dear and take a turn."

"Oh." Rachel stood so quickly it seemed as though she'd been shot out of her seat.

"Actually, I think I'm ready to rest as well," Lincoln said. "Ellen, if I may?"

He moved to sit next to Eve.

"What's wrong?" Ari appeared beside Lincoln, the man she'd been dancing with nowhere in sight. "Tired already?"

"I'm afraid I misjudged my shoes." Mariah wrinkled her nose.

"Don't be silly." Ari shook her head. Her blond hair fluttered around her as though blown by the wind of a battalion of fairy wings. "If your feet are tired, it's because you're doing it wrong. Give it another try." Ari reached toward Mariah. "It'll be fun."

Mariah grinned as she took Ari's hand. "I suppose it would be wrong to turn down a lesson when one is offered."

"Come on, Derek," Ari said. "Let us torture you."

"I think we'll make do on our own." Mariah held Ari's gaze. "Don't you?"

Ari's smile transformed from broad to playful in the space of heartbeat.

"You know what, Derek"—Ari brushed the underside of his collar with her finger—"why don't you take the night off?"

"I—" Lincoln didn't have time to beg her to be careful before Ari and Mariah wound their way to the middle of the dance floor.

66

Jerek

The tray of champagne flutes was heavier than Jerek had imagined it could be. Of course, he had been lifting trays, boxes, and tables for hours. Manual labor was not something life had prepared him for. Holden House had been a place where books and knowledge were king.

I doubt Dad could have thrown a ball if he'd tried.

A mournful itch filled his chest.

Soon, Dad. I'll finish your work soon.

The bartender's station had been set up in the parquet-floored lobby. The guests had yet to be allowed into the museum, so it was left to those in red vests to deliver the liquid fun to the feu.

"Are you going or not?" the bartender asked.

"Right," Jerek said. "Sorry."

He headed for the veranda.

Six people in fully black suits stood guard just inside the

wide, glass doors. Each of their bodies held the sort of tense awareness mixed with boredom that seemed exclusive to dangerous people forced to wait.

Maree.

They were easy to recognize even without the customary flaming shield emblem on their chests.

He quickly scanned each of their faces, searching for someone familiar. He didn't recognize any of them. There was a time in his life when that would have been shocking. A terrible thing for a Holden not to recognize the Maree.

But tonight, unknown faces were a comfort.

Balancing his tray on one hand, he pushed through the doors and out into the twilight.

Music filled the air, and dancers swayed to the rhythm of some song they all seemed to know.

Jerek weaved his way toward the outskirts of the crowd, holding his tray out to anyone who had empty hands.

The partygoers took the flutes of champagne without looking at the face of the one holding the tray. The anonymity suited Jerek just fine.

A familiar laugh rang from the middle of the dance floor.

Jerek chanced a glance.

Ari spun under the arm of Mariah Chanler, her skirt swirling around her as she twirled back into Mariah's arms.

"Excuse me." A timid voice dragged Jerek's attention away from the glisten of Ari's hair shimmering in the dim light.

Ford stood in front of Jerek, pale-faced and sweating.

"I'm so sorry to bother, but I'm afraid I need the restroom." Ford glanced nervously around as though terrified anyone would hear him.

"There's a restroom in the lobby." Jerek gave a little bow.

"Would you mind showing me?" Ford asked. "I don't think I can afford the time to get lost."

"Of course. Right this way." Jerek headed back toward the lobby, half-full tray in hand. He opened the door, letting Ford enter first.

"The museum isn't open yet, sir." A female Maree blocked Ford's path. "You still have to wait about thirty minutes."

"I'm afraid I can't wait." Ford swayed. "I've got terrible food allergies, and I think I've eaten something I shouldn't have."

"Should I get the chef?" Jerek asked.

"Do you require medical assistance?" A line formed between the Maree's eyebrows, creasing her young face.

"Just to find a restroom." Ford wiped the sweat from his forehead. "Perhaps a quiet place to sit for a moment." He took one step forward and fell.

Two Maree darted forward to help him, kneeling beside Ford and rolling him onto his back before Jerek could even wonder if he should put his tray of champagne down.

"What's going on here?" LeBlanc appeared, clipboard in hand. "Why is there a boy on the floor?"

"Ate something he shouldn't have," the female Maree said.

"Get him into the back and keep him out of sight until he can walk," LeBlanc said. "We can't have people seeing something like this. It could mar the opening."

"Yes sir." The largest of the Maree scooped Ford up and carried him, not through the door to the kitchen, but through a door to the left of the lobby.

"Shouldn't we call 9-1-1?" Jerek asked. "I don't have my phone, but—"

"What?" LeBlanc looked at Jerek as though noticing his presence for the first time. "We have our own medical team here. They'll see to the boy." LeBlanc gave Jerek a smile so brief it seemed like a trick of the light.

"Okay. If you're sure." Jerek headed to the bar table to refill his tray.

The whispered word *somb* followed in his wake.

"Why are you back if your tray isn't empty?" The bartender glared at Jerek.

"Brought a guy inside to faint, so I was already halfway back," Jerek said.

"I can accept that."

Jerek placed more champagne flutes onto his tray.

"Twenty-five minutes to museum opening." LeBlanc's voice filled the lobby.

"Better hurry." Jerek headed back out through the glass doors.

He walked into the crowd of dancers and straight to Mariah Chanler.

"Pardon me, Miss." Jerek held out his tray. "One more before the museum opens?"

Ari looked from Mariah to Jerek. "The dancing is over so soon?"

"I'm not sure about that," Jerek said. "But the tray service for champagne is scheduled to stop."

Mariah let go of Ari and lifted two glasses from Jerek's tray. "You're a dear."

"Well," Jerek said, "the museum is bound to get crowded, and I would hate for you to miss your shot at enjoying your evening."

"There are so many things to enjoy." Ari lifted one glass for herself. "Thanks."

Jerek bowed and weaved away through the crowd, heading down the steps and out toward the lawn.

He passed the cluster of seats where Grace and Eve held court. Lincoln had disappeared, absent from the group where he'd spent the first part of the evening.

Jerek scanned the crowd for a tall man with dirty blond hair as he worked his way toward the outskirts of the party, giving away the last of his flutes and picking up empties to refill his tray. He reached the edge of the lawn. Beyond were only the valets waiting for any late arrivals.

He turned back toward the museum. As he stepped toward the nearest table, Lincoln appeared.

No, not Lincoln.

The build was Lincoln's, as were the dark hair and eyes. But Jerek had changed Lincoln's hair.

The face was slightly wrong, too. A little more wary, a little more severe.

The clothes weren't right either. *This* Lincoln wore the black suit of a Maree.

Fear tensed Jerek's shoulders as he met Martin Martel's gaze.

67

Ari

Her lips tasted sweeter than champagne.

Like strawberries dipped in champagne.

That would be right.

The scent of Mariah's hair surrounded Ari, tingling all her senses almost beyond reason.

Almost.

The strong part of Ari's mind, the part that knew how much planning she and Jerek had slogged through to reach this night, was capable of thinking beyond the softness of Mariah's lips as they worked their way down to her neck.

Ari tangled her fingers through Mariah's hair, drawing her back up so their lips could meet.

Voices carried from beyond the corridor as the staff scrambled, preparing to open the doors.

"Let's go somewhere." Ari pulled her mouth only a breath

from Mariah's, letting her words whisper against the auburn-haired goddess's strawberry-flavored lips.

"Where?" Mariah moved her mouth to Ari's ear, teasing the skin left bare by her earring.

"Give me a private tour." Ari trailed her fingers down Mariah's back, grateful her gown left so much luscious skin to play with.

Mariah quivered as Ari reached the base of her spine.

"Show me the hoard of treasures before anyone else has the chance to covet them," Ari said.

"I can think of more exciting activities than staring at old things in glass cases." Mariah traced the bottom of Ari's ribs with her thumbs, teasing the possibilities that could exist if only scarlet fabric didn't separate skin from skin.

"Why do you think I want a private viewing?" Ari nipped Mariah's bottom lip, then gazed into her honey-brown eyes.

"What do you want to see?" Mariah twined her fingers through Ari's, kissing her one more time before leading her farther down the marble hall.

"What are my choices?"

"Hmm. Well, do you want pre-treaty artifacts or vampire hunting tools from the Middle Ages? We also have a nice section on werewolves, or we could go to the Den of Divs."

Ari tugged on Mariah's hand, pulling her around and into a kiss. "I want something with fire. Something with scorch marks all over."

"I have just the place." Mariah walked backward, drawing Ari along with the heat dancing in her eyes. "Scorch marks to spare, and a horrible essence of death and desperation that makes you appreciate life."

"Oh, I am definitely appreciating my life."

At the end of the hall, a sweeping staircase led deeper

underground. They ran down the steps, holding hands like two Cinderellas escaping the ball.

At the bottom of the steps, a hall led toward the vampire and div rooms. Another staircase led farther down, a velvet rope blocking the way.

"Only give them a taste at a time." Mariah unhooked the rope. "Daddy thinks it's best to save the finest pieces in his collection for last."

"And what do you think?" Ari stepped onto the stairs, waiting while Mariah replaced the velvet barrier.

"About saving the best for last?"

"Only giving a taste at a time."

"That's an old man's game."

They ran down the roped-off stairs to the lower level, both giggling as their dresses trailed along the marble steps.

A corridor led off in either direction—one long, one short.

Mariah led Ari down the shorter corridor. "Welcome to the Pre-Treaty Gallery and the best of Daddy's treasures."

Ari's heart stopped as Mariah planted her hands on the door, ready for sirens to blare and Maree to come and drag her away, but the doors flung open at Mariah's touch.

All the air whooshed from Ari's body. She couldn't even remember how to breathe as Mariah led her into the gallery.

Knowing she belonged to a people whose history reached back hundreds of years and seeing the centuries of evidence laid out before her were two wholly different things.

A golden arch rose above the entryway, stretching toward the twenty-foot high ceiling. Inlaid jewels glittered between runes, which wove in arcs, leaving no hint as to where one ended and another began.

"Wow." A hot tear tickled Ari's cheek.

"Don't get too impressed yet." Mariah winked.

She led Ari past a case that a held a silver crown. Hooks like talons extended from the bottom, poised as though ready to pierce the head of the wearer. A staff with a cracked stone lay across a bed of black velvet. A set of scorched planks with words written in soot in a language Ari couldn't read rested on a wide pedestal. A book lay open to a set of pages with drawings of magicians rising up to the sky.

Ari wanted to stop at each of the cases. To read why the ring in the red metal box was so important and who the iron chains had bound. But a wide display waited near the far wall. A sheet of deep blue glass set with a hundred jewels perched in the center of the case.

"What is that?" Ari dragged Mariah toward the Caster's Fate.

"A window." Mariah wrapped her arms around Ari from behind. "It used to be a part of the Monument to the Fallen Casters until angry feu burned the place down." She kissed the side of Ari's neck. "The window was lost for years and years. Took ages to track it down."

"Tell me about the Fallen Casters." Ari drew Mariah's arms more tightly around her, leaving nothing but thin fabric between them.

"They fought the witch hunters. Tracked them all and tried to destroy them. But the hunters were devious and more evil than the casters had imagined. The hunters fled to a village and started slaughtering all the innocents there. The casters tried to save the sombs from the flood of blood, and the hunters killed every last caster and villager. Death as payment for mercy."

"That's terrible." Ari turned to face Mariah, their noses practically touching.

Mariah's eyes danced, not with rage for the fallen innocents and casters, but with teasing.

Ari traced the line of Mariah's jaw. "If the hunters came, would you protect me?"

"I'd have a fleet of Maree stop them before their war cries even tainted our fun." She grazed her lips against Ari's.

Ari leaned into the kiss, desperate for Mariah not to back away. She parted her lips with a sigh, teasing Mariah with the tip of her tongue.

A tiny moan rose from Mariah's throat. The soft skin of her neck begged to be kissed.

Ari trailed kisses from lips to neck, and out to shoulder, shifting aside the thin strap of Mariah's dress with her teeth.

Mariah found Ari's neck.

Her head spun at the warmth of Mariah's breath on her skin.

Lips met lips again, and the two stumbled backward. Ari's shoulder met something hard and delightfully cool the moment before the alarms rang.

"Shit." Mariah stepped away from Ari, spinning to face the doors.

Ari slid down the side of the glass case, landing in a sea of scarlet fabric.

"What's wrong?" Ari reached down the front of her dress, finding the tiny, red glass sphere she had slipped from under Lincoln's collar and hidden in her bra.

Four, black-suited Maree ran into the room.

"You're not supposed to touch the cases," Mariah said.

"Stay right where you are." The Maree surrounded them. Each crossed their right hand to their left hip as though ready to draw an invisible sword.

"Would you turn off that damn alarm?" Mariah shouted over the noise. "I am Mariah Chanler. I apologize for the inconvenience, but my friend and I are going to leave now."

"Leaving sounds like great idea." Ari struggled to her feet, her fingers grazing the case as she stood.

"No one is going anywhere until we talk to Mr. Chanler," the eldest of the Maree said.

Though *eldest* held little meaning. None of the Maree were more than thirty. All had only served the knights in a post-Fracture world.

"You want to hold me here until Daddy comes?" Gone was the Mariah of dancing and luscious kisses. The girl who had been raised with the luxury of safety tipped her chin up. "Come on, Ari. We have a party to get to." She reached back for Ari's hand.

Ari laced her fingers through Mariah's, staying behind her as Mariah stepped toward the Maree.

The knights shifted to block their path.

"Do you really want to get in my way?" Mariah asked.

The Maree were saved from answering by the pounding of footsteps running toward the door.

"What's happening?" Callen LeBlanc charged into the room. "Why on earth are the alarms going off?"

Mariah stepped away from the guards, her size seeming to shrink as LeBlanc approached.

"The girls touched a case," a Maree said.

LeBlanc stepped between the Maree. His gaze left Mariah to linger on Ari.

"Mariah, you should be up at the party," LeBlanc said.

"I couldn't agree more," Mariah said.

"Then I suggest you return to your father's side at once," LeBlanc said. "Alone."

"There's no reason Ari can't—"

"This evening is for your father, Mariah," LeBlanc said. "You can indulge in the frivolities of youth at another time."

"But—"

"Mariah, now."

Her hand slid from Ari's.

"Good." LeBlanc shifted his glare to Ari. "Take that one to my office. I will not allow any trace of impropriety to mar the opening."

"Yes, Mr. LeBlanc."

LeBlanc turned and strode out of the room.

"Mariah," Ari whispered.

Mariah didn't look back. She followed LeBlanc away as though Ari had never even existed.

"This way," the eldest Maree said.

"Just let me find a bathroom and I'll look proper in no time," Ari said. "It only takes a second to fix lipstick and tidy hair."

The Maree stared at her, stone-faced and silent.

"Fine," Ari said. "If you want to shove me in a corner, I don't mind. I've had my fun."

The Maree surrounded her as they left the gallery, marching her past the treasures of the feu.

None of them noticed the shimmering dot of red glass burrowing through the case toward the Caster's Fate.

68

Jack

Bouncing from the loading docks to the kitchen, then hiding in the bathroom so no one would try to send him outside, had left Jack with an obnoxiously boring evening. The catering staff didn't even have anything on them worth stealing.

He'd slipped back into the kitchen to help fold the last of the swan napkins when his watch finally beeped.

"You're not supposed to have a phone on shift," the frizzy-haired caterer said.

"It's not a phone." Jack held up his wrist. "It's a medical reminder."

As in a reminder I won't die if I step outside.

"Well, don't let it beep around the guests." Frizz continued her death glare as Jack lifted a crate of swans and headed to the front of the kitchen.

"What's that?" Jack spoke to no one as he leaned out the

door to the lobby, getting his first glimpse of the vast space. "Oh, okay."

He ducked back into the kitchen and walked back to the napkin table.

"Sorry, someone else will have to carry these." He set the swans in front of Frizz. "I've been asked to do something else by management."

"I am management," Frizz said.

"By bigger management." Jack walked away.

"I will put you on our do not hire list," Frizz called after him.

"You do that, honey."

The shiny, wooden floor of the lobby clacked under Jack's shoes. In just a few minutes, the space would be flooded with the noise of hundreds of guests, the buzz of fools too busy enjoying themselves to notice fingers slipping into their pockets.

That's not the job tonight.

A full bar had been set up off to one side of the lobby. Jack gave the bartender his most winning smile. "I need a ginger ale for a guest."

The bartender eyed him. "A guest?"

"That's what one of the black suits said." Jack shrugged. "I guess the hors d'oeuvres didn't appeal to everyone."

"That guy." The bartender rolled her eyes. "I would hate to be his date."

"Yeah," Jack laughed. "There is nothing worse than being stuck with the sick kid in the corner at a party."

"Except being the sick kid." The bartender handed Jack a tall glass of ginger ale.

"True." Jack took the smallest silver tray on the table, placing the glass on top. "Let's just hope it's nothing contagious."

Keeping his chin high, he headed for the normal-sized door on the left side of the lobby.

A Maree in a black suit blocked the door, his hands tucked formally behind his back only accentuating the difference between his broad shoulders and slim waist.

God bless the Maree's tailor.

"I'm supposed to bring this to the gentleman who got sick." Jack raised his tray.

"I haven't been told about anyone going in," the Maree said.

"I don't think I'm really *going* anywhere," Jack said. "I'm just supposed to drop off a drink."

"You'll have to wait until I can ask if you're cleared—"

"I can just give the glass to you if that'll get it to the poor guy faster," Jack said. "It doesn't matter to me. I just don't want him to puke on anything important."

The Maree leaned forward, glancing toward the line of his fellows by the glass doors.

"Straight in, straight out," he said. "First door on the left."

"Yes, sir." Jack gave a little salute.

The Maree pulled a fob from his pocket and pressed it to the handle of the door.

A click only loud enough for Jack to hear sounded as the lock opened.

Jack stepped forward enough to stop the door with his foot, then turned back to the Maree. He leaned in close, leaving only the small tray hovering low between them as he whispered, "If the guy *has* been sick, who should I tell?"

The Maree glanced back toward the glass doors. "I rotate in fifteen minutes. Tell whoever you want after that."

"Got it." Jack winked.

He stepped into the hall and let the door swing shut behind him, the Maree's little black fob tucked in his palm.

"First door on the left." Jack counted the doors—four on

each side of the hall, all more battle worthy than the one he'd been directed to. The other doors were made of solid wood, with the narrowest bit of metal reinforcement peeking out around the edges.

The door Jack knocked on was made almost entirely of frosted glass.

A warbling voice answered. "Come in."

Jack opened the door, carefully checking all four corners before stepping inside the room. A wide desk sat at the far end of the space with a portrait of Chanler and his daughter hanging above. Couches and low tables had been arranged to give the appearance of a sitting room, though the walls and floor were made of the same marble as the rest of the museum.

Ford lay on one of the couches. His eyes shut and his face slicked with sweat.

"I've brought you a drink, sir," Jack said.

Ford sat up and opened his mouth to speak.

Don't do it.

Jack glanced up toward the back corner where a shining black disc broke the perfection of the white marble.

Ford opened and closed his mouth twice before speaking. "Thank you so much. I'm feeling better, but my stomach's still a bit off."

Jack carried the ginger ale to Ford. "Well, I hope this helps. The party should be moving downstairs soon, and it would be a pity if you missed the fun."

"Certainly." Ford took the glass and reached out to shake Jack's hand. "You're very kind."

"No problem." The weight of the fob left Jack's palm. "Have a great night."

Ford smiled and gave a little nod. Something between fear and genuine nausea filled his eyes.

Don't let us down.

Jack headed back out into the hall and through the door to the lobby.

The Maree standing guard stepped aside for him.

"Don't worry," Jack said. "No messy clean up required. Yet."

69

Jerek

He stared at Martin Martel's face. The reality of Martin being in Newport, when he should have been shipped to the other side of the ocean days ago, set a stone in the bottom of Jerek's stomach.

"Do you need something?" Martin asked.

Jerek smiled broadly, pushing the extra padding he'd added to his cheeks up toward his eyes. "Any empties?"

"No." Martin turned away from Jerek and resumed his surveillance of the party.

Did Lincoln see his brother? Is that why he hid?

Jerek headed back up toward the glass doors.

He needed to find Lincoln. If Lincoln had decided to hide from his brother, they would need to change their plans.

He didn't catch sight of Lincoln as he wound the long way

through the tables, gathering as many glasses as his tray could hold.

Mariah Chanler stormed out onto the veranda, LeBlanc a step behind her. The joy that had shone on her face when she'd been dancing with Ari had been replaced by a tight-lipped smile.

Chanler himself appeared by his daughter's side, five cronies lurking in his wake.

Jerek cut past the seating and to the doors, scanning the lobby beyond for any trace of Ari.

Where are you?

He headed back to the bar with his tray, tension creeping into his chest, his gaze fixed on the corridor that led down to the museum.

"Take those straight back to the dishwasher." Frizz waved him toward the swinging doors.

The grating sound of Frizz's voice chased Jerek into the kitchen.

"Put those in the back." A man in a white apron pointed Jerek toward the back of the room where the dishwasher spouted steam that smelled like chemicals.

But Ari wasn't in the back of the room, and neither was Lincoln.

He needed to get downstairs but couldn't be sure if Jack had gotten Ford the key to the server room, let alone if Ford had succeeded in breaking into the system.

Their flimsy plan, which had seemed so brave and well-woven while they'd sat in barns and basements, suddenly shrank to the reality of children trying to win at hide and seek. He had plotted and schemed to lead his friends into the home of a murderer.

I don't want their blood on my hands.

"Quite the party out there."

Jerek jumped at Jack's voice.

"Is it?" Jerek set his tray down amidst the mass of filthy glassware.

"Had a guy in an office almost get sick on my shoes." Jack shrugged. "I think he's feeling better though."

"Huh," Jerek said. "I saw a pretty blond girl in a scarlet dress slip off with the boss's daughter. The Chanler girl came back but not the blond. Pity. She was hot. I would have liked to talk to her."

Jack's lips twitched. "I'm a pretty good detective. Maybe I can play wing man."

"I don't know," Jerek said. "The big blond dude she showed up with is missing, too."

"Damn, that girl's having a good night." Jack laughed, his mouth opening just enough to show the tips of his fangs.

"You know"—a girl near their age slipped between them—"I have worked some epic LARP and theme parties in my day, but these people have pushed it a bit too far. Have you been to the next level down?"

"No," Jack and Jerek said together.

"It's ridiculous." The girl balanced her tray on top of the others at an angle no sane person would attempt. "I don't know if this guy bought stuff from movie sets or had everything specially made, but the fact that he spent so much money putting this magic act together yet I'm going to be paying student loans until I die really pisses me off."

"Rich people," Jack said. "No accounting for how they blow the money some of us need to eat."

"We better get a big fat tip at the end of the night," the girl said.

A gong rang in the lobby.

"Ladies and Gentlemen, welcome to the Museum of Magic." Chanler's voice carried from unseen speakers.

"Round two hors d'oeuvres to the next level," Frizz shouted. "If I don't see a food tray in every one of my staff's hands in the next thirty seconds—"

"She'll put us on the do not hire list," Jack whispered.

"I swear I will put you on the do not hire list," Frizz finished.

"There's something to be said for consistency." Jack headed to the long line of waiting hors d'oeuvres trays before Jerek could think of a way to tell him to be careful.

70

Lincoln

The guests on the veranda filed through the glass doors. Lincoln stayed at the shadowy edge of the high-top tables on the lawn, watching as Grace and Eve followed the crowd. He leaned against the tabletop, cutting a few inches off his height with the slouch.

Staff in red vests roamed between the tables, clearing away the rest of the glasses. Neither Jack nor Jerek came back through the glass doors. But they were meant to be inside. *He* was meant to be inside.

Maree patrolled the periphery of the party. He recognized a few of them.

Marta, who used to sneak the little kids candy. Lucas, who'd won recognition for best swordsmanship. There were other faces Lincoln knew, but he couldn't pull the matching names from his memory.

"The party is moving inside if you'd like to travel with the group."

Lincoln looked up into his older brother's face. The urge to hug Martin and clap him hard on the back prickled Lincoln's arms, but instead he nodded.

"I hate the hair," Martin said.

"Me too," Lincoln said.

"The eyes aren't too bad."

Lincoln glanced around the lawn. Only Maree and staff were left.

"There are more Maree here than there should be," Lincoln said.

"Word got around there might be trouble," Martin said. "Chanler appealed to the knights for extra protection."

"Word from whom?" Lincoln tensed, the horrible feeling of being watched setting his nerves on edge.

"CFH," Martin said. "Apparently, my brother's friend might have stolen an important artifact, and with so many artifacts here...."

"Damn." Lincoln straightened up to his full height, standing taller than his older brother.

"A Martel knows his duty, brother," Martin said.

"Duty bred and duty bound." Lincoln turned toward the museum doors.

"Be careful not to get rowdy tonight. LeBlanc already had us haul away the blond you showed up with."

"Haul her where?" Lincoln asked.

"His private office up in the main house. She's locked in. Even the Maree keys won't open that door."

Lincoln didn't say anything. He walked up the white steps and into the Museum of Magic, the thumping of his feet vibrating all the way to his ears.

As he passed under the overhang of the hill, the Chanler mansion disappeared from view.

Ari.

He wished he could call out and tell her he knew she was trapped. He wished he could run straight for the mansion and find a way to let her out.

The guests had begun filtering down the wide steps to one side of the lobby.

Lincoln needed to get downstairs. But going farther into the earth would take him further from helping Ari.

A flash of color caught Lincoln's eye.

Ford hurried past, grabbing a scallop from a caterer's tray.

Lincoln reached out, seizing Ford's arm.

"I am feeling much better, thank you." Ford's eyes widened as he looked up at Lincoln. "Very much better and ready to go downstairs."

Lincoln dragged Ford out of the flow of people.

"We have to find the others," Lincoln said.

"Others?" Ford said. "I assume Ellen and...and the rest are downstairs."

"Ari is locked in LeBlanc's office."

Ford's face changed from white to violently red in the span of a second.

"I'll find her," Ford said. "We won't let her—"

"You can't leave," Lincoln said. "We need you in the museum."

They stared helplessly at each other for a long moment.

"We need to get downstairs," Lincoln said. "We'll find Eve, I can take her place, she can go to Ari. I don't care if she has to climb the outside of the mansion to get there, Eve can scent her. She can get Ari out."

"Are you sure?" Ford said. "It won't be pretty."

"I can take a hit better than I can take leaving someone behind."

Ford nodded. "We should hurry."

They stepped back into the crowd. The horde slowed as they made their way downstairs.

Lincoln longed to weave through the meandering feu, but he forced himself to keep in step. He studied the signs at the bottom of the stairs pointing to displays on werewolf, div, and Maree artifacts. Tables set with swan-folded napkins waited down one branch of the hall, and red-vested caterers waited down the other, presenting tiny food to the passing people. Two Maree blocked a red-roped staircase leading to the lower level.

Hold on, Eve. Just wait for me.

As Lincoln stepped off the last stair, an alarm echoed off the marble walls, then a crash and a shout filled the hall.

71

Eve

"My sister barely has anything." Stafford leaned closer to Eve. "It's a little sad, actually. If she really tries, she can hover a pebble in her palm, but it's never extended beyond anything bigger than a gumball. I inherited my father's trace fire. It's much more useful. I'd show you but..." He looked to the nearest server. "We do still have to be careful among sombs."

"For the protection of the feu." Eve raised her still-full champagne glass.

"I do wish they'd allow somb servants," Stafford said. "You know, like the Maree but for menial tasks."

"You're right," Eve said. "Sombs who inherit the privilege of serving us would make the lives of the feu so much simpler."

"Exactly." Stafford tapped the tip of his nose. "When I'm of age, I'm going to propose the idea to the Council of the Feu. I can't think of any reason a well-educated person would reject the notion. I suppose we could always pass laws for werewolves, vampires, or divs to be servants, but they would be so much more difficult to manage."

Eve fought to swallow the growl that rattled at the back of her throat.

Gong.

The sound rang around the veranda. "Ladies and Gentlemen, welcome to the Museum of Magic." Chanler's voice carried from unseen speakers.

Chanler himself stood in front of the glass doors. His hand flew to his throat in mock surprise at the sound of his voice resonating through the air. "This way, Ladies and Gentlemen," the real Chanler said. "Magic awaits."

He spread his arms wide, and the museum doors opened. A flood of people followed him toward the lobby.

"I don't know why they're in such a hurry," Stafford said. "It's not like the displays are going anywhere."

"Well, I'm ready to go." Eve stood and headed toward the doors, weaving through the crowd to put as much distance between herself and Stafford as possible, only slowing as she reached the cluster right behind Chanler.

Mariah walked beside him, her face resolutely front even as her father tried to engage her in conversation. Ari's scent clung to Mariah's skin, but Eve couldn't catch a trace of Ari herself.

The sea of people blurred the scent of the magicians into one mass of magic.

Jack had passed through the lobby before her. That much she knew. His scent strengthened as she followed Chanler down the marble steps to the next level of the museum.

This should be beautiful. This much of our people's history in one place should be a glory for all the feu. But instead, he built a tomb.

She watched the faint beat of Chanler's pulse on the side of his neck. His hateful heart pumped murderous blood through his evil veins.

Keep smiling. I'll be ready for you soon.

At the bottom of the stairs, Chanler turned away from the tables laid out with swan-shaped napkins and toward the three rooms on the other side of the hall.

The guests branched out, scattering amongst the different exhibits.

Eve's feet carried her toward the room labeled *Werewolf Artifacts*. She couldn't have gone anywhere else if she'd tried.

A canvas of stretched leather greeted the guests. A painting in red and black showed a werewolf in full transformation. Human face replaced by wolf, hands taken over by claws. Eve shivered, her body longing for the power. The strength to break through every case in the room and free the relics of her people from the monster who had stolen them.

"I've never seen anything like it!" An older woman cooed at a case in the corner.

Passing a display of silver chains forged with iron cores, the stone of the moon breaker, and a portrait of the first Alpha in America, Eve made her way to the case that had brought the woman such delight.

Rows of pendants, rings, and bracelets hung on a black velvet background.

Moonstones of America – A collection of werewolf-empowering jewelry.

Eve's fingers floated to the pendant around her own neck as she scanned the rows of jewelry. At the top left, smaller than most, but beautiful for the intricately carved pattern on the silver—

Mom.

She would know the necklace anywhere, even if fifty years had passed.

Her mother's moonstone. Eve had never seen her mom without it.

The image of it against her mother's pale skin as she lifted Eve, throwing her out the window. How the silver sparkled as the fire of the blast devoured her mother.

The explosion had taken her family but left the moonstone whole and undamaged. And now it lived trapped inside the murderer's glass case.

"Would you like any hors d'oeuvres?"

Jack's scent wafted over her.

A thrill hummed through Eve's veins.

"How dare you!" She rounded on Jack, smacking the tray from his hand.

Finger food flew through the air, raining down a shower of meat and crudités on the well-dressed guests.

The cooing old woman screamed as sauce landed in her hair.

"What are you—" Jack began.

Eve slapped him hard across the face.

He stumbled sideways, closer to the case.

"I did not give you permission to touch me," Eve shouted.

"I didn't." Jack shifted sideways to step past her, knocking into her shoulder.

"Is everything okay here?" A Maree appeared beside them.

"Oh, hell no." Eve shoved Jack against the case.

Alarms split the air.

"Miss, please." The Maree grabbed Eve's arm.

"Don't touch me!" Eve wrenched free from his grip, knocking him to the floor.

"What the hell is wrong with you, lady?" Jack lunged toward Eve.

She pulled her fist back and swung for his face.

His head snapped back as he flew through the air. He hit the case.

The glass splintered in a spider web behind him.

"Stop! Both of you, stop!" the Maree shouted.

Eve swung again, aiming just above Jack's shoulder.

She didn't feel any pain as her fist shattered the glass.

"Someone grab her!"

Hands seized her arms, but their grasp didn't matter.

She hoisted Jack by his red vest and threw him into the case. She let her weight fall with his, carrying them both through the glass, cracking the velvet display beneath them.

Arms wrapped around Eve's waist, dragging her back.

She clawed at the velvet, trying to stay on top of Jack, fighting to wrap her hands around his throat.

A shock spun up her spine, sapping the strength from her limbs.

"Ladies and Gentlemen, if you'll just step back, I'm sure we'll get this tidied up in no time."

Her legs wobbled beneath her as two Maree set her back on her feet.

"You're going to hold me back after that sicko groped my ass?" Eve said. "I should have known this museum was just a new monument to chauvinism."

"Miss, if you'll please come with us." The Maree dragged her toward the door, holding her arms tightly enough to bruise somb skin.

"I'm going to get in trouble, and the groper is just going to dust himself off?" Eve spat.

"Don't worry. He's coming, too."

"Great," Eve said. "Lock me in a room with him. I'll make sure he never grabs another ass."

"Your ass isn't my type, sweetie," Jack said.

The crowd hadn't cleared the werewolf room. More people

seemed to have crammed in since the fight began, all eager to see the evening's entertainment.

"I'll walk nicely if you stop pinching," Eve growled.

"Just move." The Maree tightened his grip.

They reached the hall.

Lincoln and Ford waited at the bottom of the steps. Some strange worry filled their faces, but Eve couldn't tell why, and there was no time to ask.

The Maree shoved her toward the stairs.

"Don't make me punch you, too," Eve said.

Blood dripped from her knuckles, staining the floor red.

Just a taste of what's to come.

A smile touched her lips, and another alarm split the air.

72

Jerek

Alarms sounded in the werewolf room. Jerek moved away from the sound, crinkling his face against the blare of it.

A few of the Maree ran toward the commotion but not all. Not the two stationed by the red rope blocking the stairs to the next level down.

"Bite to eat?" Jerek held his tray up to the Maree.

They looked down their noses at his offering.

"We're working." The knight on the left said, though the faint paunch on his cheeks betrayed his hidden desire for pepper-crusted shrimp.

"Probably for the best." Jerek shrugged. "I heard one guest already got sick."

He passed back toward the stairs, positioning himself at the corner where he'd have the first chance of showing his selection.

"May I have one?" Lincoln stepped in front of Jerek.

"I don't know if you should." Jerek struggled to keep the warning from his voice. "Might draw attention to yourself, and that could be dangerous if big brother is watching."

"They took Ari," Lincoln said. "She's locked in LeBlanc's office in the mansion."

"Did big brother tell you that?"

"It doesn't matter. We have to get her out. If I can get Eve away—"

"Leave her," Jerek said. "We keep to the plan. Ari is on her own."

Ford slid over to stand beside them, glancing over his shoulder before speaking. "We can't just leave her locked in a murderer's house."

"We can, and we will," Jerek said. "The plan holds, or we all fail."

"Jerek," Lincoln said.

"Great," Eve's shout carried through the hall. "Lock me in a room with him, and I'll make sure he doesn't grab anymore ass."

"What would Ari want?" Jerek asked.

Ford's shoulders sagged. He pulled his phone from his pocket and pressed his finger to the scanner.

Jerek nodded and turned away, not wanting to see the look of revulsion in Lincoln's eyes.

"Don't make me punch you, too," Eve said.

The alarms on the top floor rang.

The two Maree blocking the red rope looked up toward the stairs but didn't move.

Go. Be good little knights and just go.

"Why are there alarms going off upstairs?" LeBlanc stormed into the hall, four Maree in his wake. "Someone get to the cameras and find out what the hell is going on."

One of the Maree sprinted toward the lobby while the other three stayed behind LeBlanc as he stalked up the stairs.

Jerek pressed himself against the wall, his tray of shrimp still in hand.

"Oh no!" Ford wobbled down the hall, past the red-roped staircase, grasping at his neck. "Shrimp. I think I ate shrimp." He fell to the ground, gasping and writhing.

"Help!" Lincoln shouted. "We need help."

The Maree finally moved from their posts, running to Ford's aid. A crowd closed around them as the guests clustered in to see this newest form of entertainment.

A flash of black and silver fabric dove under the rope. Jerek followed, his serving tray still clasped in his hand. He stayed two steps behind as Grace tore down the stairs. She didn't slow until she rounded the corner on the bottom level and ducked out of sight.

Jerek took the corner as quickly as he could without leaving a trail of shrimp behind. A black stiletto aimed at his head greeted him.

"It's me," Jerek said.

"Sorry," Grace panted. "Sorry."

"Are you all right?" Jerek studied her face.

A line of worry creased her forehead, and anxiety filled her eyes.

"I'm fine." Grace held up her shoes. "Just not great at running in heels."

Not a trace of doubt.

"Let's go," Jerek said.

They walked side by side to the Pre-Treaty Gallery.

"Are we really doing this?" Grace asked.

"We didn't come for the shrimp."

A golden archway greeted them. Jerek didn't let himself study the details of the ancient message etched in the metal. He couldn't let himself look at the cases of wonders they passed.

If he started looking, he would never stop. He would spend

the rest of his life lapping up the history of his people and forget to save them.

The Caster's Fate waited off to one side as though it weren't a treasure worth a museum all its own.

"It's beautiful," Grace whispered.

"Pity we have to break it." Jerek set his tray down next to the case. It seemed wrong to have such mundane clutter present for a moment generations would remember, but there was nothing else for it.

No time for glamour in the midst of salvation.

"It worked." Grace bent down, squinting at the quarter-sized hole in the case.

The shiny daub of red she'd made from a wine glass at the beach house had burrowed its way through the case, growing as it consumed, leaving a wider hole on the inside of the glass than the outside. The eater had fallen onto the black velvet and gone dormant, waiting to find more glass to feast upon.

"How big would it get if we fed it the Caster's Fate?" Grace whispered as though the creature she'd created through incantations would somehow hear its master and take offense.

"You'll have to watch and see." Jerek bent down and rolled up his pant leg. Sweat coated the sheath holding the scroll to his leg. Carefully unclasping the buckles, he pulled the Blood List free. A strip of leather on the other side of his leg held a glasscutter.

"Do you think the alarms are off?" Grace asked.

"One way to find out." Jerek inserted the blade into the burrowed hole. His heart froze as he waited for an alarm to pierce the air.

The room stayed silent as he pushed the blade up, creating a gently curving circle.

"Thank you, Ford," Grace whispered. "Only Ari would have such a useful ex."

"Ari is the best of us all." Sweat slicked Jerek's hand as he pushed the blade slowly around. He wanted to move faster, but patience was the key. "Don't be afraid to tell her I said that. She needs to be reminded of how wonderful she is from time to time."

His hand cramped as he cut the last inches of the circle. Grace reached forward, catching the disc of glass as it tipped toward the floor.

Jerek helped her guide the circle to the ground, his gaze locked on the Caster's Fate the whole time, because there, toward the top, the heliostone waited, trapped in glass for hundreds of years. Passed from hand to hand without anyone knowing the treasure they possessed.

Heat warmed his skin as he reached toward the blue glass—the soul of an age when magic was raw and magicians unafraid to use the full might of their powers. Energy surged through his fingertips as they grazed the heliostone.

Any lingering doubt that he might have been wrong about the stone disappeared as power like he hadn't felt in twelve years flooded through his veins. The dim lights of the room dazzled his eyes. The heat of Grace's magic touched fire to his flesh.

"Can you pull the stone out?" Grace asked.

Jerek dug his fingers into the indents that had held the heliostone in a staff so very long ago and yanked as hard as he could. The stone didn't budge.

"It was worth a try," Grace said.

Jerek pulled back the hand that held the glasscutter and slammed the blade against the Caster's Fate. A tiny crack appeared in the blue. He struck again and again. Veins of weakness shot through the glass, spreading out to all four corners as he chipped away at the priceless piece of history.

He pulled his arm back to hit again.

A crack echoed around the gallery as the Caster's Fate shattered in a shower of glass and jewels. The eater sprang to life, gnawing at its newfound feast.

Jerek reached into the wreckage, pulling the heliostone free.

"It's time."

73

Ari

"You know what?" Ari said. "I'm really starting to think the Maree might be homophobic."

"Keep walking."

"Catch me in the shadows with Mariah and I get dragged away," Ari said. "Is two girls too much action for the Maree? Afraid you'll blush?"

The Maree maintained their maddeningly consistent pace as they climbed the spiral staircase up through the cement tube.

Long gone were the marble corridors. This stretch of the museum wasn't meant for guests. The only trace of this stairwell on the maps she'd studied for hours on end had been a shaft leading to nowhere.

"Don't you have to charge me with something to detain me?" Ari asked.

The stairs ended at a gray metal door. The first Maree held a black fob up to the lock.

"Well?" Ari said.

"You disrupted the party," the second Maree said.

They pushed the door open and dragged Ari through.

"Couldn't you just kick me out like a normal shindig?" Ari said.

"LeBlanc's orders."

The hall they entered was better appointed than the staircase they'd left. Baseboards and chair rails ran along the walls. A soft hint of sea salt teased the air, drifting in from some out of sight window.

"You know," Ari said, "when I was young and naïve, I used to believe the Knights Maree served the feu and didn't answer to the stooges of rich assholes."

The Maree didn't answer.

"Can't blame a feu child for dreaming," Ari said.

The walls were bare in the first stretch of the hall, but as they traveled farther from the stairs, paintings were hung at more and more regular intervals.

There didn't seem to be any reasoning behind the choice of art. Some were seascapes, others people Ari didn't recognize. A few were so abstract, she had no chance of guessing what their subject was meant to be.

I'm walking through the rich man's rejected art.

A carpeted staircase led up from the end of the hall to a carved wooden door, which swung open as they climbed the steps.

"You know you could have just escorted me through the gates," Ari said. "This is a really long way to walk in heels."

They led her through the wooden door and turned left.

Ari glanced back to see the door close behind them with a click. There was no hole for a key or touch pad for a fob.

For the first time that evening, a trickle of fear dripped into Ari's chest.

They stopped at a wooden door with a gold plate on the front.

Callen LeBlanc

A Maree pulled a regular metal key from his pocket to unlock the door.

"No fob for fancy LeBlanc? How do the fobs work anyway?" Ari asked. "Are they each coded to a specific knight? Do you just have a fancy, all access pass?"

"Get in."

"It's an honest question," Ari said. "I'm not sure if your system is brilliant or the dumbest misuse of technology I've seen this month."

The Maree guided her to an armchair, shoving her none too gently to sit.

"Wait here."

"You're not going to keep me company?" Ari pouted.

"We'll be right outside."

The two left, shutting the door firmly behind them.

"Dickheads."

Ari pushed herself out of the seat, fighting the childish fear that the chair might somehow trap her.

The soft, ruddy leather was nothing more than that and let her leave without a fight.

Two wide windows flanked a desk stacked higher with paper than should be allowed in the digital age. Bookcases lined the sidewalls, filled with volumes both brand new and old enough to belong in the museum several stories below. One camera hung in the back corner of the room.

Ari waved to whatever Maree might be watching her.

She glanced back at the door. The heavy wood had no knob or keyhole to unlock from the inside.

"Well, shit."

She traced her fingers along the books, fighting the temptation to tear them all from the shelves.

LeBlanc had wanted her brought to his office.

Strange.

She pictured Jerek standing beside her, a tiny smile he didn't want her to notice on his lips as he spoke.

Why would LeBlanc want you brought to his office? There must be more convenient places to hold a prisoner. Imaginary Jerek waited for her to respond, the sparkle of suspicion playing in his eyes, but he wouldn't give her the answer. Wouldn't want to taint her journey to her own conclusion, lest Ari's reasoning be better than his.

Well, Ari thought. *Three choices. He's really pissed Mariah likes the ladies. He's dumb enough to offer his office as a holding room just because. Or he wants me away from the Maree.*

Imaginary Jerek's eyebrows crept up his forehead.

"But why me? I don't matter." Ari headed to the desk.

Bills from the catering company. Receipts from the linen rental.

"Boring much?"

There wasn't a computer on the desk or a phone, either.

Keeping her eyes on the door, she reached down, testing the desk drawers. All were locked.

Where's Jack when you need him?

She grabbed a stack of paper, flipping farther down than the party receipts.

"Why don't people just save a tree and stick to digital?"

You're only mad because you can't hack paper.

Ari rolled her eyes at imaginary Jerek.

She flipped through the endless receipts, stopping when the lines of text were interrupted by four printed pictures.

Three people waited outside the CFH. On the next page Ari, Lincoln, and Jerek stood together in the receptionist's office.

Ari clung to Jerek's arm, her face twisted with worry. Then Lincoln and Jerek in the statue hall surrounded by Maree. Last, Ari reaching up to smear Jack's explosive concoction on the hinges of the door.

The world tipped to the side, but somehow Ari's feet stayed planted on LeBlanc's carpeted floor.

"It's not a coincidence."

There's no such thing as coincidence, Ariel Love, Jerek whispered.

Her heart pounded in her chest, fighting to escape as though hoping to set an example for the rest of her body.

She stood up straight, tossing her hair behind her shoulders.

The windows behind the desk reached from waist to ceiling. Ari drew back the curtains. Headlights traveled in the distance, winding along the oceanside road. Below, the cliff led to the frothing channel that bordered the property. Waves crashed against the rocky banks, leaving no handhold for a person to climb down.

Ari tested the window. An old-fashioned lock held the window shut tight. She slipped off her shoe.

Aiming one stiletto at the center of the glass pane, she struck as hard as she could. She had expected pain to surge up her arm as the window deflected her blow, but the crash of breaking glass and the sting of slicing skin came as soon as shoe met windowpane.

"What are you doing in there?" a voice shouted as the door to the hall flung open.

Ari jammed her shoe back on and climbed up onto the windowsill.

"Stay right there," the Maree ordered.

"Screw you."

"No one here wants to—"

Ari pushed herself out the window, spreading her arms wide as she dove toward the foaming water far below.

The ocean embraced her as she met the waves, holding her close and dragging her down to the haven she constantly craved. The promise of freedom eased her fear as the muscles of her neck loosened and fresh, crisp oxygen filled her lungs. All thoughts of insurmountable odds drifted away.

Here, in her home beneath the waves, the Maree couldn't touch her. LeBlanc couldn't find her. Even Chanler himself would be powerless to fight her.

Her skirt swirled around her legs, shifting with the current as though she were a jellyfish, needing nothing but instinct to survive.

A grin on her face, Ari kicked, diving as deep as the canal would allow. She soared through the water, flying past fish and stones. Up ahead, two pinpricks of silver glimmered beneath a rock.

The two magician forged daggers waited right where she'd left them.

Just in case.

74

Jack

"I don't mind being locked in with him if you don't mind him not having a face when you come back," Eve growled.

She didn't fight the Maree's grasp as the knights dragged them into the hall where Ford had been sent to recover before the gong had rung.

"I hope you know I have every intention of suing this violent, deranged lady and all of you," Jack said. "I've been beaten, and now I'm being dragged away from work for getting punched in the chin. I better still be getting paid for this whole night."

None of their six Maree escorts saw fit to respond.

Eve twisted over her shoulder, glaring daggers at Jack. "If you didn't want to get hit, you shouldn't have touched me."

"For the last time, I didn't touch you." Jack flailed his arms.

The Maree holding him stumbled then tightened their grasp.

You want a wild time, boys?

Jack stepped backward, stomping on one of the guard's toes.

"Watch it." The guard shook Jack's arm.

Jack stepped back again, lunging away from Eve. "I will not be locked up with her. I don't know if the angry ginger decided to target me because I'm gay, black, or prettier than she'll ever be, but I demand to be held separately from my attacker. I'm an American. I have rights."

One of Eve's guards unlocked the door at the very end of the hall.

Jack yanked his arms to his chest, jerking the Maree toward him. He brushed his hand against a knight's pocket and dissolved into tears.

He didn't stop crying as the Maree dragged them into an almost bare room. If he'd had to venture a guess as to what the space's daily purpose was meant to be, Jack would have bet on *brochure assembly room.*

Boxes of printed flyers lined the walls, and narrow desks ran along the center of the space.

One of Jack's Maree reached into his pocket, pulling out a pair of handcuffs.

"You're going to cuff me?" Jack yelped. "What if she really does try to kill me?"

One of the other knights produced another pair of cuffs. They shoved Eve into one of the desk chairs, looped the handcuffs through the metal back, and cinched them closed.

"Metal handcuffs?" Eve said. "Someone like you can't do any better?"

"Be good, or we'll have more to chat about than assault and destruction of museum property," the Maree said.

"I'll sit on my own." Jack lowered himself gently into the

metal chair, reaching his hands behind his back to be cuffed. "If she kills me, my family is going to own this weirdo fetish fest."

None of the Maree said anything as they filed out of the room.

Jack and Eve glared at each other until the door shut. Even after, they stayed silent for a long moment.

"Did you get what you wanted?" Jack asked when the silence had drifted from meaningful to absurd.

"I don't know what you're talking about."

"I'm a professional, Eve. I know a grab when I see one." Jack looked to her cleavage. A slight wrinkle marred the line of her dress on the left side of her bust. "What did you want so badly you crashed my skull through a glass case?"

"I thought this was the part where you got us out?" Eve said.

"And I thought the plan wasn't to make me ribbons a la vampire."

"You'll heal," Eve said. "It's not like I stuck you out in the sun."

"Fair." Jack funneled his anger into his fangs, letting them grow to extend past his lip. He leaned down and pierced the fabric of his jacket. The horrible feeling of metal on fang shook his spine, but the lockpick waited right where he'd sewn it.

"It's not like you were in any danger," Eve said.

"I'm trying to concentrate." He bit again, making a large enough hole to dig into with his tongue.

"I had to take the chance, okay?"

"Uh-huh." Jack pulled the pick from the jacket lining, lapping it into his mouth.

"That bastard had my mother's moonstone hanging up for display."

"What?" The pick slipped toward the back of Jack's throat. He gagged, coughing the thin strip of metal back toward the front of his mouth.

"I knocked you all the way through the glass so I could get to her necklace."

"And did you?" Jack asked through pinched teeth. He twisted his head over his shoulder and spit the pick into his waiting palm.

"Yeah. I'm sorry, okay? I'll make the skull smashing up to you."

"It's all good." Jack twisted his hands in his cuffs, working the pin into the keyhole. "I've been put through worse for a good grab. Before the bite, the clan let me sit in jail for two days because they needed to use me as a distraction."

He felt the metal against metal under his fingertips. The pressure, the void. A language he knew well how to speak.

"Distraction for what?"

"Getting into a big star's hotel room." The lock on his first cuff popped open. He moved his hands around to the front to pick the other side. "They'd flown to Vegas to film a movie. The clan stole the script and sold spoilers for a huge haul."

"That's a horrible thing to do."

"Exactly what I said." Jack set his handcuffs down on his desk. "How do you think I ended up on distraction and jail duty?" He glanced to the door before kneeling behind Eve.

"I'm still sorry. Friends don't toss friends through glass."

Jack pushed the pin into the lock. "You take out the guards and get us to our next destination, and we'll call my suffering a warm-up act."

The cuffs fell away from Eve's wrists.

"Deal." Eve stood and grabbed a flyer, using the paper to wipe the blood from her hands. The skin beneath the red had already begun to knit back together.

"Wolfies and batties both heal so nicely." Jack didn't even bother checking his back for damage. The pain of healing had already subsided, and he didn't have the supplies to fix his ruined clothes.

Eve reached into the left breast of her dress and pulled out a delicate silver necklace. Her hands trembled as she lifted the chain over her head, letting the pendant fall against her chest.

"Usually, we try and hide the things we steal until we've left the premises," Jack whispered.

"I would." A glint shone in Eve's eyes. "But if I have to shift, I'm using my mother's stone."

"Shall we?" Jack bowed Eve toward the door.

She pulled off her silver heels and tucked them under one of the desks.

"Those shoes are too nice to be abandoned like that."

"I told you I didn't want to wear them." Eve stepped to the side of the door.

Jack pulled a black fob from his pocket.

"When did you take it?" Eve asked.

"Sometime around *I'm an American. I have rights.* I could help with your sleight of hand, you know. You've got the distraction part down, but you need some work on the palming portion."

"I'll stick to smashing."

"Suit yourself." Jack held the black fob up to the lock.

A faint hum carried from the innards of the door, but nothing clicked open.

He pulled the fob away, shook it, and pressed it back to the black square on the door.

The hum came again, but the door stayed firmly closed.

"Didn't happen to steal two did you?" Eve asked.

"I don't know what's wrong with it." Jack squinted at the black plastic casing. No scratches or cracks marred the surface.

He pressed the fob to the lock for a third time. The hum was his only answer.

"You like smashing," Jack said. "Wolf, smash door."

"We're going to bring more Maree."

"If we don't move soon, we'll be late. Don't worry, I've got your back."

"If you're sure." Eve clasped her hands together and raised them high over her head. With enough force to break somb bones, she smashed her fists down on the doorknob.

The screech of tearing metal dug into Jack's ears as the knob fell away.

Eve reached into the new hole in the door and yanked. With a crack, the door swung open.

Two Maree waited in the hall beyond, daggers drawn.

75

Eve

Giddy power rippled through Eve's veins. The first Maree lunged forward, the tip of his dagger pointed at her gut. She slammed the palm of her hand down on the blade and kicked out, striking the Maree's knee. He stumbled back but didn't lose his grip on his weapon.

The other Maree twisted to speak into his collar. Jack dove past Eve, tackling the knight and clamping a hand over his mouth.

Eve's Maree flicked his wrist. Lights danced from the tip of his dagger, the shape of them curling up like scorpion tails ready to strike.

Eve dove beneath the shimmer of magic. A shock caught the back of her leg, sending pain shooting up to her spine. She rolled onto her back, swiping a kick behind the Maree's knees.

The dagger slipped from his hand as he fell to the floor.

Eve leapt to her feet, seizing her Maree as he twisted to

speak into his collar. She tore the fabric from around his neck, tossing it down the hall as she slammed the knight against the wall with one hand.

"You're going to regret this," the Maree said.

"I doubt that." She threw him into the room where they'd dared try to imprison her.

Her fingers itched to open the tiny moonstone at her neck. To feel power flood her.

She stomped on the Maree as he tried to push himself to his knees.

"What do you want to do with them?" Jack dragged his unconscious Maree into the room. Blood dripped from the man's head.

"Want a snack?" Eve asked.

"Who are you people?" The Maree under Eve's foot tried to roll away.

She shoved her foot under his stomach and kicked, smashing him into the wall.

"Hell and Fury," Jack said. "Shall we cuff?"

"Let's make it a little more interesting." Eve flicked open the top of the tiny pendant that rested on her chest. Strength surged through her limbs as her hair grew and claws took the place of hands.

"Shit." The Maree dove for the hall.

Jack leapt in front of the door, baring his fangs with a hiss.

Eve raised her claws, slicing through the metal back of a chair. "Hands and feet please."

Jack tackled the Maree, pinning him to the ground and forcing his wrists together.

As though it were no firmer than wet clay, Eve molded the metal around the man's wrists.

"I appreciate your artistry," Jack said.

The metal gave a satisfying shriek as she bent it around the

Maree's feet then made a loop to bind his hands and feet together.

"The Knights Maree will consider this an attack against the sanctity of our order." The Maree fought uselessly against his metal bonds.

"Stuff his mouth with something," Eve said.

She made quick work of the unconscious Maree, tearing the collar off his coat before leaving him bound in metal on the floor.

"Shall we?" Jack asked.

He'd stuffed flyers into the conscious Maree's mouth.

"Be good, and I won't send Jack back for a snack." Eve opened the door, bowing Jack toward the hall.

"Bye now," Jack said.

With a wave, Eve shut the door behind them. Jack grabbed the torn black collar from the floor, wiping the bloodstain on the wall. "Not very absorbent."

"Leave it." Eve headed back down the hall toward the second door on the right. "Soon, there won't be any way to ignore our chaos."

Jack lifted his fob to the handle. The lock clicked open.

Eve slammed the door aside, expecting to find the room beyond either empty or filled with Maree.

An older man in plain clothes spun in his chair to gape at them. Monitors took up most of the wall behind him, showing everything from the service garage to the front veranda. Even the Pre-Treaty Gallery was there in black and white.

On the first level of the museum, partygoers milled about the exhibit halls and made their way to the food-laden tables. In the kitchen, the staff and Maree scrambled, searching for the source of the fire alarm Ford had set off from his phone. Ford's techno-magic had done its job on the cameras on the lower level as well. The Pre-Treaty Gallery on the screen was empty, without any sign of Grace and Jerek.

Unless they didn't make it.

Not looking away from Eve, the man reached for a cell phone on his desk.

"Touch that, and I break your arm," Eve said.

"Pardon me." Jack scooted behind the man, leaning over his computer.

"Who are you?" the man asked.

Eve reached up, closing her mother's pendant. The shimmer of her fading strength trickled up her limbs.

"We're not the bad guys," Eve said. "And we don't want to hurt you."

"But you will if you have to?" the man said.

"Exactly."

"What are you here for?" the man asked. "You already broke through a case. What more do you want to take?"

"It's not about taking," Eve said.

"LeBlanc won't like this," the man said. "You're making an enemy of a very determined man."

"Somehow I'm not fussed about Chanler's personal assistant," Jack said.

The man shrugged. "Your choice. But he'll find out what you're here for, and he'll come after you."

"Let him come," Eve said. "Let them all come. I'll welcome them with open arms."

"All set up here." Jack left the computers.

"You're going to come with us," Eve said. "You're going to walk calmly. Don't talk to anyone, don't warn anyone."

"Where are you taking me?" the man asked.

"Away," Jack said. "We'll drop you off on a nice beach and call a car to take you home."

The man stood. Pushing his chair back toward his desk.

"It may not matter much to you," the man said, "but I'm a good person. I've got two daughters, and three grandkids. I've arranged a private tour for them to come to the museum tomorrow. One of the perks of being in charge of installing the camera system is giving my family that treat. They're good kids, and they don't deserve the trauma of having their grandpa murdered."

"What's your name?" Eve asked.

"Stan."

"Well, Stan," Eve said. "I'm not here to hurt anyone who doesn't deserve it. I'm not sure if the museum will be open tomorrow, but maybe you can take the kids for ice cream instead."

Stan nodded. "They do like ice cream."

"We ready to blow this joint?" Jack asked.

The lights in the room dimmed and faded to red.

Ding, ding, ding.

"For your comfort and safety, please exit the Museum of Magic," Chanler's voice carried over the speakers. The message lacked any tone of panic.

For a few seconds, all the people on the screens stayed in place, frozen as though the monitors had been hacked like the ones on the lower level. Then, without any reason Eve could see, the people around the food tables surged toward the stairs to the lobby as though expecting a murderer to tear through their throats at any moment.

The guests flocked to the steps as the Maree in the kitchen ran toward the lobby doors.

The cameras on the wall flickered.

"What's going on?" Eve looked to Stan.

"No idea." Stan squinted at the computers. "The system's been acting up all night. That's why I got called in."

The monitor displaying the Pre-Treaty Gallery blinked.

Grace and Jerek knelt opposite each other on the floor. Jerek raised his hand to his chest.

"Jerek." Eve let go of Stan's arm, moving toward the monitors, unable to tear her gaze from the screen.

"Eve, we have to go," Jack said. "If the monitors are coming back on, we have to get out now."

"Jerek!" Eve shouted at the screen, knowing he wouldn't be able to hear her.

Eve tore past Jack and Stan.

"Eve!"

She skidded to a stop in front of the door to the lobby.

"Stan, run," Jack ordered. A second later, he was behind Eve. She didn't wait for him to raise the fob. She kicked the door as a thundering bang and wave of heat came from the computer room.

"What did you do?" Stan screamed.

Eve kicked again. The lock gave, and the door to the lobby burst open.

A Maree waited on the other side. She grabbed him, tossing him aside as though he were nothing more than a mannequin.

Guests streamed up the stairs as a long line of Maree fought to go down.

Eve's bare feet slammed against the floor as she ran to the steps and launched herself into the throng.

76

Grace

The cold of the marble cut through her dress as she knelt on the floor. Her fingers trembled as she reached out to unfurl the Blood List.

Richard Holden

Risa Holden

Jerek Holden

Jerek knelt on the other side of the scroll, the heliostone still in hand.

"Do I just start?" Grace's voice wobbled.

"Soon." Jerek set the heliostone on the ground and pinched the red-stoned ring on his left hand.

The red stone fell free, revealing a tiny blade on the other side.

"What's that for?" Grace asked.

Jerek didn't answer. He unbuttoned his shirt and pulled the white fabric aside.

"Jerek, what are you doing?"

"Don't worry. Your part is the incantation. You know the words. That's all you have to do."

He raised the point of the stone toward his chest.

"Jerek, don't." Panic squeezed Grace's throat.

He didn't flinch as he pressed the blade into his flesh. A trickle of blood ran down from the stone, staining skin and shirt.

He left the jewel lodged in his chest and lifted the heliostone. "Start the spell."

"But you're bleeding."

"It's only a scratch." Jerek's lips lifted into a smile. "I'm fine, Grace. Just say the words."

Grace laid both hands on the scroll. She wanted to reach for Jerek, to touch him and know he was safe.

"Just say the words."

"*Allarium finastra dothhartra.*" The words rolled off Grace's tongue as though they were fated to be there. Magic flowed through her veins, sparking against her nerves, setting fire to her soul. She belonged to the incantation. She'd been born to speak this spell. "*Imarta hontorat fini.*"

The heat of magic poured from her hands. The blood-written words on the scroll shimmered with power.

Jerek gasped as the red jewel began to glow. A stream of light shot from his chest, igniting the fire inside the heliostone.

77

Jerek

Death begins.

"It's okay, Jerek. Just say the words."

His father had written the incantation out for him on a piece of lined paper. All he had to do was speak the spell.

Jerek had protested. He wasn't strong enough. His magic was nothing more than a parlor trick. Incantations had been stolen from magicians by the Fracture.

But Father had insisted. All Jerek had to do was speak. The rest, his father would manage.

He'd pulled Jerek into a tight hug and kissed him on top of the head as he'd done years before when Jerek was a little boy.

His father had turned away to plunge the jewel into his chest. Blood seeped through his buttoned shirt.

"Say the words, Jerek. Just speak."

He'd done it. Read the words, the inflection perfect, just as his father had taught him. Light poured from his father's chest into the white stone in his hands.

How beautiful. *That was Jerek's foolish thought as he watched the pale stone glow brighter and brighter.*

He didn't notice the shaking of his father's hands until it was too late.

The last word trailed from Jerek's lips as the light in his father's chest flared. The stone in his hands shattered.

Richard Holden toppled to the ground. His face pale white, his eyes seeing something far beyond the Holden House library.

"Dad!"

Richard didn't hear his son's screams.

"Dad!"

His lips kept moving as a breeze fluttered through the library, rustling the stacks of papers that were Richard Holden's life work.

"Dad!"

Jerek leaned close to his father's lips, trying to hear his instruction, desperate for a way to save his father's life.

"Death begins. Death begins. Death begins."

Richard Holden repeated the words until death finally claimed him.

78

Jerek

Jerek watched the light pour from his chest. A rush of power flooded his veins as the heliostone filled him with magic. But the magic wasn't his to keep.

The force of the spell drew the magic from him. Pouring life into the scroll, into the air, flying to parts of the world Jerek would never see.

The Blood List shimmered. Light shone from three names written in deep red.

Soon. I'll be with both of you soon.

The pain he had feared didn't come. The fire of the heliostone welcomed him, filling him with radiant joy.

Exquisite power couldn't last long. He knew it. His body felt it.

The edge of endurance raced toward him, waiting to claim his final breath.

He watched Grace's face. Memorizing the color of her eyes.

If he could only remember the last moment of his life, at least it would be her face seared into his being for all eternity.

This is what I want, Grace. Don't hate me for my choice. Don't hate yourself for helping me.

He wished he could tell her, but the knowledge would be too cruel. Asking her to have the strength to end his life would be hideously worse than leaving her with the unknowable consequences.

The power stretched beyond his skin, pulling at the fabric of his being.

Soon, the magic would snap and there would be nothing left of Jerek Holden.

Death begins.

"*Infarso LeTurtso Malisco Maleficium.*"

The final words of the spell hung in the air.

A roar filled Jerek's ears as light burst from stone and scroll.

79

Lincoln

Lincoln watched from the side of the hall as the Maree carried Ford up the stairs and out of sight. Even knowing Ford had faked falling to the floor unable to breathe, a creeping worry gnawed at Lincoln's stomach.

The alarms on the upper level had stopped blaring.

Chanler laughed as he beckoned guests to the swan-napkin covered tables. Trays of food appeared, filled with cakes and fruit.

Mariah Chanler glared at the caterers and headed straight for Lincoln.

"Have you seen Ari?" Mariah asked.

"She was taken to LeBlanc's office," Lincoln said. "Maybe you could be kind enough to get her out?"

"From LeBlanc's office?" Mariah coughed a laugh. "Even Daddy couldn't get Ari out of there. We'd have to stage a coup and take over the house."

"It's your father's house," Lincoln said. "LeBlanc works for him, which means he works for you. Go get Ari, and bring her back to the party."

"Are you kidding? It's Callen LeBlanc's world, and the rest of us just live in it. Honestly, if he'd been born feu, I doubt he'd even let Daddy and me stay in the mansion. But who'd want to visit a Museum of Magic run by a rejected Maree?"

"LeBlanc was born Maree?" Bits of information twisted like misaligned cogs in Lincoln's mind. The rotations of the pieces had begun, but nothing fit into a useful order.

"Yes." Mariah glanced over her shoulder at her father. "He started working for the family a year before the Fracture. Then Mom died when magic disappeared and Daddy lost his powers, so LeBlanc took over to help the family. And he's never stopped *helping*. I swear if he's done anything to Ari, I'll shove him out a damn window and be rid of him once and for all."

Ding, ding, ding. "For your comfort and safety, please exit the Museum of Magic."

The guests froze as though waiting for the punchline of the joke.

"What is all this?" Chanler said, his voice carrying over the silent crowd. "Are we really having people leave because of a bit of smoke in the kitchen?"

One of the Maree by the red rope tipped his head, listening to a voice only he could hear.

"Everyone out," the Maree said. "Ladies and Gentlemen, there is a very real security threat, and we need everyone out right now."

The guests surged toward the stairs, abandoning their half-eaten finger foods.

"I demand to know what's going on in my museum." Chanler stormed over to the Maree who had given the order, swan napkin still in hand.

"LeBlanc ordered the evacuation," the Maree said.

"Why?" Chanler said. "We've been planning this party for months, and there's no danger—"

"LeBlanc gave the order, sir," the Maree said. "I suggest you leave."

Chanler twisted his napkin, wringing the fabric bird's neck. "Fine. The museum will have to rely on notoriety for success. Come, Mariah."

Chanler moved to join the back of the pack heading up the stairs.

"Mariah, wait." Lincoln grabbed her arm.

"I can't get into LeBlanc's office," Mariah said. "I'm sorry."

"How did your mother die?"

"What?" Mariah wrenched her arm free.

"How did she die?" Lincoln said. "I need to know."

"Car accident. She was driving when the Fracture hit and veered off the road," Mariah said. "That's why Daddy won't let me drive. He let Mom take the trip to D.C. without a driver. He's never forgiven himself for letting her go alone."

Mariah followed her father up the stairs, leaving Lincoln staring after her, wondering which cog in the murderous machine she'd been forced to become.

80

Jack

Jack dove into the mass of warm bodies, shoving along in Eve's wake.

Ahead of her, he watched the line of Maree heading down toward the first level.

We can't catch them.

Unforgivable hopelessness draped across his chest, slowing his steps, making it hard to breathe.

The Maree would reach the bottom level and find Jerek and Grace. All their work would have been for nothing. The feu would remain broken. The world darker and more painful than it was meant to be.

"Get out of my way!" Eve shouted, shoving guests out of her path. A growl shook her frame as claws took the place of hands.

The guests around her scattered, crushing against Jack in their panic to flee from Eve.

"Fuck it." With a hiss, Jack let his fangs grow, baring them at the feu who blocked his path.

"Vampire!" a broadly built man shrieked.

The stairs cleared, and Jack leapt down the steps to Eve's side.

A line of Maree waited on the first level, all facing the red rope.

Lincoln stood alone, blocking the path to the lower level, both hands raised as though hoping to win a twelve-to-one fight.

"Lincoln!" Eve shouted.

Four of the Maree turned to face her.

"You have to stop him," Eve said. "Stop Jerek, or he's going to die."

Lincoln's gaze darted to Eve for only a second.

"Lincoln, go!"

Eve leapt high into the air, landing in the middle of the Maree. She slashed her claws forward, catching the two knights closest to Lincoln in the back.

"Shit." Jack dove into the fight, pulling the two daggers from the Maree they'd trapped in the brochure room from his pockets.

Lincoln sprinted down the stairs, two Maree close on his heels.

Jack threw one of the daggers. Light swirled from the tip as the blade spun through the air. The bright beam wrapped around one of the Maree, pinning his arms and legs together, leaving him to topple down the steps like a defunct slinky.

The other Maree had rounded the corner before Jack could aim his other dagger.

Pain shot through Jack's ribs as a blade sliced into his back.

81

Lincoln

"Lincoln, go!"

It wasn't Eve's words that convinced Lincoln to run down the steps to the lower level of the museum. It was the look of terror on her face.

Jerek, what have you done?

Lincoln leapt over the red rope and sprinted down the stairs. Footsteps followed him, but not enough to be all the Maree. Some had stayed above.

Eve's roar of rage carried over the bedlam of the fighting.

A grunt and the thumping of someone falling down the stairs came from behind him, but the footsteps following him didn't stop.

His shoes slipped against the marble floor as he rounded the corner to the Pre-Treaty Gallery.

He saw them before he'd even made it under the golden arch.

Jerek and Grace kneeling. The heliostone in Jerek's hands glowing brightly enough to fill the whole room. A bright red light streaming from Jerek's chest.

Grace saying the last phrase of the incantation, her face filled with horrible wonder.

"Jerek!"

Jerek didn't flinch at the sound of his oldest friend screaming his name. His gaze remained fixed on Grace's face.

The scroll glistened, centuries of magicians lending their blood to the power of the spell.

"Jerek!"

Grace turned her dazed eyes toward Lincoln.

Lincoln dove on top of Jerek, knocking the heliostone from his hands. The fire inside the stone flickered out as it rolled across the floor.

"What are you doing?" Grace said.

Lincoln pressed his knee into Jerek's shoulder and ripped the red stone from his chest.

Jerek gasped, clawing at the place the jewel had pierced his skin.

"Lincoln, behind you!" Grace screamed.

Lincoln spun around.

Marta, who had given him candy when he was small, stood behind him. She reached for her left hip, drawing a sword that shimmered into being as though created through the sheer force of her will.

"Get Jerek out," Lincoln said.

"What?"

"Take Jerek and the list and get out."

"No." Grace wobbled to her feet to stand beside Lincoln.

Energy crackled from the tips of her fingers. Magic leapt from her skin as sparks of lightning.

She reached toward the shattered display that had held the

Caster's Fate. Glass and jewels rose at her command, forming a swarm of fragments. With a flick of her fingers, the shards flew at Marta.

Marta raised her arms, covering her face as the storm bombarded her.

Lincoln charged forward, punching through the glass cloud and striking Marta in the back of her sword arm.

She held tight to her blade, swinging wildly at Lincoln.

He ducked, narrowly avoiding the sharp edge of the sword, and kicked low, knocking Marta's feet out from under her.

Grace charged forward, stomping on Marta's sword arm and kicking the blade out of her reach.

"Sorry." Lincoln pulled back his fist and punched Marta in the temple.

Her head lolled to the side as unconsciousness took her.

"We have to get out of here." Lincoln didn't allow himself any time to feel guilty for attacking one of his brethren before running back to kneel beside Jerek.

Jerek's eyes fluttered, his chest heaving as he gasped for air.

"Jerek." Lincoln shook him. "Jerek."

An ear-splitting scream filled the air.

Lincoln hoisted Jerek over his shoulder.

Grace grabbed the scroll and the heliostone. She ran her hands along the ground, tracing the pattern of Jerek's blood.

"Grace, we have to go." Lincoln started for the door, waiting for Grace's footsteps to catch up to him before breaking into a run.

The sounds echoing down from the fight above set his teeth on edge.

At least they're still fighting.

He didn't know which *they* he was more afraid of falling.

Someone screamed in pain, and metal clattered to the floor.

Let everyone live. I'll accept the horrible things I've done if you'll only let everyone live.

Lincoln ran up the steps two at a time, the weight of Jerek across his shoulders nothing next to his need to know who had been screaming in such horrible pain.

He reached the top of the staircase to find the floor slicked in red.

82

Eve

Jack's gasp carried to Eve's ears above the shouts of the Maree. Blood flew through the air, shimmering on the tip of a Maree's sword.

Eve grabbed the arm of the Maree blocking her path to Jack and tossed the knight behind her.

Jack rounded on the Maree that had cut him, danger Eve hadn't expected gleaming in Jack's eyes.

Jack kicked out, hitting the Maree in the stomach. The Maree slashed his sword at Jack's leg, cutting him on the thigh.

Pain shot through Eve's shoulder, but she didn't turn to see who had attacked her. She dug her claws into the sworded Maree's back. The knight screamed as she tossed him aside.

Jack dove behind Eve.

The clang of metal on metal shook the air.

Eve spun around.

There were no enemies left behind her. She and Jack had gained the ground closest to the red rope.

Eight remaining Maree faced them, all with swords drawn.

Blood dripped from Jack's back and thigh. Still, he swirled the dagger in his hand, the tip bristling with light like a sparkler.

"Surrender, and we will take you in peacefully," a dark-haired Maree said. "There's no need to spill more feu blood tonight."

"Stand down, and we won't have to hurt you," Jack said. "We'll take our friends and leave."

The Maree didn't move. They kept their swords, which had shimmered into being, raised and ready to strike.

Eve flexed her fingers-turned-claws, the boiling rage of the wolf in her veins drowning out all thoughts of peace. In two long strides, she reached the nearest knight, grabbed the blade of his sword and wrenched it from his grip. She kicked the knight in the leg, caving in his knee with a satisfying crunch.

Another Maree screamed and fell to the floor. Jack had leapt back into the fray.

Eve jumped high, landing on the shoulders of the tallest Maree and knocking him to the ground.

Another Maree bellowed as she charged Eve from the side.

Eve raked her claws across the chest of the shouting Maree.

The Maree slashed her sword across the back of Eve's leg.

Pain filtered through her anger as Eve's leg spasmed. She tried to leap on top of the knight, but her wounded leg wouldn't obey. She lurched sideways.

The knight's blade glinted as the silver reached for Eve's stomach.

She gasped as the sword pierced her flesh and drove straight through her back.

83

Ari

The glass doors muted the voices of the fleeing guests as Ari ran down the white stairs. The sounds of fighting came from below. A Maree flew past, smashing into an out-of-sight wall with a bone-shattering crack.

She reached the bottom of the steps in time to see a blade run Eve through.

A scream tore from her throat before she understood what she had seen.

Eve toppled to the ground.

The Maree slid her sword back out of Eve's gut.

"Miss, you need to get out of here." A dark-haired Maree ran toward Ari.

"Martin?" Ari backed away from him. The name fit his face, but why he was in the museum made no sense. Nothing made sense.

The pool of red around Eve spread. Blood flecked her face as she coughed.

"Eve!" Ari ran forward.

Martin caught her around the middle. "Miss, you have to go."

Ari stomped on his foot and elbowed him in the stomach, breaking free from his grasp. "I'm not leaving them." Ari raised both her daggers.

Jack fought three Maree at once.

I'm right here, Eve. Stay with me.

Ari ran forward, whipping her blades through the air. Light danced from the tips of the daggers, wrapping around the nearest Maree. He froze for a moment before crumpling to the ground.

One of the Maree turned toward Ari, swinging his sword. Ari blocked the blade with one dagger, driving the other into the Maree's shoulder.

"Ari!" Lincoln shouted as the Maree swung again.

But the knight's injured arm wavered under the weight of his sword.

Ari kicked front, stopping the sword with her stiletto and knocking the blade from the Maree's grip.

Jack grabbed the Maree, throwing him to the ground.

"Eve." Ari ran to her, kneeling in the still-growing pool of blood.

"We have to help her." Grace knelt on the other side, taking Eve's hand.

"Where's Jerek?" Ari looked toward the stairs. "Jerek can fix her."

"He can't," Lincoln said.

Ari looked up.

Jerek lay draped over Lincoln's shoulder. Unconscious. Paler than any person should be.

"I don't know the spell," Grace said. "I don't know how to fix her."

"You have to get out of here." Martin stepped toward them.

Jack sprinted to block Martin's path.

Martin held up both his hands. His sword shimmered out of being. "There are more Maree on the estate. You have to get out before they come."

"Which way?" Lincoln asked.

"The back if you can," Martin said. "There will still be guests on the lawn."

"Jack, can you carry her?" Ari asked.

Jack turned away from Martin, scooping Eve into his arms without a word.

Ari forced herself to her feet. Her legs trembled beneath her.

The Maree around them began to stir.

"Did you do what you came here for?" Martin asked.

"No," Lincoln said. "Come with us. Help me end this."

"A Maree knows his duty," Martin said. "Go."

Ari grabbed a sword from the ground, handing the weapon to Grace.

"I don't know how to fight," Grace said.

"You do now." Ari ran up the steps, leading the bloody brigade.

84

Grace

Grace gripped her sword as she raced up the stairs, following the others into the deep red light that filled the lobby.

"All of you, stop!" The shout bounced off the marble walls.

A line of knights blocked the glass doors.

Grace's steps faltered.

"Stop, now," a Maree ordered.

The knights charged toward them.

Ari didn't pause. She led the others toward the kitchen, running in her heels and gown like a warrior princess.

Jack carried Eve. Lincoln carried Jerek. Ford had disappeared to who knew where.

There's no one left.

Grace turned to face the advancing knights. She knelt, setting her sword, the Blood List, and the heliostone aside. She pressed her palms to the floor, letting her magic flow into the wood.

Fear, hatred, and self-loathing—she funneled it all into the ground. She screamed for the pain of Eve's wounds and Jerek's unknown fate.

A wall of fire ten feet tall erupted in front of her. The flames lapped at her skin, but the horrible heat had no power to burn her.

The Maree scattered back.

Grace grabbed the few items she had to defend herself and ran after her friends, the shouted orders of the Maree chasing her.

She reached the kitchen door just behind Jack. Pulling the doors together, she threaded the Maree sword through the handles, blocking the path behind them.

The staff had fled the kitchen. Food and dishes covered every counter. Flames still leapt from the burners on the gas stove.

She followed Jack to a door at the back of the kitchen, through a tiny room, and into the concrete hall beyond. The lights held steady. There were no alarms. No signs of chaos from the fighting. Only the footsteps of the people she followed, and the weight of the scroll and stone in her hand.

"Shit." Ari's voice came from the front of the line.

Two figures dressed in black appeared at the end of the hall, blocking their path.

The Maree raised their swords, but Ari didn't slow her pace.

Honk. Honk.

Headlights blared to the left of the Maree. They dove out of the way as the bright yellow van slammed to a stop at the end of the corridor.

The side doors burst open.

Ari jumped inside and turned to drag Jerek off Lincoln's shoulder.

By the time Grace reached the door, Lincoln had lifted Eve out of Jack's arms. Jack jumped into the van and yanked Grace in after him.

The side doors slammed shut without anyone touching them. The van reversed, the sound of its squealing tires ricocheting off the garage walls. Grace fell backward as the van cut a sharp turn and raced toward the exit.

"What happened?"

Grace leaned forward to see a pale-faced Ford sitting in the driver's seat.

"I don't know if we can stop the bleeding," Jack said.

Lincoln had laid Eve and Jerek on the floor of the van.

"She'll heal," Ari said. "She's still shifted. The moonstone will heal her. It has to."

Ford laid on the horn. "Move, dammit!"

Three Maree stood in front of the opening leading out into the night.

Ford pressed the gas harder.

The Maree leapt aside at the last moment.

"What happened?" Ford asked again.

"Everything went wrong," Lincoln said.

"The incantation?" Ari looked to Grace.

"I didn't know." Hot tears streamed down Grace's cheeks. Her whole body trembled. She wrapped her arms around her middle as the fear that she might actually shake into a million tiny pieces seized her.

"Jerek used an amplifier," Lincoln said.

"What?" Jack asked.

"It's like feeding speed to magic." Ari laced her fingers through Jerek's. "At the best of times, it's dangerous. But with the heliostone projecting the spell and the Fracture blocking him, there's no way he could have been stupid enough to believe he'd survive."

"I didn't know," Grace whispered. "I didn't know."

"Then we did all this for nothing?" Jack leaned back in his seat. "We didn't mend the Fracture. Eve didn't get to kill Chanler."

"I don't think Chanler was the one to cast the curse," Lincoln said.

"What?" Ford swerved onto the oceanside road.

"Mariah." Lincoln looked to Ari. "I asked her where you were. She said LeBlanc ran the place. The house, the Museum. Chanler's name is on everything, but it's LeBlanc who's in charge. Who would destroy the feu only to hand the power they'd gained to someone else?"

They rode in silence as Ford sped through the darkness.

Grace closed her eyes, listening to the hum of the van's engine. The sounds of her friends breathing.

We're all still breathing.

I didn't know.

She waited for the blare of sirens to surround them, but the night stayed quiet.

Maybe the Maree still hadn't figured out who had caused the catastrophe at the museum. Maybe the Knights Maree didn't work like somb police. Maybe there would be no flashing lights when the Maree came for her.

"Where do you want me to go?" Ford asked as they neared downtown Newport.

"We have to find a place for them to rest," Lincoln said.

"And then we plan," Ari said. "We figure out a new way to mend the Fracture."

"Jerek is close to dead." Grace's voice cracked. "Eve is bleeding. They could both be dead by sunrise. We failed. It's over, Ari."

"No. We made a promise," Ari said. "Things went to shit today, but that doesn't mean we get to be done. Our world is still broken, and there's still no one else to fix it. So we come up with a new plan. It's what Jerek and Eve will want."

"Jerek was willing to die for the feu," Lincoln said. "I'm not giving up."

"I'm too deep in to climb out now," Jack said.

"I'm with Ari," Ford said.

"I..." Grace's voice drifted away.

Home, Sun Palms High School, her dads. All those things belonged to a girl who had never worn a blood-covered dress. Who had never understood that magic crackled through her veins and never known about a world of wonder twisted up with the world of mundane bliss.

"Okay." Grace nodded. "Okay." She lifted the blood-stained heliostone and scroll, handing them to Ari. "We'll find another way."

Ari set the stone and scroll on Jerek's chest. The heliostone shimmered with a faint light that danced around the dark interior of the van. The scroll rolled open as Jerek breathed.

Richard Holden

Risa Holden

Jerek Holden

GET READY TO LAUGH OUT LOUD, BECAUSE THIS BOY WIZARD IS NOT THE HERO TYPE.

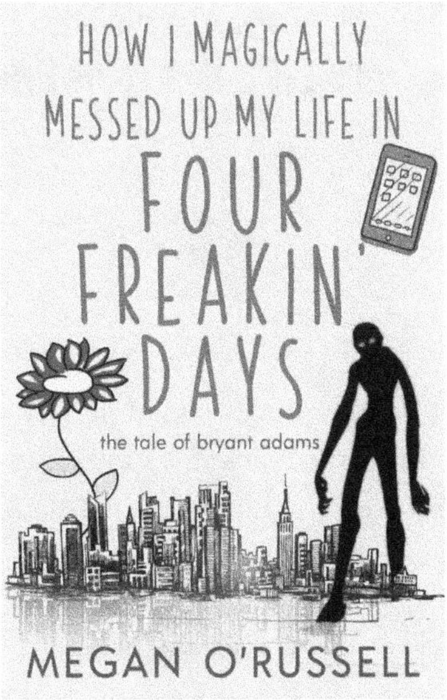

When nerdy 16-year-old Bryant Adams finds out he's a wizard, his ordinary life descends into chaos!

Read on for a preview of *How I Magically Messed Up My Life in Four Freakin' Days.*

HOW I MAGICALLY MESSED UP MY LIFE IN FOUR FREAKIN' DAYS

We walked uptown toward my dad's. I don't know if it was instinct, habit, or the fact that my keys to Mom's place had been melted by a fire. Either way, Le Chateau seemed like the best bet.

A cab would have been faster, but since I smelled like a barbeque gone wrong, I figured it was better to walk.

Devon started by giving me a blow-by-blow of what the firemen had been doing: running in and out and a lot of hauling hoses mostly. "And then Linda May, sweet little Linda May, was so terrified she needed comfort, and of course she ran to me. I'm telling you man, the fire made 8th Ave crazy."

"You do remember I was there, right?" I asked, trying not to sound snarky even though I was tired enough to curl up on a subway grate and sleep. "I was the one who saw the fire start and pulled the alarm to get everyone out."

"Really?" Devon asked, looking surprised for a second but trying to cover up his shock by punching me in the arm. "Good for you, man! Elizabeth must think you're a hero. This could be the break you've been waiting for. Did you ask her out?"

"What? No, I didn't ask her out!" I ran my hands through my hair. It was gritty from the smoke and orange paint.

Devon grimaced and shook his head, looking down at the sidewalk.

"What?" I asked again, trying not to get angry. "What did you want me to do? Was I supposed to look down, see a fire, and stop on the way to the alarm to ask Elizabeth to be my girlfriend?"

"I mean, *girlfriend* might have been pushing it, but it would have been better than nothing," Devon said.

"Sorry, I was trying to make sure everyone didn't burn to death."

"What about when you two were talking once everyone was out of the theatre then?" Devon said, nodding and winking at a random dog walker.

The poor girl had two mastiffs, three Chihuahuas, and one drooling pug. Their leashes had all gotten tangled, and one of the Chihuahuas was dangling over the bigger mastiff's back. Being a dog walker was on my top ten list for jobs I never wanted in Manhattan.

"I don't know how many more chances you can hope to get with Elizabeth."

"I've never had a single chance," I said as we turned onto Central Park West, "and now she probably thinks I'm a freak, so...." I was screwed. There was something about knowing she thought I had magically started a fire with a cellphone and was now afraid of me that made it seem more true than years of her never speaking to me ever had. My stomach felt heavy and gross.

"Why does she think you're a freak?" Devon asked. "I mean, you just saved the whole theatre class."

I pulled the little black demon out of my pocket.

"She's thinks you're a freak because you forgot to return the phone? Which, by the way, is not cool, man. You don't leave a guy phoneless in Manhattan."

"If you remember, before you *had* to tell me all about how you made out with Linda May while our school was on fire, Elizabeth wants me to get rid of the phone." I slid it back into my pocket. Somehow having it out in my hand made me feel exposed, like a big eye in a creepy tower was watching me as I ran toward a pit of lava.

"So then let's get rid of the phone," Devon said. "We'll take it to the purple restaurant and make it their problem to find the vampire dude, and you can tell her you did what she wanted."

"She doesn't want me to return the phone," I sighed, knowing full well Devon was going to laugh at me. "She wants me to throw it into the Hudson to destroy it. She thinks the phone started the fire."

I started counting to three in my head. Before I got past two, Devon had tossed his head back and roared with laughter. People stared as they walked by.

It took Devon a full minute to speak. "I'm sorry." He wiped the tears from his eyes. "Was there a stray ray of sunlight you reflected off the screen to ignite the mounds of dried grass in the set shop?"

"No." I pushed Devon in the back to make him start walking again, and he promptly skidded on sidewalk goop. "There's an app on the phone, and she thinks I started the fire with it."

"An app. She thinks you started a fire with an app on a phone you can't even open?"

"I did open the phone," I said, "and a fire app thing."

"How did you open the phone? It should have a password." Devon turned to me, his laughter fading a little. "Do you have like post-traumatic stress or something from the fire? Because I mean, we could call your mom."

"I don't have traumatic stress." I pulled Devon into the

shade of a coffee shop awning. The place smelled like vegan food and almond milk. "And I didn't use a password." I glanced around before pulling the phone back out of my pocket. I didn't know what I was looking for. No one seemed to care about the two teenagers hanging out by the vegan coffee shop. But I still couldn't shake the feeling that someone was following me. Or that the evil eye was gazing down at me from the Empire State building. "I used my thumbprint." I pressed my thumb to the button, and the phone opened, showing the same funny symbols as before.

"Whoa!" Devon took it from me, but as soon as it left my hands, the thing turned back off. "Aw, come on." He pressed his thumb to the sensor, but the screen stayed dark. "Damn. Battery must have died."

I took the phone back and pressed my thumb back on the button. The screen popped back up. Devon grabbed the phone again, and it was the same thing. Him—phone off. Me—phone on.

"Bryant." Devon's voice was barely above a whisper. "Did you buy a phone and rig it to do that to freak me out? Because I mean, good for you, but that's a lot of trouble for a prank."

"You found this in the cab. And I would never prank you. I know better." And really I did. Devon would take any reason to punk you. If you were five minutes late when you were supposed to meet him, you had to spend the next week wondering what his revenge would be. Pulling a prank on him would be the worst idea anyone in Hell's Kitchen had ever had. Except maybe the next thing I did. That may have been the worst idea anyone in New York had ever had.

Devon was still giving me the *I don't believe you* stare with his eyebrows raised and his arms crossed. And Elizabeth thought I had a possessed phone, and my mom's theatre had burned down, and I had sort of had enough.

"Fine." I dragged him over to a trashcan by the side of the street, then tapped on the app that showed the picture of the fire. There it was—the still flames with the bar below balancing perfectly centered. I held the phone out like I was going to take a picture of the can and tapped the bar, tipping it all the way to the right.

Big mistake.

Flames shot out of the can and flew ten feet into the air like the sanitation department had decided collecting trash was too hard and installing a giant blowtorch was a better use of resources.

People behind us started to scream. Devon cursed and backed away. I stood there, frozen by the sudden heat. I couldn't move. I mean, I know I had gone to the fire app to prove to Devon that I wasn't wandering the city in some PTSD haze. But finding myself in front of a ten-foot-tall pillar of fire, holding a possessed cellphone in my hands, I sort of felt like maybe I had lost my mind. Maybe this wasn't even New York and I was locked in a cell. Or even better, and less scary maybe, I was still in bed, and this whole thing was a dream. I hadn't even gotten out of bed yet, and soon I would wake up with cat ass on my face.

I squeezed my eyes tightly shut and opened them again. There was still a fire right in front of me. No padded white room. No stinky cat ass.

I tapped the left side of the bar and pulled it all the way down. Just like it had sprung up without warning, in an instant, the fire disappeared with nothing but a melted trashcan to show for itself. Well, that and the sour, nose hair-burning stench of flaming crap.

I turned to Devon who stared, petrified, at where the flames had been.

"See? Not a prank."

"What the hell?" he muttered. "Not okay. That is definitely not okay. Burning trashcans is not okay."

The rubberneckers behind us chattered noisily. One woman shouted into her cellphone, "The fire's gone out, but I think it's a gas line!" She paused for a second. "Back away. 9-1-1 says everybody back away."

People immediately scurried down the street or hugged next to the building, still transfixed in fascinated horror.

"You need to move, boys!" the cellphone lady shouted at us as sirens echoed between the buildings.

"Go!" I pushed Devon so hard his feet finally started to work again. I grabbed his arm and dragged him onto a side street out of view of the fire trucks as they pulled up to the melted trashcan.

Two run-ins with the fire department in one day is not a good thing. Especially not when you might have caused the fires. Even if it was by accident.

We cut back around the block and to my dad's building. The fire trucks had parked down the street, but from here we couldn't even see what all the firemen were staring at.

Drake was behind the desk like always. "Mr. Adams." He smiled. "I wasn't expecting to see you here today."

"Yeah." I tried to put my thoughts into an order that didn't involve a possessed demon phone with the ability to make things spontaneously combust that was currently burning a hole in my back pocket. Not literally. I hoped. "There was a fire at school. Everybody's okay, but I lost my house key, so I'm gonna hang out here until my mom gets home." If my mom still had a house key.

"Of course, Mr. Adams." Drake unlocked the safe beneath the desk. "I would be more than happy to let you into the apartment. I am so relieved you're safe. Have you called your father?"

Drake led us to the elevator and turned the key to go up.

"No." It hadn't occurred to me to call my dad. I mean, how could he be worried about me when he didn't even know my school had been on fire? Never mind the fact that the more time passed, the more convinced I was that I had caused the fire in the first place. But Drake was still looking at me all concerned, so I said, "Not yet. I'm going to call before I shower." And I did need to shower. Even though the elevator was a big one, it was still small enough to trap in the horrible smoke and burning trash smell that was stuck to me.

The door opened to my dad's apartment, and Drake waved us in. "Shall I call for a pizza?"

"Two." Devon half-stumbled into the apartment.

"Very well." Drake closed the elevator doors and was gone.

Devon walked into the living room and collapsed onto the couch. I followed him, a little afraid he might be panicked enough to start throwing up onto the carpet. And having to call the cleaning lady to tell her you got puke in the carpet was never a fun time.

I sat on the metal rim of the glass coffee table and stared at Devon, waiting for him to speak. If he could still speak. I wasn't too sure about that.

"The fire," Devon said finally, his hands shaking as he dragged them over his face. "The phone started the fire."

Elizabeth had been right. She had seen it right away.

"Both fires. And the one at school didn't go out till I put it out with the app."

Devon scrunched his face and let out the longest string of muttered curses I had ever heard. "We have to get rid of it."

"Same thing Elizabeth said. I can take it down to the restaurant and leave it with them."

"No way in *Hell*!" Devon shook his head, looking as pale as I had ever seen him. "You just burned down half the school with that thing. You can't keep it. It's arson evidence, Bry."

"So we give it—"

"We are not giving the damn phone to people who might want to do more damage with it than you've already done! That guy we saw looked evil. He looked like a vampire or demon or something. We can't give an evil dude something this dangerous. What if he lights us on fire? Or decides to take out Times Square. I can't have that on my head, man."

"So, we do what Elizabeth said and dump it into the Hudson," I said, wondering if I could convince Drake to find a guy to take the phone to the river.

No, it couldn't be trusted to a courier. I mean, who wouldn't want to open a package they had been hired to dump into a river. We'd have to do it ourselves.

I turned my wrist over, making my watch blink on. Nearly seven PM. "If we head to the water in a few hours, we should be able to find a place to dump it without getting noticed."

"No way." Devon pushed himself to sit up. "The river's way too risky. What if it washes up and someone finds it?"

"It's a phone. It'll be dead from the water."

"A demon phone that starts fires, and you think water is going to hurt it?" Devon stood up, color coming back into his determined face. "We have to destroy it ourselves. It's the only way to make sure it's done."

Order How I Magically Messed Up My Life in Four Freakin' Days *to continue the journey!*

ESCAPE INTO ADVENTURE

Thank you for reading *The Cursebound Thief.* If you enjoyed the book, please consider leaving a review to help other readers find this story.

As always, thanks for reading,
Megan O'Russell

Never miss a moment of the magic and romance.

Join the Megan O'Russell readers community to stay up to date on all the action by visiting https://www.meganorussell.com/book-signup.

ABOUT THE AUTHOR

Megan O'Russell is the author of several Young Adult series that invite readers to escape into worlds of adventure. From *Girl of Glass*, which blends dystopian darkness with the heart-pounding danger of vampires, to *Ena of Ilbrea*, which draws readers into an epic world of magic and assassins.

With the *Girl of Glass* series, *The Tethering* series, *The Chronicles of Maggie Trent*, *The Tale of Bryant Adams*, the *Ena of Ilbrea* series, and several more projects planned, there are always exciting new books on the horizon. To be the first to hear about new releases, free short stories, and giveaways, sign up for Megan's newsletter by visiting the following:

https://www.meganorussell.com/book-signup

Originally from Upstate New York, Megan is a professional musical theatre performer whose work has taken her across North America. Her chronic wanderlust has led her from Alaska to Thailand and many places in between. Wanting to travel has fostered Megan's love of books that allow her to visit countless new worlds from her favorite reading nook. Megan is also a lyricist and playwright. Information on her theatrical works can be found at RussellCompositions.com.

She would be thrilled to chat with you on Facebook or Twitter @MeganORussell, elated if you'd visit her website MeganORussell.com, and over the moon if you'd like the pictures of her adventures on Instagram @ORussellMegan.

ALSO BY MEGAN O'RUSSELL

The Girl of Glass Series

Girl of Glass

Boy of Blood

Night of Never

Son of Sun

The Tale of Bryant Adams

How I Magically Messed Up My Life in Four Freakin' Days

Seven Things Not to Do When Everyone's Trying to Kill You

Three Simple Steps to Wizarding Domination

Five Spellbinding Laws of International Larceny

The Tethering Series

The Tethering

The Siren's Realm

The Dragon Unbound

The Blood Heir

The Chronicles of Maggie Trent

The Girl Without Magic

The Girl Locked With Gold

The Girl Cloaked in Shadow

Ena of Ilbrea

Wrath and Wing

Ember and Stone

Mountain and Ash

Ice and Sky

Feather and Flame

Guilds of Ilbrea

Inker and Crown

Myth and Storm

Viper and Steel

Tower and Grave

The Heart of Smoke Series

Heart of Smoke

Soul of Glass

Eye of Stone

Ash of Ages

Fracture Pact

The Cursebound Thief

Sorcerers of Ilbrea

Spell and Secret

CPSIA information can be obtained
at www.ICGtesting.com
Printed in the USA
BVHW042326180922
647356BV00002B/79

9 781951 359539